POSTHUMAN

M.C. Hansen

Cover Image and Art by Mark Gordon:
www.behance.net/MGordon88
Author Photo by Jay Drowns
Meet the Author: Facebook.com/authorMCHansen

Print ISBN: 978-0-578-55513-3
eBook ASIN: B07WRL35FX

For my Family and Friends.

PROLOUGE

Hogtied, Hollie Cunningham lay in the jostling car trunk and, for the first time, became aware of the putrid odor of her partially digested onion bagel, three cups of coffee, and blood stew.

She'd never smelled anything so sweet.

With each breath, her body relaxed, and the panic that had enveloped her more completely than a tidal wave receded.

Good luck getting a decent resale value now, she thought. *Now that it's properly broken in, this car's nothing more than a glorified used barf bag.*

Hollie had no idea how long she'd been unconscious, but since coming to and finding herself restrained and being used as a substitute ping-pong ball, she'd screamed as hysterically as any person buried alive. Little good it did though, for even if she hadn't been gagged, her voice would have been drowned out by the roar of the engine as the car rumbled through the desert.

After all, this was Decoy, Nevada, and although prosperous with a growing population of a little over ten thousand, it was a border town in the middle of nowhere - and not even a proper border town at that. Nestled at the foot of a canyon, the city was forty miles west of Wendover and the state line and some thirty miles south of Interstate 80 - about as godforsaken as the far side of the moon. And moments earlier, that bleak thought - the thought that there was nothing out here but miles and miles of remote locations for her abductor to put his hands all over her, to put his mouth all over her - then kill her with leisurely impudence, had sent Hollie over the edge.

Hollering with vein exploding force, she'd yelled even though the gag muffled her outrage, shouted even though there was no one to hear her rage. She'd screamed and thrashed and seethed until she'd vomited; and with the gag in her mouth, Hollie had known, had been absolutely certain, she was going to die, was going to drown on her own half-digested breakfast.

Vile sticky stomach acid first burned, then caught in her nostrils like cholesterol in an artery. Chunky chyme plugged her nose, and she'd bashed her face against the ground until she could breathe again.

Now kneeling in the position of a devout worshiper, Hollie wheezed and panted and trembled. Blood misted out of her raw and possibly broken nose, and the relief of breathing again was overshadowed by despair.

Why was this happening to her? She was a good person. No saint, but she didn't tango with the law, didn't even flirt with it. She went to church, paid her taxes, tipped generously.

But...

But she did make waves.

She was no controversial starlet or revolutionary politician, yet she wasn't inconsequential either.

Could her work have something to do with this? It was conceivable, possibly even more plausible than her looks having attracted a serial killer. Except this abduction felt more personal than a corporate kidnapping, and from what she could remember, there'd only been one highjacker - not a whole goon squad of syndicate mercenaries. Then again, the identity of her abductor was far less critical than getting away from him.

Taking several shuddering breaths, Hollie calmed her nerves.

She could get out of this. Her intellect daily conquered experiential lab work and cutting-edge biochemistry; this would be no different.

Twisting and squirming, Hollie moved around the small trunk searching for anything that might be used as a weapon or could cut through her bindings. But her groping hands felt nothing but vomit soiled carpet.

Lurching, the car abruptly stopped.

Hollie froze.

The engine idled, thrummed as softly as a campfire guitar. Holding her breath, Hollie listened. She felt rather than heard the motor cut out. The resulting stillness made the cramped trunk feel like a locked coffin.

Acrid thin air wheezed between her swollen nostrils.

The suspension shifted as a door opened and someone got out.

Frantically, Hollie pulled up the corner of the carpet hoping for a tire iron or screwdriver. Something, anything! This might be her only chance to catch her captor off guard before he did...did whatever the hell he planned to do with her.

The door banged shut.

Deliberate footsteps made their way towards the rear of the car, and Hollie's heart hammered as she tore at the floorboard. She ignored the pain as skin and fingernails peeled away.

From outside keys rattled.

Biting down hard on the sour gag, Hollie wrenched the floorboard upward and with a satisfying *crack*, the paneling gave way.

Please, God, let there be a machete in there, Hollie mused in frantic bitter humor. But when she reached down, her bloody hand met only empty air.

The jack was missing, so was the tire iron.

Whoever owned the car might have forgotten to replace them when they were last used, but Hollie felt sure they had been removed in case she went looking for them.

Snorting anger, Hollie was slapped by sunlight as the trunk lid popped open.

"Oh my," said a deep male voice. "I do apologize. I had hoped the gag wouldn't be needed, but I used a minimal dose of chloroform and couldn't risk your screams being heard before we were out of town."

Silhouetted by the sun, the figure was as dark and ominous as his next words were thoughtful and sincere.

"I took extra care, however, to avoid just such an unpleasant outcome." He tsked and waved his hand, indicating the mess. "It must have been very distressing for you."

Distressing? Hollie thought, her outrage as astringent as the acidic rag in her mouth. *No, it wasn't distressing, it was fucking terrifying!* Just who was this asshole?

Squinting and batting her eyes at the sun, Hollie tried to make out the looming shadow. As the dark form slowly came into resolution, she realized he wasn't the weasel-faced and social blundering outcast her imagination had concocted, but a pepper-haired, square-jawed, handsome man. The guy could have covered for GQ.

I've been kidnapped by George Clooney, Hollie thought, as the guy smiled reassuringly.

"Don't worry about the car, we won't be using it anymore."

Hollie nodded, strangely grateful for being excused from her reeking disgorge, until realizing what abandoning the puke wagon implied; she had to fight hard to keep those dark likelihoods out of her head.

"Let's get that gag off you."

Taking her chin in his strong manicured hand, the kidnapper reached into his back pocket and withdrew an ivory-handled straight razor.

Hollie jerked away.

In the sunlight, the blade glinted and looked sharp enough to decapitate.

"Careful," said the Clooney doppelganger, his sturdy fingers squeezing. "I wouldn't want to put an eye out. That brain of yours is far too important to damage. Now, I'm only going to cut the tape, so hold still."

The blade snapped upwards.

Hollie felt its cool kiss, but not its bite.

The stroke had been surgically precise and confidently delivered. It was, though, unnecessarily dangerous; a move meant to cow her. Even now, as the hunky abductor unwound the duct tape, he continued to assert his dominance - despite being gentle, his cupped hand held her chin the way a dog trainer would hold the muzzle of a misbehaving pup.

Hollie glared defiantly.

He might be in control, but she still had her dignity.

Dark, confident eyes held her gaze, and in those unwavering orbs was a depth of confidence and will that overwhelmed Hollie, making her feel…insignificant.

Hollie looked away. She hated this man. Hated him for making her less than she was, for making her subservient to him.

The tape was removed and the tennis ball-sized gag plopped heavy to the ground. As it came free, the remaining spew sluiced out. But still, the hand held.

Even while Hollie spat and hacked and coughed to clear her throat, it never moved, as steady and firm as stone. Foul liquid dripped from the fingers of her kidnapper. If he minded, Hollie couldn't read it with the quick glances she stole - peeking upward between fallen bangs.

"Better?"

She nodded, feeling like a child.

"Good. I'm glad," he said and beamed.

That smile could have sold an endangered species fur to a paint wielding PETA activist. It was the most awe-inspiring and terrifying thing Hollie had ever seen.

"Now…" said the smiling man, and his hand blurred. Where moments before the tape had parted like a zipper without incident, now a gaping gash appeared.

Hollie tried to scream, but her previous tantrums had left her voice as empty as her stomach.

"That's just so you know I'm serious," he said, wiping red lines from the steel onto his pant leg.

The gash would surely leave a scar for life. Her tongue darted in and out of the hole in her cheek and anger sparked in Hollie. But one look from the smiling man's intense amethyst eyes put out the embers of rebellion before they even had time to fully ignite.

He was in charge. She would obey. The razor had made sure of that.

"Come on."

Legs wobbled to support Hollie after she was freed and helped out of the trunk. The rocky grey ground was infected with jaundice grass and brittle sagebrush. From the vista, it was immediately apparent that they were high up on a mountainside, higher up than any of the surrounding summits. Hollie believed this meant their location was Spruce Mountain. Somewhere north was Shafter Army Base and Testing Grounds surrounded on three sides by the Pequop mountain range. The range formed a J, and Spruce Mountain was both its highest and southernmost peak. Back in the late 1800's it had been home to a dozen different mining operations. Nowadays, it was scarred by crumbling ghost towns and pockmarked with abandoned mine shafts - nothing more than a used-up and dead piece of landscape.

The area seemed to foreshadow Hollie's own fate a little too overtly, and as she swallowed the blood pooling in her mouth, she asked her escort from hell just what he wanted.

"All with be made clear soon," he said, grasping her high up on the arm and leading her down a narrow path.

They ended up at a mine entrance that might have been mistaken for a cave if it hadn't been secured by an old rusty gate.

"Open it."

The smiling man produced a key from his pocket. It was shiny and new, as was the lock that secured the metal bars meant to keep out trespassers and overly adventurous teenagers. Hollie noticed too that the decaying hinges had recently been greased.

Just what was this place?

"It's not far, but we need to hurry."

Closing the gate, the smiling man plunged them into darkness. A moment later, an oil lamp was lit, and devil shadows sprang to life, darting behind boulders and clinging to the ceiling.

"Come on."

A hand at the small of Hollie's back guided her forward.

The shaft descended steeply, and roughhewn side passages snaked off in all directions. After approximately a hundred yards, a man-made cavern opened up before them - a staging area for preparing to move deeper into the mine. The ceiling was low and flat, and the space economically packed.

A kitchen area in one corner was stocked with canned goods while a plastic Porta Potty leaned off-center in the opposite corner. The centerpiece was a worn wooden picnic table littered with medical equipment: first-aid supplies, syringes, an IV drip line, defibrillator, even a battery-operated heart monitor.

Hollie wondered what the supplies were for when she spotted a cell carved into the stone wall. Approximately eight-feet-by-four, the repository had probably once been used to store mining equipment, though no doubt it would secure a human subject just as easily as it did pickaxes, drills, and dynamite.

The sight of those iron bars made Hollie pull up short. She now knew the real horrors of what awaited her. The food, the medical gear, the cage - the smiling man meant to keep her here. He wasn't just going to rape her and be done with it, he was going to hold her prisoner, possibly torture her, and with all his provisions, he could probably keep her alive until she longed for death, even begged for it.

Down here in the cold dark earth, she likely wasn't even the first to suffer such depraving atrocities.

"Now don't go faint on me," said the smiling man. "It's not what you think. Oh, the cell is for you, yes, but the rest—" he motioned to the supplies "—is for me."

Too overwhelmed to understand what that meant, Hollie let herself be imprisoned in the cage. She was too tired, too sore, and too numb to be scared anymore. She turned to ask this sadistic wanker just what he wanted - maybe even hawk a bloody loogie in his handsome face - but halted when she saw the gun.

"Now, I know you're familiar with human biology - DNA, RNA, chromosomes, and all that, but you're no physician. So, let me explain what's going to happen."

He shot her.

The bullet blasted through abdominal tissue, and instantly Hollie folded in on herself. Forgotten were her lacerated check and battered nose; they were nothing compared to this. This was the pain of the damned.

"Being gut shot is a terribly slow and painful way to go," said the smiling man putting down the gun. "But I need you dead."

He then took off his pants, and an acute chill coursed down Hollie's spine. *Oh, this freak is truly one sick bastard,* she thought. *He's a goddamn necrophiliac!*

As if reading her mind, the George Clooney lookalike halted his undress. "Regardless of what you may think, I'm not going to ravish your body once you die."

He finished disrobing, and Hollie gasped.

Woven into the guy's skin from neck to wrists to ankles was an intricate unitard of blood-red tattoos. However, these weren't random pictures or even gang markings, but a collection of occult symbols, hieroglyphs, astrological charts, swastikas, and satanic goat heads.

Suddenly Hollie was mouthing the words to the twenty-third Psalm, and she felt on the verge of falling into an abyss of mindless hysteria. Pain and primal fear filled her, and hot tears burned in her eyes.

Damnit, keep it together! You can't lose it now, Hollie yelled at herself, and took several deep breaths, choking down her despair.

There was more than basic first aid supplies just outside this cell; she just had to get to them. First, however, she needed to incapacitate this demonic sociopath.

The gun wasn't an option - too far away. What she needed was something in or near the cell to use as a weapon. Then, once this pervert tried to rape her, she could knock him out. For despite his claim, Hollie believed he would try to use her sexually. What other explanation was there for his nudity?

The rough granite ground seemed as likely to conceal a weapon as a baby's crib, yet Hollie's searching hand brushed up against a nail, and not just any nail, but the king of nails: a railroad spike! Perfect. She could hit the creep in the head, club him until he was unconscious, or better yet, thrust it into his face - put out an eye, break his nose, shatter his perfect gleaming teeth.

I hope you like eating food pumped directly into your stomach, because once I'm done with you, you won't have a face left.

Hollie hadn't lost her sense of humor, which was good because she was going to need it when this was all over.

"Now, before the loss of blood makes you too delirious, I want to ask you a critical question."

The smiling man swabbed iodine circles on his chest. The orange spheres marked the contact points for the heart monitor electrodes, though why they were needed was as elusive to Hollie as her freedom.

"Some people can last up to an hour before dying from a wound like yours, but I don't think you're going to make it that long; so, what I want to know is - are you a believer? Not in God, I know where you stand with that, but in yourself?"

Hollie nodded. To her devout Catholic parents, her schooling, Ph.D., and career were all failures. Each success was a slap in the face to their antiquated values, but she had never once doubted her aptitude.

The smiling man beamed his Oscar-winning smile. "Yes, I see you do. Good. So do I. That's why I'm doing all of this: because of you."

A thoughtful expression crossed his face. "It wasn't easy though, being a man who only believes in himself, but…I saw the light."

With the electrodes in place, the heart monitor beeped, indicating a strong heart rhythm.

"Now, Adam Murakami was not a believer."

"Dr. Murakami!?" The name bought Hollie out of her pain and sharply back into focus. "What does he have to do with this?"

The smiling man ignored the question.

"A visionary man perhaps, but the problem with visionary men is that their obsession makes them blind. All they can see is what they want, not what's really there. He didn't believe in you like I did."

What was this creep talking about? Dr. Murakami had hand-selected her, put her in charge of a highly skilled team, and had given her every resource she'd asked for. If that didn't show the billionaire's trust in her, Hollie didn't know what would.

"I can see that you don't understand. My terminology is perhaps too metaphysical. Let me put it another way; Adam Murakami used you. He deceived you. Your theoretical research has been tested and applied since day one - with the help of the government no less. Today, in fact, is the first human trial."

"Impossible!" Hollie blanched, spitting coppery tasting blood.

There was no way that her research was even plausible. She was only indulging the whims of an eccentric old man. Of course, the project did have the potential to be the springboard to many exciting possibilities - possibilities that could change the world - which was why she'd gotten involved in the first place. She'd wanted to be part of something amazing, something truly revolutionary. But to actually be experimenting - and with human test subjects - was ludicrous.

"You're full of shit."

"No," said the smiling man, and although there was madness in him, Hollie saw he also spoke the truth. Had there been hints? Had she truly been so myopic? So naïve?

The smiling man continued.

"The ultimate indication of faith is to act, to plunge into darkness and the unknown with the expectation of results. The fool Murakami lacked the faith to fully submit. He thought he could achieve the ultimate goal without paying the full sacrifice - a delusion that leads to death, a folly made by many. However, since he started what I could only hope for, I spared him. I wanted him to see the error of his ways. I wanted his faith to be genuine. But to do that, I first had to purify him."

He paused for emphasis, "And do you know what the greatest purifier is?"

Hollie didn't answer.

She knew where this nightmare was heading.

"Pain."

The man's perfect smile flashed in the light.

Why had she ever thought it charming? The sight was pure evil.

"Adam Murakami was an obstinate man. It took me a good while to convince him of your doctrine."

Despite her own suffering and the precarious position she was in, Hollie's heart went out to Dr. Murakami. How this lunatic had bypassed security to capture and torture the entrepreneur was a mystery, but she had no doubt he'd done it, and the indignation that she hadn't been able to fully form for herself now blossomed for her mentor and friend.

"You cock-sucking bastard," she spat, her hand squeezing the railroad spike with white-knuckle anger. "How could you kill one of the greatest minds of our time?"

Eyes widening, the smiling man was genuinely shocked. Not by the insult, but by the accusation.

"I didn't kill him. What would be the point of that? He's still in the basement of my house - completely secure, undetectable, and alive."

Hollie straightened. The knowledge that Dr. Murakami wasn't dead - hurt and possibly dying but alive - bolstered her determination to get out of here. Adam's survival depended on it.

"No, no, nooo, the esteemed geneticist won't die until after he beholds me in all my glory. Murakami is my Thomas. He doubts, but will weep bitterly once he sees. Only then will he die."

The smug superiority with which the smiling man spoke sickened Hollie. She was convinced that this freak must be some kind of missionary serial killer. His obvious God-complex would have been as pathetic as the end-of-the-world ravings by some doomsday derelict of the street, pathetic that was, if his threats weren't so real.

Naked as he'd come into the world, the smiling man took up the ivory-handled straight razor and stepped towards the cell.

"Now we're out of time. Consider my shooting you an honor. You shall be my first angel."

"You're insane," Hollie declared.

Wagging a finger like an adult reprimanding a misbehaving toddler, he said, "Now, now, you disappoint me, Hollie. That's the talk of a nonbeliever."

Then, with a final grin as luminous and broad as a retiring stage performer, he raised the blade to his throat.

"Behold!"

A spray of blood arched across the room, shimmering in the flickering lamplight.

The heart monitor sang and the smiling man crumpled.

"Fuck..." Hollie exhaled, and the railroad spike slipped from her fingers. For a while, she just listened to the electronic flat line.

What was the point of shooting her if the psycho's plan all along was to kill himself? Did he believe that if she died with him she'd serve him in the afterlife? Was she some kind of retainer sacrifice like the servants of an ancient Egyptian pharaoh? Or did he just need an audience?

Screw why, Hollie was getting out of here.

Bright pain flashed anew as she hauled herself upright. Reaching through the bars, Hollie touched the old iron latch. The wacko hadn't even secured it, but stranger still, Hollie couldn't feel it. Her hand held the latch, but it seemed like someone else's.

Leaking blood and trembling, Hollie managed only a single shove of the gate before sliding heavily to the ground.

God, she was tired.

Perhaps she'd take a short nap.

'*Short*' *my ass,* Hollie thought, as a hard bubbling cough escaped her. *Close your eyes now, and you won't ever wake up.*

But she wanted to. She wanted nothing more than to just lie down and rest.

Her head listed to one side and her eyes fell on the burgundy tattooed freak. Hollie found herself fixated on the elaborate canvas that was his skin. A large inverted cross caught her attention, and suddenly it came to her that the smiling man had it all wrong.

She was the doubting Thomas.

Could Dr. Murakami actually have done it? Had he really found the solution to the paradox? If the military was starting human trials, then that must mean they'd already been successful with animal testing.

That possibility alone was enough to make Hollie no longer want to sleep.

But closing her eyes, that's precisely what she did.

Eternally.

CHAPTER 1

Kaufman Striker almost didn't hear the stranger come through the front door. He froze, listening - a small blue flower in hand.

This wasn't his house.

He was trespassing, and not for the first time.

Jingling keys advocated that it was the homeowner, because what were the odds that two voyeurs would hit the same house at the same time? More likely to win the California state mega lottery. Yet, even standing in the room of a teenage girl, what Kaufman was doing was not voyeurism. He hadn't entered the house out of some sordid sexual fetish.

No, his perversion was much more disturbing, much more deeply-seated.

From downstairs came the insistent beeping of the house alarm.

Kaufman knew that the correct seven-digit security code needed to be entered within two minutes, or the police would be notified of an intruder.

In this case, the system was deactivated in less than thirty seconds.

Definitely the owner. This was bad.

Worse, heavy footfalls indicated that it was not the tall, graceful, and kind Ms. Green that had unexpectedly come home but her three hundred plus pound husband. Both a pit boss and a one-time professional football player, Anthony Green had a reputation at The Paradise Hotel and Casino that made even the thug security guards timid at his passing.

Kaufman wondered how much punishment his body could sustain if discovered - probably about as much as a field of wheat in a hailstorm. Although he was well-muscled with tough, calloused hands, his own stout twenty-eight-year-old frame was shaped from years of digging and landscaping, not fighting. Anthony, on the other hand, had earned the nickname "Raging Bull" in his brief season with the Chicago Bears defense - both for his physique and his temperament. All these years later, the handle he'd acquired in the NFL remained, and if the rumors were true, so did the track record of concussions he still dealt out; although whether justified or just to make a point wasn't always clear.

Slowly, Anthony made his way up the stairs.

Why was he here? He was supposed to be at the funeral of his fourteen-year-old daughter. A large public presence was expected as Dominique Green's death had been front page news. Anthony must have forgotten something. He would never intentionally miss his only child's funeral; unlike Kaufman, who was specifically avoiding the event.

"Forget me not, Mr. Striker!"

It was the playful saying Dominique had always used when leaving the nursery. She'd been a beautiful girl - quick to smile with raven hair and skin the color of creamed coffee. Kaufman always looked forward to her biweekly visits, notably since she never showed any of the awkwardness that others displayed around him. He'd even contemplated offering her a summer job when she turned sixteen.

Forget-me-not.

It wasn't just a farewell; it was also a request.

The botanical name for the flower was Myosotis arvensis - the state flower of Alaska. Dominique had wanted the five-petal blue perennial ever since she'd seen a picture of it in one of Kaufman's horticultural books. Yet he'd never ordered her one. His procrastination wasn't due to laziness or forgetfulness, but because of his warped nature - his emotional unconnectedness. Getting her the flower didn't serve his self-interest. However, here, now, with flower in hand like an awkward prom date, he would only be able to deliver Dominique's special request - and in some small way exorcise his own atrophied soul - if he wasn't discovered.

Lingering in the doorway, though, left him exposed. Surely when the Raging Bull saw this interloper in his little girl's bedroom, he'd give new meaning to the term "gratuitous violence" that even director Martin Scorsese would be ashen to reproduce.

Regardless of his innocence, even kind intentions, Kaufman needed a place to hide.

Before him, Dominique's bedroom stretched out like a jungle canopy. On the far side of the room, large bay windows gave a sweeping panorama of the grey-brown desert beyond, while directly below a green waterfall of flowers and ferns, palms and pines, cactuses and herbs cascaded from the expansive curving window seat. But it was the two colossal climbing rose bushes to the right and left of the doorway - woven along and covering the ceiling - that was most impressive.

Overhead, a sky of red roses bloomed.

But for all its wonderment, the room offered very little concealment. Besides the pink four-post bed with a translucent silk canopy, there were no other furnishings; no bookcases or desk, not even a dresser - which all boiled down to nothing to hide behind or in.

Kaufman was about to dive under the bed, when the massive bulk of the Raging Bull crested the stairs.

Quickly stepping sideways, Kaufman pushed himself up against the rose-covered wall and listened.

The muffled whoosh-clump of dress shoes on carpet drew nearer, and each step reverberated through the floorboards and into his bones.

Why had he waited so long to hide? Why had he chosen *this* room to hide in? He could have easily ducked into the nearby office. Now he was trapped.

His actions had been careless and reckless. Of course, a father would be drawn to the bedroom of his offspring on the day she was being laid to rest. This outcome was easily anticipated. But perhaps, just maybe, he would get lucky, and Anthony would only glance in - would want to keep the room as pristine and undisturbed as his memories.

To give luck every opportunity, Kaufman needed to get as close to the wall as possible, become part of the paint. Unfortunately, the rosebush acted as a buffer and he risked making his presence known if any branch snapped while he mashed further up against them.

The footsteps approached, accompanied by heavy breathing.

Anthony was close and getting closer.

Kaufman didn't have a choice. Gritting his teeth, he flattened himself into the roses.

Thorns bit deep and Kaufman chomped down on his tongue to keep from crying out. The sacrifice was worth it. Anthony stopped just short of the doorway.

Embraced in the organic iron maiden, Kaufman felt his nostrils taunted by Anthony's expensive cologne and he suddenly became aware of his own sour stink. The scent of stale sweat poured off him, seemed almost visible, and if he could smell Anthony, could Anthony smell him?

As if in answer, the Raging Bull's sasquatch hand reached into a suit pocket and pulled out a knife. He flicked it open with a practiced snap, and impatient fingers gripped and re-gripped the rubber-coated handle.

This was no gentleman's folder, no inconsequential penknife either, but a four-inch tactical folding dagger, and Kaufman's imagination raced with the possible ways the blade could inflict bodily harm: gouge out his delicate eyes, flay him like an expensive fish, or just stab him in the kidneys like some prison shanking. Yet for all the nightmarish possibilities those four inches of black steel represented, Kaufman remained passively detached, as always. He knew his cool mental state would typically indicate either advanced military training or his being a total sociopath.

Yet, he was neither an elite soldier nor a homicidal maniac. No, his near-perfect stoicism was a birthright, an inheritance passed down to him by his father - the famous architect Göttlich Striker.

"You either own or are owned, Kaufman. Never forget that. Life is about pushing yourself beyond what you're capable of and becoming something new and powerful. Your legacy - your very worth - is determined by the degree to which you obtain control over yourself and everything around you. That is why you must not become dependent on anyone or anything. It makes you weak, and worse, it makes you a possession."

Those words had been drilled into him over the years more thoroughly than any celebrity-endorsed, internet-spread, multimillion dollar-backed slogan. Dominism wasn't just the new and controversial architectural style his young, ambitious father had introduced to the world, but the doctrine he lived by. Those twisted and truculent ascetic ideologies also guided Göttlich's parenting, and Kaufman's upbringing was about as traditional as women's rights in the dark ages. Even the house he'd grown up in was more a stockade than home. Indeed, as a joke, Göttlich had named the edifice *The Dwelling* when Kaufman - in a rebellious juvenile tantrum - stated that they didn't truly live, they only "dwelled."

Reared in near-total indifference, Kaufman had never owned a single toy, never played with another child, and while he'd had plenty of books to occupy him, they were only dry, sterile texts full of cause and effect. Homeschooling had begun early, although success or failure - like crying - elicited neither compassion nor irritation, only the next lesson. However, as part of his educational progress, he had to be periodically tested; and since the exams were conducted at the public library, it afforded Kaufman brief moments of escape from his father, The Dwelling, and Dominism.

The public library became his land of liberty, and the books his freedom fighters. Every narrative he was able to get his hands on fascinated him, plunged him into worlds that he never knew existed; and yet they mystified him too, puzzled him more deeply than any abstract philosophy. Love and hate were baffling, jealousy confused, and compassion was an alien planet. Indeed, emotions as a whole generally perplexed Kaufman. That didn't stop him from reading, but in time those stories did reveal just how rice-paper thin and deficient his life was.

He'd always known he was different, but at the tender age of eight, he'd also swallowed the odious reality that his isolation and esoteric upbringing wasn't just was making him into a coached introvert, but an android. He came to understand as well that, although literature would forever be his sanctuary, it was not the impregnable treetop fortress he'd once imagined it to be; rather, it was a dilapidated couple of two-by-fours in a rickety old pine - a place to escape to for a time, but not a place capable of sustaining long-term habitation.

So, to rein in his abnormality - and possibly discover the key to his elusive emotions - he'd taken to sneaking out of The Dwelling and into the real world. Observing the microcosm of Decoy offered a wealth of insights, although it wasn't until he started entering people's homes that he learned what normal really was.

At first, he'd just knocked on doors and asked to use the restroom. That worked until he got caught a few times in rooms other than the bathroom and word spread about the freaky architect's kid. That led him to take up full-blown trespassing. Most people usually left a door or window unlocked; if not, he'd move on.

Kaufman never broke in.

He wasn't a criminal or a thief, just an emotional squatter.

At fifteen, though, all that changed.

That was the year he began living on his own. Kaufman suspected his effortless emancipation had less to do with his father's plan to move to Siberia (to live and work in an abandoned gulag) than to the fact that Göttlich was as silver-tongued, as efficacious, and as quick to grease palms as any corporate lobbyist. But whatever the reasons, the day he'd been recognized as a legal adult had severed Göttlich's autocratic umbilical cord and freed him from The Dwelling. The separation also dissolved his need for clandestine home invasions, and for twelve years now, he'd been an upstanding citizen of the community - albeit a socially outcast one.

Until today.

Once again - like the emotionless haunted youth he still was - he'd entered the home of someone else to try and understand what wasn't in him, what had been sired out of him.

A week ago, a drunk driver had hit and plowed over Dominique Green as mercilessly as a runaway train. The guy had been so inebriated he'd driven three blocks before realizing the pedestrian he'd just killed was still stuck in the undercarriage. The entire police force had been called out, and a quarter-mile stretch of public road was closed for the cleanup. Dominique's death was a tragedy, an outrage; the newspaper had reported as much, and the town agreed, yet Kaufman felt nothing.

Even now, the sight of Anthony's handheld bayonet didn't cause his heart to race with dread or his brow to trickle with nervous sweat. Intellectually Kaufman knew the blade represented danger, pain, even death, just as he recognized that he should be moved in some way by Dominique's untimely and horrific demise; except he was emotional vapid, as empty as a black hole, and it was this bareness that had led him to the bedroom of his friend - or more correctly, to the bedroom of a girl who had been friendly to him - to try to evoke some emotional response and prove to himself that he wasn't wholly a heartless machine.

Though, if Anthony found him, there would be no opportunity to feel anything other than physical pain. Kaufman wondered how much longer he could maintain his precarious position; already, the sharp strain of flexed muscles had given way to a dull ache and his legs were quaking.

What was Anthony doing? Kaufman was confident he hadn't been seen, so why *had* Anthony drawn the knife?

Perhaps he should announce himself. He might talk his way out of this. Kaufman immediately dismissed the thought. He might be emotionally lacking, but his survival instincts were well-honed - as finely pointed as a syringe. The small forget-me-not would be an impossible sell.

Abruptly Anthony's heavy breathing changed from a steady rolling rhythm to a series of sharp, quick inhalations. Surely, he'd just caught Kaufman's sent - if he hadn't already smell him before now.

Anthony entered the room.

The Bull didn't so much walk as plod, and his sniffing was so robust as to be classified as snorting.

Kaufman waited to be seized and pounded, have his bones crushed, be stabbed, mutilated, mangled. Even when Anthony passed him by without so much as a glance, Kaufman expected the ex-defensive lineman to wheel around and charge, and the thought persisted well after the childless father started cutting roses.

A held breath slipped out of Kaufman as he watched the knife worked with utilitarian efficiency. Looking at the situation without himself as the epicenter, he realized Anthony hadn't come to Dominique's bedroom to confront an intruder, but rather to gather flowers for the girl's headstone. Also, Anthony hadn't been sniffing to smell - hadn't gotten a whiff of Kaufman's bodily reek - he'd been sniffling, trying to hold back grief and tears. However, as he worked, his reserve broke, and suddenly, Anthony was blubbering.

"Baby, my sweet baby girl," he sobbed softly, over and over, as he cut roses and delicately placed them on the bed as if they were fragile as dreams.

Kaufman's chest tightened.

For all the hard edges and wildness of Anthony 'Raging Bull' Green, underneath was a soft, doting father. Dominique had been the classic beauty that tamed the beast.

Kaufman suddenly felt that intimacy, felt his stoic straitjacket momentarily slip free, felt…felt what? Joy? Sadness? Empathy?

He couldn't identify the sensation, and as much as he wanted to stay and be a part of it, he knew he had to get out. He'd gotten lucky when Anthony had first entered the room, but as soon as the teddy bear dad was done reminiscing and collecting the velvety blossoms, he would turn, and no amount of luck would help Kaufman then. He would be as trapped and visible as a deer in headlights.

Now was his opportunity to flee.

Lowering himself off his tiptoes, Kaufman felt relief immediately flood into his aching back and legs. He hoped they wouldn't cramp. He needed to remain flexible to be able to creep silently out of the room.

But as he stepped towards the open door, it wasn't his legs that held him back - but the rose bush. His denim work shirt was tangled and ensnared. The thorns may have let him down, but they weren't going to let him go. Kaufman worried the effort required to pull free would cause enough noise to bring Anthony out of his reverie.

But he had to get away - and soon.

Already a pile of a dozen or more roses had been cut. It was unlikely he had more than a minute or two left in which to escape.

Kaufman considered unbuttoning his shirt and slipping out, yet if he was seen shirtless he wouldn't just be an interloper but a pervert, for only a sick sexual deviant would be in such a place at such a time, and never was an animal so ferocious as when they were protecting their young, or in this case, the memory of their young. Seeing a half-naked man standing in the bedroom of his late teenage daughter, Anthony's grief would transform into wrath that would obliterate Kaufman.

No time to think, act.

Undoing his shirt, Kaufman slipped out. The blue fabric hung limply like a forgotten battle-scarred flag. Even if his name and nursery hadn't been embroidered on the front right pocket, he couldn't leave it; the presences of that article of clothing would alert Anthony to a trespasser, and as it would be too time-consuming to unpin each thorn, so Kaufman just yanked.

The shirt came away cleanly and with only the slightest tearing sound.

It must have been loud enough though, for Anthony's rich bass voice boomed.

"You!"

Kaufman froze.

His heart missed a beat, and suddenly clammy hands held the torn denim. With his bareback to the huge man, Kaufman knew fear, understood terror.

"You…" came the voice again. Although instead of being an accusing lash, the vocalization was drawn out and oddly musical. It was in that melodious timber that Kaufman realized he wasn't being called out but was the unwitting observer of more of Anthony's mourning.

As if in confirmation, the bereaving father began singing *You Are My Sunshine*.

For a second, Kaufman listened - breathlessly, reverently. Anthony's familiarity with the tune suggested that this had been a lullaby sung to a beloved daughter, except the usually cheery ditty was now melancholy and laden with sadness - more blues than bluegrass.

With the melody, Kaufman's distress dissipated, and as much as he wanted to stay and be part of this moment, it wasn't his to claim. To remain would be more than stealing; he would become an emotional vampire, a ghoul feeding off another's pain, when what he wanted - what he needed - was to feel his own sense of loss.

Quietly slipping out of the bedroom, Kaufman left the grieving father to his memories. He entered the adjacent office and put back on the puncture-riddled shirt. He then closed the glass-paneled French doors. Here he would wait until Anthony left.

Two large flat-screen computer monitors stood prominent on a polished desk. Black lacquer bookcases flanked each corner of the back wall, separate by a rectangular mirror. The room had the feel of a power broker's office.

As Kaufman took in the space, his breath stuck in his lungs. Near the bookcase on the far side of the room, was Dominique, smiling her signature double dimple smile.

Kaufman stood transfixed.

The photograph perfectly captured the girl, and he could see why the Greens' had had the image enlarged and framed, for it was not a posed shot but had been taken in a moment of pure joy. Dominique's features shone warmly and softened the otherwise managerial and impersonal quality of the office.

This was the Dominique he remembered, and he was drawn to her. Without realizing what he was doing, he grasped the snapshot and plucked it up. The action was as unremarkable as someone tying their shoe, but, for Kaufman, this was akin to pulling the Mona Lisa off the wall of the Louvre. He treated the homes he entered like museums, something only to observe and contemplate. Touching or interacting with objects destroyed the enchantment, reduced everything to the mundane. But Kaufman could no more have stopped himself than he could have commanded the sun to rise.

He'd reached out for the girl in a way he never could have in real life, had taken up the photo as if the connection could somehow save them both.

Kaufman's hands shook and the thin glass rattled in its wood encasement. Even strangers who had never met Dominique felt sympathy and pity at the news of her death. Yet his own firsthand acquaintance with her wasn't enough to stir remorse in him or even create a sense of selfish loss.

"Forget me not, Mr. Striker!"

Dominique's witty farewell statement suddenly came to mind with the force of a branding iron, except now her tone wasn't merry but mocking, and in the photograph, her eyes no longer sparkled but accused.

Kaufman was trying to logically work out the proper emotional response to this reproach, was so focused on conjuring up *any* feeling that he was barely aware of Anthony standing at the glass-paneled entryway. Any sane person would have had their gaze drawn upward to see if they had been noticed, but Kaufman couldn't take his eyes off the photo.

"Feel," he demanded through clenched teeth. He was breathing hard now, shaking.

The Raging Bull seemed to glare at him, yet still, Kaufman did not look up.

"Forget-me-not!" Dominique shouted in his head. *"Forget-me-not!"*

The statement was no longer a request, but a plea - a command.

Anthony's solid hands curled into fists.

"Feel!" Kaufman spat under his breath, as his shaking evolved into rigid convulsions.

At the door, Anthony finally exploded. His fist hammered into the door. The impact should have shattered the wood and glass, should have sent fragments flying through the room, but this was a well-crafted expensive home and the door only banged against the wall.

Now was the time of Kaufman's destruction, yet his gaze never wavered from Dominique's imploring eyes. He didn't even blink when the door crashed open. He was determined, so close to an epiphany.

Squeezing the frame harder, Kaufman clenched violently as if he could somehow crush an emotion out of the photograph.

"*Feel!*" he demanded and, rather than speaking the word, it shook from his body like a dead throw.

Under his fingers, the glass cracked.

Kaufman looked up and peered into the face of the now childless father. They regarded each other.

Set firmly in Anthony's features was a hateful and slightly disgusted expression, but Kaufman remained detached; and as a true master of Dominism, his aloofness allowed him to see that the abhorrence in Anthony was not projected outward, was not focused on an identified trespasser. No, Anthony's haunted bitterness was directed inwards, was a growing self-loathing as terminal as cancer.

Indeed, from his position at the distant wall of family portraits, Kaufman was entirely out of view, hidden and safe. What he was seeing was Anthony looking at his reflection. The Bull had been on his way out when he'd walked by the office and saw himself in the back wall mirror, saw injustice, saw a cold and indifferent universe.

The father still lived while his innocent daughter did not. In those angry eyes quivered the question of God's plan and the purpose of life. After a long while, Anthony turned away without an answer and descended the stairs.

Kaufman sighed.

He had narrowly escaped the Raging Bull again. It was perhaps Dominique's last gift to him. Her smile had saved him, for if he hadn't been drawn to her photo, he would have been spotted. Better not to tempt fate any further. It was time to leave. Besides, with the breaking of the glass, his own fixation had shattered. In his hands was just another fairytale that he could not make real. This was just another house that was not his home.

Hearing the front door close, he watched the Audi R8 Anthony owned drive off.

The glass lining of Dominique's portrait was ruined, a cobweb of razor-sharp crystal. Kaufman knew he couldn't take the picture with him. So instead, he hid the broken fragments deep in the trash, figuring it might go unnoticed. Then he wiped the frame where his fingers had left prints and re-hung the photograph.

Although the flower would mark his visit, he decided to leave it anyway.

"Forget me not," Kaufman breathed, resting the blue blossom lightly on the top of the frame. It would have looked marvelous in Dominique's hair.

Downstairs he stood before the alarm system keypad. Leaving would be easier than getting in.

Earlier, he'd disable it using a generic worker's code obtained from a neighboring house he'd landscaped and since all the mansions in this particular gated community were secured by the only local service available - and the affluent owners were all too indifferent to change the codes more than once a year - it had worked.

Pressing the REARM button, he was now free to walk away. Theoretically, after sixty seconds, the alarm would reset, and no one would be the wiser about his visit. Yet at the door, he hesitated.

Something bothered him.

The house was quiet, as it should be, but Kaufman's hackles were raised.

Racking his brain, he came up with nothing that might betray him. He hadn't forgotten anything, hadn't overlooked anything, all the loose ends had been taken care of.

Still, something was not right.

He supposed that anyone would be on edge after narrowly escaping the Raging Bull, twice - while in his own home, nonetheless.

Kaufman shrugged off the apprehension and opened the door.

On the porch, waiting for him, arms crossed, was a cop.

Kaufman recognized him immediately. This was not their first encounter.

"Somehow I knew I'd find you here," said the policeman.

Apparently, dodging Anthony had exhausted his luck.

Strike three.

He was out.

CHAPTER 2

"Turn around and put your hands behind your head," said the blond officer. In his mid-thirties, fit and immaculately dressed - complete with a trim mustache and aviator sunglasses - the cop was the poster child for justice.

He was also a religious zealot.

Sergeant Donald Graeci; pronounced GRAY-see, but behind his back, he was known as Greasy by those not interested in what he was proselytizing - which was almost everyone. The thing that turned people off wasn't so much the self-made brand of Christianity Graeci preached, although there was that, but how he tried to sell his religion: fast, slick, and polished.

Donald was God's used car salesman.

"I said, turn around!"

The authoritative tone was now laced with irritation.

Kaufman didn't wait to be told a third time. He wasn't ashamed about being arrested, but he was surprised by it.

Donald had never handcuffed him before.

When he was younger, it had been Officer Graeci, fresh out of cadet school, that had picked him up when watchful neighbors tipped off the police to his trespassing. During those times, Kaufman had been lectured, preached at, even severely warned, but never taken into custody.

Slapping the cuffs on, Sgt. Graeci roughly turned Kaufman around and pushed him sharply down the walkway. Stumbling, Kaufman went down hard. One knee scraped against the concrete and he bit his tongue. Blood filled his mouth, and the coppery taste made him aware that he ought to be feeling bitter or angry at Donald's actions - his betrayal. Even with the awkward wedge Donald's ever-present desire to convert created, Donald was a friend or the closest thing to a friend Kaufman had. Yet other than his stinging knee, Kaufman remained as emotionally anesthetized as any lips after dental surgery.

Emotional emptiness: his father had sought it all his life, but it was Kaufman who had obtained it. And didn't want it.

"On your feet," said Graeci, pulling Kaufman upright.

Friend he may be, but Donald was still a cop, and this wasn't the minor leagues anymore. Kaufman was now an adult, subject to the full penalty of the law, and he'd just broken into a private residence, something he'd never done as a youth.

Prodded forward roughly, Kaufman reached Donald's patrol car. He resisted as his head was pushed down, and he was forced into the sedan. His own truck was parked at the end of the street, a beat-up old Dodge, yet that wasn't the reason for his resistance. Donald's patrol car was too clean, sparkled with fresh wax and fanaticism. Indeed, Donald was so adept with the idea of cleanliness being next to Godliness that he could have owned a mansion in the breast pocket of the Almighty. It was that level of monomania that reminded Kaufman of his father, echoed Dominism, and made him reluctant.

Kaufman shifted in the back seat.

As they neared the community entrance, a guard stood waiting, arms planted on hips and a bothered expression on his round face. As if having to get out of his air-conditioned shack was akin to having to answer the phone while performing heart surgery.

Donald slowed to a stop and rolled down the window.

"There's nothing to worry about. It was just the landscaper."

"The Droid?" asked the pudgy guard bending over to get a better look. The buttons on his dress shirt strained to hold back the massive girth underneath.

"Kaufman," corrected Donald sharply.

"Oh…right," said the rent-a-cop, blushing as stood up and tugging at his wrinkled uniform.

At least he had the decency to act embarrassed. So many of the town's folk openly gawked at Kaufman. Though he was used to the whispered remarks and finger-pointing. It came with the territory of his peculiar celebrity.

"So…uh…what do you want me to do?" asked the guard, identified as 'Lee' by his Wal-Mart-sized name badge.

"Nothing," responded Donald. "I'm taking him in for questioning. I'm sure the whole thing is just a misunderstanding."

Nodding, Lee said, "I still got to fill out a report. It's procedure." The last word was drawn out.

"He was just working, so you don't need to take any further action," said Donald. "I'll handle it from here."

Lee seemed more than willing to let someone else take responsibility; he didn't want the extra work, but he also didn't want to lose his cushy job.

"Still need to call it in."

"You already did. I'm here."

Lee fidgeted, not satisfied. He resembled an overweight forty-year-old hall monitor.

"Look, I insisted on making the report myself," said Donald, feeding the guy lines, "Who were you to argue?"

The security guard smiled. His brown tobacco-stained teeth matched his brown rumpled uniform. He was being given an easy way out, and he knew it.

"Right, it's your jurisdiction anyway."

"Exactly," said Donald. "Now, open the gate."

Security guard Lee did his duty.

Giving a little wave as the patrol car drove off, Donald said, "I sleep much easier at night knowing the citizens of Golden Hills are *so* well protected."

Kaufman regarded his one-time friend.

The unrestrained sarcasm surprised him. Had something happened to turn Donald cynical? Had a decade of rubbing shoulders with lowlifes day in and day out made Donald misanthropic? If so, then being arrested was more serious than Kaufman had previously thought. In fact, if their tentative friendship no longer existed, Kaufman might be royally screwed.

Pulling away from the gated community, Donald rounded the corner, parked, and twisted to face his detainee.

"You shouldn't have come, Kauf." Reproach furrowed his brow. "I know you haven't been in anybody's house since your father left. I've been watching out for you, like I promised, but this was too much. It was reckless. Understandable, but reckless. Not to mention stupid. If Anthony had discovered you, only God's grace would have saved you because my hands would have been tied. Understand?"

Kaufman thought he did. Donald still saw him as thirteen, still regarded him as a service project. While sincere, even admirable, Donald's behavior was just the charitable version of gawking - his way of dealing with the town oddity.

"I understand," said Kaufman, more in response to his insight than to the question.

"Good," said Donald, getting out of the patrol car and coming around back.

"Sorry about the handcuffs and all the rough stuff, but I had to make it look official. A neighbor called in a 10-66: suspicious figure."

"Uh…sure, no problem," said Kaufman, rubbing his wrists. Then, as custom demanded, he added, "Thanks."

The sentiment seemed hardly appropriate. Donald had stuck out his neck for him, had risked his job, his reputation, and it wasn't the first time. When Donald had learned of Göttlich's less than ideal parenting, he'd donned the protector role, made Kaufman his personal crusade. He'd kept homeowners from pressing charges and the local newspaper from writing slanderous reports.

Even if his motives were derived from some sort of misdirected big-brotherly benevolence, Kaufman knew he ought to feel more; at the bare minimum, feel regret for doubting Donald's loyalty. But there was nothing. Kaufman was as empty as a shucked oyster. All he could do was lamely voice his counterfeit gratitude again.

"I…I really appreciate it."

"This was a heinous accident, Kaufman. The murder of Dominique Green is utterly reprehensible. The Bible warns against drunkenness, and more, it states: Whosoever shall offend one of these little ones that believes in me, it is better for him that that a millstone were hanged about his neck, and he were cast into the sea, Matthew 18:6. Now, why don't you come ride up front, and I'll take you home." Kaufman nodded and moved to the front passenger seat. On it was a Bible, heavily cross-referenced and well worn. It marked Donald as much as his neat military mustache - he never went anywhere without it.

Would you hold that for me? I don't want to lose my place. God's word is too important to keep closed."

"Right," sighed Kaufman, shutting the door. Left open, the bible was about as subtle as a billboard, and Donald hope that by just handling the book, any passenger would have an uncontrollable desire to read, an unquenchable thirst for truth, a burning desire to be saved.

Kaufman has never been so inclined.

Getting back on the main road, Donald licked his lips, popped his knuckles, and cracked his neck. A sermon was brewing. Kaufman felt it.

"You know your father walked in darkness at noonday," said Donald, and, in the blink of an eye, gone was the model police officer replaced by the pushy auto salesman. Like the classic dual character of Dr. Jekyll and Mr. Hyde, Sgt. Graeci had just transformed into Greasy.

"Göttlich is an unrepentant heathen, a corrupter of minds, a spreader of lies, and you were never taught correct Christian principles." Graeci suddenly paused thoughtfully and looked at Kaufman. "You're not alone, though…I can relate. I was Catholic growing up. Did you know that?"

Kaufman hadn't; he'd always presumed that Donald had been brought up in a less traditional Christian environment - something with venomous snakes perhaps.

"As a child, I believed it was God's true church. I attended faithfully, sang in the choir, was even an altar boy, and for my dedication, I was lied to, duped, and swindled. The Bible warns of apostasy, says that the very elect shall be deceived and that wolves shall enter in and not spare the flock, 2nd Thessalonians 2:3, Matthew 24:24, Acts 20:29."

The references were clipped off like a junior executive reporting end of the year sales figures. It was an annoying habit, and although Kaufman supposed it was proper pastoral etiquette, it had the air of conceit.

Unaware of his passenger's silent criticism, Graeci continued. "I grew to know the truth, though. Catholicism is no longer a holy sect but a fallen institution. To this day, my parents still refuse to believe. They have closed their eyes to the truth. Have chosen to walk in darkness at noonday, like your godless father. I'm sure you've seen the news - another priest molesting children. Abominable! It should be obvious to everyone that these atrocities are not just a blot on the church but another stain on an already filthy garment, proof that Catholicism no longer has the authority to act in the name of the Holy One."

Kaufman suspected all religions had their bad apples, just as it was absurd to think all politicians were corrupt or that the good ones were infallible. People were people, imperfect and prone to mistakes. That didn't excuse an individual's actions, but he was disturbed by how easily people judged others by their worst deeds yet measured themselves by their best intentions. He supposed that in this age of digital hustling and twenty-four-seven exposure, where culture was as volatile as a trending YouTube video - the current mainstream truism was that of a heckler: expose someone else's flaws to cover your own.

Opening his mouth to comment, Kaufman stopped himself. He didn't feel like raising an objection and being dragged into a debate. Besides, Graeci preferred a more passive audience.

Staring out the window, Kaufman watched the town give way to the seemingly endless desert - a visual blur to accompany Donald's auditory droning - and kept watch for the tall piñon pines that marked the entrance to his driveway.

As the desert passed by, Kaufman thought about his house. The Pueblo structure never failed to impress. It belonged, seemed to be a part of nature rather than a creation of man. Indeed, the brawny tan stucco and the graceful curving arches mimicked the surrounding windswept hills.

Constructed in 1940 on ten acres, the adobe-style farmhouse preceded the establishment of Shafter Military Base and the city of Decoy by a few years. Back then, the landscape had been home to a few ranchers and a scattered population of miners.

The house was cozy and inviting, built with calloused hands and honest labor. It had the quaint personality that came with age and simpler yesteryear. It was the epitome of everything his father's architectural style was against. Buying the home had been a step towards normalcy, though that's not how the newspapers and magazines had reported it.

The adobe was as far away from his childhood residence and architectural "wonder/blunder" of The Dwelling, his father's most recent "masterpiece/outrage," as one could get and still be within the city limits.

Choosing to buy the house at fifteen as his first act as a legal, court-recognized adult, instead of continuing to live in The Dwelling, was seen as an act of rebellion, heralded by critics as clear proof of the crimes against the architectural world - let alone humanity - that Göttlich Striker was committing.

Kaufman had wanted to keep the house as purchased - lived in and homey. The fully furnished rooms had been a major selling point for him, yet when he'd moved in, he'd felt like a trespasser. It was as if he were a kid again and bold enough not only to visit for a few hours in someone else's home, but sleep and eat there as well.

For a year, he'd kept up the charade. However, the dim hope that getting out from under his father's shadow and the oppressive house of his childhood would somehow transform him into a normal person wasn't realized.

There was nothing normal about him.

He was as alien to most people as any beetle-eyed space traveler would have been. He'd gone from the cold and uncaring world of his father to the cold and uncaring world at large.

After the public had become bored with the strange architect's son and latched onto a fresh new subject to sensationalize and exploit, Kaufman had cleaned out the house room by room. Although he was no longer living in The Dwelling, the ideologies behind that monstrosity were still living in him.

As the cruiser came to a stop, dusty rooster tails kicked up from the rear tires.

Turning to look at Kaufman, Donald said, "Now I want to offer you something." A crease furrowed his brow. "What I want to offer is not false hope, not a false religion or false doctrine. No, my offer is for you to come study with my fellowship. Help us prepare for the restoration, become a brother in Christ. What do you say? Will you join us?"

Kaufman had heard this pitch a hundred times. His pseudo-friend preached hellfire and talked of damnation as if it were the weather. It was all stuff he neither cared about nor understood. Still, maybe being part of something bigger, participating instead of observing was precisely what he needed. The invitation to join Donald's congregation did have a certain appeal, even if it meant swallowing the parochial elements. Kaufman wasn't ready to say yes, but he didn't say no either.

"I'll think about it."

"Really?" Donald exclaimed in disbelief. "Well…that's great…fantastic actually. If I could just open up peoples' minds, plant the seed of faith, I'd be a rich man in the sight of God and the harvest would be bountiful indeed."

Nodding, Kaufman got out. The early morning air was already as hot and dry as a baker's oven. He shut the door and waved as the patrol car drove off.

Nearing the front door, he stopped. He figured it was late enough to check the mail and so he headed back down the driveway.

Never one to receive more than an occasional bill or local advertisement, he was surprised to see a large white envelope slicing through the black of the rusty mailbox. Pulling the letter out, Kaufman stiffened. The crisp, precise handwriting was his father's.

Suddenly the air felt thin, the sky low and oppressive, the sun too bright.

This was no inconsequential credit card offer, nothing so trivial as junk mail. This was a disquieting and harrowing shadow from his past, a buried ghost resurrected. Kaufman never expected his father to contact him again, never in his most extravagant nightmares believed Göttlich would try to rekindle their relationship.

Left with a substantial endowment and an empty soul, his inheritance had been bequeathed, the relationship neatly severed. Yet now here, all these years later, was a letter and with it came instant despotism. Kaufman had thought himself free of that demeaning condition, but here it was with just a mere note from his dad.

He held the letter at arm's length. The envelope had an official appearance. Whatever it contained could only be bad news.

Kaufman wanted no part of his old life. He would shred the letter without reading it. He had enough problems dealing with the scars of his past to open up any new ones. Whatever his father had to say would be left unsaid.

Entering the house, determined to burn the letter once it was shredded, Kaufman abruptly stopped.

There, in the kitchen - just beyond a collection of tarnished brass pots - hung a thick hangman's noose.

Seeing that execution device, Kaufman dreaded the contents of his mail more than ever.

CHAPTER 3

Kaufman stared at the noose.

Two inches thick, the heavy cord was weathered, worn, and stained a dark maroon. The dark color made the noose seem more like a guillotine block soaked in blood, as if it administered death through decapitation, rather than asphyxia.

Kaufman looked around, expecting to find someone waiting for him. But he was alone.

His solitude gave him no comfort.

Neither did knowing that no one had come here to lynch him.

Kaufman himself had tied that most infamous of knots. Three days ago, the notion came to him after hearing the terrible way in which Dominique had been killed, and his utter lack of a response. In anyone else, the stupor would have been diagnosed as shock. Except, Kaufman knew, if that were the case, his condition was a perpetual state of shock - a life of numb existence. For even the tragedy of a girl struck down just as her life was beginning, stirred nothing in his stagnant soul.

As a reminder of this deficiency, he'd left the noose hang empty. Waiting.

Though in the aftermath of narrowly escaping Anthony and being apprehended by Donald, Kaufman had forgotten about it. Originally the idea had been strangely rational. Now though, with the unexpected arrival of his father's letter, the noose seemed not only malevolent but a conscious evil.

Looking away from the rope, Kaufman's gaze went to his father's letter. It called to him - a siren song that shouldn't have tempted him, yet inexplicitly did.

Fingering the lip of the envelope, Kaufman caught himself holding his breath. Had something happened to Göttlich? Perhaps he'd died or been killed.

Kaufman didn't care one way or the other. His father had taught him too well for that. There was neither dark glee nor sadness. There was, however, curiosity.

All at once in a reckless impulse, Kaufman ripped open the envelope and crushed the letter between his fingers. But before he looked at it, his good sense reasserted itself.

He gained nothing by knowing the contents of this note; in fact, it might do irreparable damage.

Something in him knew that if he read the letter, what little sanity he'd gained since getting away from The Dwelling would be dashed to pieces as completely as any ship upon a stony shore.

Kaufman looked around his starkly furnished house and speculated.

Could his father still be testing him? Was he even now, after all this time, and from another continent, trying to continue his lessons?

Revolted, Kaufman flung the unread document away and stomped on it. The hard rubber of his work boot left a dusty print.

The noose had been a stupid idea.

He had no intention of killing himself, which was why he'd gone to Dominique's house, thinking that there - in the now silent room of that innocent child - he would finally be able to mourn, finally feel remorse.

Or at the very least, feel a selfish loss.

Now home, his failure was sharper than ever. Though he didn't feel the failure as an emotion. It was an empirical knowledge - a dagger in his mind, not his heart. Göttlich would be pleased by this response, see it as a strength, as getting that much closer to perfect self-mastery.

Kaufman saw it as missing the most vital part of being human, and he moved to take the rope down. A bucket under the sink made a workable step ladder.

Inches from his face, the noose swayed hypnotically.

Maybe he *should* end his life, stop wasting resources that could be used by more deserving people, deny his father the satisfaction of molding his son in his own image.

Reaching up, Kaufman slipped the rope around his neck. Calloused knuckles press hard into the soft palate under his chin and his breathing quickened as he felt the power of the cord to end his life. It had no compassion for him. It was mechanical, moved only through the laws of physics. It was as unsympathetic and inexorable as the passing of time.

A second ago, the threat had been empty. The rope only had the potential for death - just as hundreds of daily household items did. Its true ability to force an emotional response was only proportional to the proximity it came to actually terminating life. In other words, an unloaded gun locked in a safe wasn't scary; playing Russian roulette was.

At this height, if the bucket slipped, Kaufman knew the fall wouldn't be enough to break his neck – rather, death would be slow and panic riddled.

Kaufman's heart race. His face flushed, and a tear welled in his eye.

This…this was exactly what he'd longed for, what his father had taught him to do without. In this moment, there wasn't time for his mind to metastasize his emotional response through an intellectual filter. Death was near. Death was a rough cord that chafed his neck and smelled strongly of sawdust and oil. Death was only held back by the wedge of his fingers curled tightly around the rope.

This was masochistic behavior!

He ignored the thought. He wasn't getting off on some version of autoerotic asphyxiation and it wasn't pain that electrified him - it was the extreme condition a brush with death elicited. With death so near, life seemed much brighter.

Oddly, though, the sensation was fading.

As quick as a fish escaping a hook, the brief excitement slipped away. Logic exerted itself, and Kaufman noted how precarious his position was. He ought to get down, but his heart…his heart and soul longed for more!

How far could he take it?

Tipping the bucket onto its edge, Kaufman felt it wobble and give. The hard tiled floor beneath was clean and slick, and the effort required to maintain the balancing act caused his heartbeat to surge again. But this was different.

Cold sweat beaded Kaufman's forehead and his knees knocked.

If the bucket slipped, he would die.

Period.

And what then?

His theology was undecided. He certainly didn't believe in heaven or hell, for what was the point in caring about an afterlife when he couldn't even care about the life he was in? If he did cease to exist when he died, all the more reason to obtain the love and relationships that eluded him in this life. Maybe then, once he'd gotten to a point where had something to hold onto, something to believe in, he could hope for an existence after death.

"Hope!" Kaufman spat, suddenly exhausted.

Hope was nothing but a cruel torturer.

As a child, he'd lived and breathed hope. Hoped that his father would love him, pay attention to him. Hoped that he could escape, find a family that would want him, be normal, and when those hopes turned sour, he'd hoped death.

Eventually, even that cynical hope faded until there was nothing. Nothing but numbness and other worlds - the worlds of books; worlds that mocked and ridiculed him, worlds forever denied him.

How was he ever to hope again if he couldn't even feel regret or pity or remorse of any kind for the slaughter of a young girl? A girl he'd known, whose smile he'd been gifted with many times.

Kaufman trembled with rage, and the bucket quivered.

He was a monster - a Frankenstein. Nothing but the parts of a human, yet unlike the Hollywood creature, he wasn't ugly on the outside and tender and misunderstood on the inside. Just the opposite. Although he looked normal, inwardly, he was as hideous and terrible as the mob's prejudice suggested: worthy of destruction.

From the floor, the white beacon of the unread letter taunted him.

Not only was he a monster, he was a coward too - just a scared kid, too frightened to even read a little note from his dear old dad.

A mad laugh exploded from Kaufman.

For all these years he thought he was free but really he was trapped within himself and unable to face his father. He laughed again, and this time it was hard and dark, and sounded just like Göttlich's. That sound startled Kaufman. He realized not only didn't he possess the nerve to face Göttlich, he also didn't have the power to stop himself from becoming his father either. That insight dissipated Kaufman's intensity and he suddenly felt drained.

Cautiously he lowered the bucket from its perch.

He would not accidentally lynch himself this day.

Breathing heavily, he thought about the rage that had just overwhelmed him, had flowed through him as hot as lightning. The reaction made sense. Emotionally he was an infant, prone to tantrums and uncontrollable outbursts. Tapping into his emotions would require careful treading. He needed to learn to bridle his anger, rein in—

Outside, a gun boomed.

Kaufman jumped at the explosion.

The bucket snapped out from under his feet, and the noose cinched tight.

Flailing legs sought support.

After an instant of blind panic, Kaufman realized he was still able to breathe, albeit with great difficulty. Luckily his fingers were still curled around the rope, and he pulled himself up into a chin-up position. This brought immediate relief and made his breathing easier. Yet how long could he maintain this posture?

Surely no more than a few minutes. His arms were already quivering from the strain.

Kaufman looked for the bucket.

It was close. No more than a foot away, and still upright.

Stretching out his leg, he eased the bucket across the floor with a toe. Abruptly the lip caught on the grout between two tiles. Only a few centimeters wide, the gap was a canyon of destruction if Kaufman couldn't navigate it successfully.

But no matter what he tried, the bucket wouldn't budge.

Stretched out and contorting, desperate for air, and with arm muscles burning, Kaufman decided to try and stand even though the bucket was not directly under him.

Kaufman took a breath and lowered his weight.

Immediately the bucket overturned, skittered sideways, and rolled away.

Kaufman dropped two feet and bounced.

He bit through his tongue and had to fight to maintain consciousness. He'd just pulled himself pull himself back into the chin-up position when a knock sounded at the front door.

"Gggaaa…" Kaufman croaked.

Through the kitchen window, a UPS van was visible.

Kaufman knew he had to get the guy's attention. Had to. It was his only chance to get out of this mess.

"Help!" Kaufman screamed, except what came out was a wheezy huff.

Seething and thrashing, Kaufman desperately tried to make himself heard; tried to kick out and knock down the overhead pots. But instead of helping, his jerking movements caused his arms to give out.

Bony knuckles crushed deeply into his esophagus and he partly blacked out.

Somehow, he managed to get his body weight off his throat, but each breath burned like molten lava, and his arms trembled violently.

That's when something clicked in Kaufman's mind.

He was going to die.

Hanging there, slowly being strangled, he understood the thrill he'd experienced moments before was a farce. At best, it'd been an imitation of the genuine emotions he sought. He was no longer looking over the edge of life but had fallen headfirst into the hands of death, and he knew for certain that he didn't want to die.

There were things to live for.

He wanted to see his sapling trees grow into mighty umbrellas of shade. He wanted to revisit the familiar and comfortable worlds in the many novels he loved and explore new ones in books he hadn't yet read. He wanted to know the embrace of a woman and the love that united two people.

He wanted to hope again.

Through the window above the sink, Kaufman saw the UPS delivery man get in his truck. Apparently, on-time deliveries were more important than rescuing idiot people who inadvertently hanged themselves.

As the van drove away, it backfired - the explosion from earlier, the gunshot that had startled him.

No savior was going to rescue him. He'd gotten himself into this predicament. He'd have to get himself out of it.

The nearby marble countertop was his only option. If he could reach it, he might be able to plant his feet and support his weight long enough to slip off the noose.

Twisting his body, Kaufman began gathering momentum for a lunge. Using his legs, he rocked back and forth, and once his pendulum motion had gained enough momentum, he snapped out his feet.

The heels of his boots landed squarely on the counter.

A smile broke across Kaufman's face.

Then the reverse force pulled him off his landing. The sharp drop wrenched free his hands and without obstructing fingers, the noose closed with deadly precision.

Like so many who had worn that terrible necktie, Kaufman's windpipe was crushed.

Eyes bulging, feet kicking, Kaufman clawed at the rope, fought with every last shred of strength to pull himself up, but his oxygen-deprived muscles were already losing their grip.

Desperately he searched the kitchen for salvation.

He didn't find any.

What he did see was the letter from his father.

No, not a letter - a document.

Kaufman blinked.

The paper was government issued, with decorative scrollwork along the edge.

He blinked again as his body slackened and twitched.

He could not accept what he was seeing.

His father had sent him a Nevada state death certificate.

Kaufman's name was at the top.

But it was the date that really sent his mind reeling.

That set of numbers almost kept Kaufman's heart pumping and his blood circulating, almost caused the life that was leaving his body to rush back in.

Almost.

With a final spasm, exhausted arms went still, and death closed in, but Kaufman's eyes never left the paper.

Unblinking, he stared on…

The date was today.

CHAPTER 4

"Hurry, Jess! Mom's dying."

Holding both her favorite doll and prized stuffed pony, his little sister came up behind him.

"Just bring one," said Matthew.

Clutching the toys to her chest, Jessica shook her head; blond pigtails swished. Her stubbornness might have aggravated someone else, but Matthew could never get mad at her.

Jessica was too cute, too sweet, too special, and in his dark moods, when black thunderheads of depression settled over him, she was a godsend. Her freckled face and ever-present pixie smile always lifted his spirit.

He'd promised to take care of her and although only a kid himself, Matthew took that promise very serious. In fact, like many children afflicted with a physical disability, he was mature beyond his years.

"Alright, give me one to put in the suitcase, and you can hold onto the other one."

Jessica considered and kept Mr. Horsey.

Snapping the latches close, Matthew whispered the pledge he'd been repeating all week.

"Hang on, mom, we're coming."

His mother - Samantha Sterling - *was* dying, or at least that's what Matthew believed. At the age of ten, he knew adults didn't always tell the truth. He recognized when someone was coddling him to cover up some unpleasant news - being handicapped had exposed him to more sugar coating than his average peer - however, these days, he was also seeing through the more subtle lies.

So, despite what his Aunt Lucy and Uncle Bernard said, he knew his mom was not getting better.

At the end of his last visit, she'd tried to hug him, but she couldn't lift her arms. She'd been more frail and feeble than even he was, which had scared Matthew because the condition he was afflicted with - BMD: Becker's Muscular Dystrophy - was slowly making his prepubescent body resemble that of a ninety-year-old man.

The disorder was characterized by slow progressive muscle-weakening of the legs and pelvis, and although medical technology had advanced tremendously since the disease was diagnosed, no known cures were available. This meant that his leg braces were not only going to be a permanent necessity but in time, would likely be upgraded to a wheelchair.

Yet regardless of how frail he became, it seemed he would outlast his mom.

Patting the bed for him to sit, his mother had looked as pale and as weak and as doomed as a newly hatched bird fallen from its nest. Her skin was thin and brittle, and it tore at Matthew to see her like that. He'd sat fidgeting, wishing he could change things and hating himself for knowing he couldn't.

His mother had dropped a tarnished necklace into his hand.

"This was a gift from *my* brother when I was a little," Samantha had said in a tired voice. "I want you to have it now, to give to Jess."

Matthew looked at the silver pendant - a flowing robed angel on a slender chain - and in that instant, he had known that just like his father, she was leaving him.

Five years ago, after Samantha had gotten sick with the cancer and his father had walked out, and he gone from big-boy to man-of-the-house. He hadn't wanted the promotion, but he'd shouldered the extra responsibility. He always did.

Now he was being given the title of protector.

"No…" Matthew breathed and shook his head.

This mantle shouldn't be his. It was too much, too heavy, and tears had streamed down his face. He was so scared and hurt. He didn't want this, couldn't do it. He was just damaged goods.

Samantha Sterling touched her son's cheek.

"Don't be afraid," she'd said, brushing away tears, "you won't let me down."

Matthew wasn't so sure.

"I know you won't."

She smiled, and her eyes had shone as proudly as a lioness.

"You never have."

Matthew turned the angel pendant over in his hands.

That had been three weeks ago and although they went twice a week to visit, he and Jess were always forced to wait in the lounge while Uncle Bernard and Aunt Lucy talked to the doctors and returned from Samantha's room ashen and red-eyed.

That's when they'd tell him that their mom was doing fine, getting better even, and would be home soon.

Lies.

It was only a matter of time before his mother was dead and gone, gone to heaven, gone forever. But before that happened, Matthew was determined to see her again.

That's what the suitcase was for.

The most difficult part about a clandestine and solo visit to the hospital was not the six-mile walk but getting past Lucybean. That was the nickname he and Jess had come up with for their Aunt Lucy and Uncle Bernard, who were overprotective to a fault.

Matthew didn't know if it was his condition that made them so prudish and overly protective, or because they didn't have any kids of their own to experiment with and screw up on. But whatever the case, his aunt and uncle ran their house like a maximum-security prison.

Doors were always locked, curfews were upheld, rounds were made by one or the other every half hour just to make sure everything was "A-OK." It infuriated Matthew to be checked up on so often, so much so that he'd taken to committing minor crimes to shake up the joint. And this morning, he'd planned a felony; a prank that would easily get him five to ten years - if not life - and while doing hard time, he planned to slip out and go to the hospital.

Of course, once Lucybean found them missing, all hell would break loose. It would be worth it though, if only to see and be with his mom for a few minutes.

He missed her terribly. So did Jess.

Putting the angel necklace back into his pocket for safe-keeping, Matthew thought about his plan.

He knew two kids - one ten and one six - would be stopped if seen wandering down the road alone. So, to give them a reason to be out there, he planned to wear his Cub Scout uniform and pretend to be selling chocolate bars to raise money for summer camp. He just hoped no one actually wanted to buy any, because the only thing in the suitcase was clothes. Well, clothes and Jessica's doll, a map, snacks and a picture of the family before all the bad stuff happened.

In it, Jessica was only a baby and Matthew was four. The next year he would be diagnosed with BDM, but in the photo, he looked like a healthy boy without a care in the world. Mom and Dad were young too, and in love. It was the perfect family: idealistic and full of promise.

What the photo didn't show was how everything would fall apart in just a few short years. But that's why Matthew liked it; the snapshot was a memory of a happy, worry-free family.

Perhaps the last time it had been…or ever would be.

As Matthew went over the scheme in his head, looking for any flaws, the doorbell rang.

No more time to think - it had started.

"Jess, I'm going to disappear."

"Magic?" she breathed, eyes sparkling.

She was adorable, so innocent, so believing. She was the real magic.

"Right, you have to find me."

She nodded.

The front door was unlocked and opened. Matthew slid the suitcase under the bed. He had to hurry if he was going to make it to his pre-arranged hiding place.

From down the hall, muted voices hummed like a conversation through the pipes of an old apartment building.

"I have your three large pizzas fully loaded," said a landlocked surfer voice. "That'll be $42.38."

Matthew jumped down; his legs were stiff and swayed as they struggled to support his weight.

"What!?" came the flabbergasted response of Aunt Lucy. "I didn't order any of this. Who orders that much pizza at ten o'clock in the morning?"

Trying to make a dash of which he was incapable, Matthew's legs buckled. He stumbled forward, catching the nearby dresser.

"You'd be surprised. I once delivered twelve pizzas to an all-night party at 7AM. They didn't even want the pizzas - just the boxes, for what, I have no idea. So, three pizzas at this hour…uhhh, that's an early lunch for someone with a big appetite."

Sudden movement after long periods of inactivity was not recommended for individuals with BMD. Matthew had been sitting for nearly an hour and should have worked up his muscles gradually before trying to move quickly.

"Well, I'm not paying for it. Nobody here ordered it."

"This is 319 Caliber Road, is it not?" said the pizza delivery man, not backing down without a fight.

The only problem was that he had never come up against anyone as uncompromising as Aunt Lucy. "I don't care what it says. You'll have to take it back. I didn't order it, and what's more, I don't want it. Pizza is disgusting."

Jessica giggled. She confided in Matthew, "I like pizza."

Holding onto the dresser for dear life as his lower body wobbling, Matthew nevertheless agreed, "I know, me too."

Then he heard the words he dreaded. The pizza man wasn't as dumb as he sounded.

"Uh, one Clint Sterling made this order. Is that someone you know?"

"Clint?"

It was his father's name.

When ordering, Matthew hadn't known what to say when the pizza place asked for his name, so he'd used the first thing that came to mind. Unfortunately, Aunt Lucy wasn't stupid either. As quickly as a two-point connect-the-dots, she put together what was going on.

"Matthew!" she hissed.

This was going all wrong.

Losing his grip on the dresser, Matthew's knees finally gave way and he went down hard. Luckily, he caught himself before eating DuPont Berber. Yet to his horror, Aunt Lucy paid and dispatched the pizza delivery guy with the speed of a celebrity denying drug charges and came storming down the hallway.

Laying prone, Matthew listening to his approaching annihilation.

Bursting into the room, seemingly without turning the doorknob, Aunt Lucy's fists went to her ample hips.

"You are sooo grounded, young man."

Matthew grinned.

Everything was going perfectly to plan.

"Oh, you think that's funny? Well, how much fun do you think you're going to have sitting in the office for the rest of the day?"

That took the smile off Matthew's face.

"That's what I thought. Now come on, let's get you up."

Matthew groaned, as much from his sore muscles as from being sent to the study.

Even if the stairs hadn't posed a physical difficulty for him, they creaked and moaned as loudly as an old man. They were also visible from the living room where Lucybean ran a small tailoring business. That's why he was sent there when they wanted to keep an eye on him. There was no escape.

Trudging up the wooden staircase, Matthew berated himself. Stupid not to think of this.

His original plan had included escaping out his bedroom window, a feat that would have been difficult on the first floor; from the second, it was going to be impossible.

"What'd we do now?" murmured Jess at the bottom of the stairs.

Matthew stopped and looked back.

"I don't know. Go and wait in the bedroom. I'll think of something."

In the slanted roofed room, Matthew took in his surroundings. Old bolts of cloth and other sewing junk lined the walls. On the far side of the narrow space, by a large oak desk, a single square window let in the morning light.

Matthew slid up the heavy timber frame and removed the outer screen.

Twenty feet below, lawn furniture and a barbeque looked like miniature dollhouse toys.

It was a long, long way down, but he would have no better opportunity to go see his mom than right now. Lucybean wouldn't check up on him for hours, so somehow he would have to climb down, which meant he was going to need some rope. And a lot of luck.

Searching the room, Matthew discovered a heavy-duty extension cord. Not exactly climbing gear, but it would have to do.

He lashed one end of the rubber cord around his waist and the opposite end to a heavy tailoring mannequin. He tugged on the line to tests it was secure, then backed out onto the window's edge.

Swallowing hard, Matthew tried to bolster the courage that was slip-sliding around in his belly with his breakfast by chanting his mantra.

"Hang on, mom, I'm coming. Hang on, hang on…hang on."

What was he doing? This was crazy, completely Looney Tunes.

Far below, thorny bushes looked ready to impale.

But it was now or never.

Taking a last deep breath, Matthew leapt.

Or he thought he leapt. With his weak legs, he actually tumbled backward and fell six feet, banging and scraping the side of the house, before the cord snapped taut and jerked him to a halt.

"Holy crap!" Matthew gasped as the loop around his waist slid up under his armpits, and he fought to hold on.

His plastic-covered legs clacked uselessly against the slick vinyl siding. Then, as if he'd been holding on for hours instead of seconds, his arms betrayed him, and the cord slipped from his grasp, and the ground rushed up to meet him.

Matthew screamed as he contemplated the pain he was about to feel when he became a human shish kabob on the spiky plants below.

Slamming into the hedges, Matthew's world flipped upside down and his head whacked the ground with enough force that solar systems flashed into existence in the sky above him.

For a minute, he hung there, upended, before flopping over and working his way free. Upon standing up, however, there was hardly a scratch on him. The hedges, on the other hand, looked like they'd been hit by a Howitzer.

"Cool," Matthew laughed and suddenly wished one of his friends had been here to witness his daredevil stunt because they were never going to believe what he'd just done.

He looked up at the window and realized that the dangling orange extension cord was blaring evidence of the breakout. But there was nothing he could do about it. Not that it mattered. As soon as he and Jess were found missing, Lucybean was going to go ballistic.

Hurrying around back, Matthew met his sister at their bedroom window and helped her out. Pulling a red wagon loaded with their suitcase, he didn't breathe easy until the house was well behind them.

On Decoy boulevard, shoppers moved among stores, delivery trucks dropped off goods, and the flow of traffic moved as steady as oxygen through a body. The city was healthy and prosperous, and it didn't take notice of two small children.

Swinging Mr. Horsey, Jessica skipped along. For her, this was just an adventure, and she trusted Matthew totally. Which she should, because Matthew was never going to let anything bad happen to her. That was true until a police car flipped a U-turn and pulled up alongside them.

Squeezing Matthew's hand, Jessica whispered, "Are we going to jail?"

"No, so don't start crying."

He didn't need to tell her not to talk. Jess was a shy girl, almost catatonic with strangers, sometimes even with people she knew, so it wasn't what she might say that would give them away. However, if she started to cry, the gig was up.

Leaning over to shout out of the passenger window, the police officer said, "Hey there, where are you kids off to?"

Acting as if he hadn't heard, Matthew kept walking, which only forced a confrontation.

Pulling over, the policeman stopped and got out of his car. He took up a position in the middle of the sidewalk directly ahead.

"Well now," he said, removing his dark aviator sunglasses. "Looks like I found me a pair of lost lambs."

With a huge gun at his hip and a badge pinned to his chest, the blond cop reminded Matthew of an old west gunslinger: very cool, but also a little scary.

"And where might you two be heading?"

"I'm selling chocolate bars for scout camp," said Matthew reciting his pre-prepared line.

"Kind of far from home, aren't you? Do your folks know you're out here?"

Matthew opened his mouth to respond when, to his amazement, Jess beat him to the punch.

"Our mom's in the hospital."

"My, what an angel you are, sweetheart," said the cop, squatting to be at her level. "What's wrong with your mommy?"

Matthew eyed the cop, and for some reason, he didn't like what he saw. The policeman seemed honest and friendly, but there was something in his look - like the excited expression somebody gets when eating a tasty treat.

No, that wasn't quite right, but not quite wrong either.

Whatever it was, Matthew didn't like it.

He pushed Jess behind him.

"Nothing's wrong with her. She works there. She's a nurse."

The lie came so easy. He'd just lied to a police officer. Matthew didn't think it was a sin that could damn him, but it definitely wasn't good. Once started, however, he found he couldn't stop.

"We're supposed to meet her there. My dad said we could. He works around here…at the casino. I'm selling chocolate for scout camp along the way."

He was babbling. Better stop talking.

Matthew ran a hand through his dusty blond hair and glanced at his shoes. That always worked with grownups.

Looking at the suitcase and wagon, the cop said, "There's not many houses along this road. On the other hand, there is a lot of traffic. So why don't you two get in and I'll drive you to meet your mom?"

The offer of a ride directly to the hospital should have been great news, but once the cop found out he'd been lied to, he'd be pissed.

"Ummm..." Matthew exhaled, stalling for time. His eyes darted about, frantically searching for a way out. He might have outrun the policeman with perfect legs, but with Jess and pulling a wagon - it was hopeless.

The cop took Matthew's hesitation as fear.

"It's okay. I won't hurt you."

Matthew believed him. In fact, it would be awesome to go racing around in a real cop car, and as if reading his mind, the officer opened the rear door and encouraged them.

"Come on, get in. I bet none of your friends have ever ridden in a police car."

Matthew was still trying to think of a way out, still looking for an escape route when the cop stepped forward and took hold of Jessica's arm. He was only assisting her into the car, but at the touch, she whimpered, and that snapped something in Matthew.

Exploding in a defensive fury, he lashed out and with reflective speed, knocked the offending hand away. Then, before the cop could react, he grabbed his belt and head-butted the guy in the groin.

Folding over with a *whoof*, the police officer cupped his bruised testicles. Matthew seized the opportunity and fled.

"Come on, Jess!" He shouted, pulling his sister towards a nearby alley.

Behind them came an angry voice.

"Come back, you little brat. He that spareth the rod hateth his son: but he that loveth him chasteneth him betimes, Proverbs 13:24."

Weaving a tangled route through brick and mortar canyons, Matthew ran as fast as his rocking gait would carry him. He could hear the cop pursuing - shouting and cursing. The policeman's words promised mercy, but this time Matthew didn't believe him.

After a while, the stalking voice faded, and a chain-link fence halted the getaway.

Matthew looked over his shoulder. Somewhere back there was the cop, angry and hurting. Lying was one thing, but beating someone up was a major sin. He might even go to jail, was definitely going to hell.

What had he been thinking?

He hadn't; he'd only reacted. Trying to justify his actions, Matthew thought about the cop grabbing Jess. No, he'd only been helping her into the back seat. But that look...what look? Everyone was mesmerized by Jessica. She was adorable.

"I'm in deep crap," Matthew muttered to himself.

"Doo-doo," Jessica corrected.

Matthew sighed.

Better make his screw up worth it.

Past the fence was a cement aqueduct, and beyond that, towering over the other buildings was the hospital.

They were so close.

Only the aqueduct kept them from their mom.

Finding a hole in the fence, Mathew and Jessica wiggled through.

For most of the year, the manmade creek was dry. Today though, terra-cotta water swirled and gurgled lazily downstream. It didn't look deep, but Matthew couldn't see the bottom.

Going back the way they'd come wasn't an option. They might run into the cop; couldn't risk that. That left swimming.

The braces on Matthew's legs wouldn't be a problem. They were sleek and made of a light, durable plastic. Getting Jess across, on the other hand, was going to be monumental.

Holding Mr. Horsey tightly under her chin, she stood shaking her head, knowing what he was thinking.

Maybe they could use the wagon.

Taking the suitcase out, Matthew pushed the red Radio-Flyer out into the water.

It floated.

Perfect.

Turning to reassure his sister, Matthew said, "Don't worry, this will be fun, just like riding the Pirates of the Caribbean at Disneyland."

Jessica continued to shake her head as the Radio-Flyer drifted out into the canal. The wagon floundered and was pulled under.

Maybe that hadn't been such a good idea.

Watching the wagon disappear, Matthew was surprised to see the suitcase he held bobbing up and down.

Of course! The wagon sank because water had gotten in, but the plastic suitcase was like a balloon or a submarine, it wouldn't sink because water couldn't get in. This would work even better than a boat.

"Okay, the wagon was a bad idea but look at the suitcase. It won't sink, see." He pushed up and down to demonstrate the suitcase's buoyancy.

"All you have to do is just hold on, and I'll pull you across."

Jessica still refused. "I'll slip off."

Matthew thought about it for a minute then unlaced his shoes.

"Here, we'll use these to tie ourselves on."

Matthew tied a knot around the handle and both their wrists. "See now the suitcase won't float away."

Jessica didn't say anything, but she still didn't like the idea.

The murky water wasn't very strong along the shore, but as Matthew kicked out from the bank, the current picked up speed. That didn't worry him, for he was an excellent swimmer. It was the one exercise he could do without pain, and he went to the community pool three times a week.

In the pool, he was normal; the other kids didn't know anything was wrong with him. Most couldn't keep up. But right now, the braces were making it hard. He'd never swum with them on before. Not only that but pulling his sister and the suitcase was wearing him out fast.

Suddenly Jess yelped.

Looking over his shoulder, Matthew saw the suitcase sinking.

Panicking, Jessica scrambled up, pushing down hard, which caused the front end to sink even faster.

"Hang on," Matthew shouted, turning back to the opposite bank. It wasn't far, they could still make it.

Oblivious of their plight, the current pushed and pulled and spun the children.

Matthew took in a mouthful of water as he was pulled under. Resurfacing in confusion, he looked around, but before he could understand what had happened, he was turned about and dragged back under again. And this time, he didn't come up as quickly.

Kicking desperately, he finally reached air.

He looked around trying to figure out what was going on and something clawed his leg.

Down in the brown creek, the water wasn't dark enough to blot out the sight of his sister fully submerged and drowning. Mouth open, hair billowing, Jess writhed in slow motion. The suitcase, which had earlier been a buoy, now acted as an anchor. And they were tethered to it!

Diving down, Matthew grabbed Jess in a bear hug and kicked for the surface. They broke free into the sparkling morning light only to be pulled back under.

Below the surface, Matthew tried to untie the shoelaces, but Jess fought him as much as the current did. She thrashed about violently, knocking him away.

After struggling for a minute, he had to go back up. It took everything in him to reach the surface and grab a snatch of air. That's when his mantra changed from the benefit of his mother to that of his sister.

"Hold on, Jess. I'm coming."

Diving back down, he could see Jess had stopped moving, and the image of her sill form almost drove him mad. He had to save her. She was so much more important to the world than he would ever be.

Descending to the bottom of the canal, Matthew grabbed the suitcase and yanked. If he couldn't untie her, he would walk her to safety.

High stepping and tugging, Matthew inched the suitcase along.

Above, the sun sent swirling flashes through the cloudy water.

Soon the demand for oxygen forced Matthew to let go.

Swimming up for air, the string tugged hard at his wrist and pulled him up just short of the surface. His right hand broke free and he tried to pull himself up, but the water dissolved around his fingers.

Air was only inches above, but he couldn't reach it.

Lungs screaming, heart hammering, Matthew reached out and he knew he'd failed - failed to see his mother and failed to protect his sister.

No longer able to hold his breath, Matthew sucked in a lungful of water. His skinny body shuddered as the dirty liquid poured in.

He was going to die, was going to heaven. But that was okay, he would be with Jess, and they would wait for their mom.

Hang on God, I'm coming, Matthew thought, and he drank in more of the filthy liquor. One last gulp and his body convulsed - shaking off life.

Above, the sun sparkled and shone, careless of the children gently swaying, swaying, swaying to the rhythm of the river.

CHAPTER 5

Cold.

Why was he so cold?

Blackness everywhere, and a numb body that wouldn't respond. Then out of the arctic nothingness, something exploded.

Thud.

Like an ancient machine slowly coming to life, his heart constricted, expanded, constricted, expanded.

Thud. Thud. Thud.

Pins and needles surged through a frigid torso and stiff limbs. It was as if he'd been drained of heat and frozen in snow.

Shivering uncontrollably, his diaphragm hiccupped as lungs gathered air.

Thud.

Pain now replaced the coldness as blood coursed through veins - a thousand swarming ants biting and tearing flesh with razor sharp mandibles.

Thud-thud.

As he opened his eyes, blinding whiteness dazzled, and a hard, smooth surface lay underneath.

Thud.

Distortion everywhere, blurry images, and pain - fiery pain!

Thud.

His body screamed as heat poured out of his ribcage.

Thud-thud, Thud-thud.

White-hot pokers seared and burned and boiled his flesh.

Thud-thud.

What was going on?

Thud-thud.

He gasped again, and it was as if a cheese grater had been rammed down his throat.

Instinctively he reached out.

Nothing. His body was as responsive as a sack of potatoes.

Thud-thud.

Convulsions racked muscles as spasms shot through stiff arms and legs. He flopped on the hard, slick surface as a gale-force migraine raged in his head.

Thud-thud.

Then through the haze of confusion and agony he realized something was wrapped around his larynx.

Tortoise arms slowly inched up to remove the obstruction, and when his fingers touched the object memory flooded back in.

The noose!

Kaufman sat up, and a universe of stars popped behind his eyes.

Was he really alive?

As he extended a hand to steady the spinning world, that point didn't seem at all important. All that concerned him right now was water.

Like a bloated dead rat in his mouth, his tongue was dry and gagging, and each shallowed breath felt as if he were taking shots of acid. Standing, sausage fingers plucked at the noose. Once off, Kaufman flung it away. It flopped heavily on the floor, sliding into the far wall.

At the kitchen sink, cool water poured over his cupped hands. Slurping up mouthfuls, Kaufman abandoned using his hands and put his lips directly to the faucet, drinking deeply.

Nothing had ever tasted so wonderful.

Kaufman knew he should take it easy, drink slowly, be cautious of the damage done to his esophagus, but rational thought had no power to stop the primordial drive of thirst. He sucked down a river then flopped onto the floor, arms wide.

Above, the exposed ceiling rafter to which the noose had been tied, bristled with splintered ends. At some point, his weight must have been enough to snap the beam. The previous owner had probably never inspected the wood for termite damage or other weakening's - and neither had Kaufman.

A giddy laugh escaped his lips.

He was alive!

In the empty kitchen, Kaufman howled. Each hoot ripped his raw esophagus anew, but he could not stop.

Tears streamed down his face and his cheeks felt as if they might split. In his entire life, he had never laughed so hard. It was the kind of laughter experienced only with extreme drunkenness or pubescent single-mindedness; it was pure joy. The most natural and beautiful thing Kaufman had ever known. He'd finally broken through, finally crossed over. He was no longer objectively observing but was finally actively participating! This is what he had been seeking his entire life, what had been taken from him as a child.

Through the kitchen window, warm sunlight streamed in and the world seemed right.

Still giggling, Kaufman stood, basking in the revelry of being alive. Heading out of the kitchen, it felt as if he was floating rather than walking, flying even…until he spotted the death certificate.

Like a welcome mat embroidered with an obscenity, it leered up at him.

For a full minute, he stared at it.

The euphoria of being alive blinked, out and uneasiness settled in his gut.

It must be some kind of joke. It definitely stank of his father's black humor.

Picking it up, the paper seemed exceptionally heavy, the text not merely printed but chiseled. No way could his father have known that today of all days, he'd accidentally hang himself.

That's when he noticed the cause of death: Suicide.

The death certificate rattled in his hands.

Coincidence?

It had to be. Looking at the signature near the bottom, Kaufman noticed it hadn't been signed by the county coroner, nor by any state employee, or even a city intern. It was signed by his father, and although that neat little scribble completely undermined the validity of the document, it didn't erase its malignancy.

Was his father trying to encourage him to take his own life?

Kaufman's jaw tightened.

On the next line down, in the box indicating time of death, the truth seemed indisputable: Between 10:00AM and 10:30AM.

Somehow Göttlich must have been keeping tabs on him, must have known about Dominique's death and when her funeral was. From that, he could have all too easily deduced his son would be vulnerable, ripe for the picking, on the edge of suicide.

The death certificate was nothing more than an elaborate test, a final exam to see if Kaufman had perfected Dominism.

He should never have opened the damn thing.

Pitching it aside, Kaufman wanted to dismiss the whole event and forget it had ever happened. But a dark residue of despair remained.

What he needed now was something that would restore order and sanity to the day. He rubbed his throat where the grim reaper's necktie had been. It was sore and swollen. He should go to the hospital and have it checked out. Nothing like filling out tedious forms and sitting in a waiting room to help him feel normal again.

A sterile hospital would be just the thing to help rid him of the lingering gloom the death certificate had imparted. Exiting through the front door, Kaufman discovered a tall, broad package resting against one wall of the porch: the delivery of the UPS man.

He hadn't been expecting anything, and he felt certain he would have remembered ordering something so large. Roughly eight feet by six and a foot deep, the brown box seemed perfectly sized to contain a painting.

The return address confirmed the deduction, a company in New York called: *Children of God Fine Art Gallery — Oil Portrait Paintings*.

This could have been a calculated recruiting technique by Donald, some picture of Christ meant to invoke feelings of wonder and awe to open him up to further indoctrination, but Kaufman doubted it.

Although it was not from Siberia, Kaufman had a hunch it was from his father. It also likely had something to do with the death certificate, and doubtless, encapsulated in that cardboard shell, was something far more terrible than the prediction of his demise. Kaufman had no intention of discovering what that might be.

Not now anyway, maybe not ever.

Picking up the box, he put the package inside the foyer. He'd had enough of Göttlich's continuing education for one day.

On the front porch, the warm afternoon air stung the angry red abrasion around Kaufman's neck.

He couldn't shake the feeling of being pronounced dead. As intense as his feelings of jubilations had been, now a foreboding surrounded him although the day was bright and cloudless. Typically, Kaufman would have dismissed the sensation, wouldn't even have given it a second thought - except, standing on the stoop, the morning did indeed feel different.

The air quality was odd somehow…thicker, heavier, filled with the intense energy that precedes a powerful thunderstorm. Potent on the windless day was the odor of ozone and something that caused Kaufman's skin to tingle.

He raised one arm to examine his flesh.

The invisible goosebumps didn't itch or burn or sting; however, they were eerily unnatural and definitely had a physical quality that seemed to have more to do with the strange atmosphere rather than a lingering reaction to being mailed his own death certificate.

Then Kaufman noticed the light.

Less than three feet away, a blazing beam of sunlight streamed down through a bare patch of branches in a half-dead almond tree.

The light was rich and vibrant...too rich and vibrant, like the oversimplified yellow of a child's crayon drawing, and it seemed to wriggle and ripple as if alive.

Kaufman stepped forward, compelled. His breathing quickened and he lifted a hand to the sunbeam. It was warm and substantial; waving, phosphorescent fingertips left long, languid tails of glitter.

Kaufman blinked, but the streaming neon colors remained.

Closing his eyes, he shook his head to try and clear his vision. When he looked again, the glittering comets were slowly fading away like the afterimage on an old television set after being switched off.

What was going on here?

A dubious impression formed in his mind: *this is what it's like to be dead.*

At the thought, Kaufman shivered despite the dry desert heat.

What if he *had* died?

Kaufman's heart quickened, then jackhammer logic began pounding away at the ludicrous thought. The failed suicide might have set his feet on the emotional path he'd sought his whole life, but he wasn't about to be blown around by every irrational fear and groundless impulse that came to his mind. This hyper-reality was nothing more than a bad trip, the byproduct of too little oxygen to the brain while he'd been asphyxiated by the noose. Nothing more.

Except he found he couldn't swallow his impending sense of dread, couldn't shake off the premonition that clung to him like a desperate lover. He felt certain that something far stranger than cerebral hypoxia was happening here.

Around him, a perfect silence gathered. It was the silence of a funeral procession.

Kaufman realized he was holding his breath, anticipating something. Waiting for the storm to break, for whatever nightmare he'd stumbled into to reveal its face.

He didn't have to wait long.

Out of the placid afternoon, a shrill scream split the air.

Sharp and incredibly high pitched.

The shriek went on and on, and the longer Kaufman listened, the more confident he became that it wasn't feline after all. It was human - the scream of a dying infant.

Breaking into a run, his own bizarre situation forgotten, replaced by a need to find the source of so wretched a cry and provide assistance.

Rounding the end of his long dirt driveway, Kaufman turned into a new housing development.

He tried to orient himself to the tortuous scream, but the nearby stucco houses with their brown, parched lawns, acted as baffles, fracturing the sound in multiple directions and making it impossible to pinpoint. He headed north on impulse and the choice seemed to be the right one, for the shrieking grew louder. Maybe only a block and a half further, maybe more - it was hard to tell. This neighborhood had no straight roads but instead twisted and lumbered along. The design succeeded in getting away from traditional boxy zoning, yet the result was a labyrinth of streets and intersections.

Kaufman had entered an urban maze.

Still running hard, he took a right, then a left, then another right and would have sworn he just past these same residences' moments before. Like sugar cookie cutouts, the track houses repeated endlessly, varying only by minor external differences.

After another minute of mindless sprinting, Kaufman staggered to a stop. Bending over, he breathed as raggedly as an asthmatic jogger. It felt as if he had a fatal case of strep throat. There was no way he was going to be able to keep up this pace.

Unexpectedly, the sound ebbed away and, in that instance, Kaufman knew he was close.

Very close.

Just around the corner on the right.

There he would find the child…or what was left of it, and now he wasn't so sure he wanted to. An eerie hush blanketed the neighborhood.

Kaufman looked around.

No one and nothing stirred.

Where was everyone?

That horrible scream should have brought both aid and gawkers. Even more timid neighbors would peak out of doors and windows to see what the commotion was about. Yet Kaufman looked from house to house and saw no faces; no elderly grandmothers on front porches wringing hand towels with worry, no young children fighting at the windows for the best position to see what on TV was only make-believe, no housewives peeking down the road on tiptoes to be the first with new gossip.

As he listened, he didn't hear any traffic or the low hum of the city. No birds chirped, no dogs barked. This stillness was too exact, too complete…everything fell subject to it.

Kaufman began to wish for the scream again - it was far less oppressive than this unearthly quiet, however as he turned the street corner, he immediately retracted that desire.

If the God of Ordinary hadn't abandoned him as a child, he certainly had today.

Before him was one of the strangest sights of Kaufman's life.

In the middle of a cul-de-sac where half-formed homes were wrapped in dirty plastic and chicken wire, some thirty black-tailed jackrabbits had gathered. Most stood on hind legs, some reached towards the sky, all were gaunt and resembled the haunting death casts of ancient Pompeii: cowering and pleading victims petrified in an instant.

Although equipped with poor eyesight, the rabbits would have easily heard Kaufman's approach, yet not one turned to look in his direction. These were prey animals, wary of predators at all times. They should have scattered the instant he'd come into sight or at the least been eyeing him with ears perked, ready to dash off at any sudden movement.

But none of the hares acted as millions of years of instinct and evolution demanded.

Inching forward, Kaufman's stomach turned.

Something was horribly wrong.

The jackrabbits weren't just unmoving; they were misshapen.

Spines were wrenched like jagged bolts of lightning and paws and legs jutted and twisted at unnatural angles as if mimicking gnarled tree branches.

The rabbits might have been stuffed, the grotesque positioning the invention of some taxidermist from hell, for no one in their right mind would purposely make such an arrangement. But Kaufman abandoned that notion, for at ten yards he could see furry chests rising and falling, noses wiggling and muscles twitching. In fact, the small bodies trembled so much they might be having full body spasms, and such intense spasms that they were twisted rigid.

The jackrabbit nearest Kaufman was large for its breed - easily fourteen pounds.

Without thought, he leaned down and reached out a hand.

Fingers traced the bones beneath the fur, which weren't broken but somehow bent.

The touch unnerved Kaufman, and for once, he was glad of his impassive nature.

What could have caused this?

Muscle convulsions - even immobilizing ones - couldn't account for these warped limbs, nor could it explain why the majority of the rabbits were upright perked on their hind legs.

More disturbing was how this particular specimen's head had corkscrewed around nearly one-hundred-eighty degrees.

Picking up the rabbit, Kaufman slowly turned its face to him.

Thick red mucus tears oozed from the eyes, the color of arterial blood, and the tiny maw was locked open in a nightmarish scream, displaying long, switchblade incisors.

Heart hammering in his chest, Kaufman couldn't tear his gaze away; instead of viciousness or rage, the jackrabbit exuded utter despair. Then it screamed and became the demonic beast of nightmares.

Lurching and spinning away, Kaufman dropped the ruined creature. It thudded pitifully to the ground, but it continued to shriek, which acted like a triggering domino that set off all the other bleeding-eyed monstrosities.

Suddenly, the shrill was not unfamiliar to Kaufman. He'd heard it before. Once while at a sporting goods store, he'd tried a fox call. The wooden whistle was meant to reproduce the high pitch squeal of a rabbit in distress.

But this was no hollow replica.

Magnified many times, this shriek of suffering was devastating.

Kaufman covered his ears, though it did little to muffle the fingernails-on-chalkboard sound.

His throat be damned, he ran.

All at once, he knew what had happened - knew why the jackrabbits had congregated so unnaturally for their kind; why they were mangled and inert.

They were sick, diseased, dying of something dreadful. Something unnatural. Something manmade.

It must also be this poison or disease or biological weapon that had silenced the streets of Decoy.

Kaufman didn't want to believe it, but what else could it be? Certainly not his earlier notion that he was dead - that the change in weather and his tingling skin were signs that he was in limbo.

No, the narcissistic scientists at Shafter Army Base, in their ever-present obsession to create the next weapon of mass destruction, must have inadvertently released an agent. Only this wasn't a nuke. This time every human was a potential walking bomb once contaminated.

Or maybe it was the civilian researchers at NewLife, the genetic engineering building on the outskirts of town. What did it matter? Someone had screwed up, there'd been an accident, and *it* had gotten out, gotten loose in the air or water supply, and had infected everyone.

Images of red-eyed families, bent and writhing, flashed through Kaufman's mind.

He stopped.

What if they were already dead? All of them?

The surrounding houses were silent and solemn.

There was only one way to find out.

He would have to go in and see.

But what if he exposed himself by going in? Kaufman thought of the disfigured rabbits; they could have been the source - patient zero - and he'd touched them! Picked one up and handled it! What had he been thinking? He was more than likely already contaminated...

Still, maybe he should head into town, contact the police, bring help, and let someone else play the hero.

However, there was no way to be sure that whatever had happened in this subdivision hadn't already swept thought the entire city too.

"Hello? Is anyone there?"

Silence.

"Can anyone hear me?"

Only silence.

"Heeellllooooo?"

Kaufman waited.

Nothing.

The entire neighborhood looked as utterly deserted as a ghost town.

There was no point going downtown. Whatever he found here would be exactly what he'd find everywhere else.

His footfalls echoed softly as he approached the nearest front porch.

As a kid, the homes he'd entered weren't just adventures but sacred places. Each might be explored, but they were also to be venerated. Now, standing in front of this house, with the screams of thirty mutilated rabbits ringing in his ears, Kaufman felt no excitement, nor any reverence.

This abode was no longer a refuge for the living, but a tomb.
He twisted the steel doorknob.
It was unlocked.
Tombs housed bodies.
Kaufman went inside.

CHAPTER 6

In the dim murkiness of the living room, flat supine eyes gazed on. They weren't red or bloody, but they were lifeless.

Nearly a hundred porcelain dolls lined the walls of this otherwise unremarkable living room. On any other day, the pale blank faces, permanent rosy cheeks, and flawless smiles would only have appeared sickeningly cute. Today, though…today the dolls seemed like soulless husks in a demon's perverse trophy room.

Kaufman ran a hand over the stubble on his chin. On a day that was anything but ordinary, he'd stumbled into the house of a miser. He didn't like this.

As a trespassing child, he'd found that most people lived very analogously. After a while, creating imagined histories and life stories for these homogeneous homes became highly repetitious. Even the wealthy - in their extravagance and luxury - existed like most other people, just with more accessories.

There was one singularity, though, that fit no framework. An atypical category that was as rare as it was diverse; it was this group that he'd named "misers."

He used the term loosely to describe someone who collected, hoarded, or secretly, sometimes fanatically, lived hobbies. Most misers were eccentric at worst, but some were certifiably deranged; and although this collector of curly-locked figurines seemed harmless enough, Kaufman knew it was the ones who seemed the most innocent, that turned out to be the most cloven foot.

As nine-year-old, he'd entered the shanty of what he'd believed to be an elderly retired couple. Their smallish house was nothing exciting: drab furniture covered in doilies, a few outlandish and gaudy garden gnomes, fuzzy wallpaper reminiscent of scratch-n-sniff stickers, and shrines of photographs devoted to their children and grandchildren.

They were as ordinary as male-pattern baldness, or so Kaufman believed. That was until he discovered a hidden room in the basement. Then his opinion changed…drastically.

Covered in dimpled gray paneling that matched the rest of the basement, the opening led deeper underground to what was once a canning cellar. There, in the carved out earth, the elderly couple apparently indulged in their ghoulish taste for studying birth defects.

Even if Kaufman had been a zoologist with a medical background, he might not have been able to identify everything he saw. Sealed in beakers of formaldehyde floated every kind of strange mutation imaginable: pigs with two heads, dog and cat fetuses with no eyes, fowl with extra wings, baby calves conjoined, dwarfed creatures and gigantism of every description. Some of the jars contained fleshy blobs so twisted and malformed as to be nothing more than genetic porridge - lumpy piles, missing half the ingredients.

At the center of the collection backlit and glowing in amber baths were the human abnormalities. The array and breadth of congenital disorders was enough to curdle even Kaufman's stagnant soul.

As if from some dark fairy tale, these ostensible grandparents were the modern-day equivalent of the witch from Hansel and Gretel. Except instead of eating unsuspecting children, these crones devoured fetal refuse with their eyes; and although this doll collector might be more socially acceptable than those macabre grandparents, Kaufman knew he was in dangerous territory.

Any encounter with a homeowner on their turf was potentially hazardous. By nature, people were protective of their personal spaces, and technically he was trespassing. Adding to the risk today was the fact that this miser - already quirky and paranoid and possessive - now might be contaminated, possibly even brain damage - which meant no standard of aggression or behavior could be prepared for.

Surveying the room, Kaufman found it to be in perfect order. There were no visible signs of frantic departure and no immediately apparent infected occupants. No one might have been home when the calamity had struck; however, he felt certain for some reason, that wasn't the case.

Announcing himself, Kaufman waited for a response.

None was forthcoming. No moans of pain, no cries for help. Yet he did hear something.

From up the stairwell came a continuous beeping, and like with the modern compulsion to answer a ringing phone, no matter the circumstances, the persistent beeping drew Kaufman up the stairs.

On the second floor, he stopped. The noise was much louder here and somehow more insistent. Each indignant squawk grated nerves and, the longer Kaufman listened, the more convinced he became that it hadn't been accidentally left on. This wasn't an alarm left on due to a dead or incapacitated homeowner, crippled by whatever had ravaged the jackrabbits. No, Kaufman suspected a darker purpose, suspected he was walking into a trap.

As if his thoughts had been heard, a *thump* came from beyond the closed bedroom door.

Suddenly Kaufman wished he had a weapon.

Looking around, he spotted a vacuum cleaner. He disengaged the plastic extension tube. It made a poor club, but he felt better for having it.

Placebo mace held high, Kaufman inched forward.

He wanted nothing more than to burst through the door and smash the life out of the annoying alarm clock. However, logic dictated that if this paranoid suburbanite had set an ambush, then caution wasn't just prudent - Kaufman's life might depend on it.

He turned the doorknob, flung open the door and quickly stepped aside.

From the room came neither angry or terrified screams, nor a gunshot. What did come out, brought Kaufman to his knees. A dense, pungent stench of human feces - thick and nauseating.

Gagging, Kaufman reached into his back pocket. He pulled out a handkerchief and pressed it to his nose. Inside the master bedroom, the source of the smell was evident - an abstract expressionistic painting on the far wall dripped sewage, was splattered with excrement and glistened with brown and yellow streaks.

Disoriented by the reeking partition and constant buzzing of the electronic alarm clock, Kaufman only took a moment to look around before quickly exiting the house for the fresh air of the backyard.

Nothing in the bedroom made sense.

When falling ill, a person was most likely to hunker down and try to ride out the sickness from home. That's where they would feel most comfortable and be most able to take care of themselves. So then where were the bodies? Where were all the dead and dying? Or at the very least, where were the signs of a hasty departure as victims struck with violent symptoms rushed to the hospital?

The withered lawn - more weeds than grass - rustled underfoot as Kaufman tried to shift his paradigm, tried to open his mind to other possibilities. If he hadn't stumbled across a lethal germ, then what? What would cause a person to create a guano mural then abandon their house? Some kind of city-wide brain aneurism? Mass hypnosis? Aliens?

Kaufman felt like he was grabbing at rejected storylines from *The Twilight Zone* for answers. No, there had to be a logical, scientific explanation for what was going on. He just needed to look around some more to find it.

A tall fence to the east inhibited his view of the neighboring yard, but it didn't impede the aroma of an afternoon barbeque. Kaufman decisively scaled it.

A blinding white rock garden greeted him on the other side.

Kaufman's feet crunched through the jagged alabaster stones, and it felt as if he were walking over broken bones.

Next to the pool, a polished steel grill emitted anemic smoke. Inside blackened, shriveled hot dogs resembled petrified wood. Nearby, full cups of soda waited next to plates arranged neatly on a patio table.

Kaufman switched off the gas.

The incinerated cow flesh seemed a dark omen. Images of crisped human bodies, cooked black from thermal burns as a result of a nuke, conjured in Kaufman's mind.

Born of cold war paranoia and countless movie plots, could that unlikely explanation be the source of his permanent goose flesh? Were radiation and nuclear fallout what had mutated the jackrabbits?

He knew it was ludicrous to give any credence to such notions, for an explosion of that magnitude would have reduced the entire city to rubble. No, there had been no nuclear war.

But the thought was troubling and persistent, nonetheless.

To determine what had happened, however, he needed to find a survivor.

Either that…or a corpse.

Like an open sepulcher, this new house waited with its back door wide open. Kaufman took a deep breath and entered.

The space felt instantly familiar. Its layout was nearly identical to that of its neighbor. A precursory walkthrough of the bottom floor revealed no bodies - burnt or otherwise.

In the living room, though, among the beige walls, cream carpets, and minimal design, the glow of a laptop drew his attention. Kaufman saw a miniature version of himself mirroring his movements; the camera was on.

Next to the computer was a cell phone. He picked it up, but it displayed a **No Service** signal. He tried the landline and rather than a dial tone or a deadline, a strange bubbling static, unlike anything Kaufman had heard before babbled.

He tapped the switch-hook, but the line remained unresponsive.

A virus wouldn't have jammed communication systems. Maybe radiation, but he'd ruled that out as a serious possibility. He supposed the inactivity might be a defect found solely in this house, but how many other dead phones in other dead houses would he have to put to his ear to conclude that Decoy was utterly cut off? Five? Ten? A hundred?

A chill coursed down his spine - it was another feather added to already bright and full plumage.

Kaufman bit at his nails. Suddenly a hard grunt escaped him. He examined his fingers and smiled at the nervous action. He'd never chewed his nails before. How easily these new emotions pushed through his years of conditioning. It buoyed him to know that he was human after all and that his usual unfeeling veneer was beginning to crack and chip away. He took a deep breath and turned his attention back to the computer.

Although there was no internet connection, a recent video call had been recorded, which explained why the web camera was on.

Sitting down, Kaufman scrolled over and clicked the play button.

A platinum blond with blue eyes and heavy mascara popped up on the screen. The woman resembled a more angular Marilyn Monroe, and Kaufman recognized the room she was in as a standard suite at The Paradise Hotel and Casino.

"That little orangutan is *so* cute," she crooned in a New Jersey accent. "Oh, and guess what...I already won fifty bucks. Can you believe that? First slot machine I put a coin in: *ka-ching!* It was—"

The woman froze. Her smile slackened, and all her features went loose as if she were a robot powering down.

Then, without warning, she snapped to.

"Wha...huh? What was that?" She looked around, apparently trying to regain her bearings. "Man, was that weird? Felt like somebody hit me with a shot of heroin. If only, huh?" She laughed. "Anyway, what was I say'n?"

Head cocked to one side, the woman's right eye twitched, then twitched again, and again, and again, until it was as spastic as a miss wired lightbulb. After a moment, it subsided, but the woman remained perfectly still. It was as if the pause button had been pressed, except the time bar continued to slide right, counting seconds.

A cold sweat trickled down Kaufman's armpits.

This was it. This was what happened, whatever *it* was.

In a trance, the woman sat unmoving. Her eyes glazed over and she started to pant. In time, a pearl of saliva built up at the corner of her mouth. The liquid ember spilled out in a long transparent ribbon that slowly stretched until it met fabric and created a splatter of darker blue on the woman's blouse.

For what seemed like minutes, the woman continued to sit as frozen and as zoned out. Kaufman finally skipped forward a few seconds, then a few more, and then stopped when the pixelated image jumped.

In one hand, the woman now held a fistful of her own hair. Bloody roots and skin matted the ends of the blond filament. With an epileptic spasm, the other hand shot up and pulled out another clump of hair.

"What the hell!?" Kaufman muttered, leaning forward.

Over and over, the hands tore out golden locks until the white scalp resembled a botched sheep shearing.

The pain must have been intense, yet the detached faced woman never cried out, didn't even whimper.

How was that possible? Kaufman checked the volume. It was all the way up.

Abruptly standing, the woman turned away from the camera and walked zombielike over to the nearby bed. Half out of the frame, she stopped and rummaged through a bag. Finding what she was looking for, she hunched over and began twisting violently. Her body heaved and jerked as she continued to labor on whatever it was she was doing.

After a minute, she turned around. Bloody multipurpose pliers were clenched in one hand. The other hand dripped blood where all the fingernails had been stripped off.

"Jesus!" Kaufman blurted, bracing himself in the armchair.

Next, the shiny red pliers went up to the woman's mouth and without any hesitation, she began popping out teeth as casually as if she'd been shucking oysters.

It shouldn't have been possible for teeth to come out so easily – nevertheless, bright bicuspids and molars plopped into a growing pool of crimson. As the woman worked, she lost her dead-eyed stare. Her brow narrowed with focused determined.

Suddenly she grew more frantic, breaking off the remaining teeth at the gum line and leaving behind a jagged line of ivory.

"Nononono…" Kaufman exhaled, reaching for the computer power button, knowing where this was heading, what this frenzied crescendo was building up to.

But he wasn't fast enough.

Grunting and gurgling, dark blood streamed out over the self-mutilating Marilyn Monroe's chin and down her throat, as she reached into her now toothless mouth, and yanked out her tongue. Blood gushed and the spongy muscle smacked the camera turning the screen black.

And now Kaufman heard screaming, low and horrified; except this bellow came not from the computer's speakers, but from his own lungs.

Staggering, he pushed the laptop away and fled the house, fled the horrors on the monitor.

Yanking open the front door, he flung himself into the dry afternoon air, and instead of feeling oppressive, the heat was welcoming, as abrasive and cleansing as a scalding shower.

No microbe or bacteria, no escaped superbug from Shafter, could account for the erratic insanity he'd just witnessed. As Kaufman passed forsaken homes and deserted cars, his mind searched for answers, tuned over possibilities.

That's when he noticed the birds.

Like belly-up fish in a polluted pond, dead birds peppered the landscape. Apparently, whatever had reduced the jackrabbits to red-eyed horrors had also killed the local avian. That didn't surprise Kaufman. Birds were fragile creatures, which was why they'd historically been used by miners to detect deadly odorless and colorless vapors.

That notion formed a new theory in Kaufman's mind: chemical gas. The pre-nuclear doomsday device.

Used on the battlefields of World War I and steadily enhanced as a weaponized agent - the ruined rabbits, the eradicated birds, as well as the biological wall paint and deranged Jersey woman - they all seemed easily explained by a manufactured gas designed to cause instant insanity.

Absorbed through the skin and quickly entering the bloodstream, a psychotropic gas would spread throughout the body and into the brain, causing adverse psychological disorders and even mutations. It was just the kind of thing a military testing facility looking for a new synthetic weapon would invent. Yet if that was the answer, why hadn't he been affected too?

Then again, his tingling skin might be a sign he already had.

Who was to say that even now, he wasn't strapped down on a gurney, restrained by a straitjacket with a rubber ball in his mouth, and all this was a fantasy, the never-ending nightmare?

Around him, the lifeless piles of feathers seemed to stretch on endlessly.

That might be the case, except no dream was ever so real, so colorful, laced with such convincing smells and textures, and plated with powerful emotions and physical discomfort. The answer might indeed be altering fumes of some kind, and he might eventually succumb to it, but he hadn't yet.

No, in this bleak phantasm, he was wide awake.

The only logical thing to do now was to get in his truck and drive. Drive as fast as he could, as far as he could. Just leave. Leave this city and its scourge behind him. Forever.

He should go to Wendover, or Elko, get medical attention and let someone else deal with all this.

Making his way across town, Kaufman thought the moon probably contained more life than the streets of Decoy. Even driving through the city in the middle of the night on Christmas Eve, the roads had never been so uninhabited. It was as if every man, woman, and child had dried up and blown away, and that un-accounted-for singularity punched a big hole in every one of his theories - viral, nuclear, *and* chemical.

Where *was* everyone? Where were all the bodies?

Kaufman had no answers, nor any more theories.

At Golden Hills, where he'd left his truck after Donald had apprehended him, the massive wrought iron security gates were twisted outwards. Kaufman walked by without a second glance.

Passing by the finely manicured yards Kaufman appreciated the quality of the grounds. He'd landscaped many of these homes, and they represented the pinnacle of his creativity, as well as the success of his business, in spite of all obstacles. The thought of leaving it all behind troubled him, and he felt the briefest pang of regret. But it was gone in a heartbeat. There would be other yards, other jobs.

Reaching his battered pickup, Kaufman got in and turned the key in the ignition. A fast click sounded, but the engine remained silent.

"Reliable as old faithful," Kaufman grumbled, banging a fist into the steering wheel. The truck gave out a tired honk like the agitated moo of a disgruntled heifer. Kaufman laughed and shook his head.

Unlike the luxurious houses of this neighborhood that displayed wealth without personality, his old truck dripped uniqueness and was dented and scratched with more character than any vehicle had a right to.

Today, however, it wasn't personality he needed, but performance and Kaufman knew where to find not just a set of wheels, but the crème de la crème.

Anthony Green was a car connoisseur, and his house was a hundred yards away.

Exiting the truck, Kaufman pulled a hand ax from the back and made his way once again to the mansion.

However, his resolve wavered when he reached the back door. He wasn't worried about the alarm - indeed, he would welcome any response it might bring. He'd love to explain himself to some living people, but that's not why he hesitated.

His dilemma was a moral one, and the sensation was odd since he didn't have moments like this. His condition had always allowed him to act logically and without any hesitation. Except right now - even though the situation was extreme and arguably reasonable - he was stymied by the feeling that, by stealing a car, he'd somehow failed. It was a crazy irrational reaction. Anthony Green's death was not his fault. He didn't even know for sure that the Raging Bull was dead, but images of the big man clutching at his chest, struck down by some unseen agent (or possibly the victim of his own traitorous hands like the woman in the video) gnawed at him. Never before would he have reacted in this fashion, but since coming back from nearly hanging himself, well...

He'd wanted these emotions, and that meant taking the good ones with the superfluous ones.

Shaking his head, Kaufman reached back and smashed the window.

The alarm was immediate and blaring.

Ignoring the noise, Kaufman made his way to the garage. Four of the six bays were occupied. Besides the high-end Audi Anthony had been driving earlier, the other missing car must have been in use by his wife. That left a choice between a posh Jaguar convertible, a thuggish but stately old Cadillac, a rare vintage Ferrari, and a Humvee - not the civilian Hummer, but a converted military transport Humvee.

Of all the automobiles, though, it was the classic cherry red Ferrari that spoke to Kaufman, sang to him. He'd always wanted to drive one of these magnificent machines, and if he was going to be bothered by guilt over taking a car, all the more reason to indulge now.

In a metal box on the wall was a series of waiting keys.

As he slid behind the wheel, soft leather conformed to Kaufman's body. All instruments, levers, and knobs were in easy reach.

The engine rumbled to life.

The sound was a mixture between a roar and a purr, the perfect blend of power and refinement.

Pulling out of the driveway, Kaufman was surprised to find that he had to hold the sports car back. Heading out of the city on northbound State 229, he could no longer hold back. The road was empty, and Kaufman let loose the more than 600 horsepower engine. The performance machine not only responded but seemed to anticipate his every action.

A giddy laugh escaped Kaufman as he tapped the gas for more speed, and at 70 mph, the tires chirped, surging forward.

The Ferrari wasn't even close to topping out.

How fast could this baby go?

Giving himself over to the thrill, Kaufman momentarily forgot about the empty city. The pleasure of driving erased the madness around him. In all directions, the desert stretched flat, with withered mountains on the horizon. As the car raced over asphalt, Kaufman whooped. This is what the Ferrari had been designed for. At 110 mph, it ate up the miles.

And still, there was more.

Wholly consumed by speed and the need for more of it, Kaufman figured he'd be able to top 160 mph, and the thought exhilarated him. He floored the accelerator.

Rounding a subtle turn in the highway at 130, the G-forces pulled hard. Kaufman belted out laughter; he was flying!

However, as he shot around an outcropping of rock, a massive traffic jam stretched out before him.

Kaufman stomped on the brakes.

The Ferrari shuddered and fishtailed. In its wake, ribbons of serpentine black painted the asphalt.

Still, the barricade of vehicles rushed closer.

Rising out of the seat, he pushed down with both feet trying to ram the brake pedal through the floorboard. But there wasn't enough room.

At the last moment, Kaufman twisted the wheel in a desperate attempt to turn away from the traffic jam. He wasn't sure how fast he was going when he slammed into the first car, but it was enough to send him airborne.

Spinning, the Ferrari flipped and rolled and skipped off the hoods of the metal sardines, like a pebble across a pond.

Kaufman found himself at the mercy of impartial physics.

His head shattered the side window, and in the next instant, his right foot was tangled in the pedals and wrenched sideways. The last thing he remembered before the car stopped its mad tumble, was being jerked forward so hard the restraining harness snapped his collar bone.

For a long time, he hoped to pass out, to drift off into a world of nothingness and embrace oblivion. Yet after hanging upside down for what seemed like hours, he finally resigned himself to trying to get out. Locating the belt latch by touch, he released it and dropped to the roof. The impact sent a wave of pain through his shoulder. He wriggled out the rear window and flopped heavily on the hood of another car.

Rising to his feet, Kaufman surveyed his surroundings.

At least a quarter of the city's vehicles were present: mini-vans, campers, pickups, convertibles, SUVs, even some limos. Some were running, most were parked, and almost all, especially those at the front, were wrecked.

It was an interstate junkyard.

A few vehicles imprisoned dead motorists, those that died in the initial impact, but the cars further back were all abandoned. Open doors and broken windows, where the occupants had no other way out, showed the traces of human passage; otherwise, the scene was as empty as the town had been.

Where had everyone gone?

Scanning the horizon, Kaufman saw the answer to his questions. At first, the dark line in the distance seemed to be a ragged trench created by mountain runoff, but then he recognized it for what it really was.

And for a man who didn't drink, Kaufman suddenly needed one.

Desperately.

CHAPTER 7

The sound of a hundred voices mumbled.

The babble went on and on like the multilayered hum before a theatrical production. Except this murmur wasn't chatter, not people's voices anyways, but similar – something else though...something familiar, something organic, but not alive. Not living in the way animals or even plants do but filled with life, brimming with it.

Whatever it was, if it could be identified, everything else would be made clear. Clarity was on the tip of his tongue, but ultimately it was the movement, not the sound that restored him.

A wet wave pulled and ebbed, pulled and ebbed, pulled...

Sitting up, dirty water gushed out of Matthew. Repeatedly he purged himself, coughed and spit and vomited, yet still, he felt bloated - felt like the liquid was coming out of his eyes and ears and even the pores of his skin.

The saturated feeling was nothing more than an illusion, however, for he was dry. The sun had warmed him, baked his clothing, and dried his hair. Besides the damp earth under his chest and his shriveled feet, still half in the aqueduct, he was not only dry but dusty.

That was strange, since he'd drowned, gulped more water than a fish.

Flopping on his back, he saw that he was on a sandy shoal far downstream from the swift currents of the cement aqueduct. It was probably only by dumb luck that he hadn't croaked. It had been a crazy, stupid idea to tie himself and Jess to the suitcase.

Matthew sat up.

Jessica!

He scanned the waterline. Where was his sister?

He stood and called out. There was no response.

He had to find her. *Had* to. She might be hurt. Worse, she might be dying.

Heart racing, Matthew surveyed the surrounding bank. Apart from a plethora of empty and broken bottles, miscellaneous trash, and a fat dead rat, there was nothing - no signs of Jess.

In a fast waddle, he started upstream and was almost yanked off his feet by the shoelace lashed to his wrist. The suitcase - cracked open - slid along the ground, its innards washed away. Towing the stupid thing was going to slow him down; it would fight him every step of the way like a willful dog, but he also couldn't carry it. What Matthew needed, and didn't have, was some scissors.

From the wet sand, the dead, bloated rat seemed to laugh at his dilemma. Major decomposition had widened its already sinister grin, and razor-sharp teeth gleamed where flesh used to be.

Was Jess like this rodent, washed up and rotting?

No, he would never let her end up like that.

In a fury, Matthew bit at the shoestring - gnawed and chewed. After a savage minute, he was free.

Moving upstream, his leg braces squeaked as he stumbled over discarded refuse and driftwood. He kept expecting to see Jessica's swishing pigtails as she played along the riverbank. But there were no signs of her.

She couldn't be dead, couldn't be. If she was…well, he might as well be dead too.

Picking up his pace, Matthew passed through a tall patch of reeds and stepped on something soft.

Looking down, his breath caught in his throat.

Under his sneaker was Mr. Horsey. The stuffed animal's pink imitation fur was matted with mud, and oily cotton stuffing spilled out of the pony's belly.

Numbly, Matthew searched the area, his heart in his throat. Then, there, a few feet away, face down in the water, he saw his sweet sister, bobbing among cattails, her golden hair a shimmering nebula about her head.

"Jessica!" Matthew howled.

He was supposed to be her protector, not her executioner.

Storming into the creek, Matthew wrapped his arms around his sister and dragged her toward shore.

Laying her out flat on her back, he knew what needed to be done. Matthew had taken CPR classes at the community pool; except the instructors never said how your mind would go blank when it was your kid sister you pulled from a dirty ditch, never said how heavy a limp body would be. They didn't prepare you for the gray pasty discolored quality of the skin and the dead look in the eyes.

The eyes!

The rubber mannequins Matthew had practiced mouth-to-mouth on all had closed lids, but Jess looked right at him and those unblinking lifeless orbs questioned him. Asked him how he could let this happen. Why'd he let her drown? How? Why? How? Why?

Matthew began to hyperventilate.

His breaths came in short hiccupping gasps. All the while, the dead eyes stare on.

If he lost it now, he'd be no help at all; he slapped himself before he could slip into hysteria. Hard. Stinging cheeks brought focus, and instantly, practice sessions drilled into him annually over three years were in his mind.

It was as if his teacher was kneeling right beside him speaking into his ear, telling him step by step what to do, 30:2 - that was the ratio of compressions to breaths. First, though, Matthew needed to make sure nothing was obstructing Jessica's airway. Tilting her onto her side, he let the water drain out of his sister's mouth. He depressed her tongue and looked in the back of her throat.

No debris.

Tilting her head back, Matthew breathed twice, then pumped. Over and over, he repeated the cycle for what seemed to be forever. Indeed, after ten minutes, his arms and shoulder ached from the effort. The pain started as a warm cramp but soon spread to a throbbing fire. Tears streamed down his face, partly from the soreness but mostly for Jess. She looked dead, felt dead, and she didn't seem to be responding to the CPR.

Maybe he was doing it wrong.

Growing frantic, Matthew pushed more oxygen into her small lungs but dared not press any harder for fear of breaking a rib.

Through clenched teeth, he counted off each depression.

"One. Two. Three. Four. FIVE. Come on-SIX-Jess-SEVEN-wake up. Eight-you've got-NINE-to live. Ten. Live! Eleven. Live! Twelve."

Giving up the count, he tried to coax Jessica back through sheer will as he pumped. "*Live. Live. Live. Live. Live.*"

He hated himself for what he'd done, for forcing her across the creek. She hadn't wanted to go, had possibly known what would happen. But he'd pushed her. From the start, he should never have let her leave the house, should never have invited her along. He'd put her in harm's way. *He'd* killed her.

"This. Wasn't. Supposed. To. Happen," Matthew grunted, clipping off each word as he jabbed at his sister's chest. His command for her to live slowly soured and grew venomous. It was so much easier to blame himself; the supply of guilt and self-loathing was bottomless.

"It-was…my-fault. My-fault…mine…mine. Damn-me. Damn. Damn. Damn."

Matthew's arms gave out.

He'd gone well beyond thirty depressions, probably beyond a hundred and still Jessica's eyes didn't blink, didn't shine with life.

He'd broken his promise to his mother. He'd failed to protect Jess. What was he supposed to do now?

With his last ounce of strength, he took Jessica into his arms and held her. Without even realizing it, he began rocking her, his self-destruction giving way to anguish.

In between sobs, he prayed.

His plea was simple: "I'll be your cripple, God. If that's what you want. I won't ask to be healed. Not anymore. I don't need to be normal. The pain's not so bad, I can bear it. Just let her live. Let Jess live, and I'll be your cripple, God. I'll be your cripple for life. Amen."

But his prayer wasn't answered.

Life did not return. Jess didn't start to breathe or move, didn't wake up - just hung limp and wet, and dead.

Maybe God didn't want another cripple. It was a stupid offer. Nobody *wanted* a cripple. Not God and not his father. Cripples had nothing to offer. They were weak. They let people down. *He* let people down. He was a worthless cripple that had let his little sister drown.

Holding Jess, gently swaying, Matthew began smoothing her hair. It was matted and caked with dirt. It had always been so lovely - decorated with ribbons and bows, flowers and barrettes. Now it was gnarled and soiled just like the bloated rat he'd seen earlier.

No, never!

So, while stroking the golden mane, Matthew's nimble fingers removed the knots, and his soft hands combed out the tangles. It was all he could do, and soon it was as straight and glossy as it was going to get without a brush.

That's when Matthew realized he was going to have to put Jessica aside. He would have to lay her out, leave her on this muddy shore among the feces of feral animals and scattered garbage. Jessica hated getting dirty. Moreover, she deserved better.

Matthew's ears burned in humiliation.

Not only had he taken away her life, but because of his debilitated body, he would be forced to leave her without dignity as well.

His father had been right. He *was* a burden - a broken-bodied gimp. He couldn't even carry Jess out of this toilette. From this day on, no matter how twisted his body became, his soul would always be the more deformed. Every breath he took would be a reminder of his shame, a reminder of the life denied to his sweet sister.

Hating himself for what he was about to do, Matthew suddenly remembered the suitcase. It offered possibilities, perhaps redemption.

The cavity was just large enough to hold Jess. Inside she would be kept off the ground, and it could double as a sled. Dragging her dead body still wasn't very dignified, not to mention how slow and tedious the going would be, but at least he wouldn't have to abandon her.

However, making it back to the suitcase - a mere half dozen yards upstream - might as well have been a mile, for there was no way he was going to be able to stand and carry her that far.

But he would try anyway.

For once, he had to be strong.

Working his legs under him in a squat position, Matthew prepared to stand. If he fell, he wanted to fall directly downward so Jess wouldn't tumble out of his arms.

To his amazement, however, he stood without difficulty: no shaky legs, no weak muscles. His upper body felt good as well. Not great, but capable.

Somehow, Matthew reached the suitcase without incident, and he gently lowered his sister as delicately as if he'd been cradling a porcelain sculpture. At some point, her eyes had closed, perhaps during the grooming, but whatever the case, Matthew was relieved, because now he wouldn't have to shut them…wouldn't have to see the blame in them.

Curled in a fetal position, Jess looked asleep - at peace.

With the makeshift stretcher set, Matthew put his head down and pulled. His feet slipped as they sought traction, but the hard plastic of the suitcase slid easily over the ground.

Pulling until his legs ached, Matthew glanced up to see how far he'd come. It was barely fifty yards. Before him, the path stretched on as long as a marathon. He would, however, not be deterred. Lowering his shoulders, he continued plodding forward, knowing that once in town, he would be able to find help…

Except, unexpectedly, help found him.

Moments ago, where the path had been empty now stood a pair of feet.

For a second, Matthew thought it was the blonde cop, and his heart skipped a beat, but this guy wasn't wearing any shoes, and his hair was dark. He was also wearing tan khakis with the cuffs rolled up and a loose white shirt, not a uniform. With the sleeves pushed up high and the top three buttons undone; the guy looked like the picture-perfect vacationer on a Hawaiian beach.

Except this wasn't a tropical paradise, it was a dirty aqueduct. No one walked around here barefoot since broken glass and unidentifiable metal shrapnel were as plentiful as weeds.

Matthew supposed the guy might be homeless, but in his spotless clothes and with his purposeful stride, the clean-cut dude gave off a celestial vibe. Indeed, he looked so powerful and resourceful, Matthew thought he must be sent from God.

Pulling up short, the barefoot man looked down at Jessica curled up in the suitcase.

Feeling shame and humiliation burning in his cheeks, Matthew blurted out, "She's dead."

"Remarkable," the man whispered, almost reverently, never taking his eyes off Jessica.

Matthew cocked an eyebrow at that. That wasn't the response he expected. The guy must not have heard him right.

"No…she's *dead*."

Blinking, the beach bum shifted his gaze to Matthew as if he was just becoming aware of the boy's presence for the first time. He stared intently, and Matthew felt his guilt consume him.

"I…I tried to save her, I even did CPR, but it…it didn't work. She drowned."

"Yes, but what's she doing now?"

Matthew frowned, confused. Again, this was not the reply he expected.

The guy continued to stare; his searching eyes didn't seem to hope that Matthew knew the answer as much as accuse him of withholding information.

Again, Matthew babbled his initial statement, "She's…uh, she's not doing anything. She's dead…she died."

The calculating eyes softened and looked past Matthew, back into the suitcase.

"No, not dead, she's alive."

The guy spoke with such conviction that Matthew whirled around, half expecting to see Jessica standing up with her head cocked to one side, smiling her ever-present pixie smile. The blow of finding her still lying motionless completely deflated him. Absent was the slow rise and fall of her chest. She was still gone.

Duped, Matthew wanted to tell this butthead that he wasn't funny, maybe even to go to hell, when Jessica's nostrils flared.

Matthew blinked.

He waited for the movement again, but it didn't come. What did come was a memory of something his lifesaving teacher had once told him. Matthew couldn't remember the medical term, but his instructor had said that when a person drowns, their throat constricts when water enters the airway. This shuts off the lungs to protect the victim, resulting in a loss of consciousness. A small portion of people still died even after being rescued because the sealed lungs wouldn't reopen; however, some people began to breathe spontaneously once the muscles relax.

In his grief, Matthew hadn't checked for a pulse or airflow. He did so now.

Dropping to his knees, he felt Jess' wrist. He'd never been good at this part and didn't feel a pulse now. Giving up, he put his cheek close to her mouth and nose and tried to feel any expelled air.

The slightest of breezes caressed his face. Matthew's heartbeat quickened, but he couldn't be sure it wasn't just the wind.

He waited, but he didn't feel the breeze repeat.

In desperation, he turned Jessica onto her back and placed his ear to her chest. He couldn't make out a second independent rhythm over his own thudding heartbeat.

"I...I just can't tell," stammered Matthew, flopping to the ground.

"I can," replied the beach bum, scowling.

Kneeling, the guy used a hand to push Matthew away, clearing a space around him. Matthew shuddered at the contact. The touch had been mild, but it left him feeling grimy - the kind of grimy he'd felt once when he'd stolen a piece of candy from a grocery store.

Of his own accord, Matthew moved further away from the dark-haired man who hunched over Jess. As if testing her temperature, the guy placed his hand on her forehead.

She squirmed! It was quick, but she'd definitely moved.

"Did you see that!?" Matthew said, leaning forward.

"I didn't suspect this, not at all. You caught me completely off guard; you didn't figure into any of my contingencies."

Matthew was about to ask what the guy meant when he realized he wasn't the one being spoken to.

"You're quite the sly one," said the guy, still addressing Jessica. "You must have known right away, sensed me somehow. Well, that works both ways, and you were right to hide, but enough of this foolishness. Come forth!"

Upon the command, the guy wrenched back his hand, hissing as if burned, and indeed, Matthew thought he detected the faint odor of burnt flesh.

Jessica's eyes popped open.

They focused on the man above her and bore into the peculiar savior with a death glare. In the same instance, she spoke slowly and denunciatory, "Bad man."

Smirking and holding his hand, the guy took a few steps back. "Cute."

Matthew rushed over to his sister. She continued to eye her reviver even while he hugged her.

"See, not dead," said the man. Then added, "Well, I guess that depends on how you look at it. But never mind that. All's well that ends well, or so the saying goes. Now, let me introduce myself. My name is Shane—"

"Liar," Jess cut him off.

Matthew was taken aback. Never had he heard his sister talk so confidently or so boldly to an adult, to anyone.

"Yes, that may be."

"Usurper!" she spat, and instead of being offended at the accusation, the man's smile widened.

"Hopefully, but for now, you can call me Shane."

Matthew tried to calm his seething sister. He didn't understand why she was so upset.

"It's alright, Jess. This guy…uh, Shane, he's here to help us."

However, immediately after speaking those words, Matthew wasn't so sure.

"You should listen to your brother Jessica, he's right, I am here to help. It's a changed world out there. Different from anything you've ever seen or known. You need to be careful. Be extra wary of strangers. Don't trust anyone, because everyone you meet will be jealous of what you've become. They'll try to use you, even hurt you. So stay away." The man paused for emphasis, "Especially from *me.*"

The last was said with such repressed violence that Shane's teeth clacked together, and his eyes seemed to flash.

Had they always been purple?

Matthew was surprised that he hadn't noticed the intense coloring before. He'd looked right into those eyes. Suddenly, he felt like he was seeing the beach bum for the first time. The clothing hadn't changed. Shane's face was still inviting and charming, still held a supernatural quality, but now it had soured. For Matthew, it inspired the power felt on those rare occasions when he dropped the F-bomb or when he belittled someone to make himself feel better, a feeling that never failed to leave a bad taste in his mouth.

Also, Matthew now noticed the tattoos. Had they always been there? Rosy ink markings, covered Shane's chest where his shirt was open at the throat and along his muscular arms down to the wrists.

"You can't surpass me," continued Shane, apparently not done helping. "It will never happen, so don't try. If you do, if you try and approach my level, you'll be just like Icarus - the closer you fly to the sun, the faster you'll burn. It's better to stay in my shadow. Better yet, keep away entirely. Because if you get too close, get any crazy notions of standing in my way, I'll destroy you. I'll tear you apart and devour you, piece by piece. Got it?"

Matthew nodded.

Even Jess dumbly bobbed her head.

Gone was her spit-fire attitude; she was scared. They both were.

"I doubt you do. You have eyes, but you do not see; ears, but you do not hear; you understand naught but fear."

Shane leaned towards the cowering pair, and terror filled their youthful faces.

"Perhaps that is enough. Yes…" Standing erect, he placed a hand on both Matthew and Jessica's heads.

Light shunned this man, bent away from him, but darkness seemed his lover; it surrounded him, shrouded him in a cloak of evil, and when he touched their heads, a transfer of that vile shadow oozed over them. A physical sickness of body, heart, and soul cried out against such corruptness, but Shane held fast.

"Fear me. This is my gospel, my blessing."

Fingers dug painfully into Matthew's head. Jess whimpered.

"Obey me, for inasmuch as ye keep my commandments, ye shall live."

Matthew tried to pry the hand from his skull as fingernails punctured flesh.

"Fear me. This is my will, my endowment."

Talons of impossible strength and sharpness threatened to crush bone and brain. Jessica cried in earnest.

"Because ye feared, ye are my disciples; the first of my flock. If there be others, teach them my word, for in the heart of fear the seeds of insurrection and subversion can never grow."

The vice grip grew stronger, inhumanly strong.

"Go forth in fear. Remember, always fear. Fear be with you."

The pressure and pain was too intense. Matthew went wild. Gone was any rational effort to remove Shane's hand; instead, he clawed and scraped and plucked at the fingers, hoping to break one. Break one, then another; break them all until he was free.

Matthew yelled, begged, pleaded for Shane to stop, to let go, but he didn't relent - only squeezed tighter.

Hands shaking, heads rattling and on the verge of popping - Jessica screamed, loud and shrill and piercing.

It was an unearthly sound and acted like a crowbar, tearing Shane's clasp away. Fingers peeled off with the resistance of soldered iron, but Jessica's continued shriek was so powerful as to cause a concussion in the air, staggering the false messiah backwards.

Matthew used the brief freedom to run.

Grabbing Jessica's hand, they made a hasty escape. Looking back over his shoulder, Matthew stopped.

Shane was no longer behind them. As quickly as he'd appeared, he'd vanished. Only the empty suitcase remained.

Not waiting to find out where he'd gone, Matthew led his sister towards town. The guy had been nuts - a homeless wacko. However, once back among the main streets, Matthew saw that there was truth in what he'd been told.

Decoy was different.

No cars cruised the streets, no pedestrians strolled the sidewalks, and dead birds dotted the ground.

Shane was right. The world had changed.

Jessica clung tightly to Matthew's waist. It felt so good to have her back. He would shield her from all unpleasantness, let nothing stain her shining life, be valiant in his guardianship. He resolved to redouble his efforts.

But as they drew nearer to their home, he questioned his ability to accomplish such a feat. The neighborhood was quiet, spooky. Beyond the haunted quality, Matthew perceived a wrongness that he could not put into words; Jess apparently felt the same, for as they neared Lucybean's little brick rambler, she stopped.

Shaking her head, she refused to go in.

"What's wrong?" he inquired.

Jessica didn't respond. He didn't want to push her; her refusal reminded him of only a short while ago when he'd insisted that she cross the creek.

"It's okay. You wait out here, and I'll go inside."

"No. I'm coming too," Jess pouted. She put on a brave face and took his hand.

Matthew felt confident that once they were inside, everything would be fine. Aunt Lucy and Uncle Bernard might be pissed, would certainly overreact, but maybe in light of whatever had quieted the city and killed the birds, they'd just be glad to have them home. That's what he hoped anyway, and he convinced himself that's exactly what would happen.

Until he found the front door unlocked.

Lucybean never ever left the front door unlocked; they never left any door unlocked.

As the door swung inward, a wave of hot stifling, muggy air rolled out.

From inside, the sound of the heater running was unmistakable. The old furnace - used sparingly in the winter – clanked and popped and rattled. It was far too warm to need extra heat, and Lucybean was a stickler about wasting energy. If it was broken, Aunt Lucy would be clucking at her husband, while Uncle Bernard cursed the ancient machine in the process of trying to fix it. In the worst-case scenario, Aunt Lucy would call a repairman, squawking at the outrageous rates, while Uncle Bernard paced back and forth, complaining about not having the right tools to fix it himself.

In either event, the sound of those old birds would have been heard throughout the house. Thus, the stillness inside was clear evidence that everything was not alright.

Matthew moved to cross the threshold, but Jessica held him back.

"We should leave," she said, with wide-eyed fright.

"We can't. We have to find Aunt Lucy and Uncle Bernard. Wait here if you're scared."

Matthew instantly regretted being sharp with her, but if he didn't keep moving, he was going to lose his nerve. Jess again refused to be left behind, and this time she took to clinging, tucking herself in the crook of his arm like the frightened child she was.

Matthew stopped short of the living room. They were both sweating hard - the heat must have been turned all the way up. In fact, the air was so thick that it almost had to be chewed to breathe, but that wasn't what caused Matthew to halt. In the space beyond where Lucybean ran their tailoring business, someone had arranged all the mannequins in the middle of the floor.

Broad-shouldered male models and thin waisted females - all cut off at the neck and shoulders and ending in metal poles at the bottom. It was a forest of headless torsos. These fabric bodies weren't meant to display clothing but to shape them. Usually, they weren't scary - now though, in the dark room amongst shimmering heat waves, the mannequins weren't just menacing but seemed like a vision of hell: condemned souls, limbless and suffering damnation.

Matthew could almost swear he heard tortured moans.

The only interruption in the darkness was a glowing rectangle of light from the kitchen beyond.

Heading in that direction, Matthew halted as movement flashed past the door.

Someone was in here.

Someone or something, for the more the movement repeated in his mind, the more he was convinced the shape hadn't walked upright but was hunched over, shuffling.

"Aunt Lucy?" Matthew called out. "Uncle Bernard?"

Mannequins crashed to the floor, and the kitchen door slammed shut.

If Matthew hadn't already been drenched in sweat, he would have been now because, for an instant, the light had illuminated the face of his Aunt Lucy, and she'd looked...wrong. As if he'd caught a glimpse of her in a funhouse mirror.

Shakily, Matthew called out. "Aunt Lucy, are you alright?" He took a tentative step forward.

Jessica pulled at him. "No, don't."

"We have to help her, Jess, she's...sick."

But something told him that wasn't entirely true. Swallowing his unease, Matthew picked his way to the closed door.

From the gap below the door where the light spilled, a shadow swam across the floor; swam literally, because the carpet was covered in water. In the kitchen, Matthew could hear his aunt pacing back and forth, sloshing through a couple inches of liquid.

The heat and now the water...something very bad had happened - was happening - for Aunt Lucy would never allow the house to be in such a state.

Matthew called out again as the shadow continued to slice back and forth through the light. Still, there was no reply.

Nervously, he reached out for the doorknob and stopped when the dark figure's shadow fell still at his feet.

"Aunt Lucy?" he whispered.

From the other side of the door came a wheezy reply, a low guttural slur, barely audible.

"AuntLucyAuntyLucyAuntLucyAuntLucy," the voice repeated.

Somehow Jess must have heard that quiet murmur because she spoke. "No, not Aunt Lucy."

A self-assured knowledge filled her eyes, though it was also troubled and tinted with sadness and fear.

"What do you mean, not Aunt Lucy?" asked Matthew, but before his sister could respond, the voice from the kitchen began shouting.

"Whatdoyoumean?Whatdoyoumean?Whatdoyoumean?"

Jessica answered the mocking question, "Changed."

The raspy voice mimicked this revelation. It was louder now, more insistent. "ChangedChangedChangedChangedChangedChangedChanged."

Matthew's grip tightened on the doorknob, not in preparation for opening it, but to hold it shut.

In the dark, his heart thudded. Surging blood conspired with the rising temperature and dizziness buffeted him. He had to fight to keep upright.

Yet even in the suffocating dry temperature Jess's next word's chilled him: "No, not Lucy. Not human. Changed."

The continued bleating suddenly took on an enraged quality.

"NOTHUMANNOTHUMANNOTHUMANNOTHUMANNOTHUM ANNOTHUMAN…"

The hoarse voice suddenly crescendoed into a scream, and something banged into the door.

Banged again and again - with the aggressive tempo of a death metal band.

Matthew reeled backward.

His aunt wasn't hitting the door with her fist or even her body but seemed to be head-butting the wood like a deranged woodpecker.

A sharp crack noted progress, and soon the shoddy door split open and revealed a face.

The face resembled Aunt Lucy - had once been Aunt Lucy - but wasn't anymore.

Jess was right. Somehow, she'd known.

Not Lucy. Not human. Changed.

"God, what has she become?" Matthew breathed.

He stood transfixed, watching as the mindless animal performed its destructive ritual. Phlegm and spittle shot forth as the changed Lucy parroted her nephew's new question.

"Whathasshebecome?Whathasshebecome?Whathasshebecome?"

Splinters and cuts, gouges and abrasions, littered the once stern but kind face. Although Lucy seemed oblivious of the multiple injuries she inflicted, oblivious even of the children, she fixated on rhythmically pulverizing the weakened section of the door. Or maybe she was fixated on pulverizing her own wretched existence.

Matthew couldn't tell. Couldn't tell which fractures were on the door and which were on the face, was so hypnotized by the constant reverberation of both door and voice that he didn't feel Jessica tugging at his arm, didn't feel her take his hand and didn't realize that he was being led away until they were outside, and down the road.

Behind them, in that abominable sauna, the demolition continued. However, long before the feverish intonation faded away, Matthew noted a disquieting modification to his question.

From that unholy house, among the headless mannequins, the aunt, once known as Lucy, repeated an unanswerable prayer:

"GodwhathaveIbecome?WhathaveIbecome?WhathaveIbecome?…God?"

CHAPTER 8

Survivors.

Among all the bodies, there had to be at least one.

Scattered over the dusty ground were hills of men, women, and children - thousands of them.

The sight looked like footage from a World War II concentration camp, except these corpses weren't emaciated prisoners. There were no signs of starvation or malnutrition, no sores or other evidence of disease, no thin coating of gas residue either, only the stiff faces of the recently deceased.

Inexplicably, at least a quarter of the population of Decoy had simply fallen to their death.

A repulsive, nauseating odor surrounded the bodies. By the end of the day, the air would reek of the dead.

There was no escape here.

The town had become a coffin, an island of death. Leaving meant taking a ride down the river Styx.

Kaufman felt certain this graveyard of metal and flesh was not an isolated event. Similar scenes of massive car wrecks and mounds of bodies would be found at all the exit points of Decoy.

Above the cadavers swarmed a black cloud of scavenger birds. In silent turmoil, the vultures circled...circled...circled as if sensing this was a contaminated banquet, and if they drew nearer, they too would be damned. Some of the braver or more desperate birds had already flown too close, and now, partly covered in sand, they resembled winged cacti.

Kaufman shaded his eyes with a hand. Somewhere in the midst of the dead was an invisible line, a threshold where life ceased to exist. A space that once crossed allowed no return.

Taking a step closer, Kaufman could almost feel the wall of hidden death. It didn't radiate, wasn't a visible shimmer, but he could sense it nonetheless, for it ceased to make his skin crawl. And that scared him.

His skin had been tingling more or less continuously since leaving his house. Now, the sensation was very faint, and its absence was alarming rather than being a relief.

Kaufman scanned the bodies and noted all states of dress (and undress) from nightwear to work clothes. Whatever had compelled these people here, it had done so irrespective of whatever activity the townspeople had been doing when the calamity struck.

A sudden gust of hot air whipped across the dead, rustling fabric and crusting blank faces with sand.

In the sky, the living cloud twisted and writhed. Dark wings beat the air in growing frustration - a storm on the edge of breaking.

Kaufman understood their frustration. Somehow, he'd been spared insanity, slipped through the fingers of doom that had raked over Decoy and been left an observer. Why he should be singled out, left untouched while so many others perished, was a mystery.

Searching the glazed faces and slack expressions of his neighbors, Kaufman realized all were unknown to him, only the moving background of his world. Each had been a unique life that he'd never known, and now never would.

The thought saddened him - more, it enraged him.

These people had been robbed, had been forced between a rock and a hard place like victims of a sky rise fire. The choice was to be consumed by flames or jump to the unyielding cement below.

Damned if they did, damned if they didn't.

Perhaps he should join them.

Only a few more feet, and he too would be just another piece of human roadkill, struck down by an intangible semi.

Kaufman didn't move.

Whatever the Decoy Madness was, unlike these people, who might have seen death as the more favorable option to the insanity that pursued them - the insanity that perhaps was already in them - he felt no threat.

For him, there were no consuming flames, no advancing fire. He would not be propelled over that edge, and that deep-seeded need to live in the face of so much senseless death infuriated him.

Picking up a rock, Kaufman hurled it into the air, roaring with exasperation.

Overhead, the avian tornado erupted.

In a frenzy of pent-up energy, the birds wheeled and exploded in every direction.

Spiraling downward, some two dozen carrion eaters made for the corpse mound. At some point, they passed through the unseen barrier, and abruptly, the birds dropped out of the heavens. In a tumbling ballet, fowl rained down in a hailstorm of sharp beaks and razor talons as gravity claimed its nemesis and rocketed the lifeless birds to the ground.

Each impact was marked by a hard *thwack* and puff of dust.

Raising his good arm protectively, Kaufman turned and ran. All around birds slammed into the hard pack and ricocheted off cars.

Amongst the storm, a large turkey vulture struck Kaufman in the back, and he stumbled, landing hard on his injured shoulder. He felt the broken clavicle shift and grind under his skin.

"Ahhh..." he moaned, as hot pain lanced through his body. He lay there for a moment waiting for the hazardous precipitation to end. The right side of his body and his chest throbbed with each breath. It felt as if he might have broken a few ribs.

Breathing slow stinging breaths, Kaufman sat up and noticed something out on the horizon. Silhouetted against the turquoise skyline - past the cars and inanimate birds, and several miles past the mountain of death - were tiny dark moving shapes. Holding up a hand to block the glare of the sun, Kaufman scanned the objects, and the longer he looked, the more convinced he became. There were people out there.

Probably state troopers or the military. They must be setting up a perimeter, playing damage control and preparing to collect their damn test results. Soon the government would come in and hush up any remaining survivors. They'd call it quarantine, but it meant the same thing. The media would be pitched some red herring to misdirect public attention, and any living subjects would be "disappeared." They would be held against their wills and forced to undergo endless medical experiments.

For a moment, Kaufman was tempted just to lay there and let those bastards come get him, let this screwed up world have its way.

But that was escapist behavior.

Yesterday, he might have tried to wait out this unpleasantness, but not today. Not anymore. He had a second lease on life, and he wasn't going to shirk from any challenges. He held destiny in his own hands - maybe not by the balls, but at least he was partially in control, and that grip on fate meant facing up to the hard parts of life to get where he wanted to go and become what he only imagined.

He also realized that ever since hearing the screaming jackrabbits, he'd been running scared; that was an outfit he wasn't familiar with, that didn't fit him well. His suit was logic, tailor-made for him since he'd been a boy. And if any situation called for a calm, calculating, level head, this did.

It was time to dress for the occasion.

If he, the forsaken Kaufman Striker, had survived, then surely there must be others. There had to be others, and he would find them - more, he was going to find some answers.

First things first, get patched up and get provisioned.

Holding his injured arm against his body, Kaufman left the fallen, as well as the immaterial wall of death, and trudged back through the obstacle course of mangled cars. Reaching the end of the massive pileup, he felt the strange tingle of his skin deepen with each step. Kaufman welcomed it.

However, instead of grabbing a vehicle to head back into town, his feet moved with purpose towards a low squat building. It was if his body knew where it wanted to go but hadn't told his brain.

Kaufman remembered that the outlying ranch was a veterinary hospital, and although it catered to horses and pets, it would nevertheless stock medical supplies, supplies that he could use to treat himself. That's what his subconscious must have put together.

However, as he neared the animal shelter, Kaufman found himself breaking into a frantic run. Legs hammered the asphalt propelled by a deep hunger in the pit of his stomach unlike anything he'd ever known. It was an irresistible impulse, a raging compulsion, an urgency to gorge that surpassed any natural craving. He was famished, starving, and this he realized, was the real reason he'd skipped taking a car back into town.

He wanted food. Now!

The front door of the clinic was locked. Kaufman kicked without hesitation. The wood frame cracked and exploded inward.

With the single-mindedness of an addict desperate for a fix, Kaufman raced from room to room, driven by his preternatural hunger. Ransacking cupboards, emptying draws, and pilfering the trash, he searched for anything edible. But there wasn't a snack to be found, just sterile white floors and polished metal countertops.

Snatching up a piece of paper, Kaufman shoved it in his mouth. He masticated the printout into a mushy pulp and swallowed, then ripped off another bite.

It wasn't even close to being enough. If he didn't find real food soon, he was going to head back out and gorge on dirt. Luckily, before he began devouring terra firma, he located a room at the back of the building marked **Feed and Supplies**.

Crashing through the door, Kaufman found himself in a small warehouse. The far wall consisted of a single roll-up metal door. To the right and left of the docking station were chain-link stalls stacked high with hay and blue plastic barrels of dry grain.

Kaufman made a beeline to a cache of dog food.

For minutes he stuffed his face, not caring what anything tasted like and not repulsed in the least. How he could eat anything, let alone pellets of mystery meat and brown jelly in the shape of tin cans, was baffling. Less than twenty minutes ago, at the foot of a hill of his dead neighbors, he had been on the verge of vomiting. Now he was stuffing his face.

While he ate, he hardly even tasted what he put in his mouth; however, once satiated, he realized his breath was repulsive. He would have given anything for a stick of gum. Then again, he doubted that even a few packs would have been enough to get rid of the awful aftertaste.

Spitting and trying to clean out his mouth, Kaufman wiped a hand on his pants. They sagged loosely on his hips. Somehow, during the last hour, he'd shed ten or more pounds. He didn't even know how that was physically possible, but it sure explained his ravenous appetite.

The weight loss wasn't the only sudden change either. He'd always been fit, but now he realized he was suddenly toned, muscles on top of muscles - a Calvin Klein underwear model waiting to be discovered.

Contemplating both his new physique and his eating splurge, Kaufman didn't hear the dog behind him until it growled.

Low and threatening, the throaty rumble wasn't just a warning - it was a prelude to an attack.

Stiffening, Kaufman slowly turned around.

What greeted him was a German Shepherd - ears plastered to its head, fur bristling. The dog was in full attack mode, but Kaufman found himself wishing the thing was riddled with rabies and foaming at the mouth, because that would have been preferable to its current condition. Although it was not contorted and screaming like the infected jackrabbits, the Shepherd had nonetheless been contaminated by the same dementing elixir.

The German Shepherd stood upright on its hind legs. The posture might have been comical, except that the dog wasn't the least bit awkward. Somehow it appeared more agile, fierce, and far more threatening.

All at once, like an attacking Velociraptor, the dog sprang forward.

Kaufman swiveled and backed into the nearest food locker just as the dog reached him. Bouncing off the gate, the German Shepherd yelped and landed on its side before eerily standing erect once more.

"Just what is making you do that?" Kaufman wondered to himself, strangely fascinated by the dog's aberrant behavior.

As the Shepherd growled and clawed at the latch, Kaufman knew waiting for the animal to tire or give up wasn't an option. The lunatic pooch might never lose interest - worse, it might get in.

"I guess the better question is, just how am I going to get out?"

To escape, the German Shepherd would need to be incapacitated - or killed - and the prospect of having to destroy the beast didn't bother Kaufman.

He'd done it before. He could do it again.

As a child, his father had owned a huge Irish Wolfhound named Temüjin, the birth name of Genghis Khan, and the dog was as ruthless and antagonistic as her namesake.

Kaufman hated the beast, not only because of her surly disposition but because his father showed affection to the animal. The praise was rare and dispensed with an eyedropper - still, it was something he never received and, at an age before his heart had hardened, he'd vowed to eliminate the competition.

In his coursework, Kaufman had learned that canines were unable to absorb a naturally occurring stimulant in chocolate called Theobromine. So, Kaufman decided to poison Temüjin. Feeding her dense squares of baking chocolate, the Wolfhound began urinating more, started vomiting, and having uncontrollable diarrhea. He felt a giddy satisfaction each time the animal was reprimanded for these offenses.

For a month, the mean-spirited dog took the full brunt of his youthful hate and jealousy.

Towards the end, Temüjin panted constantly and her muscles twitched so severely she could hardly walk. Still, he increased the frequency and amount of her dosage until one night, the chocolate finally caused the Wolfhound's heart to give out in a massive epileptic seizure.

Standing over the animal, Kaufman had watched triumphantly as his rival died. If he, Göttlich's own blood, wasn't the recipient of infamous architect's adoration, then no one would - especially not some dumb, mean old dog.

After Temüjin's death, he'd waited for his father to say something, imagined an angry confrontation, but Göttlich never accused him of treachery, or even hinted at it.

At first, Kaufman didn't understand why. He'd expected to be called out - part of him even wanted the recognition, the pleasure of seeing his father mad. Except the silence continued, and soon Kaufman realized what it meant, what it had to mean. Göttlich had known all along what his son was doing. And worse, he'd possibly even planned it.

A week after Temüjin's death, Kaufman broke down and cried. He wept not for the dead dog but for his own actions, for his loss of innocence.

It was the only memory he had of crying. The event had been a defining nail in his emotional coffin.

So if at the age of seven, he could methodically murder Genghis Khan out of envy, for survival, he could whack Rin-Tin-Tin without blinking an eye.

Kaufman would have preferred that his continued existence didn't come at the expense of the animal's life. He was not cruel. He would, however, do what needed to be done. For the time being, however, he didn't see how he was going to escape, period - let alone avoid killing the Jurassic Park fleabag in the process.

In the stall, there was nothing of use to help him escape, other than a few fifty-pound bags of oats. Scanning the surrounding room, though, Kaufman spotted the perfect solution.

To the right of the door through which he'd entered hung an animal control pole. A simple device, the pole was nothing more than a metal rod with a loop of wire at end. The rubber-coated noose was designed to be placed over an animal's head, which allowed a person to keep a safe distance and avoid sharp teeth. To reach the pole, though, meant going toe to toe with the mutant devil dog. It was risky, but really there were no other options.

Kaufman sighed and contemplated using one of the sacks of oats as a shield to protect himself against the German Shepherd as he made his mad dash across the room. He ultimately decided against it; he couldn't wield the bulk with busted ribs and only one good arm. No, his best option was speed. He needed to be careful and time it right, because if he wasn't able to use the door as a ram and knock the dog backward, the giant German Shepherd would knock him over instead, and pin him in the narrow stall. In that scenario, Kaufman would be lucky if all he lost were some fingers.

Growing more frantic, the German Shepherd threw itself at the chain-link door again, snapping with bear trap ferocity.

Kaufman stepped back. Better get on with it.

Kicking up the latch, he lowered his shoulder and exploded out of the stall just as the German Shepherd made its next lunge.

Except the timing was off and in the ensuing impact, Kaufman felt the individual diamonds of the chain-link fence smash into his forehead and split his scalp.

Both he and the dog fell backward, but he was quicker to regain his feet. The rubber soles of his boots providing better traction on the slick cement floor than the German Shepherd's leather paws.

Kaufman knocked the gate wide and darted across the room.

Ripping the pole from the wall, he turned just as the German Shepherd flew at him. Without thinking, Kaufman brought up the pole with both hands and swung. It connected with the dog, and a stabbing pain flashed through his left side as the pole was torn from his grasp.

Clutching his injured arm back to his body, Kaufman snatched up the aluminum pole with his good hand and tucked it under his right armpit like a knight holding a lance. Jabbing downwards, he swung the snare over the dog's head just as the mongrel German Shepherd rose and twisted away.

Lean and powerfully built, the Shepherd stood nearly five feet tall on its hind legs, which caused Kaufman to lose the his leverage. Now instead of being able to pin the dog down with his weight, he found himself struggling to keep balance as he clung desperately to the bucking pole.

Suddenly overbalanced, Kaufman reeled backward and was slammed into the nearby wall. The impact snapped his head forward, and he nearly lost his grip. Reflexively, he yanked upwards and kicked off the wall, driving the German Shepherd back.

Unbelievably, as he blazed forward, he found himself picking the German Shepherd up and carrying it as easily as he might hold a small brook trout at the end of a fishing pole. He knew what he was doing was impossible. There was no way he possessed the strength - even with two good arms - to achieve such a feat. It was incomprehensible, as uncanny as the seemingly living shaft of sunlight he'd seen earlier this morning pouring through the almond tree at his house.

On the other side of the room, Kaufman dropped Fido into the same food locker he'd just occupied.

Immediately, he braced himself, expecting the dog to thrash, except the animal though lay placid. Kaufman backed away and reached for the gate.

That brought a reaction, but not the fury Kaufman had been expecting.

Whining and whimpering, the ferocious beast of only moments before was now a scared pup. As if afraid to be left alone, the German Shepherd eyed Kaufman with a doleful expression. It was the same torment he'd seen in the rabbits. Except in this dog, it was more profound, and more easily recognizable for what it was.

In those brown orbs, there was a longing to die.

Kaufman scowled.

That couldn't be right. He had to be viewing the mutt through an anthropomorphic filter. There was no way the German Shepherd was asking to be killed...and yet the longer he looked the more pain, confusion, and suffering he saw.

Quivering, the German Shepherd seemed to sense Kaufman's hesitation, his unwillingness, and suddenly the dog clawed at the floor, snarled and snapped, and tried to stand. Kaufman staggered back, not out of fear but out of bewilderment. The Shepherd was trying to force his hand! More, the dog's renewed aggression wasn't calculated just to coerce him, but to try and make the killing easier, to make it an act of self-defense.

No way, Kaufman thought, shaking his head and nearly letting go of the restraining pole. The knowledge that the dog had somehow reached a level of consciousness where self-destruction was more desirable than life made him shudder. It also brought to mind his dead neighbors out on the highway.

The first casualties might not have known that they would die once they reached a certain distance from town, but surely people afterward must have. They would have seen friends and relatives methodically drop dead, would have had to climb over those still-warm corpses to reach their own demise.

That realization both angered and saddened Kaufman. Whatever madness had been in those fleeing citizens of Decoy was also here in this dog, and as he watched the miserable creature struggle to mount an attack, he spoke.

"It's okay, pal. Just calm down...relax."

At the sound of Kaufman's voice, the canine quieted.

"That's right, good boy," Kaufman soothed, kneeling and stroking the dog's head.

Moments ago, Kaufman had been callous to the idea of killing this animal; now, though, he wasn't so sure he could do it. Although it might be euthanasia, it felt like cold-blooded murder.

Continuing to speak in a tranquil tone, Kaufman twisted the pole until the cord was taut against the dog's throat. He knew he wouldn't be able to do the job with only one hand; he would have to stand and use both. Gritting his teeth, Kaufman rose and stretched out his injured arm.

Limp fingers curled around the pole, and when he forced his grip tight, a cry of agony escaped his lips. The sound mixed with the dog's pathetic mewling, which echoed hollowly in the empty storage room.

Bearing down with all his weight, Kaufman leaned into the pole and twisted. He had to fight to keep control as each rotation caused a fiery pain to shoot through both his injured arm and his heart.

Below him, sprawled on the floor, eyes bulging and tongue hanging loosely, the German Shepherd morphed into Temüjin, and Kaufman suddenly saw himself as a boy. Hands clenched into jubilant fists, standing over the lifeless body of his childhood rival, and Kaufman wanted desperately to reach back in time and stop himself, wanted to save that boy, save his innocence.

"I'm sorry," Kaufman moaned. "I'm so sorry."

Kicking and clawing at the floor, the German Shepherd fought him, fought death. Trembling, Kaufman willed himself to hold tight, and after a time, the pole stopped shaking. Eventually, Temüjin stopped thrashing and closed her eyes.

Letting the pole clatter to the floor, Kaufman staggered away. This time there was no pride, no triumphant sense of victory, only hot tears and heartache.

Blindly he made his way to the front of the building, and by the time he reached the door, the poignant anguish in his chest had withered to a dull pang. As evasive and slippery as an eel, these emotions were, but also powerful and haunting. For even now, with only the memory of it, a profound sadness seemed ready to spring up.

For Kaufman, though, this taste of grief, although bitter, reminded him of his newfound purpose, his desire to truly live - as well as his determination to find others and somehow get out of this malign dimension he'd woken up in. Because in him now burned the faintest flicker of renewed hope, and if it soured this time, as it had for him as a child, he knew, was absolutely certain, that he would be lost forever - a truly damned man.

Outside, the day had grown hotter, and the sky was a clear blue. Before leaving, Kaufman located some bandages and wrapped his injured arm tightly against his body. He'd planned to walk back the way he'd come and secure a car for his trip into town, but he stopped when he noticed a Vespa parked at the side of the animal hospital. Although the scooter would be slower, he decided to it would also be more accessible, agile, and easier to steer than a car.

Locating the keys, he squeezed into a helmet and slapped down the visor.

Tawny rocks, white salt flats, and red mineral deposits blended together and blurred by in swirling ribbons of color. Kaufman had the distinct sensation of being a lone astronaut stranded on some distant planet as he drove back into Decoy. But once the houses and buildings came into view, the illusion was shattered.

Without having told himself to go there, he knew he was heading to the police station. Any survivors of the Decoy Madness would have gone there too, as it was the logical place to find help and would be the central point for restoring order.

An array of bland stucco buildings made up the downtown section of Decoy. A few were more daring in their design, but most, especially the government offices, were as dull as cardboard boxes, which made the modern steel and glass structure of the police station stand out all the more.

Göttlich had once described the edifice as a metallic and glass pile of dung, dropped from Modernism's bunghole. Pulling up to the "sparkling jewel" of northern Nevada's law enforcement agencies, Kaufman was forced to agree. Today though, even as the building glinted in the sunlight, it looked like a sadistic version of an amusement park funhouse.

Kaufman might have dismissed this ominous quality to the weird events of the day if there hadn't been a large pool of blood beside an idling car parked in the middle of the front promenade.

In the blistering siesta sun, the blood resembled fresh tar: dark and shiny.

Parking the scooter, Kaufman slowly approached.

The car - a late model Plymouth - was held together with duct tape and desperation. It was the type of jalopy found in the many white ghettos located on the outskirts of town, a true chariot of the trailer park, and it wasn't until he was close enough to touch the bumper that Kaufman noticed the footprints.

The shimmering trail of red led straight towards the police station.

In the silent street, Kaufman listened to the pounding of his heart.

Never had he been more aware of the remoteness of Decoy than at that moment. In between buildings were vast oceans of sand, interrupted only by ancient weathered mountains. The nearest cities were more than sixty miles away, and he knew that whoever had left those prints wasn't the source of the blood - but the cause of it; and all at once, a premonition took root in his mind. He was going to meet this bleeder of bodies. Soon.

Kaufman just hoped he'd leave that encounter alive.

At the entrance of the police station, another massive lake of blood was darkening in the afternoon heat, pooling out from some source just beyond the main doors. There was so much of the crimson liquid that it was possible to believe that it might be spilled paint, except the odor was of slaughter rather than latex.

As distasteful as it was, Kaufman crossed through the viscous liquid - each step making a sickly sucking sound. He peered in through the tinted glass.

Beyond, something vaguely human-shaped waited. Kaufman tried to identify what the blurry mass was, but before he could, the sliding glass doors retracted and revealed the object.

A tremble took hold of Kaufman's hand and it spread quickly through his body until he was quivering uncontrollably. He shook not out of fear or shock, but in anger, and his eyes never left the savagery before him.

It made the self-mutilating Marilyn Monroe on the computer seem almost paltry.

In the vaulted lobby, suspended from his feet, was a nude man gutted from groin to chin as casually as a buck disemboweled in the wild.

Every ounce of blood had drained from the filleted man, and the sheer volume of the formerly life-sustaining fluid was mind-numbing. Kaufman knew that the average male body contained a little more than five quarts of blood, which was the standard for a man of one-hundred sixty pounds.

However, there was easily twice that much here, twelve or thirteen quarts, maybe even a little more.

That much blood came from an enormous human.

A true bull of a man.

Even in death, Anthony Green was anything but average.

CHAPTER 9

There had been no struggle, no battle for life, no last-minute reckless brawl.

Seemingly as docile as sheep led to the slaughter, Anthony had been killed and hung out like a side of beef waiting to be sectioned and sold.

How that was possible was beyond Kaufman.

Anthony Green hadn't eviscerated himself, hadn't performed an extreme and grotesque form of seppuku. This also wasn't a crime of passion, wrought in the heightened frenzy of the Decoy Madness. No, this had been the work of a cold, calculating, Machiavellian killer.

And the proof was literally written on the wall:

Unclean, Unworthy, the Herd has been thinned.

Even if the meticulously crafted calligraphy hadn't been written in blood, the message came through loud and clear - there was no help here: no mayor initiating city emergency disaster procedures, no police fighting to maintain order, not even a level-headed civilian leading an evacuation. Just like the suburb with the polio jackrabbits, the station had been forsaken.

Kaufman also now knew that although he might be on his own, he was not alone.

Someone was out there.

A killer stalked the town, or perhaps this very building.

The sane course of action was to get out of there, but as Kaufman looked at Anthony, he knew he couldn't. He couldn't leave that doting father in such an ignominious death. The man deserved to be cut down. Kaufman could do that much.

Except he didn't move. He felt immobilized by fear, and it wasn't so much the possibility of Anthony's killer waiting in the shadows that troubled Kaufman, but Anthony himself. It was absurd, illogical - the man was dead. Yet Kaufman couldn't shake the image of Anthony rising up, some undead creature, moving in to attack him as soon as his back was turned.

It surprised Kaufman how easily the big man, both alive and now dead, caused him to be afraid. He knew it shouldn't have; while his father's indifference had left him devoid of feeling joy - fear, by its very nature, was much more instinctual, and thus much harder to suppress and root out. It was love, devotion, selflessness - those higher, nobler feelings - that were so elusive to him, emotions that went beyond mere biology, beyond survival and the impulse to pass on one's genes – traits prized and honored by most societies, qualities that were the pinnacles of human history and achievement.

His brush with death had been a breakthrough, but he was still mostly an animal reacting. Kaufman desperately wanted to embrace humanity and transcend those baser instincts; wished his theoretical knowledge could translate into authentic experiences.

Except wishes weren't reality.

So although he wanted to be brave, wanted to stroll over to the desk and locate a box cutter, be like the unflinching hero of the novels he read, that didn't stop Kaufman from instead backing away, and repeatedly glancing over his shoulder to check and make sure Anthony hadn't moved.

Some protagonist he was shaping up to be.

But in his own personal narrative, the plot had gone places he didn't like, dark and disturbing places - places akin to the depths plunged in Dante's *Inferno*. Except this was no poetic account, but a true glimpse into the bowels of Hell.

At the reception desk, as Kaufman rummaged through drawers, images of walking corpses plagued his mind.

Behind him, dead eyes fluttered to life.

Kaufman forced himself not to give in and look back.

Suddenly Anthony seized him and bit into his skull. Bone cracked and soft pink brain spilled out.

Kaufman shook his head. Shook it again, trying to rid himself of boyhood phobias about monsters coming out of the TV to get him. The fears were silly, beyond foolish - he hadn't even had a TV while growing up - but they also lingered.

Trying to focus on the task at hand, Kaufman steadied his breathing. He located a pair of scissors and tried not to ride himself too hard about being afraid of Anthony's untapped potential to become the living dead.

But perhaps he shouldn't have, for suddenly the Raging Bull's voice boomed forth.

"YOU!"

Dropping the scissors, Kaufman spun around.

Anthony was still dead. Stone dead. He didn't even sway - not a zombie.

Kaufman swallowed hard.

For years his imagination had been his escape, his refuge, but now it was playing tricks on him, betraying him. Or maybe it was the Decoy Madness finally wreaking havoc in his cerebral cortex. Whatever…he was getting out of here.

So what if he was a coward? No one would blame him. He was the screwed-up son of Göttlich Striker - a damaged and awkward social burden. Maybe not quite fallen through the cracks of society, but definitely on the outskirts, a sideshow freak.

His escape, while so many others perished, was just another example of the world's ever-increasing pessimism towards Nihilism.

But when he reached the exit, Kaufman stopped.

White-hot panic drained filled his mind and he felt confused.

Why he was leaving the police station when he hadn't even found help?

No, he had tried, but there were no survivors here and no help, only the grim leftovers of a religious sociopath.

Kaufman took several deep breaths, cold logic returned, and he went back to the lobby, intent on finishing what he'd started.

With scissors in hand, he climbed the stairs to the landing on the second floor. Kneeling, he reached out past the safety railing to the exposed scaffolding where the rope was tied off. With his arm in a sling, he wobbled a bit as he sawed with the scissors, but the edges were sharp, and soon the individual strands of the rope burst apart.

After a few seconds, the ruddy brownish exterior of the rope gave way to lighter fibers. This didn't surprise Kaufman since he'd assumed the dark coloring came as a result of the rope having lain in Anthony's blood at some point. Except the rope didn't smell like blood, didn't carry the sharp scent of iron. Instead, the fragrance was musky, reminiscent of oil and sawdust and dirt.

Suddenly Kaufman knew this rope.

This was *his* rope. The rope he'd hung himself with; the rope that had almost killed him. Frowning with distrust, he stopped cutting.

What was going on here?

He'd asked that question a thousand times since leaving his house this morning, but each repetition was due to another layer of this twisted world being pulled back to reveal yet another puzzle. It was the proverbial riddle wrapped in a mystery inside an enigma.

Unexpectedly, the rope snapped, and the sickly slap of flesh hitting wet linoleum brought Kaufman out of his stupor.

Rushing down the stairs, he flung some jackets atop Anthony's sprawled body. It wasn't very dignified, but he couldn't take the time to straighten it. He had to get home. Now. He had to know; had to confirm the impossible and see if his kitchen floor was empty.

At a desperate speed, he bolted out of the police station and into the stark streets, his mind sprinting as quickly as his feet.

If that was his rope, it meant someone had been inside his house. Someone had come looking for him...no, not someone - Anthony's killer. Kaufman wasn't alone anymore; he was being hunted.

At the end of his long driveway, Kaufman slowed his pace to a jog.

Everything about his house was as he had left it.

Except the front door.

It was wide open.

Deciding that the best approach was a direct one and hoping that by being bold, he would catch the killer off guard, Kaufman picked up a fist-sized rock and rushed forward.

Bursting through the foyer, Kaufman glanced right. No one in the kitchen. Directly ahead was the living room, on his left, the stairs. The second floor contained the library, a full bath, and the master bedroom. Figuring he would hear anyone descending the stairs to attack from behind, Kaufman continued to the back room.

Turning the corner, he came face to face with a dark-haired man, arms extended in the manner of Christ's ascension into heaven, standing - no, *holy shit* - floating three feet off the ground.

Instinctively Kaufman hurled the rock at the guy and immediately felt like an idiot. The stone hit the wall and exploded.

Although not the savior painted by so many Christian artists, the dark-haired figure was a painting and not a real person.

With his heart yo-yoing in his chest, Kaufman warily approached the overly effusive artwork.

Trimmed in an ornate gold-leafed frame, the life-sized portrait was gaudy enough to reside comfortably in a rococo-style cathedral; but in this simple space, it wasn't just out of place, it was utterly overwhelming.

Drawing up short, Kaufman noticed a Polaroid tucked neatly into one corner of the frame.

He picked up the headshot.

It wasn't anyone he recognized, but it was clearly the model used for creating the painting.

Apparently, the Children of God Fine Art Gallery designed works based on real people. For a fee, anyone could see themselves being visited by an angel, talking with the apostles, or walking in Jerusalem with the Lamb of God. It probably wasn't standard procedure to reproduce a client as if they were the Almighty Himself, but for the right price - mountains could be moved.

Here was Anthony's murderer, the bleeder of bodies, the man who left footprints and calligraphy in blood.

With a full smile and bright eyes, the portrait was meant to show a benevolent, merciful, and majestic deity; however, the artist had failed in Kaufman's opinion.

Walking on clouds, this mock messiah seemed to be leering rather than kindly reaching out, looked more likely to strike down than lift up. The artist might not be to blame, though, since it was an accurate reflection of the man in the photograph. His dark hair had been drawn wavy and long, and the eyes were the correct purple, but his smile was a kind interpretation.

Many people would probably find the man's expression charming, the perfect presidential grin; for Kaufman, though, it was too aggressive, something between a grimace and a donkey's bray. It was like the guy had been given a new face and wasn't quite sure how to make it work properly. Yet whoever he was, and however he presented himself, Kaufman knew that underneath was not a demigod, but a demon.

The painting leaned casually against the wall, and it occurred to Kaufman that the killer wasn't lying in wait. Suspending Anthony Green's body with the rope had been a way to get Kaufman's attention, a means to draw him home - not to spring an ambush, but to show him this self-aggrandizing artwork.

Except that wasn't right.

Immediately Kaufman recognized that his logic was flawed.

The police station crime scene had been staged as precisely as a movie set. Every detail had been accounted for and no effort had been made to draw attention to the rope. It had been nothing more than a prop. The killer hadn't left it for him to find, couldn't even have known Kaufman would go there, let alone get close enough to recognize that the rope belonged to him.

No, the religious crackpot had come here specifically for him, found the house empty, and let himself in. Then, noticing that his gift hadn't been unwrapped, he'd opened it and propped it up against the wall. On his way out, he had taken the rope; and whether he'd grabbed it because of what he intended to do to Anthony or whether it had just been a spur of the moment thing, was inconsequential.

What Kaufman couldn't begin to comprehend was, why him? Why had he been singled out? He was less than special - a nobody. Then again, perhaps he wasn't the only one. Perhaps others had been mailed paintings too. But why? Why?

He searched the canvas for answers. The brushstrokes revealed nothing new, but among the swirls and looping laurels at the bottom of the frame, Kaufman spotted a slender brass plaque inscribed with bold print:

-The Face of God-
Exodus 33:20

At first, he thought the title was some portion of the scripture; but the more he looked at it, the more convinced he became that the reference was another message entirely.

The verse might be worth looking at, might give him an insight into the killer's mind. The purpose wasn't to psychoanalyze the murderer so that he could better understand him. Kaufman didn't want to understand him - hoped never to come close to that type of empathy. No, by reading the scripture, he hoped for an edge, some advantage that would help him survive the foreboding encounter he'd felt coming outside the police station - that he would meet Anthony's killer - a premonition that now seemed inescapable.

Upstairs in his library, on his mahogany desk, a bible had been left open. It didn't surprise Kaufman. The killer had a message he wanted understood.

Cracking open the heavy leather-bound volume, Kaufman discovered that the verse had been marked for him as well. He set aside the folded piece of paper that acted as a bookmark and read:

Exodus 33:20 - *And he said, Thou canst not see my face: for there shall no man see me, and live.*

The 'he' referred to God.

The killer believed himself to be God.

Kaufman had now seen his face, the painting - The Face of God - and suddenly, he felt watched.

Skin crawling, Kaufman's testicles drew up inside him, and he spun around, fully expecting to see the mock messiah waiting for him, smirking hungrily with a raised cleaver.

Except the room was empty.

No god watched him - at least not any mortal ones. Kaufman was still alone. But for how long?

The painting wasn't just the killer's calling card, but his black dot - his mark of death. All at once, Kaufman wanted to be anywhere but there. He didn't care anymore about the rope or Anthony or why he'd been singled out.

As he slapped the bible shut, the paper that had been marking the passage fluttered to the ground. Reflexively, Kaufman bent to scoop it up. Five inches above the ground, his hand froze.

Mouth dry, Kaufman swallowed hard.

This was no scrap piece of paper. It was the death certificate.

A starburst tread mark marred the corner of the document where his boot had stomped on it earlier this morning.

Had the killer stumbled across it and decided to use it as a bookmark because he'd thought it would be funny? Or had he somehow known about it?

The throbbing in Kaufman's shoulder suddenly accelerated with his heartbeat.

Was it possible that this madman was working with his father? Was Göttlich in some way involved with the Decoy Madness? Had he orchestrated the outbreak?

Fingers curling into a fist, Kaufman's jaw bulged as he clenched his teeth.

Göttlich was a master gamesman, capable of planning many moves ahead; and he not only had plenty of followers but a handful of fanatical fans, even a few devotees.

Twice while growing up, Kaufman could recall disciples showing up at The Dwelling asking to be taken under his father's tutelage. They had been allowed to stay, although both times the neophytes had washed out, been unable to hack it, and endure the demanding tenets of Dominism.

Upon awakening and finding their sleep niches empty, Göttlich had told Kaufman that they'd been unworthy. Envious of their departures, but not realizing that was what he was feeling, Kaufman would sneak outside, look at the distant horizon, and wonder when those skinny college kids would be back. He knew now that he too could have left at any time and his father wouldn't have stopped him. But Göttlich had been too adept at Dominism, and too subtle in his control, for that idea to ever occur to Kaufman as a child.

After all these years, though, had his father finally found a pupil who was a crazy as him?

It was possible; certainly, there were enough nutjobs out there in the world, but Kaufman had a hard time imagining his dad partnering up with someone. Göttlich would never allow himself to be dependent on anyone else, even a pupil, because, for him, that would be akin to being owned by them - a core axiom of Dominism. If anything, his father was using this follower. But to what end? What could he possibly hope to achieve by wiping out an entire city?

Kaufman traced the tidy, almost unfriendly signature of his father on the death certificate, hoping for an insight. Up and down, his finger moved, looping and crossing and dotting.

What proof did he have that this ink mark was genuine? It could so easily be a forgery. Perhaps the killer had known about the death certificate precisely because he'd been the one to fabricate it. Perhaps this lunatic had just rolled up his obsession with Göttlich, Dominism, and Christianity into some perverted hybrid and was now living out the delusion where he saw himself as the returning Redeemer of the World, foreordained to dispense justice as the whim struck him.

That seemed to make a lot more sense than his father reentering Kaufman's life after a thirteen-year hiatus in the form of a death certificate telling him to commit suicide. Didn't it?

Then, an even more likely plausibility blossomed in Kaufman's mind, one that halted his finger.

What if this was a coup d'état? What if this guy *had* been a disciple of Göttlich's and was now seeking revenge for being rejected? Or more frightening, saw himself as the true heir to the kingdom, and, like the bitter disgraced bastard of some Russian noble, was planning to kill the czar, wipe out his bloodline and rewrite history? What if Göttlich was already dead and the cryptic painting and death certificate had been a mocking invitation for Kaufman to opt-out rather than face being slaughtered?

What if he, Kaufman, wasn't just another of the herd to be thinned, but the ultimate sacrificial goat?

Crumpling up the death certificate, Kaufman let it fall to the ground.

Whatever the case - whether his father was maneuvering the mock messiah like a puppeteer or the religious assassin was working on his own - Kaufman needed more information to draw a firmer conclusion.

And he needed a gun.

Originally, Kaufman planned to go to The Paradise to look for survivors and then head to NewLife and Shafter to look for answers. He still intended to do that, but first, he had a quick detour to make.

Tucking the photo into his back pocket, Kaufman hurried to the garage. There, he pushed open the heavy carriage-style doors and rode his bicycle out into Oz - although in this land, the Munchkins weren't friendly, but self-mutilating schizos and the wizard wasn't wonderful, but a deistic megalomaniac that passed out death instead of courage and ruby slippers.

. . .

Twenty minutes later, Kaufman parked the second vehicle he'd commandeered from Anthony Green's garage at Warrior Pete's Military & Outdoors Supplies. The Humvee was massive, a true urban tank. It might not be eco-friendly, but it was exactly what he needed for toting some gear.

In front of him, the converted aircraft hangar - complete with curved ribbed aluminum siding - advertised everything from gasmasks and sleeping bags to inflatable rafts and ammunition.

It was a militant's wet dream.

Inside, the aisles were filled with the heavy scent of wood and metal, oil and wool. The merchandise ranged from secondhand army and navy equipment - going all the way back to WWII - to extraordinary lightweight and compact modern camping gear.

Kaufman felt like a kid in a toy store.

Indeed, as he strolled down each aisle, he selected at random whatever fascinated him - a fantasy of window shoppers the world over. Although what he'd come for was some firepower.

Warrior Pete's sold mostly hunting rifles, but in the back office, Kaufman discovered the owner's personal stash. Either a collector or, more likely, an extreme survivalist, the hidden stockpile of illegal firearms wasn't huge, but it did seem to be evidence of a militaristic approach to a feared social collapse.

Assault rifles, flashbangs, fully automatic pistols with extended clips, shotguns, plastic explosives, even a grenade launcher - the hoard offered more than what Kaufman was looking for, but perhaps not more than he might need.

The Benelli M4 Super 90 combat shotgun was not illegal, but it was certainly top of the line. Gas operated, the semi-automatic pistol grip shotgun with collapsible buttstock boasted twin self-cleaning pistons and was self-regulating for cartridges of varying length and power levels.

He selected the Royals Royce 12 gauge for both its extreme reliability and ease of use.

Despite never having fired one, Kaufman knew guns.

Autodidactic by nature, he studied a different trade, art, or scientific topic every month. He felt a broad general knowledge was a good thing, and by design, he'd shaped himself into a spectacular bookworm Renaissance man - all theoretical knowledge, no real experience.

Now was the time to put his education to the test and get his hands dirty.

Pocketing extra shells, he looked over the handguns and decided on a revolver. Although the capacity of the Glock and other 9mm pistols were tempting, he desired the stopping power of the Smith and Wesson .41 caliber model 357PD magnum.

Light and more powerful than a standard .357 MAG, this four-inch barrel six-shooter was exactly what he needed. It might not have the stopping power of a .50 Desert Eagle, but it also didn't have its recoil, and, with only one good arm, that was a major consideration.

Leaving the arsenal as heavily armed as a SWAT team member, Kaufman was now ready for the casino, ready to face whatever he might find - be it suicidal dogs or counterfeit god.

CHAPTER 10

Hollie felt like shit!

And not just a garden variety turd, but an excrement as foul and repugnant as parasite-riddled diarrhea.

Opening her eyes, nausea buffeted Hollie and a migraine screamed in her head. For a moment, she was under the impression that she was suffering from a hangover.

The cut in her cheek, however, now gummy with clotted blood, dispelled that notion - not to mention the deep throb coming from her second belly button, the product of a metal slug which left a trail of shredded organs and tissue in its wake.

Hollie was the epitome of death warmed over.

Speaking of, why wasn't she?

If this was Heaven, it sure needed to step up its pampering services. Hollie was *not* enjoying herself. Even Purgatory ought to be nicer than this...which meant somehow, against all odds, she'd survived.

But for how long?

The catch-22 was that, if she stayed put, she was going to die, and if she moved, she would likely die faster.

Hell, that was hardly a choice at all. No way was she going to curl up and do nothing, but she didn't need to prove her toughness either - didn't need to cauterize her wound with a blazing hot knife and a bottle of whiskey like some hardboiled gunslinger. There were more than basic first aid supplies just outside the cell. All she had to do was move carefully so as not to reopen the wound, clean and wrap the sucker, then cross the mountainous desert back into town - a measly twenty miles or so - locate a doctor, and not pass out in the process.

Piece of cake.

Hollie barked a hollow laugh.

As if she'd ever even made a cake. She was not a proficient chef, not even a modest cook; her culinary skills fell into the realm of cold cereal and take out.

Better be a three-step box cake, or you're screwed, Hollie dear.

As she sat up, the room spun a slow waltz. Her abused body protested every movement, and there seemed to be something wrong with her eyes because all that blood couldn't be hers. Could it? Only half-seen in the flickering lamplight, the spot of red was too large, too large by far. It shouldn't have been possible to have lost so much blood and still be alive. Hollie was baffled by the sight; however, she could wonder about her survival later, once she was certain of it. Right now, though, she needed to worry about that latch, which had defeated her before.

Her fingers probed the darkness and located the latch above her head. She worked at the simple lever that, once sprung, would set her free; but it resisted. After several attempts, Hollie tilted her view upwards to discern the problem.

In her now upside-down world, the mechanism looked unnecessarily complex - a clockwork of gears and levers. The reality was much more straightforward: the door was locked.

Glistening dully against the rusty faceplate was a shiny new padlock.

Hollie scowled.

Where had that come from?

The tattooed freak hadn't locked the door after he shot her, she was sure of it. She'd watched his every move up until the psycho cut this own throat. Besides, what was the point of locking somebody up *after* killing them? The corpse wasn't going to rise up like Lazarus and walk off.

Apparently, though, that's precisely what her kidnapper had thought.

Looking over to where she'd seen the smiling man's naked and lifeless body fall, Hollie saw only the heart monitor electrodes, dangling in empty air.

The corpse was gone, the tomb empty.

The revelation not only brought disbelief - as it had for the disciples of Christ - but terror and dread as well, for although it might have been a trick, some elaborate sick joke - the magnum opus of a demented magician - Hollie feared otherwise.

She had inside knowledge. Might, in fact, be partly responsible for such a feat.

"Today is the first human trial."

Impossible!

That had been her initial response, and she still believed it.

"Adam Murakami used you, deceived you."

Even if that were true, the technology wasn't available to test her research or put her hypothesis into practice. Science, especially genetics, was a slow process; her work was only the seed of an idea, not the fruit.

Imagining her theories were practical was as absurd as believing in faster-than-light speed or time travel. Humankind didn't do these things; they only dreamt of them. To believe otherwise was pure speculation, and to believe the world currently possessed that ability was sheer self-delusion.

"Your theoretical research has been tested and applied since day one - with the help of the government nonetheless."

Impossible...but doubt, had taken root in her conviction, and the AWOL stiff shook her to the core.

A sudden sharp twinge caused Hollie to look away.

"Do you know what the greatest purifier is?"

Warm blood began to seep out of the bullet wound anew.

This was bad.

"Pain."

Clamping a hand down over her hemorrhaging abdomen sent a sharp pang through her gut. Her own pain hadn't brought her any nearer to God, but it sure as hell had focused her, had stripped away the frivolous and the unnecessary.

She wasn't the only one that needed saving.

"He's still in the basement of my house - completely secure, undetectable, and alive."

Hollie's resolve deepened.

"Murakami is my Thomas, doubting, but he will weep bitterly once he sees. Only then will he die."

Hollie wasn't about to let that happen. She was going to live, and so was Dr. Murakami.

Tugging at the lock confirmed that the device was securely fastened. There would be no easy escape due to an oversight. Hollie wished she'd worn her hair up this morning because then she could have used one of the bobby pins as a lock pick. Perhaps she still might find a thin piece of metal and tease the tumblers open.

Yeah, and while you're at it, MacGyver, you can create world peace with a pair of pantyhose and some duct tape.

Even if she could steady her shaking hand, she had no training in picking a lock. Blind luck like that only worked on TV and in the movies.

The idea was stupid, yet still, it persisted.

But what good was a bobby pin if not to try and pick the lock?

Stopped assuming, Hollie demanded of herself. She closed her eyes and allowed her subconscious to work at the problem uninhibited by visual prejudices. It wasn't so much the function or material of the bobby pin that was important as the term itself. Pin could also mean needle, but a needle wasn't quite right either. A needle was similar to a small nail, a nail—

Hollie opened her eyes.

The railroad spike!

She had planned to use *that* pin to save her life.

And it still would.

Looking down, she spotted the heavy nail. Worn and marred and covered in rust, it nevertheless looked better than the golden spike used at Promontory Point.

Envisioned how it could be used as a makeshift crowbar to break open the padlock, Hollie pulled herself upright. She sagged unsteadily against the barred door, then threaded the offset head of the spike through the lock.

Hollie prayed she wouldn't bust her bullet-riddled gut in the process of busting free, for if she lost consciousness again, there was no guarantee that she'd wake up a second time.

Breathing heavily, she considered her risky plan.

Simple physics stated that the longer the lever, the less force need to pop the lock. Which meant, with a five-inch railroad spike, she was going to need superhuman strength.

Where's Superman when you need him, Hollie thought. *I should have been a journalist.*

Clamping down on the stubby pry, Hollie grit her teeth and pushed.

Screw you, Lois Lane.

Lancing pain immediately shot up Hollie's spine, and blood sluiced out of her wound.

Tears streamed down her face, but Hollie ignored the pain and bore down harder. She was rewarded with the sound of creaking metal.

That's right, Hollie encouraged, throwing all her weight behind the makeshift lever. *Break like a Made in China useless POS.*

The latch pinged and moaned in metallic agony as the decaying bolts began to give way.

Blood was steadily streaming out of the gunshot wound now, and a cold blackness began creeping in at the corners of her vision.

Damn you, break!

It was only a matter of time until either her strength or the forged iron gave out…and Hollie was sure as hell not about to yield. In a last-ditch effort, she began violently jerking and wrenching the spike back and forth.

In protest, the metal framing screeched and popped.

Knowing she was almost there, feeling the ancient iron giving way, Hollie gave out an exhausted but triumphant laugh.

Then, without warning, the railroad spike slipped free, and Hollie was off-balance - falling. Her exuberance morphed into panic as the floor rushed up to meet her.

Reflexively, she put out her hands to catch herself but was too late. The unyielding ground slammed into her face with the force of a sledgehammer. The impact rammed her teeth together so hard it cut off her scream and cracked open a filling.

In the distance, the clatter of the railroad spike bouncing off the ground rang in her ears, but Hollie was barely aware of it. The pain and failure were too much and enveloped her completely.

Spent, Hollie cried.

In the car trunk, bound and terrified, she'd kept it together. She hadn't allowed herself to cry. She hadn't even whimpered after having her face slashed or being shot. She'd been strong, proud, unbeaten. Not now, though…now she wept. But that was okay. It was alright to feel the injustice of the situation, to let out her inadequacies and frustrations, and gain strength from an emotional release.

She was scared and hurt, and her tears of trauma mixed with sobs of self-pity, but after a while, she felt better.

She sniffled, allowing her eyes to refocus on the world.

Not more than a foot away, the railroad spike was blurry and distorted. Looking past the overgrown nail, Hollie spotted another sort of nail, with its own hammer.

On the corner of the table where the smiling man had folded and placed his clothes was the gun.

Hollie's ears burned as bitterness filled her mouth.

That's the taste of your foot, you hypocrite.

She was indeed. She'd jumped to conclusions, assumed her mind had come up with the railroad spike as a substitute crowbar - when in reality, her subconscious had been using it as a steppingstone to direct her attention to the gun. More than a steppingstone, the railroad spike could also be used as a tool to retrieve the gun.

Like an alcoholic lecturing about the hazards of drinking while giving a toast, she'd fallen into the assumption trap she preached against. It wasn't the first time, and probably wouldn't be the last, but at least she had time to repent.

Easing onto her back, Hollie removed her blouse. The bloody shirt was simultaneously crusty and wet with blood. Using her teeth, she tore the fabric into strips and tied the ends together. At one end, she fastened the spike.

It took a few casts to hook and reel in her lock-buster; the handgun might not be the master key a shotgun was, but it would do the trick.

The M9 military sidearm was similar to the service pistol her brother Sean used as a police officer. He'd taken her to the firing range a few times, but she'd never developed a taste for shooting. However, she did have basic knowledge of firearms, and it served her well now.

Taking up an angle to deflect the ricochet away from her, Hollie aimed at the padlock and pulled the trigger.

The gun bucked and roared, but the padlock remained intact. Firing three more times, she blew the thing away, and in a bloody bra, with a smoking pistol in hand, Hollie felt like one badass femme fatale.

"I'm ready for your next film, Mr. Quentin Tarantino."

Exhausted, Hollie smiled briefly at her joke before letting the gun slide out of her hand; and in a less dignified manner than a Hollywood heroine might take, she scooted on her ass over toward the medical supplies.

Wading through her abductor's thickening blood, Hollie stopped to retrieve the lantern.

Somehow the freak was alive - a walking miracle - but she couldn't care less. She'd worry about that later, as long as it was from a comfortable hospital bed while doctors and nurses attended to her every need and reassured her that she'd be all right. In that position - being spoon-fed and sponge bathed by muscular and hopefully handsome orderlies - she'd write a book about the damn thing, even sign away the movie rights, but right now, all she cared about was taking some painkillers.

Aspirin, Tylenol, Ibuprofen - a whole cocktail of drugs mixed with Codeine and OxyContin and washed down with a shot of Morphine. Whatever - just give her some beautiful drugs.

The harder, the better.

Having reached the supplies, Hollie attempted to play doctor. She rummaged through the containers, throwing down every pill bottle and bandage she laid hands on. In moments, the ground was littered with gauze, compresses, splints, ointments, sprays, and Band-Aids. Once satisfied, she set to work. Hollie cleaned the wound and applied sterile wraps to both the entrance and exit points, then secured the thick pads with heavy medical tape. The patch job wouldn't win any awards, but it was good enough for right now.

Sitting back and panting, Hollie looked through bottles until she came across a package of Demerol - perfect.

Popping a handful of tablets into her mouth, she chewed until the pills were a bitter, chalky paste. Feeling the cut in her cheek stinging, Hollie snatched up a nearby jug of water and washed down the meds. She drank desperately, and as she gulped, she became aware that not all the wetness in her pants was caused by the overflow of liquid spilling down her chin. Apparently, both her bowels and bladder had relaxed at some point and given up their delightful treasures.

Revitalized to the point that she could be disgusted, Hollie tried to wiggle out of her jeans, a much more difficult process than she would have imagined. The foul mess glued the fabric to her skin. After a moment, Hollie gave up and just cut the suckers off with a pair of EMT scissors; but in peeling away the denim, a horrid potpourri of urine and feces was released.

"Ugh…" Hollie gagged, doubling over. "This has got to be a Guinness record for biggest blowout."

In disgust, she began washing herself. The cool liquid felt good, and the repetitive wiping motion was soothing. Soon she was humming without being aware of it and her mind drifted with the repetitive, hypnotic movement.

She had cleaned her baby brothers and sisters many times this way. In a small basin, she'd sponge bathed their soft pink flesh, and the task had never been a chore. Indeed, she was naturally good with children and enjoyed taking care of them. Hollie always felt she would have made an excellent mother, except she'd been afraid that in accepting that role, she'd lose her individuality and become just another drone…become just like her mother.

As a child, Hollie had been taught repeatedly that her place as a woman was in the home, bearing as many children as her body could produce - nothing more than a baby factory. She'd never taken to those lessons - drivel, taught by zombie parents who couldn't think for themselves.

Misdirected good intentions had the potential to retard as much as any genetic underdevelopment, and Hollie promised herself that she would never end up like that.

So, she'd shunned men and their advances. The result of locking herself up to study while her sisters got knocked up was that she'd become the proverbial hiss and byword in her parish, while her sisters gave birth and were praised.

How odd that here, in this dreadful mine, she felt different - could see things as they could be instead of fearing what they might become. It was her right, her privilege, to be a mother if she so chose. Not as her parents viewed it, but on her own terms.

Nothing clarified what was truly important in life, like a brush with death.

Yeah, and if soiling yourself brings enlightenment, I ought to be sitting in Nirvana between the Dalai Lama and the Buddha, Hollie thought, fling aside a particularly disgusting wad of dripping gauze.

After washing, Hollie sat shrouded in shadows, and although she was alone, she felt as exposed and vulnerable as if she'd stepped out of a shower into the bright lights of a TV news camera. Clothes were in order.

The obvious and only choice was the psychopath's black outfit folded neatly beside the heat monitor. The freak might not mind traipsing around the desert in his birthday suit, but Hollie did. Her sense of modesty was high - rivaling that of a nun - so, as unpleasant as it was, she would have to wear the madman's clothes.

The shirt was one thing but dressing in the guy's pants was another. Being exposed in that way, having her bare skin touch where his had so recently been, was not going to happen, and there was no way she was going to wear his jockeys. So instead, Hollie loosely wrapped herself up in a few ace bandages down to her mid-thigh. Only then was she ready to put on the pants.

The black khakis were far too big for her waist, which required that she cinch tight the belt to keep them up. As she did so, a sharp bulge pressed against her thigh. Reaching into the right front pocket, she withdrew an automotive key with remote.

Hollie turned the key in her hand. Her abductor hadn't driven away!? The car was still here - just outside the mine. Leaving the vehicle made about as much sense as locking up a corpse; however, up until that moment, Hollie hadn't considered how she was going to get back into town. The drama of her gunshot wound had been too consuming to think about anything else.

Now, by luck or providence, she had her means of escape, and that wasn't all. From the other pants pocket, she withdrew something flat and stiff like a credit card, which turned out to be a military ID badge. The color photo showed the face of the smiling man and at the bottom, his name: Shane Málin.

Possessing damning evidence of the kidnapper's identity should have been reassuring, yet Hollie wasn't reassured. If anything, it alarmed her. She felt that she'd intentionally been left the car key and was meant to find the ID badge. But for what purpose? Was this some kind of sick game? Was the Clooney freak

- this Shane Málin - outside waiting for her? Had he staged his death only to give her false hope so he could capture her again just to relive the thrill of her terror?

Hollie almost wished that were true because it was better than the alternative - that Shane was alive, and didn't care if she, or anyone else for that matter, came after him. He believed himself to be untouchable and, with what she knew, he just might be.

Putting the ID back into her pocket, Hollie pushed that possibility out of her mind. She needed to focus on getting out of here.

Working her way back to the entrance took far longer than she expected. Hollie got turned around several times and felt near panic, but seeing a spot of sunlight in the distant quieted her fears that, rather than going deeper, she was actually ascending.

Outside, the heat of the day felt fantastic, a warm embrace. The sun was high and on its western arc. Had she spent half the day in that cavern? It didn't seem possible, but it also didn't matter. In less than an hour, she would be back in town. She slipped in behind the steering wheel of the sedan.

The drive down was a lot more enjoyable than coming up. The new car all but glided over the rocky road. How different had been the nightmarish ride in the trunk earlier this morning.

At the bottom of the mountain, the painkillers began kicking in, and Hollie felt good...better than good, great! Even though she'd been shot and was still critical, Hollie had never felt more alive. Colors were brighter, smells stronger, and there was a crispness to everything.

The sensation couldn't be all drug-related, could it?

"I'm stoned!" Hollie giggled, but even as she said it, she knew her high was due to some internal change rather than pharmaceutical aggrandizement.

She wasn't buzzed, but at peace - centered and experiencing tranquility, unlike anything she'd ever known before. This also wasn't just a sense that she was going to make it out of her current predicament, but a knowledge that she would no longer die. As counterintuitive as it might be, she barely gave it a second thought. Her mortality was somehow no longer something to contemplate.

"These are some great drugs," Hollie asserted, smirking.

Ahead, the dirt road straightened out and turned to pavement. It was a black line in the desert sand, and Hollie pressed on the throttle.

Suddenly the car jerked hard.

"What the—"

Correcting the steering, Hollie angled the vehicle back onto the road.

She'd just fallen asleep.

When had her eyes closed? She hadn't even felt drowsy.

The road hummed by, as empty of answers as she was.

Little by little, a lulling quality enticed her. The sandman was whispered in her ear, saying—

Boom!

A cactus exploded over the hood of the car.

Hollie shook her head and rubbed hard at her eyes.

She'd drifted off again.

"Fucks going on…" Hollie slurred.

This was no normal drowsiness. Although she'd probably taken way too much Demerol, this was no drug-induced slumber. She could feel her body shutting down, and although the abnormal sleep was as peculiar as her seemingly enhanced vision, Hollie knew she couldn't stop now. Pulling over was certain death. Forget her grandiose sense of everlasting life; if she fell asleep out here, she *would* die. People regularly succumbed to heat exposure, even in cars with the windows open.

The desert was as unforgiving to stranded motorists as shark-filled waters were to a bleeding man.

Less than halfway to town, she still had easily fifteen miles to go.

Cement eyelids pulled at her vision. Hollie shook her head again. She wasn't going to make it. Then again, she didn't have to. Not all the way, anyhow. Although most people in desert environments lived close to civilization, there were still a few outlying ranches. If she could reach one or stop a passing vehicle, they could assist her.

The car bounced hard, kicked like a bucking colt, and Hollie smacked into the ceiling.

Damn, she'd fallen asleep again.

Get it together!

Using her finger, she dug painfully into the bullet hole. A surge of heat brought momentary focus.

Back on the road, she spotted a house.

Liquid heat waves rising off the near molten blacktop made it difficult to tell how far away it was.

Probably only a quarter-mile; she could make it - had to make it.

God, let there be someone home.

Hollie woke up a hundred yards from the house racing through the open desert.

No time to get back on the road. Instead, in her last waking moment, she aimed for the back door and prayed she could hold the course as the car pitched and yawed violently along the rocky ground.

Hollie hit the farmstead like a bullet. The crash was massive - a roaring explosion that rocked the foundation.

Timber and drywall, glass and insulation erupted in every direction as the vehicle blasted through the house. But Hollie didn't hear a thing. She was deep asleep in a dreamless world.

CHAPTER 11

Taller and more majestic than the Taj Mahal - after which The Paradise had been designed - the hotel and casino's whitewash exterior sparkled in the late afternoon sun . The black parking lot, on the other hand, resembled a nonstick frying pan decorated with yellow parking lines.

With the Smith and Wesson in hand, Kaufman traversed the long shallow reflecting pool adorned in a colorful mosaic. His goal was to locate the security room and use the surveillance cameras to quickly scan the hotel; however, just inside the golden multi-door entrance, he stopped.

Stale cigarette smoke filled his nostrils - the cheap perfume of casinos everywhere - but it wasn't the heavy odor that had reined him in. From deep within the casino came the sound of grunting, low and primitive.

The sound caused Kaufman's flesh to break out in goosebumps.

He'd finally found a survivor - just not a human one.

Merah Gunung bellowed.

Like the booming of a massive Japanese stage drum, the roar swept through the casino.

It didn't at all sound muffled by the primate habitat's glass.

Kaufman raised the revolver and stepped through the doors.

Merah Gunung meant "Red Mountain," and he was a shaggy, broad-faced 250-plus-pound male orangutan. His arm strength alone was seven times as strong as that of a human. The confrontation with the crazed German Shepherd might as well have been a scrimmage with a field mouse for all the good it would do in preparing Kaufman for squaring off with this giant of the jungle.

Quickly moving across the green-and-silver-patterned carpet, Kaufman put a wall to his back.

Crisp and clear, the inhumanly long hooting rumbled through the casino again. The grunting calls were not only a way for Merah Gunung to mark his territory but a warning, a caution to others not to come near.

Standing in a maze of flashing slot machines, Kaufman suddenly wished he'd brought the shotgun. Even if he wasn't capable of wielding it with only one good hand, its mere presence would have been more reassuring than the revolver. With the Smith and Wesson, he'd have to get a head shot…and probably more than one.

The gambling floor was ripe for an attack.

In between the rows of slot machines were dense arrangements of large potted plants. The dark tropical foliage offered pristine ambush points, and Kaufman didn't like leaving so many of them unexplored, but there was no way he could search every one.

Moving deeper into the casino, empty gambling venues spread out in all directions. They waited, ready to entertain, but without the laughter and curses of luck, the place had lost not only its charm but its very soul. The constant background chatter and hum of human activity was the true lifeblood of casinos and, now abandoned, The Paradise seemed haunted - a purposeless ghost, brooding and malevolent.

The casino hadn't deteriorated to the point of being sadistic but stripped of its essence, the jaunty electronic slot machine music - meant to be exciting and enticing - was abrasive, the flashing lights too bright, the colors too cheery.

Everything conspired to put up a front - a blatant attempt to misdirect, like a prostitute with too much makeup and the clap.

It hadn't always been this way. Only yesterday, Kaufman had considered the building classy, elegant even. Indeed, The Paradise had been the shining gem of Decoy, just as much as the police station was its hairy wart.

At the time of its construction, the resort was an ambitious and unprecedented building. During a time of financial crisis in the mid-1980s, Decoy's three small casinos decided to merge. The purpose of this merger had been twofold: first, a new building would be built to retain the local gamblers, such as servicemen that were leaving town for the more modern casinos at Wendover; and secondly, the owners wanted to encourage out-of-state tourists and weekend-warriors to come an hour further inland past the state line and stay in Decoy.

To accomplish these goals, the strategy was to build a hotel and casino like no other. Hence, the mega-resort was born. Three years before the Mirage opened and instituted a revolution along the Las Vegas strip, The Paradise vaunted its massive hotel, colossal casino, and orangutan preserve.

Home to three rescued Sumatran orangutans, the 5000-square-foot habitat was the central attraction and primary selling point of the new resort.

But the new casino had been only moderately successful.

Although the town's economy prospered, it wasn't until the birth of Pohon Sepupu that The Paradise really began to pay off.

With the species on the edge of extinction, and with the lowest birthrate of any mammal (only one infant every six to eight years), the arrival of the baby orangutan brought publicity that made the great apes local celebrities overnight.

Along with the town, Kaufman had been instantly captivated, which afforded him the opportunity to openly observe and not elicit as much judgment as his public people-watching regularly drew.

But the orangutans had become more than an obsession, more than exotic window pets. Over the years, Kaufman had grown to know each one's personality, and they had become a kind of surrogate family - although it was Pohon Sepupu that he had deeply connected with. In many ways, they'd grown up together. As Pohon Sepupu had evolved socially and emotional, Kaufman's own understanding and development had expanded. He often wondered what he would have become without the orangutans, for they'd given him a glimpse of what natural altruistic relationships were - what kindness, devotion, and love looked like - pulling him back from fully succumbing to his father's teachings, and the listless, grim world of Dominism.

Kaufman had even given them all secret nicknames. Pohon Sepupu had become Seibu, which, in Indonesian, loosely meant half-brother.

In the last few years, he'd even gotten to meet his orangutan family as a local flora consultant for the habitat. His first face-to-face meeting had been a dream come true.

Stepping inside the manmade rain forest, the female orangutans had approached Kaufman with interest. And, like a long lost relative, he'd been instantly accepted, whereas strangers were usually treated with timidity. Taken by the hand, he was made to sit and was examined head to foot, even groomed - a social behavior reserved almost strictly to the mother-child relationship in this socially independent species. The experience had been profound.

As a trespassing child, Kaufman had been nothing more than an intruder. He deceived himself into believing he was part of the families in whose houses he wandered into, but with the orangutans, he truly felt like he belonged.

Although his duties only required him to visit the habitat twice a month, Kaufman always looked forward to the visits, and he wondered if it was that bond that had brought him here now.

Kaufman suspected that his intentions had less to do with finding survivors than in discovering the fate of his proxy family.

Though with gun in hand, he wasn't dropping by with treats and idle chatter, but with bullets and death.

If the orangutans had been people, even infected ones, would he be so detached about hunting them down and annihilating them too? Kaufman didn't know, but as he made his way towards the habitat, self-preservation kept his eyes on the lookout for lurking figures.

Passing beneath columns of fake vines that climbed upwards and arched out overhead like gothic buttresses, Kaufman both felt and heard Merah Gunung's next roar.

The sound was close and unnaturally loud.

Unlike chimpanzees, which hunted in packs and could be as brutal as a cartel, orangutans were generally nonaggressive and solitary primates. The thought of them ranging as a troop, crazy-eyed and jacked up on the Decoy Madness, did little to ease Kaufman's already substantial nerves.

"Headshot, it has to be a headshot," Kaufman reminded himself, sliding along rainforest-inspired wallpaper.

At blackjack tables, neat stacks of cards and chips were piled high. The fact that there was visible cash and little to no signs of mass confusion or dementia, other than a few spilled drinks and overturned chairs, did not bode well for the likelihood of survivors. Even amongst a panicking mob, there would be patrons who'd use the commotion to snatch up as much money as possible. For many, greed trumped survival.

Yet the Decoy Madness had struck so deep here that even that ignoble proclivity had been repressed. As if out of some 1930's horror novel about mass vanishings, the casino was a dispiriting uninhabited life-size diorama.

Kaufman moved through the empty floor. He was close now.

He was also hesitant, jumpy, and for some reason, extremely angry. It was odd that he should be upset. Trying to puzzle out his incoherent rage, he came within sight of the terrarium.

Strewn about the floor was one entire section of the supposedly, unbreakable habitat glass.

Inside the enclosure, Kaufman had an unobstructed view of what was left of the orangutans. The older female, Tua, had put out her eyes with a pair of sticks, and her body was slumped over the wooden skewers, resembling a civil war soldier impaled on battlefield spikes. At least the other female - Seibu's mother, Besinar Mata - hadn't been driven to such torturous suicide because even with her immense arm strength, there was no way she could have twisted off her own head.

The decapitation was ragged and messy. Kaufman turned away.

This was why he was angry; this wanton violence was what he'd known he'd find.

Through the habitat's broken glass came the sickly-sweet mélange of tropical flowers mingled with blood.

It wasn't the only thing to have escaped.

Covered in thick shaggy dreadlocks, Merah Gunung hunkered at the far end of the corridor. In shadows, he was like some monster out of a children's dark fairy tale. His usually demure face was currently pinched in a brooding scowl. Looking down at bloody hands, he seemed not only perplexed by the sticky substance but bothered by it. As if a moral conscience had arisen in him and he knew what he'd done was not only wrong but a sin.

The sharp squeak of work boots on hardwood brought the great ape out of his introspection. Glancing up, Merah Gunung spotted Kaufman, and all at once, his self-loathing turned outward, transformed into a seething contempt. Eyes narrowed, and although his aggression was usually reserved for claiming females in heat, the Red Mountain suddenly gave an unrestrained demonstration.

Snorting, the hulking orangutan slammed down his fists. A nearby bench shattered. Floor bolts popped as Merah Gunung ripped up the seat and smashed it against a wall. Wood cracked and splintered as shrapnel ricocheted wildly off the cement floor.

Picking up a section of the bench, Merah Gunung raised it overhead and rushed down the corridor, a true berserker charging into war.

Accustomed to seeing the animal in a slow lumbering, almost lazy gait, the sudden speed caught Kaufman off guard.

He hastily took up a shooter's stance.

Unsteady in a one-handed grip, the first shot went wide, and during recoil, Kaufman pulled the trigger twice more. Both shots went into the ceiling, and the sharp crack of the gun did nothing whatsoever to slow Merah Gunung. If anything, it further enraged the beast.

Kaufman ducked as the bench was flung at him and fired again. Unfortunately, Merah Gunung had already moved and was now swinging along the artificial vines overhead in huge strides. Only fifteen feet away, the orangutan's close-set eyes were hard and focused.

Kaufman had a clear shot; the sights were on target...but he hesitated. There was no confusion or pleading as with the Shepherd, only rage, which should have made taking the shot easier, but Kaufman wanted to save, not to execute. How could he commit premeditated manslaughter and call it mercy?

Before Kaufman had time to consider the question, Merah Gunung dropped to the ground and launched all his considerable weight, sinew, and bone-crunching ferocity forward.

In the blink of an eye, Kaufman steadied the gun.

This wasn't a moral debate or even a philosophical one - it was either kill or be killed.

The next shot missed, but the one after that caught Merah Gunung in the shoulder.

Not a headshot.

The orangutan went down but was quickly up.

Frothy with rage, wild with hatred, the Red Mountain charged again.

This time Kaufman didn't hesitate.

He fired.

Click.

The cylinders were spent.

Click.

Click.

Click.

There were no more bullets.

Five shots and he'd only managed to wound the creature, only succeeded in pissing it off.

Arms extended, teeth bared, and with murder in its eyes, the Red Mountain flew towards Kaufman.

There was no time to reload – no time to run.

Slammed to the ground by nearly a quarter ton of hairy enraged flesh, Kaufman gasped as the air exploded out of his chest. It felt as if he'd just been hit by a wrecking ball. From above, Merah Gunung began delivering tremendous jackhammer blows. Doing his best to cover up with one arm, Kaufman tried to breathe. It was like sucking air through a straw. His ears rang in between meaty thuds that caused his vision to flash and darken.

An impossibly strong hand suddenly seized his bad arm in a vice grip and wrenched. Kaufman screamed as tendons and ligaments gave way. He was literally going to be torn limb from limb, was about to have his arm ripped from his shoulder as if it had been made of nothing more than paper-mâché when something shot out of the habitat, and bowled the Red Mountain over.

Clambering away, Kaufman wobbled to his feet and pointed the empty gun at the giant orangutan, which now seemed to have an extra set of limbs.

Through a haze of mental fog, he realized that the additional arms and legs belonged not to Merah Gunung, but to Seibu. Although he hadn't seen the young orangutan's body, Kaufman had assumed him dead.

Grappling like a Brazilian Jujitsu wrestler, Seibu was anything but deceased. The younger and smaller orangutan broke free of the tangle and leaped to his feet. He raised something short and shiny above his head. By the time Kaufman recognized what it was, the metal pipe had arced downwards and split Merah Gunung's head.

Again, and again the club fell, like a kind of sinister oil drill, bringing up blood and flesh where it struck rather than black gold.

Kaufman watched as the pipe continued to rise and fall, continued to strike, even well past the point where it was necessary.

Abruptly, Seibu pivoted towards Kaufman at the height of the next blow. Looking at the revolver, he slowly backed away, as if recognizing the threat it represented. His eyes were deep pools of fear as he dropped the club, sat down, and curled into a ball.

Shaking and hugging himself, the orangutan resembled a scared orphaned child huddling in the rain.

Kaufman's long, deep, and deliberate breaths were the only sound in the now silent corridor. The ruthlessness of the assault, its sheer unrestrained brutality, the spreading pool of blood around Merah Gunung's caved-in skull, the fact that he was still alive and his body screamed with pain - all crashed together in his mind.

He couldn't move or think, but still he aimed the empty gun.

Peeking out from his protective position, Seibu slowly reached out a finger.

Stunned, Kaufman watched Seibu gently push aside the weapon, throw himself forward, and burry his face in Kaufman's knees.

Was this really happening? Was it wise to let Seibu live after the savagery he'd just displayed? The orangutan seemed docile enough now, but what guarantee was there that the ape wouldn't lose it at any moment and attack? Then again, there was no guarantee that Kaufman himself wouldn't turn homicidal either. Latent in his body, the Decoy Madness could surface at any time, could force his hand against himself just as it could be forced against others.

By trusting in Kaufman, Seibu was taking as big a risk as he was.

Besides, Seibu had just saved his life - by killing his own father nonetheless - and if that didn't engender trust, what would? Kaufman's instincts told him to be wary, yet it was difficult to give credence to such feelings with Seibu trembling against him; and when Kaufman looked down into those pleading eyes, he was ashamed. There was no anger in Seibu, no malice, and whether it was their unique history and kinship, or the onerous and isolated circumstances they found themselves in, Kaufman decided they should stick together.

Patting Seibu on the head, he slowly led them away from the gruesome carnage.

Moving through the casino, Seibu remained extremely timid, hiding behind Kaufman and using him as a shield, much like a shy toddler scared of the big unknown world. Then again, where Kaufman had awoken to a mysteriously empty city, Seibu's world had become a nightmare in the blink of an eye. His aunt had committed suicide, and his mother had been murdered by the father he'd just been forced to kill; plus, at eleven, Seibu was still a sub-adult, barely a teenager.

Stepping off the elevator, they made their way to the presidential suite. Kaufman figured, why not indulge when in hell? Inside the huge room, opulence and luxury stretched before them, but Kaufman still locked the door. The deadbolt slid home with a satisfying *clack*.

The noise seemed to bring Seibu out of his funk. Grabbing hold of a heavy armchair, the orangutan dragged it over to the door and wedged it up under the knob. After it was secure, the bow-legged hominoid waddled over to the bed. He pulled off the comforter, twisted it into a nest, and promptly fell asleep.

"How did you know to do that?" Kaufman wondered, looking from the chair to the sleeping red furball.

In a day when he'd seen screaming bloody-eyed jackrabbits frozen and twisted, discovered dung painted walls in abandoned home, and observed a horrific self-maiming - in a day when he'd witnessed the grisly work of a mad man who thought he was god, and had stood at the foot of a mountain of human lemmings before mercy-killing a bipedal German Shepherd - this simple act of wedging a chair against the door to further secure it was the most astounding.

All the former events were dark and destructive, whereas Seibu had not only displayed creativeness and intelligence but a creativeness and intelligence beyond his capacity. And that insight scared Kaufman more than all the previous experiences combined, for it suggested that whatever had happened was more complicated than just an escaped biological or chemical weapon...and more historic than the atom bomb.

Something was affecting the very being of every animal species in Decoy that it didn't kill, something that caused madness as well as created intelligence - something, something.

But what?

Tomorrow, Kaufman planned to find out.

CHAPTER 12

Hollie woke up.

She was no longer in the car, no longer outside.

Someone had moved her, and by the distinct pillow sections beneath her, she'd been laid out on a couch rather than a bed.

Peeking out through crisscrossed eyelashes, she followed her intuition and continued to feign sleep. It seemed irrational to hide her wakefulness from whomever had aided her, but her gut reaction was strong. She was sure her life depended on it.

In the dark room beyond, watery waves of blue light radiated along walls covered in gaudy wallpaper. The swimming illumination was the result of a black light coming from a saltwater fish tank somewhere deeper in the house, and a big one by the sound of the filters.

Out one window, Hollie could see the moon, and she realized she must have been out for hours if night had settled in. The thought unnerved her. In her unconscious state, anyone could have done anything to her. As she took inventory of her body, though, she was surprised to find it free of pain and remarkably whole.

Hollie would have liked to examine her restored health closer, but as she shifted her position, the couch creaked beneath her.

Freezing, she wondered if she'd been heard. She sensed she had.

Someone *was* watching, and it didn't feel like a concerned citizen.

Murmuring softly, Hollie tried to cover her movement as a shift in sleep. It was evident that the ruse failed, though, when something struck her. As if hit with a sandbag, Hollie cried out and instinctively curled up into a fetal position to protect herself.

Again, she was hit, and again, and again - the blows growing faster and more intense, even as they oddly become less physical and somehow more internal. It felt as if she were being assaulted by emotions; confusion, loathing, envy, mistrust, greed, all crashed into her. Raw and invading, the metaphysical beating left Hollie feeling as violated.

Bolting upright, Hollie frantically looked around for the source of the attack. No one was near, but deep in a shadowy corner, motionless sat a figure - her Samaritan.

Head bowed, fingers steepled, with elbows resting lightly on a worn leather armchair, the guy might have been a prime minister contemplating world peace, except he was dressed in nothing but stained tighty-whities and was as emaciated as a heroin addict.

Bald and gaunt, it was impossible to tell the guy's age; yet for all his hollow-eyed thinness, there was nothing frail about him. The Samaritan appeared as lithe and powerful as a warrior elf out of a fantasy book. Indeed, the only thing that ruined the man-boy's ethereal quality was his profuse sweating. Likely burning up with infection, the man sat as calmly as a meditating swami.

Without looking up, he spoke in a low, gravelly voice tinged with a southern accent.

"It's taking every bit of humanity left in me not to jump up and smash your face in."

Hollie flinched, but she didn't take a step back. Insanely she took a one forward.

Although only moments ago she'd felt defiled, now for some reason, she was filled with compassion for this wrecked human, whose suffering was so great that she could physically discern it. She was picking up on this man's emotions not as a well-trained listener empathizing, but within her as if those emotions had been her own, and she now felt compelled to give succor.

Where these angelic sentiments came from was beyond her, but she had to fight hard to resist the ludicrous yearnings.

"I can sense you want to help me...and your compassion disgusts me," said the skeleton with skin. He opened his eyes, and this time Hollie did take a step back, not because of the outpouring of hate and revulsion in those eyes, but because of the eyes themselves. They were completely red. Not just bloodshot, but bloody.

The sanguine orbs should have stood out against the creep's flesh, except instead of being blotchy or pale - as someone in such an advanced state of starvation would have been - the skin had a distinct sheen, a result of the silver sweat that covered his body.

"What you've become disgusts me," growled the Samaritan. "And I plan to kill you. But before I do, I want to give you a sporting chance. I want to make this fun…Hollie *Cunt*ingham."

As if slapped, Hollie stiffened.

Only one sleazeball had ever called her that before - a slimy researcher at Shafter who was as immature as he was crass.

A real live walking, talking dick, Hollie had always thought*, small and useless.*

"Captain Mills?"

"Bingo!"

Thin lips pulled back into a smile, revealing gums that had receded so far as to make each tooth look like a fang.

Hollie gasped. "What happened to you?"

"Don't play coy with me, you stupid cow!" Mills snapped. "You know exactly what's happened."

"I swear I…I don't know anything," Hollie stammered, inching away with arms out behind her, searching for anything that might be used as a bludgeon.

"And just where do you think you're going?" asked Mills, suddenly playful.

"You need help, Ryan. You need a doctor," she said, trying to mollify.

"What I *need* are answers, and you're going to give them to me…hopefully unwillingly."

Mills' pink tongue ran obscenely over his shiny sharp teeth.

Hollie felt sick. She wanted to run, wanted to turn and flee, but she didn't dare expose her back to those demonic-looking chompers.

"You were at Shafter, what were they working on?"

"I didn't have clearance to know what the big project was, but it had your name on it," Mills snarled, abruptly angry again. "It had something to do with enhancement. Do I look enhanced to you?"

"No," breathed Hollie automatically, but she lied.

Mills had always been vulgar, as quick to spin a tale and brag about his sexual endeavors as a sailor, but he was also all talk. Hollie had known from the moment she first met him that he was full of shit - a perpetual teenager who would say anything to get a reaction. Now though, besides the visible physical change, Mills' personality had also been augmented. He'd gone from boorish to malicious, but Hollie knew commenting on any change would be unwise.

"What's the matter?" asked Capt. Mills teasingly, back in good humor, his backwoods twang more pronounced than ever. "Cat got your tongue?"

Hollie shook her head as she watched sparkling beads of sweat rolled down Mills' cadaverous golden skin.

"You know, speaking of cats," he continued, "I have this friend down in the animal labs who told me some really weird shit. Said their orders over the last few months have been to sever limbs, put out eyes, stab and shoot the animals…not your usual injections and blood test-type stuff, eh? I even heard one guy was court-martialed when he refused to execute five monkeys for that day's testing. Just what kind of research do you need dead monkeys for, huh Dr. Cuntingham?"

Hollie shook her head, not because she didn't know - she knew exactly why - but in surprise that Dr. Murakami had convinced the military to take the testing so far.

Could they really have gotten to the point where they were experimenting on recently deceased animals?

Yet, perhaps it hadn't been him.

"Did you hear anything about…human experimentation?"

"No," said Mills, "but I wouldn't have put it past them. The brass had a hard-on for your little brainchild, and it wouldn't be the first time the United States Armed Forces conducted unauthorized human trials. All in the name of the national security, of course."

Carefully Hollie reached into her pocket and pulled out the ID badge she'd discovered earlier. She held it up so Mills could see it.

"Did you know a Shane Málin?"

"Nope, who's he?"

"I don't know; someone involved, I think."

"You think?" Mills blustered. "Is that all?" He stared at Hollie accusingly. For a long time, his crimson eyes bore into hers, as she desperately tried to come up with something to say, something that would give her an edge, anything to buy her more time, but her usually nimble mind came up blank.

"Well then," Mills smacked his lips, "if that's all you know, how 'bout we have some fun."

Jumping up, he crossed the gap between them faster than Hollie could blink, faster than she could react - she barely had time to get her hands up before he seized her and shook with neck-snapping ferocity. Yet as quickly as the violence started, it stopped.

Ripping himself away, Mills suddenly looked contrite.

"I'm sorry," he pleaded in a meek voice. "I can't control myself, but just now when I touched you, I saw myself through your—"

His voice broke and became a strained plea.

"Look, you have to get out of here, whatever good is left in me is being stripped away...I...there on the dresser is a key to the truck in the garage. Take it, go, get out of here before I do something...before..."

Mills stepped back. He shook his head, like a madman hearing a bug buzzing in his brain. His hands shot up and covered his ears as if to hold in whatever voices or demons were trying to break out. The scene reminded Hollie of Gollum from the Lord of the Rings films. Bald and gaunt, Mills not only shared that twisted and aberrant creature's features but his split personality too.

Ryan Mills had clearly undergone something traumatic, something that had radically changed him, something the smiling man - Shane - must have known about, even triggered, yet Hollie didn't believe Mills was being insincere or trying to trick her when he offered her the truck key. She needed to act quickly though before whatever virtue had passed from her to him in the moment he'd grabbed her - and had briefly turned him docile, even helpful - evaporated like his sanity.

Snatching up the key, Hollie made for the stairs when Capt. Mills' voice caused her to halt, caused the very hairs on her neck to stand on end.

"Going so soon, Dr. Cuntingham?" he asked, no longer any trace of kindness in his voice. "Goodie! More fun for me. I like a chase."

Hollie ran.

Even when she heard him crashing down the stairs after her, she didn't look back, didn't stop until he grabbed a fistful of her hair and yanked.

Hollie's head snapped back while her feet kept going. She struck the stairs with her back and skull so hard that she momentarily blacked out. Wildly she reached out for something to stop her slide down the washboard steps and caught Mills by an ankle. She pulled him off balance, and the two crashed down the remaining steps in a tangled heap.

At the bottom, Hollie scrambled upright; and as Mills rose to his hands and knees, she dropkicked him in the face. Cartilage and bone gave way, but Mills didn't seem to mind. In fact, a bloody smile spread across his face like a dazed prizefighter.

"Wee!" he coughed. "Now, I can say I took a tumble with the closed-legged bitch, Cuntingham."

"Here's your tumble," Hollie spat back as her foot darted out again, connecting with ribs and stomach and groin.

After the barrage, Hollie stepped over Capt. Mills and into the foyer. There, in a pile of twisted metal, fragmented drywall, and broken timber, was what was left of the car she'd driven into the house. The front entrance was completely obliterated, and the sagging roof looked on the verge of collapse. A hole in the ceiling showed the starry sky above, and with the massive gurgling fish tank washing everything out in a blue-black light, it felt to Hollie as if she were in a kind of post-apocalyptic-themed night club. All that was missing was the deafening blast of rapid-fire techno music.

Staggering over to the nearest door, Hollie yanked it open, hoping for the garage.

Suddenly the door slammed shut.

Her fingers were crushed in between the door and frame, and Hollie screamed. Behind her, Mills - or whatever the hell Mills was now - stood inches away, holding the door shut. He smiled maliciously, a luminous Cheshire cat grin in the black light. Then he bit her, driving his face into her shoulder, and began to chew.

Blood gushed, and Hollie's scream went up an octave.

She tried to hit the ghoulish face with her free hand, but Mills' weight pinned her against the wall and drove her to the ground. Unable to break free, Hollie kicked and squirmed as she was masticated. Breath escaped her, and in the watery illumination, as her flesh was torn away, Hollie suddenly believed she was deep in the ocean being devoured by some medieval leviathan.

And being eaten alive was a thousand times worse than being shot.

In wild desperation, as the Gollum-Mills thing came in for another bite, Hollie bit back. Instantly her mouth was filled with foul, diseased-tasting blood and salty sweat. But still, she held tight until Mills pulled back and his ear tore away. Hollie spat out the vile flap of cartilage and clawed free as Mills howled.

Racing down the hall, she opened the next door, which *was* the garage, and rushed in. A diesel pickup sat parked inside, and Hollie hoped to God it wasn't locked.

Her prayer was answered.

Throwing herself into the driver's seat, she started the engine, put the truck in reverse and turned to back up when the window beside her head exploded. Fragments of glass sprayed across her face, and the handle of a gardening tool struck her in the temple.

For a moment, everything went white.

Mills reached through the broken window and got a hold of the steering wheel. Hollie floored the gas even as her world spun. The truck flew backward, and the garage wall caught Mills in the chest and ripped him away.

Tires screeching, Hollie fought to maintain control as massive torque yawed her left and right. Stomping on the brakes, she came to a shuddering stop.

Blinking, Hollie tied to clear her vision and locate Mills.

He was nowhere to be seen.

Popping the truck into drive, she revved the engine, but she didn't drive forward - for there, in her headlights, stood the *enhanced* Capt. Ryan Mills.

He should have been a wreck, should have been smashed and broken as a secondhand action figure. But he looked whole - didn't appear hurt at all.

What have you done, Dr. Murakami? Hollie wondered as Mills stood like some demon from hell, with his crimson eyes and impossibly thin and sinewy form glowing in the muddy yellow of the headlights and dripping blood.

He smiled delightedly. "This is so much fun."

Hollie gripped down hard on the steering wheel.

"Then you're going to love this," she said and stomped on the gas.

Launching forward, the truck shuddered as it hit Mills and plowed him into the ground.

Slamming on the breaks, Hollie looked back into the rearview mirror. The Gollum impersonator was struggling to stand.

"Fuck no!" she barked and backed up.

The wheels bounced when they struck their target, but unlike with a speed bump, the impact was soft and squishy. And when she drove over Mills the third time, she made sure to aim for his head, which popped like a ripe watermelon under the weight of the pickup.

"Just like Lord of the Rings," Hollie muttered bitterly, applying pressure to her gnawed shoulder as she pulled out of the long driveway and made for Decoy, the hospital, and a tetanus shot.

CHAPTER 13

Clink.

Matthew snatched up his weapon.

The knife shimmered in the early morning light.

A ten-inch all-purpose chief's knife, the blade was a short sword in Matthew's small hand. The fine edge and sharp point could eviscerate and stab just as easily as it sliced, diced, and minced. However, the weapon offered no protection if the wielder slept, and Matthew had dreamt the night away.

Tilting his head, he waited for the noise to repeat.

How easily he'd lost the battle with sleep. Some guard he'd turned out to be. He'd promised Jess to stay up all night, but he'd failed…again. At least she wouldn't know of his failure, for she still slept - although not soundly and certainly not peacefully. In her makeshift bed, his sister wrestled with some imagined bogeyman, tossing and turning. Or possibly her nightmare was real - a recent experience replayed, an unpleasant memory remembered.

Matthew was about to wake her when her struggle ceased, and she drifted into calmer currents of sleep.

They'd ended up staying the night at their old house, not daring to return to Lucybean's place. The house had been for sale since they'd left it five months ago, and their mom had gone to stay at the hospital.

All the furniture had been sold to pay medical bills, so Jess had made a bed out of old blankets. It had also been her idea to come here. Last night she'd been clear-headed, quick and smart, while Matthew had felt clumsy and unsure. The horror of Aunt Lucy and the creepy Shane guy had numbed his mind. He'd been unable to think or act, as useless as ear hair.

Now though, it was his turn to take charge, be the big brother, be the responsible one; and although their old bedroom felt safe with its familiar Disney-themed wallpaper, Matthew knew they couldn't stay here. He worried about going to the police after ball-busting the blond cop, but what other choice did they have?

Looking around, he hoped something in the room might give him an answer. The ceiling was covered in glow-in-the-dark stars, a remnant of the days when he'd wanted to be a pirate. His dad had helped him arrange the constellations, and then they'd gone outside to look at the real Orion's Belt and the real Big Dipper. His dad had even shown him how to locate and get directions using binary stars.

"There, now you'll always know your way. If you get lost, just find the North Star and BAM, you're on your way."

His father had made everything sound so easy. The truth was Matthew didn't know where to go or what to do; looking at the five-pointed plastic decorations gave him no insights either. He was not the confident swashbuckler he'd once imagined himself to be, able to navigate any situation, but a bowlegged kid, scared and way out of his league.

This was real life, not make-believe.

Matthew wished for the millionth time that his father was here, but it was a tired wish and one that never helped. Life was hard, sometimes unpleasant; perhaps that's why Clint had left. He'd been a dreamer, someone who shied away from hard times, sought the path of least resistance, a person in perpetual playtime. Matthew wasn't like that at all.

At the age of ten, he was more adult than his father ever had been, maybe ever would be.

That insight was both empowering and sad.

He'd been forced into adulthood, his childhood stripped away, snuffed out by BMD; and if he was already an adult now, what would happen once he grew up?

Scroogehood was definitely on the horizon.

Matthew sighed.

He yearned for carefree days and the innocence of youth - except boys with plastic-covered legs were not meant to be fun-loving, life-filled people.

So be it. He might not be full of life, but he certainly was full of pee, and whatever had woken him was just in time because he was ready to burst.

At the toilet, Matthew struggled to unbutton his pants. As he worked at the button, the chef's knife slipped from his hand and stuck firmly in the linoleum, inches from his foot. Carefully he pulled it loose and laid it by the sink.

He might not be able to avoid becoming Ebenezer, but he could avoid circumcision.

Clink.

Matthew jerked up his head.

It was the same noise he'd woken too.

Finishing his business, he went to investigate.

Holding the knife high, he crept through the house.

Near the den, he slowed his approach.

This was where the sound had come from.

The room was empty, and the windows were free of curtains and blinds, which meant he had an unobstructed view of a dog with forepaws pressed to the glass. The dog stared intently into the room, searching for something...or someone.

Matthew froze. He hadn't yet left the short hallway, and his gut told him to keep still. He knew that dogs had far better hearing than humans, but that their eyesight wasn't very good. That was true for most domestic dogs, but this was no tame animal.

Cousin to the wolf, the coyote was an efficient hunter of small animals, and this particular specimen looked ready to take on bigger game. With pointy ears and an angular muzzle, it was also smaller and leaner than its forest-dwelling relative.

Spotting Matthew, the coyote snarled; and in its eyes was a malicious desire to kill. Matthew somehow knew the coyote hadn't tracked him down out of hunger, but because it hated him.

Rushing back to the bedroom, he heard again the sound that had woken him.

Clink.

Looking around, Matthew saw the coyote at the window panting and fogging up the glass as it glared down at Jessica.

Glancing over to his sister, Matthew thought she looked as delicate and easy to break as a China doll. Dropping to her side, he shook her awake.

"What's going on?" she asked sleepily.

At her movement, the coyote went wild, clawing and snapping.

"Shane was right," said Jessica, watching the possessed coyote.

Matthew frowned, not following.

"He said they'd be jealous," Jessica reminded him.

"Never mind that," he said, taking her by the hand. "We're leaving."

"What if it doesn't let us out?"

"Then we'll just have to let it in," Matthew said coyly and smiled.

"What do you mean?" Jessica asked.

Behind them, the glass suddenly cracked.

"Come on!" he shouted.

Shutting the door, the two raced through the hall, and Matthew explained his plan.

He went over it three times to make sure Jess understood. Then, he made himself as conspicuous as possible in the middle of the room. Jessica took up a position behind the front door, and they waited.

It didn't take long.

Clink.

Eyes appeared in the front door's window, as hostile and aggressive as an assassin locked onto its target.

Matthew waved and stuck out his tongue.

The coyote bristled. Yellow teeth appeared beneath snarling lips.

Continuing to taunt the beast, Matthew slowly backed up. Halfway through the house, he signaled.

"Now!"

Jessica opened the door.

The coyote shot in, and for an instant, Matthew couldn't move.

He watched the coyote bear down on him like some kind of freak dinosaur - for instead of attacking on all fours, the thing ran upright on its hind legs and was twice as terrifying in its prehistoric blitzkrieg.

Screaming as claws and fangs reached out for him, Matthew pivoted and took off.

Hot breath puffed in his face as the coyote's teeth flew by, missing him by mere inches.

Why had he thought this was a good idea?

Wobbling down the hallway, he felt as slow and awkward as a fat baby hippo being pursued by a cheetah. Scratch that, he wasn't being hunted by a cheetah - nothing so mundane as a quadruped - but a miniature furry T-Rex.

Slipping out from behind the door, Jessica stepped outside and made her escape.

Turning sharply into the kitchen, Matthew knew the coyote was gaining on him, but the back door was only a few feet away, so maybe he could avoid becoming lunch after all.

Hurrying, he reached the rear exit and yanked.

The door didn't budge.

Matthew yanked again and realized in his haste he'd forgotten to unlock it.

From the far side of the kitchen, the coyote chuffed and growled.

It sounded like mock laughter.

In blind panic, Matthew fumbled and slapped at the deadbolt as the sound of claws rattled across the linoleum.

Disengaging the deadbolt, Matthew knew he couldn't escape, knew he didn't have time to swing open the door. The coyote sprang into the air, and Matthew screamed as fur and claws slammed into him.

The impact knocked him off his feet and knocked the wind out of him.

For a moment on the floor, hunkered over and gasping for breath, Matthew didn't know where he was or what was going on.

Exploiting the boy's vulnerability, the coyote pounced. Biting full force into Matthew's leg, it whipped its head to tear away soft skin and flesh - except instead of ripping into muscle, the coyote got a mouth full of hard plastic. In anger and confusion, it gnashed its teeth at the unyielding leg.

Using the confusion to his advantage, Matthew twisted and kicked. The blow landed solidly in the coyote's snout, and the beast yipped as it spun backward. Scrambling to his feet, Matthew flung open the door and stumbled outside, slamming it behind him. Jessica stood waiting for him with fear and worry, lining her usually cheery face.

"I'm alright," he said, gulping at the air.

Inside, the coyote batted against the door.

"Let's go," he wheezed, and the two siblings set off.

Cutting through patchy backyards, they put as many fences behind them as they could.

"Where are we going?" Jessica inquired.

"To the hospital," Matthew said, breathing a little easier now.

Jessica faltered.

"What's wrong?" Matthew asked, but his sister didn't reply.

"Before, we wanted to see mom to make sure she was okay. Now we have to see her," he explained. "She's the only one that can help us."

Jessica shook her head, and Matthew dropped her hand.

He was suddenly angry, as furious as a hornet. Where else could they go? Aunt Lucy had gone crazy and who knew where Uncle Bernard and everybody else was. They couldn't go to the police, not after what he'd done to the cop, so that left Samantha. Their mom would know what to do; she always knew what to do.

"I'm sorry," Jess said, looking at her feet. "I just have a bad feeling."

Tentatively, she took hold of his hand again, and Matthew didn't stop her. He felt awful for being angry at her. Really he was angry with himself - frustrated and scared. Also, his legs were aching, yet he knew they couldn't stop.

"It's okay. I'm not mad at you."

She wanted to believe him. "Promise?"

"Promise."

Reaching the open road, they took to walking down the center of the street. Somehow it felt safer.

Roughly a block from their home, they were far enough away not to hear the breaking of glass as it exploded outward with the escaping coyote; however, Jessica must have sensed it, because she turned and looked back the way they'd come.

Breaching some low hedges, the sleek hunter approached quickly, but with a new respect for its quarry.

As soon as Matthew spotted the lean prairie wolf, he was ready to bolt.

"No," Jessica whispered.

Matthew looked at her, but she hadn't been talking to him. She was staring at the coyote.

Twenty feet away, the thing slowed as if suddenly unsure of its intent.

"No!" she said again, more forcefully this time, and the coyote halted. It regarded the small girl, and Matthew watched the contempt in the animal's eyes give way to curiosity.

"Go away from us. We're not the cause of your suffering, so go away. Just go away!"

Jessica stood straight, hands fisted by her sides.

The coyote growled and whined, battling between its own will and the spoken command. In the end, though, Jess was obeyed. Dropping to all fours, the coyote tucked tail and scampered off.

Matthew was stunned; his sister had *made* the creature leave.

"How did you do that?"

Jess turned to him, shoulders slumped, looking exhausted.

"We should go. It won't last long."

Not arguing, Matthew took his sister by the hand. All around them, silent, empty houses loomed.

At the end of the block, they looked back.

The coyote had slowed its retreat. In agitation, it snorted and chuffed, trying to fling off confusion, dislodge its mental fog. After a moment, it stood, and there was no longer any befuddlement in its behavior.

The wolf cousin howled long and hard.

From elsewhere in the neighborhood, the call was answered.

"Run!" Matthew shouted.

The chase was on.

Coyotes appeared, as if from everywhere, and for a species that tended to avoid human encounters, these individuals seemed eager to make the children's acquaintance…violently.

Two, five, six - the pack grew and gained ground. Matthew knew outrunning them was hopeless. With each step, a pinching pain shot throughout his arthritic legs. It was a different ache than he was used to, but even without the cramp, his top speed barely matched his sister's; and although she could outdistance him, it wouldn't matter in the end, for they would surely be caught if they didn't find shelter soon.

Up ahead, the road T-boned, and a wall of houses blocked their escape. Several garages stood open though, and Matthew made for an empty one.

Pushing Jessica ahead, he watched her race up the driveway; and by the time he reached the entrance, she'd pressed the button for the automatic door.

Slowly, it rumbled downwards.

The charging coyotes bayed and howled. Jess put her hands over her mouth as Matthew pulled her near. The door was almost closed when the lead dog slipped its snout under.

Immediately the garage door halted and began to retract.

Matthew broke away from Jessica and slapped the button to freeze the door. Five inches off the ground, it now had sprouted several searching jaws and even more probing claws. Matthew wished he could press the button again to crush every one of the coyotes, except he knew a safety feature prevented just such an incident from occurring. In its current position, however, the garage door was down far enough to deny entry.

For the moment, they were safe.

Sitting down, Matthew pulled down his pants and examined his legs. He expected them to be red and swollen, but to his surprise, they looked healthy, evenly proportioned and…normal.

Carefully, he removed his braces, and the cramped sensation immediately eased. It was as if the plastic were the cause of his discomfort and not some genetic defect.

As he rubbed his muscles, the pain all but vanished.

Jessica looked on expectantly.

Wiggling his toes, Matthew watched them dance and responding without difficulty.

Bracing himself, he stood and didn't wobble, didn't need support.

Walking, he jumped, spun.

His legs were healed.

"Did you..."

"No," Jess interrupted, but she didn't look surprised.

"How then?"

She shrugged, "We've changed."

She'd said that before. "Like Aunt Lucy?" he asked.

"No. She changed...bad."

He thought about that. "Just like the coyotes?"

Jessica nodded.

Bang! The garage door rattled with the impact of one of the coyotes.

Bang, bang, bang - like mortar rounds, the mutant canine flung themselves at the aluminum paneling.

This was not the time to have a conversation. He and Jess had to get out of there, get someplace safe, and the sooner, the better. The adjoining house door was locked tight, which meant the only way out was back the way they'd come.

Matthew still had the chef's knife tucked away in his waistband, wrapped in a sheath he'd made out of cardboard and some packing tape, and as cool as it might be to hack his way out like some Jedi Knight, he knew that was only wishful thinking. But the garage didn't offer any better solutions.

A few gardening tools might be used as weapons, although the long handles would make them awkward to wield, and the weed whackers and chainsaw - while even more tempting - were completely out of the question. Matthew had no idea how to start them and doubted he was strong enough to swing them around without cutting off one of his own newly healed legs.

A line of bikes hung from hooks on the back wall, but even the child-sized ones weren't an option, as Matthew had never learned how to ride. His braces hadn't allowed him to push the pedals properly, so there'd been no point; and if he tried now, a simple fall wouldn't only result in a few bruises and scrapes, but in him being torn apart.

Bang!

The next coyote that rammed the garage door yipped in pain, yet its suffering was not in vain - as one of its brothers was now able to almost completely slip under. A few more assaults like that might knock the sliding door off its track, and then a flood of prairie wolves would swarm in. Matthew needed something that would help them escape now - but what? The garage was unnaturally clean. The owners were most definitely not average Americans, for tools were arranged neatly on pegboards, the bikes were ordered from biggest to smallest, and even the paint cans and gasoline canister were labeled and carefully tucked away.

Matthew did a double-take.

Of course! The gasoline!

One night he'd awoken to the laughter of teenage boys as they lit zig-zagging lines of gasoline along the blacktop. Their irresponsible entertainment was interrupted by the arrival of flashing police cars, but Matthew had never forgotten how quickly the petroleum took flame.

Grabbing the nearest canister, he found it full, and once he had located a long-stemmed BBQ lighter, Matthew set to work.

Sensing his approach, the coyotes grew more frantic. They were reaching further in now because of the newly created dent, and Matthew made sure to stay well out of their range.

Twisting off the cap released a pungent vapor, and as Matthew poured, the fuel rolled out from inside the garage and down the driveway. The coyotes retreated right away but quickly returned, and in their reckless frenzy to get in and kill, they ended up rolling in the gasoline as casually as pigs in slop.

Matthew focused his dousing where the attackers were most concentrated, and in moments the dogs were saturated, walking Molotov cocktails.

As if sensing their impending demise, the Kamikaze coyotes pounded the door with even greater ferocity.

Bang, bang-bang, bang!

The five-gallon container wasn't quite empty when the wheels of the garage door suddenly popped off its track. Matthew hurried back as several furry T-Rexes began to wriggle under the new opening. Dropping the gas canister, he pulled the trigger on the lighter.

A blue flame flicked to life, and the moment he touched the tip of that thirsty tongue to the pool of refined oil, it lapped it up in a great *whoosh* of flames that surged out under the garage door.

Everywhere coyotes erupted, grew heavy coats of orange and red. They yelped and whined as skin bubbled, popped, and sizzled. The sickening sweet scent of burnt hair and flesh filled the air as consuming fire burned down the driveway. Half-lit coyotes scattered in every direction, while others lay down and were consumed in flames.

Matthew let the inferno burn for a while before signaling Jess, but when she pushed the button for the garage door, it only groaned upwards a foot.

"Great, it's busted," he said, pulling at the door ineffectually. "We'll have to crawl under."

On his belly, he squirmed through the roiling black smoke and out into the chaos of burning coyotes. A moment later, Jessica emerged covered in greasy smudges. Most of the pain-filled yipping had fallen silent, but a few coyotes still whined and twitched, their charred carcasses shriveled and brittle.

Matthew almost hurled.

The carnage was awful, but for all the damage he'd done they still weren't safe. A handful of coyotes materialized out of the wispy smoke as soundlessly as a death squad. Most were burned to some degree, but all stood upright, their forelimbs hanging low like freak kangaroo crossbreeds, and in a slow coordinated maneuver, the coyotes surrounded the children.

"Can you make them go away like you did before?" Matthew hoped.

With a sad expression, Jessica shook her head. "There's too many."

Pulling out his knife, Matthew prepared to fight.

He swung the blade, trying to widen the tightening circle of bipedal predators. If they all attacked at once, he wouldn't stand a chance.

One large and particularly badly-burned coyote stepped forward. Sporadic patches of singed hair speckled its blackened skin, and a gaping vacant hole where the right eye used to be was an exclamation point above permanently peeled back lips. But in its good eye, the physical suffering had focused the earlier mindless bloodlust into cold, calculating vengeance.

In a burst of speed, the creature attacked. Lashing out, Matthew felt the knife strike deep, felt skin and muscles part, and the blade drag along bone.

Retreating, the bloodied coyote howled. The rest of the pack joined in, and the chorus was shrill and primal and siren loud. Matthew almost wet his pants, almost dropped the kitchen knife that wobbled in his hands.

He was as scared as he'd ever been in his life, and behind him, Jessica cried.

In his mind, he could see himself being torn apart; could see intestines ripped out and flesh rendered; could even hear bones snapping like gunshots.

Unexpectedly three coyotes crumbled to the ground.

Dark blood pooled beneath them.

Those pops hadn't been Matthew's imagination - someone was shooting.

Down the street, in front of a flashing patrol car, stood a cop with a smoking gun. Matthew thought he looked cool as hell, like Batman or something, until he realized it was the same blonde and mustached policeman that yesterday had offered them a ride.

"Come on!" he waved, motioning them towards the cruiser.

Matthew hesitated for an instant before pulling Jessica away, as more bullets whizzed by. The cop continued to shoot until all the nearest coyotes were dead.

"Damned spawns of Satan," Officer Graeci spat, slamming the car door shut. "Infected by the Evil One himself."

He turned to the huddling children in the back seat. Matthew knew he should say something, apologize for whacking the guy in the nuts, but he couldn't quite think of the right way to say sorry.

"It's okay, son. I'm not mad at you. Vengeance is mine saith the Lord, Romans 12:19. God's already punished the sinners of this world and you're not one of them - not among the tares that have been sifted."

Matthew smiled weakly. He had no idea what that meant.

Outside, the remaining coyotes circled.

"It's lucky that you found us when you did," said Matthew, wanting to change the subject. "I don't think I could have fought them all off."

Buckling up, the cop adjusted the rearview mirror.

"Luck had nothing to do with it," he said, his serious eyes framed in the sliver of mirror. "I was *sent* to find you."

"Sent? By whom?"

It was Jessica that asked.

His eyes flicked over to the girl, a switchblade glance.

"God."

That should have been comforting. It wasn't.

Matthew shrunk down in his seat as Donald stomped on the accelerator, and the car took off.

CHAPTER 14

A videoboard of flat-screen monitors lined one wall of the surveillance control room. Each monitor showed several thumbnail images; every gaming station, hallway, stairwell, and alcove was covered and recorded.

Big Brother was watching.

Right now, though, except for about a half dozen bodies and a handful of signature Decoy Madness exploits, there were only rows and rows of empty slot machines, blackjack tables, and keno chairs.

The bizarre suicides would have been gruesome, even in black and white. On high definition color monitors, they were like morbid hyper-realistic photographs.

Kaufman had seen enough.

He'd spent the morning searching for and gaining access to the control room, only to confirm what he'd suspected. Perhaps there were others about town, but as far as the resort went, he and Seibu were the only ones breathing.

"Alright, let's get out of here," said Kaufman, moving to the door.

Seibu waddled over. His short legs weren't really designed for walking - his strong, flexible feet and long arms were more at home with arboreal locomotion. Yet he looked quite comfortable in his erect posture. Then again, if the city's calamity could make dogs run upright, then an orangutan forgoing his species' normal knuckle-walk was almost insignificant; and it was trivial compared to what Kaufman himself had to add to the puzzle.

Waking up this morning, his broken collar bone and cracked ribs were completely healed. Yesterday his arm had been rendered as useless as decaf coffee; today, however, only a minor stiffness lingered. Kaufman was certain he hadn't misdiagnosed the injury. Somehow during the night, his body had mended itself, had knitted up splintered bone in a matter of hours instead of weeks.

The restoration was stunning, miraculous even, and now more than ever, Kaufman was determined to find out just what was going on.

NewLife and Shafter were only a car ride away; illumination was just around the corner.

Leaving the casino, Kaufman opened the Humvee's trunk and repacked a few items. In the process, Seibu let himself in and situated himself in the passenger seat. Kaufman got in after him and watched as he examined the seat belt. Comprehending its purpose and function, Seibu buckled up before Kaufman could demonstrate the straps function.

"I suppose if you could reach the pedals, you might even like to give driving a try?"

Seibu nodded and grinned as if he understood.

"Yeah, well, unfortunately, in this country, they only give licenses to immature *human* teenagers, so you only meet half the requirements."

Seibu's grin broadened, and Kaufman tousled his hair before pulling out onto the main road.

Heading to NewLife, the streets were as empty as any ghost town, as silent as any grave. Images of the mountain of dead bodies out on Highway 229 played through Kaufman's mind, and he struggled to push them away.

As they drove, Seibu played with the radio; but it only produced the same strange bubbling noise Kaufman had heard yesterday when he tried the landline at the house with the abandoned BBQ. It wasn't the normal static between channels, but a steady gurgling on all frequencies. The sound was uncanny and desolate, a stark reminder to Kaufman that he was trapped in this dead city with a mad man hunting him.

Lost in thought, Kaufman was caught off guard when Seibu suddenly pounded on the window. He jumped and braked hard.

Looking around, Kaufman thought Seibu must have spotted someone, but he didn't see anybody. Tapping the window, Seibu pointed at a grocery store and clacked his teeth together.

Kaufman raised an eyebrow.

He knew great apes were among the few mammals that were self-aware, able to use tools and could acquire and interpret language signs. However, the ability to identifying a grocery store among other buildings without ever having seen one before placed Seibu into a completely new range of intelligence.

Or perhaps he was crediting the orangutan with more brainpower than was due. Most likely, Seibu had noticed the giant fruit bulging off both sides of the store's main sign. The colorful plastic bananas, grapes, apples, and watermelon wedges had no doubt caught Seibu's attention as easily as fireworks.

Finicky eaters by nature, orangutans spent the majority of each day searching for and eating fruit, so it was likely hunger and not advanced intellect that had caused Seibu to point out the grocery store. It was something Kaufman himself should have responded to. Except for the mid-day dog food splurge, he hadn't eaten anything for almost forty-eight hours.

Seibu continued snapping his jaw - mimicking eating.

"Lunch it is," said Kaufman, turning into the parking lot, which twinkled like a disco floor.

Shattered glass from broken car windows blanketed the tarmac, and in the center of the blacktop, half a dozen shopping carts had been arranged in a semicircle around a massive pile of spoiling food.

Cereal and pasta had been removed from boxes; soup emptied from cans, milk dumped from plastic jugs, even fresh fruit peeled of its skin. Then, for some reason, after piling up all the edible portions - as if they had been poisoned or were rotten - the empty containers had been replaced in an orderly fashion back into their metal shopping carts.

The scene was familiar: random chaos followed by total abandonment - the trademark of the Decoy Madness.

Driving over the transparent caltrops, Kaufman worried less about puncturing a tire than about Seibu cutting his feet. He supposed he could carry him, but it might be difficult, especially if Seibu wasn't willing. Kaufman's worry was misplaced, though, for once parked, Seibu walked through the remaining glass without any hesitation.

Nature had designed the soles of his feet over eons of time, and they were armor leather tough. Kaufman's boots might not be as well-engineered - for instead of trusting in their craftsmanship, he carefully picked his way over the razor-sharp sidewalk as if he'd been wearing moccasins.

Once inside, Seibu wasted no time and made a beeline straight for the produce section. Kaufman watched the short orange-red fur ball look around in wonder. Displayed to their best advantage, the rows of fruit were an utter smorgasbord, and when Seibu looked back, he beamed. He was in orangutan heaven, and with uncharacteristic zeal for his species, he hurried around nibbling and tasting everything that caught his fancy.

Seibu savored each bite, rolling his eyes in pleasure, but he moved through the vegetable aisles with less enthusiasm. When he picked up a stubby jalapeño, Kaufman cleared his throat.

"Ah...I wouldn't do that if I were you."

Seibu popped the whole pepper in his mouth and smugly grinned.

"Alright, but I warned you." Kaufman waited as Seibu chewed. All at once, Seibu scrunched up his face and stuck out his tongue. It was covered in green mulch, and he put half a hand in his mouth and scraped it clean. Panting and wagging his long lips, he looked around miserably, fat tears and snot streaming from his face.

Laughing, Kaufman snatched up a cucumber and cut it open with a pocketknife. He handed it to Seibu, who sucked at it and ran it over his lips as if applying ChapStick.

Kaufman continued to chuckle as he handed over a wedge of cantaloupe, and Seibu rubbed it over his head and face, hooting delightedly.

"You're worse than a baby with spaghetti."

Seibu bobbed his head as he messily devoured another slice of cantaloupe.

His innocent mirth was infectious, and suddenly Kaufman had a desire to indulge himself.

As a child, he'd always wanted to do just as Seibu was doing - taste and try everything in a grocery store that caught his attention. The food he'd eaten under his father's roof had been bland and strictly regimented for nutrition. Göttlich Striker didn't believe in sugar, salt, butter, or anything that flavored food for that matter. He taught that although all appetites of the body were to be mastered, food was a particularly tricky desire to overcome.

"Lust and sex are nothing compared to hunger," Göttlich had explained. "Give a starving man the choice between a steak and a naked woman, and in this case, the meat will always come before the milk."

He'd chuckled at that.

"The desire for food isn't just about satisfying hunger, but pleasing the palette, and people are so unaware of how completely it controls their lives that they become willing puppets to those cravings. Slavery can come from within, as well as from without."

But Kaufman enjoyed food, liked cooking, and after leaving The Dwelling, he'd become a self-taught chef. However, he followed recipes like a math equation - never varying, never experimenting. But there was so much he hadn't tried, so many exotic flavors he'd never savored, and with Seibu leading the way, the empty grocery store was too tempting to resist.

Giving in to his desires, Kaufman jumped up on the cart and raced it through the aisle, snatching up spicy Mexican candies, strange dried Asian delicacies, dark European chocolates, and colorful South American fruit drinks. This particular grocery store had an extensive range of imported goods, as well as the traditional, homegrown snacks and beverages, and soon his cart was overflowing.

A kid at Christmas must feel like this, Kaufman thought - never having celebrated any holiday.

He didn't know which present to open first.

But among all the gems, one prize stood out: a brightly wrapped candy bar - a caramel and nugget concoction crafted by old-world confectioners.

Carefully opening the wrapping, Kaufman peeled away the gold foil and was awash in rich nut and cocoa aromas.

Opening wide, Kaufman took a huge bite—

—and almost gagged.

Coughing and spitting, Kaufman thought the candy bar must be moldy or have spoiled. Eventually, he realized that the chocolate wasn't rancid but intensely sweet, sweeter, and chocolatier than anything he'd ever experienced before.

The explosion of flavors was overwhelming; the candy bar was sensational, bordering on a religious experience. It was as if his taste buds had been magnified; each ingredient could be discerned from the others but completely relished as a unifying whole.

It was incredible; he'd never experienced food so thoroughly and wondered if this was some freak side effect of the Decoy Madness. The thought didn't give him pause, though, as he ripped into new delights. Everything was beyond wonderful. Flavors were bolder, nuances were more subtle, complementing seasonings popped. Eating had suddenly become euphoric, and Kaufman might have gone on trying everything in the store, not just what was in his basket, except for the explosion.

Outside, a distant boom rumbled.

Inside, all the lights blinked out.

Kaufman shot to his feet.

The store was engulfed in darkness, and Seibu howled.

Stumbling in the gloom, Kaufman located the shotgun and ran. Seibu followed at his heels, ululating.

Outside, the day was bright and clear, which ruled out the sound being thunder. Scanning the skyline, Kaufman noticed a wisp of smoke a few blocks away, suggesting that the source of the detonation was NNRP.

Standing on the bumper of the Humvee, he could just make out Northern Nevada Rural Power's main transformer on fire.

Had the electric company been sabotaged? Was this the work of some NNRP employee ravaged by the Decoy madness? Or was his father's new deranged disciple - the wannabe leader of Dominism - responsible?

Whatever the case - even if it had been a natural mechanical failure - Kaufman didn't plan to investigate. There was nothing he could do. He was no electrician.

He was, however, a citizen of the information age, and the lifeblood of modern society was electricity. Turn off the power, and existence in the twenty-first century stopped. People were dependent on digital information and electronic gadgetry; life was automated, and civilization today was far more fragile than its historical ancestors of just a hundred years ago. Technological advancements were growing exponentially, but Kaufman didn't feel like humanity's moral responsibility was keeping up.

Just because something could be done didn't always mean it should be, and Kaufman was certain that whatever had caused the Decoy Madness would be the perfect case-in-point.

With the loss of electricity, finding that truth was now going to be both easier and harder.

NewLife would be wide open. Without juice, there would be no security system to bypass, no need to worry about setting off alarms or breaking through electronic locks. Yet it also meant no retrieval of electronic data. His search of the genetic engineering building would be limited to hard copy documents only, and with the day waning, it was time to make use of the remaining light.

"Come on, Seibu, lunch is over."

. . .

The name NewLife was meant to invoke feelings of hope, prosperity, and energy, but underneath its soft exterior was a fully-functioning, state-of-the-art biological lab. It was one of the world's foremost scientific facilities, but since the facility worked closely with the military - specifically Shafter Army Base, only ten miles away - being innocuous had become their forte.

NewLife's architectural style was inviting, the landscape lush, which was all by design. Millions had been spent on PR for the express purpose of reducing fears the general public had about genetic engineering and making the NewLife industrial compound more approachable.

It was a trend the world over. For Kaufman, the style came across like a New Age religion, and the high fences, security cameras, and guard booths protecting lush gardens, sleek open-air galleries, and iPod-chic designed buildings, made the pseudo-church feel all the more cultish.

Today though, NewLife didn't just seem duplicitous, but reprehensible.

Approaching the main building, Kaufman toted the Benelli while Seibu dragged a long crowbar. He wondered if lead or steel would protect them inside, for surely NewLife not only housed the source of the Decoy Madness, but many other abominations.

As they pushed through the rotating front doors, red emergency lights threw up amber fountains at regular intervals. It made sense that a facility working with fragile genetic materials would have its own backup power, and Kaufman was glad not to have to wander the halls in darkness with only a flashlight and his courage.

At the main reception desk, he was also relieved to see no dead bodies or traces of odd behavior. He wanted to deal with as little death and psychosis as possible; he'd seen enough of both to last a lifetime.

Rummaging through a directory at the receiving desk, Kaufman decided to focus his search on senior-level offices, where classified reports and restricted documents would most likely be. The most promising, and the top of his list, was the suite of the Advanced Programs Director and Special Projects Leader - one, H. Cunningham, Ph.D., Sc.D.

Unfortunately, Dr. Cunningham's office was on the upper level of a vast research lab, which meant taking the stairs up five floors and exposing themselves to whatever unseen microbes might be floating around. Although they appeared immune to what had already been released, Kaufman didn't plan on nosing around any sites with biohazard warnings. He did, however, worry about Seibu. Things could quickly get out of hand if the young orangutan got spooked. What would happen if they came across tainted survivors in the full grip of the Decoy Madness? Or worse, the mock messiah, the thinner of herds?

Kaufman preferred not to dwell on those possibilities.

"Alright, let's keep moving," he said, heading for stairwell.

Reaching their destination without incident, Kaufman was glad that his worries hadn't materialized, and the laboratory adjacent to Dr. Cunningham's office wasn't as ominous as he'd had imagined either. There were no airlock doors or rubber suits, no refrigerators housing Ebola or any other dangerous and exotic pathogens. The most threatening items in the spacious and clinical area was a collection of large microscopes that resembled giant pressure cookers topped with binoculars, some test tubes, and a bunch of Petri dishes. Most work appeared to be done on huge computers sitting on top of control panels that had more buttons and knobs than a stealth bomber. Presently all the computer screens were blank, but Kaufman had no trouble picturing the room full of doctors seeking to identify and manipulate gene sequences. Perhaps not as evil as comic book geneticists creating super villains, but no Norman Rockwell physicians either.

Entering the corner suite of Dr. Cunningham was like stepping into a dry sauna. The room didn't have any backup lights, but several large windows were trapping in plenty of the late afternoon sun. The air was so thick and stagnant it could have bred mosquitoes the size of Volkswagens.

Kaufman took in his surroundings.

Contemporary steel and white leather furniture decorated the space, presenting a professional demeanor while maintaining a level of comfort. Kaufman would have bet that it had all been ordered directly out of an IKEA catalog.

There weren't many personal touches, but in the center of a collection of degrees and awards on one wall was a framed portrait of Albert Einstein sticking out his tongue.

Apparently, Dr. Cunningham hung the picture as a reminder to not take himself too seriously.

Kaufman disapproved of the notion. Maturity should be guiding the advanced-programs director, not some schoolboy creed of reckless experimentation. Kaufman was forming a strong dislike for this Dr. Cunningham, and although he tried never to prejudge anyone, he felt certain that the large filing cabinet in the corner would hold damning evidence of the man's imprudence.

More of a safe than a flimsy tin filing cabinet, the armored armoire was not going to be easy to get into. Half-inch steel doors surely secured folders full of incriminating documents; however, the spacing was so precise that there was no gap in which to gain leverage with the crowbar.

"I could try the shotgun, but that might freak you out," said Kaufman to Seibu, who sat tongue out, panting in the stifling room.

Kaufman was also worried that the shotgun pellets would shred whatever contents were inside the filing cabinet. What he needed was an industrial drill, one that could bore through the lock - either that or the jaws of life. And since he had neither, Kaufman searched the room for anything that might be useful.

His eyes didn't find anything, but his mind turned to an emergency fire ax he'd seen in the stairwell.

Retrieving the ax, Kaufman stood in front of the miniature bank vault, feeling unkempt and desperate. He was no stranger to swinging this type of tool. Over the years, he'd chopped down and uprooted more stumps and boulders than he could remember. This would be no different. Entrance might not be easy, but at least now, it would be possible.

Taking aim, he reached back and swung hard.

The pick end stuck the steel door with a loud *gong* and bounced off. Kaufman had just enough time to duck as the blade came rushing back at him.

"Glad that worked," he said, irritated with himself for being so dim-witted. Ripping open one of the nearby couch cushions, he wrapped it around the curved blade and then secured the foam in place with some tape from the desk. His new sheath looked like a marshmallow wrapped in a rubber band. The job was sloppy and crude, but at least it would save him from decapitating himself.

With the guard in place, Kaufman set to work in earnest. After five minutes of steady work, he wiped a forearm over his brow. It came away dry, rather than slick with sweat. After ten minutes, he ought to have been drenched - especially in this greenhouse of a room. But no moisture beaded his forehead nor darkened his shirt.

The phenomenon was unnatural, as strange and unexplainable as his weight loss and newly developed taste buds. He didn't break his rhythm to contemplate just how bizarre, for the front of the filing cabinet was beginning to look like the surface of the moon, and one deep crater was close to splitting open.

Kaufman worked at the crack until the gash was big enough to get the crowbar in. After that, it was only a matter of minutes before he twisted the lock out of place, and he had access to the cabinet's confidential contents.

Inside were rows of external hard drives, neatly arranged and labeled, as well as two industrial laptops. But likely everything would be encrypted, at the very least password-protected. Kaufman set those aside as a last resort.

Below the rows of digital data were three deep drawers full of paper documents.

The carbon copies took up half the cabinet spaces but represented only a tiny fraction of all the information stored in this vestibule. However, the tradeoff was that the high-density storage capacity of digital media required special equipment to access that information, whereas the paper files needed nothing more than the eye to read.

He fingered through the folders; most seemed to be highly detailed technical biochemical reports, but after searching for a few minutes, Kaufman found a group of records that looked promising. The contents appeared to list the different projects being run at NewLife.

"Jackpot!" said Kaufman, selecting a few of the more interesting ones. Loading his arms, he went to the window to look over what he'd uncovered.

Sitting, he glanced over at Seibu who looked as hot and miserable as he should have been, but for some reason wasn't. The orangutan turned to him and pointed outside.

"We'll go in a bit," said Kaufman, interpreting the gesture as Seibu's desire to leave.

Still pointing, Seibu made a flicking motion that resembled someone brushing lint off a shoulder. Kaufman didn't understand what this meant, so he waved his hand back in the same manner.

Frowning, Seibu huffed and stood. He walked to the nearest window, and all at once, it hit Kaufman. Seibu had been asking him to open the window, yet before he could move, his furry friend had released the lock himself, and clean, dry air blew in.

A broad, toothy grin spread across Seibu's face, and despite his recent strenuous labor and the heat of the room, a chill rose up Kaufman's spine.

Just like last night with the chair used as a doorjamb or this morning with the seatbelt, Seibu was displaying knowledge that he shouldn't have possessed. Kaufman didn't doubt an orangutan could be trained to do these things, or even imitate actions they'd seen demonstrated before, but Seibu had never had access to chairs or doors or windows in his enclosure. He had probably never even seen any of those items in his entire life before today.

Once again, the ramifications of Seibu's transformation were somehow more troubling than all the horrors Kaufman had witnessed so far, and he wondered if he really wanted to know the source of the paradox that mangled jackrabbits, wiped out whole cities, and created ultra-intelligent apes.

Doubt lingered for a moment, then passed and was forgotten as quickly as a cool breeze on a scorching hot summer afternoon. He'd never learned to master his curiosity, but after reading the papers in his hands, it would be the one time in his life that he wished he'd taken to his father's teachings.

Packaged in a brown military envelope and marked classified, the report was as thick and ominous as a suitcase filled with explosives.

Entitled Project Osiris, the reading was laborious. So much of it was intensely technical and filled with such specialized language that Kaufman could comprehend only the beginning and end of sentences. However, in between phrases and words like "RNA bridging," "exponentially increasing cell growth," "metabolic dormancy," "species genomes," "enriched molecules," "mutations," and "self-regenerating genes," he was able to distill that NewLife's flagship project had something to do with manipulating DNA; and after another half-hour of slogging through the document, he came across a paragraph that made his mouth go dry.

He reread the section five times.

The ramifications seem absurd, a B-budget movie script at best. The segment made reference to cells, but they weren't bacterial.

Kaufman shut his eyes.

Not fungal or plant, or animal.

He examined the report again. It hadn't changed.

Not human cells either.

The two words that were causing his heart to race seemed to jump off the page.

ET cells.

Here was the answer to the Decoy Madness.

Calloused hands rubbed over bristly stubble, rubbed as if they could push back time and erase the information in the report.

At the heart of NewLife's top-secret venture with the military, they'd been experimenting with extraterrestrial cells.

Not a believer in the tabloid little green men himself, Kaufman nevertheless felt it was possible, probable even, that life wasn't solely limited to planet Earth. Now here, not only had the government apparently discovered some type of microbial space life but were splicing human DNA with it!

This was H.G Wells *The Island of Doctor Moreau* on an interstellar level. The government - along with these civilian scientists - weren't just satisfied with playing god, they were mixing chimera cocktails, throwing into the blender genetic materials from vastly differently corners of the universe to see what would come out.

And what they got, even a child could have predicted.

A square peg doesn't fit in a round hole. Dogs don't breed with cats, elephants aren't born with wings, and horses wouldn't swim underwater if they mated with dolphins because, in all those scenarios, the embryo would be rejected by the host.

Nature regulates very precisely what genetic information can combine with other genetic information, and it was glaringly obvious that the human subjects in Decoy not only rejected these extraterrestrial cells but had utterly self-destructed when subjected to them. There was a city full of empty houses and empty streets, leading to a mountain of corpses just outside of town that testified to that.

Even the animal life hadn't been receptive. The ones that hadn't been instantly killed went insane or desired death - as in the case of jackrabbits and the German Shepherd.

Thinking of those pitiable creatures made Kaufman ill, made him stand with disgust. The thick Osiris report sloughed to the ground.

The memory itself was not why Kaufman felt ill, but because he realized that, although the ratio of failure to success was well over 99.99%, there had been survivors.

More than survivors.

He and Seibu were the repugnant silver lining of the abhorrent experiment.

Clearly, the orangutan's intelligence was a singular event, something not found in earthly evolution. And even his own body had somehow accepted these foreign microbes, for nothing else short of a miracle could explain the rapid healing of his broken collar bone and new physique.

And this morning, at the grocery store, his taste buds had experience food on a level beyond human design.

He'd changed, was changing, and the question he didn't want to face now was, how much longer before he lost his identity? Wasn't just a social oddity, but a physical one?

Outside, a loud gunshot cracked.

Kaufman was slow to react to it, slow to recognize the significance that it represented.

But the second blast brought him fully out of his stupor.

Someone was alive out there…alive, but in what condition? Would they even be classified as human anymore? If the Decoy Madness had struck deep - if this genetic alteration hadn't enhanced, but reduced this individual to a mindless pod person that might even now not be shooting in defense, but firing off rounds at anything that sparkled - would he want to meet them? Could this gunman even be the reason behind the explosion that knocked out the power? Could it be the mock messiah trying to draw him out?

156

Yet even with those possibilities, Kaufman hesitated only for an instant. The risk be damned. He had never felt more alone, more desperate for human companionship - not even as a child. He wanted a sympathetic ear, needed an understanding soul. The information in the Osiris report was a burden too heavy to bear alone.

Looking out the window, he could see no shooter, but the third crack of gunfire didn't seem very far away. Collecting the Benelli and the military report on ET cells, Kaufman raced back through NewLife with Seibu at his heels.

Somewhere beyond what he could see from the front door, the gunman was still firing off rounds, although at a more irregular speed.

Jumping in the Humvee, Kaufman twisted the key, and the diesel engine roared to life.

Exiting the parking lot, tires squealed as Kaufman floored the accelerator. He stuck his head out the window, trying to gauge the direction from which the gunshots were coming. Racing down the road at more than fifty miles per hour, he had no chance of stopping when, three coyotes ran out in front of him.

The Humvee plowed through the upright dogs and barely shuddered as their frail bodies exploded against the grill.

Kaufman hit the brakes far too late, and the massive SUV skidded to a stop, leaving black and red tread marks fishtailing along the asphalt.

Gasping hard, Kaufman got out.

Two of the coyotes were unrecognizable – a third lay dying, twitching in a growing pool of blood.

Down the street from which the mutts had come boomed the crack of another gunshot. Spinning in the direction of the sound, Kaufman could see a car in the distance. Leaving the Humvee without closing the door, he headed for the shooter on foot.

As he ran, the distinctive black and white of a patrol car came into view. The sight caused Kaufman to sprint faster.

Donald Graeci stood over a downed coyote. He put another bullet in the dying animal, then spat on the corpse.

Elated, with legs pumping and hands waving, Kaufman shouted at his friend. Donald turned.

His eyes went wide, and, as if seeing an approaching threat, he raised the pistol.

"Don't move!" he yelled.

Kaufman staggered to a halt, and Donald aimed right at his head.

CHAPTER 15

"Wait," screamed Kaufman, arms outstretched, feet backpedaling.

"Don't move!" demanded Sgt. Graeci.

"Donald wait, it's—"

"I. Said. Freeze."

Kaufman slowed but didn't stop, his hands still out in a defensive position.

Donald's face was red and sweaty, and a vein pulsed rhythmically in his forehead.

"Stop or die!" he shouted, finger tightening on the trigger.

Kaufman halted and stared down the barrel of the Glock.

Had he come all this way - survived his own suicide and discovered the truth of the government's insane science experiment - only to be gunned down by his quasi-friend? Donald looked more than prepared to kill. His eyes were cold and hard, and even a little giddy, but they also weren't focused on Kaufman.

Behind him, Seibu hurried to catch up.

Although not built for speed, Seibu was moving quickly, flinging himself forward with his long arms.

Taking a quick step forward, Donald pushed Kaufman aside and raised his gun. Seibu tumbled to a stop, but not before Donald fired.

The gun boomed as loud as a cannon.

His aim was true, and the bullet would have ripped through Seibu, except at the last second, Kaufman lunged forward and knocked the shot wide.

Whirling around Donald roared, rage transforming his features into a demonic mask.

"Woe be it to the heathen that stands in the way of my servant, sayeth the Lord, for I have given him power to crush the head of the serpent and smite his followers!"

Kaufman didn't know if that was actual scripture, as Donald didn't state the reference as he habitually did, but if his friend was so far gone as to see himself as a warrior of God or some kind of avenging angel, then it would have been safer staying with the pathogens at NewLife. Although invisible, at least those microscopic killers were straightforward, whereas Donald was pumped full of otherworldly DNA and was about as predictable as quantum mechanics.

"It's alright, Donald," said Kaufman stepping in front of and shielding Seibu. "Seibu's no threat. He's not crazy like the dogs. He even saved my life."

Kaufman hoped the last bit of info would intrigue Donald, open up a dialogue, or at the least give him pause. However, instead of being pacified by that noble news, Donald grew angrier.

"That *thing*," he said, jabbing the gun at Seibu, "will always be a threat as long as there are men that delude themselves into believing that we somehow evolved from such creatures.

"The Holy Word states: God created man in his own image, Genesis 1:26. But the teachings of men seek to reduce us. Men would have us believe we are nothing more than an accident, a cosmic fart - the Big Band indeed!"

Donald huffed, and his nostrils flared. Beads of sweat streamed down his forehead; yet Kaufman was at a loss about how to respond. Donald's logic - his faith - was as strange to Kaufman as any of the things he'd seen in the last day and a half - maybe not as horrific, but just as incomprehensible.

Kaufman decided it was better to let the preacher finish his sermon, better to be a silent congregation than an objecting one.

"You even named it!" Donald spat.

"I should shoot it as a favor to you, Kaufman," he said, his eyes fixating on Seibu's cringing form. "I should shoot it to help you see."

The stare narrowed, intensified, and disgust grew.

"I should shoot it to cleanse the darkened human mind. I should shoot it just because."

This was bad. Donald was working himself up, convincing himself to pull the trigger. Kaufman had to say something. Silence would no longer avoid a confrontation.

"Please, Donald, put the gun down. It's okay. Seibu…I mean the orangutan, he isn't going to hurt us. I promise."

But the sergeant wasn't buying it, didn't even seemed to have heard - talked right over him.

"I should shoot it. I should. I should shoot it, shoot it. I should shoot it."

Donald drew a bead on Seibu, and Kaufman might as well have been transparent glass; Donald was entirely fixated on destroying the offense before him that he didn't see anything else.

"We're all alive for some reason," said Kaufman, trying an appeal to Donald's piousness. "Everyone else was taken, but we were spared - even Seibu. God must have some plan for us. Remember, the Lord said: For as the heavens are higher than the earth, so are my ways higher than your ways, and my thoughts than your thoughts."

Kaufman didn't remember the reference, or whether the scripture was from the Old or the New Testament, but he was aware of the risk. He was fighting fire with fire, except Donald was a roaring inferno ready to consume, and his own ammunition was a flickering flame. But something must have gotten through.

Donald's head snapped up.

"Do you know what's happened?" he asked skeptically, almost accusingly, advancing on Kaufman and searching his face like CIA agent waiting for a lie.

Leaning back, spooked by the abrupt change in focus, Kaufman stammered, "I...I think so."

Donald's sweaty face suddenly split into a jack-o'-lantern grin, and when he spoke, his voice was breathy and fervent.

"Praise God, brother!" he said, extending a hand.

Kaufman shook it.

It was moist and clammy and...confusing.

Was the recital of one scripture enough to convince Donald that he was a believer? Kaufman expected a much harder sell, especially when seconds ago his pontifical friend had been fixated on shooting Seibu, had been utterly obsessed, and now he was pumping hands like a politician at a fundraising convention.

"I have been praying for your soul these many years, and the good Lord has finally answered. When did you find out?"

Kaufman took a step back, tried to regroup.

"Uh...just now, at NewLife."

Donald's smile faded. "That building and everything it stands for is an abomination. It's one of the follies that brought us here today."

"It's not *one* of the reasons," said Kaufman, shaking his head, his mind going back to the report on recombinant DNA. "It's *the* reason."

"No," Donald disagreed, wiping the sweat from his brow and holstering his sidearm. Kaufman watched, relieved to see the weapon put away.

Did Donald really know what had happened? The military might have fed the local authorities scraps of information on what they were up to, but they wouldn't have told them everything. Indeed, it was more likely that whatever Shafter had divulged was a total fabrication, a dog-and-pony show meant to misdirect and hold back public inquiry.

There was no way Donald knew the real truth, but he was wholly self-assured.

"No, mankind has been heading down this dark road since Cain slew Abel, since Adam's transgression. History has shown us that we love darkness more than light, that we are lovers of pleasure rather than God. We cannot abide truth but are seduced by corrupt governments and silver-tongued corporations, led so easily by diverse lusts and told, by the harlot Babylon, that we deserve everything, shouldn't have to work for anything, have responsibility for nothing. And so, just as in the time of Noah when God flooded the earth to purge it of wickedness, so too now has the chaff been shifted from the wheat.

"For behold!" said Donald, extended both arms wide. "The day cometh, that the earth shall burn as an oven; and the proud, yea, and all that do wickedly, shall be stubble, Malachi 4:1. But the day of the Lord will come as a thief in the night, 2nd Peter 3:10. And I looked, and behold a pale horse: and his name that sat upon him was Death, and Hell followed him, Revelation 5:8."

Revelation? The apocalypse?

In all Kaufman's speculation, the end of days had never occurred to him; however, it made perfect sense that someone religious like Donald would see scripture fulfilled in the face of such chaos. Besides, was the second coming of Christ any more farfetched than a government-bankrolled alien invasion - albeit on a molecular level? In many respects, the apocalypse was easier to swallow than Project Osiris, and in either case, the result was the same: human's arrogance had brought down destruction upon its own head.

"Let there be no mistake, this is the beginning of the end," said Greasy in full stride now, a man in his element - a preacher in the midst of a prophecy. "Judgment Day has arrived!"

The soundless and desolate street didn't contradict him – seemed, in fact, to add authority to what he said.

"Preceding the Lord's return, the Holy Word words tell of plagues, pestilence, famine, and disease such as the world has never before seen; of scourges, tribulations, calamities, and disasters without parallel; of strife, wars, rumors of wars, blood, carnage and desolation which overshadows anything in ages past; of evil, iniquity, wickedness, turmoil, rapine, murder, crime, and commotion among men almost beyond comprehension.

"For there shall be great tribulations, such as was not since the beginning of the world to this time, nor ever shall be, Matthew 24:21. Brother," said Greasy, leaning forward on the hood of the car, as if it was a pulpit, hands fisted, "you might have recognized what has occurred, but it is not enough. You must accept Christ and be baptized, or elsewise live in fear for your immortal soul. The time to choose is now. What say you? Do you accept Jesus as your Lord and Savior?"

Kaufman opened his mouth to speak, but nothing came out. He needed to be careful here. It would be too easy to say the wrong thing and give offense without meaning to. He certainly didn't believe as Donald did, although he hadn't come to terms with the NewLife report either. What he wanted was to change the subject, go somewhere safe where he could think, and let his unemotional Sherlock brain mull everything over for a while.

Looking around for a distraction, Kaufman's eyes landed on two children in the backseat of the patrol car. Amidst all the gun-waving and threats, he hadn't noticed them. There was a little girl in pigtails and a boy in a Cub Scout uniform.

"Who are the kids?" asked Kaufman, genuinely interested, and not just trying to avoid answering Donald's question.

"Lost lambs; scared, and in need of a shepherd."

"But where did you find them?" pressed Kaufman, wanting more information, excited by the fact that there were other survivors.

"I was directed to them, told to protect them."

Donald's cryptic response abruptly checked Kaufman's enthusiasm. He was about to ask, "told by whom?" when a snarling scream split the air.

This was not the same shrill shriek of the jackrabbits from earlier, but the unmistakable banshee cry of a mountain lion.

Everyone turned to the nearby hills and the sound of the scream.

The cat was close, and although they were typically long-range stalkers, this feline hadn't been far enough away to be out of reach of Shafter and NewLife's altering ET cells.

Kaufman felt Seibu's grip tighten on his legs, and amid a half dozen dead coyotes, it didn't take much imagination to realize that this bone-crunching cougar was no longer a bashful puss.

In the evening light, the chilling growl came again sharp and homicidal.

"We should get out of here," suggested Kaufman, but Donald didn't respond. His eyes were wide and jittery. Not from fear of a possible encounter, but the anticipation of it.

"Donald?" Kaufman inquired cautiously.

He had never been on a battlefield, was not a soldier, and so had never seen what others described as blood lust, but Kaufman was convinced - as Donald hungrily licked his lips - that his Bible-thumping friend was in the grips of such. Donald didn't just want to shoot the animal; he wanted to hunt it down and massacre it.

No way was Kaufman going to reach out and touch his friend. Donald was as tense and focused on the surrounding mountains as an ambushing crocodile on the shore of a river. So instead, he spoke more forcefully and firmly.

"Donald!"

"Yes," said Graeci, his eyes still fixated on the distant peaks, his index finger caressing the trigger of his gun. "You're right. We should find someplace to retire for the evening."

"Okay, good, how about my nursery? I have a few generators there, and we could rig up some work lights."

Finally tearing his gaze away, Donald nodded once, sharply. The gesture seemed more for himself than to confirm Kaufman's suggestions.

"Right that would be…sensible," he said, retrieving his aviator sunglasses from his breast pocket. "Lead the way."

Kaufman took Seibu by the hand and led them back towards the Humvee. The cougar's scream filled the air once more, and the walk back seemed very exposed, and to take forever.

Reaching the SUV, Kaufman swore he would never again leave his gun behind. Bullets couldn't cure the Decoy Madness, but at least they would give him a chance to survive it.

• • •

On the road, the hum of rubber on asphalt was hypnotic. The low sun turned the sky pink and gave the dead landscape a healthy glow. Long shadows stretched out towards the distant horizon, and as Kaufman drove, he felt at ease for the first time since reading the NewLife report. The thought of his nursery and greenhouses brought him as much tranquility as anything in life. The nursery was not merely a livelihood, but his calling, his asylum, for the plants not only needed him, they also never judged him.

When he was close enough to see the onetime frontier general store from a distance, Kaufman slowed his approach. It was really nothing more than a large glorified barn, but it had always suited him, and it would now be ideal for offering protection with its narrow porch and small front-facing windows.

The setting sun bathed the wood-shingled roof an apricot orange, but even from afar, Kaufman had no trouble reading the tall sign that ran along the rooftop: Decoy Landscaping and Nursery.

He'd always felt the name wasn't very creative, unlike the names his father chose, which were often cryptic and mocking.

Indeed, his own name was a joke.

Back in the 1930s, a successful businessman named Edgar J. Kaufmann Sr. had commissioned Franklin Lloyd Wright to build a house for him, and thus Fallingwater was born.

The residence was one of the Great American Architect's most famous buildings, and Göttlich saw Mr. Wright and his architectural style - that of harmonizing nature and architecture - as his nemesis, or at the very least, his polar opposite. So as a wry jib, he picked the name Kaufman for his son.

The irony was that Kaufman much preferred Wright's work to his father's, and perhaps Göttlich had intended that too to be part of the jest. It wouldn't have surprised Kaufman if that had been the case. He was well aware of how deep his father's influence had and still was, directing the course of his life. He might live to be a hundred and never succeed at getting out of its shadow.

Pulling up in front of the store, both Kaufman and Donald stopped at the curb well away from the nursery. There was an unspoken understanding between them that they needed to be able to see whatever might approach during the night - be that coyote, cougar, or other.

Standing with the driver's door wide open, Donald scanned the surrounding buildings - one hand on his holster.

After deciding there was no threat, he opened the rear door and let the children out.

Kaufman had not seen them closely back on the country road. Both had blond hair, although the boy's was much darker, and both looked scared, even as they wore brave faces.

The children's resilience and fortitude were impressive. Most kids in their position would be inconsolable messes, and Kaufman was glad of their resolve. He would have understood intellectually if they had been sniveling and catatonic under such circumstances; however, he didn't possess the emotional tools it would have required to console them.

No, these children were special.

The little girl especially had enormous presence. Kaufman had only ever met one other individual with similar poise and magnetism: his father. However, where Göttlich exuded power and intimidation, this small girl engendered courage and hope. And Kaufman found himself drawn to her.

As he approached, the girl waved.

"Hi, I'm Jessica. What's your name?"

Kaufman smiled and felt none of his usual social awkwardness. Indeed, he felt strangely serene.

"My name's Kaufman," he said, offering her a handshake.

Jessica beamed as she shook.

"Is this your house?" she asked, staring at the nursery in wonder.

Kaufman laughed. Had he ever been so innocent? No, he'd never been allowed to, and with that thought came the intense desire to protect this girl, to make sure nothing happened to her or her brother. It was now no longer enough to just survive.

"Nope, I don't live here, this is where I work. But we're going to stay here tonight because it'll be safe. Okay?"

Jessica nodded, and Kaufman felt his chest tighten at her utter faith in him.

Turning to Donald, he said, "I'll go around back and get a generator."

Donald nodded and took off his sunglasses.

"Do a sweep of the perimeter while you're at it. I'll secure the front entrance."

Kaufman opened his mouth to respond, then thought better of it. Donald might be a used car salesman for God by choice, but he was also a trained officer of the law. Kaufman hoped that meant Donald wasn't just bossing him around to stroke his ego but was following some tried and true procedures.

As he turned to leave, Jessica shrieked; and even though the squeal wasn't filled with terror but rather one of surprise and glee, Kaufman still whirled around expecting to see her being run down by some mutant mountain lion.

Standing in front of the two children, Seibu had one hand draped comically over his head. He seemed fascinated by these miniature humans, and the kids were equally enamored.

Donald, on the other hand, was less delighted.

Clenching his jaw, the cords in his neck bulged. Any more pressure and Kaufman could imagine those pearly whites shattering, popping like fluorescent light bulbs in a trash compactor. But before Donald hurt himself, Kaufman hurried Seibu away.

Feeling Donald's icy stare on their backs, Kaufman looked down at his furry friend.

"In case you haven't noticed, not everyone thinks you're irresistibly cute."

Seibu scowled and stuck out his tongue. Kaufman chuckled and returned the gesture. Seibu's eyes widened, and he pushed out his pink tongue even further. Not to be outdone, Kaufman blew, making a loud wet farting sound, and put his thumb to his nose, wiggling his fingers.

Seibu hooted and clapped. Kaufman had never blown anyone a raspberry before. It felt awkward, giddy, and...normal.

Giving Seibu a stiff little bow, he said, "Seriously, though, you better steer clear of Donald for a while."

Seibu's soft brown eyes looked up, and he raised his arms as a sign that he wanted to be carried. Kaufman picked him up, and Seibu buried his head into his shoulder. Kaufman felt the little guy understood, even without his enhanced intelligence. Donald was someone to avoid.

As they walked the property line, they passed half a dozen plastic-covered greenhouses. Unlike in cooler climates, where such structures were used to focus light and keep plants warm, here in the desert, their primary purpose was to minimize direct sunlight and control evaporation. Seedlings in Nevada often needed to be hardened and acclimatized to the blistering desert sun before being introduced directly to its wilting rays. These accordion-style greenhouses were ideal for such protection.

As they passed an area of more mature outdoor vegetation, Seibu let his long fingers brush over a stubby shrub. There were no giant trees here, no vine-covered canopy to swing and frolic from, only prickly pines and other knobby foliage which were as utterly foreign to an orangutan as any flora that a distant galaxy might produce.

Still, surrounded by plants - even of a temperate zone rather than tropical - Seibu seemed more at home than at any time since leaving his jungle enclosure.

Kaufman intended to keep it that way.

He and the other survivors of Project Osiris might be held against their will under the guise of quarantine, but there would be no pretense about Seibu's fate.

Reaching the generator, Kaufman sat Seibu atop it. He wheeled it out from behind a pile of fertilizer, and as they made their way back, the portable engine bucked and bounced along the uneven ground. Seibu grinned and let his arms wave above his head. He clapped and clacked his teeth delightedly, and Kaufman swore to himself that no scalpel would ever touch a hair on his friend's head. If he somehow made it out of this mess, he'd go underground, leave the country, and get Seibu out of this arid hellhole.

Kaufman set the old generator well away from the main building - as it was deafeningly loud - and ran a long extension cord inside the building to a tripod of work lights. As he turned them on, deep shadows appeared on the polished wood floor.

Donald had already laid out the sleeping bags from the Humvee, and the group sat down on their thin beds to pick at their dinners. MREs made for a silent meal, but in between bites, the children stole avid glances at Seibu.

Having twisted a few large, leafy house ferns into a nest, Seibu lay flat on his stomach and was flipping through a gardening book. He seemed for all the world to be comprehending the drawings that demonstrated tips on how to trim and shape bushes into animal sculptures.

"Is he reading?" asked Jessica excitedly.

"Of course not," Donald snapped. "He's just a stupid monkey."

The girl looked down at her feet as an uncomfortable silence settled over the room.

"Actually, he's not a monkey; he's a great ape," explained Kaufman, trying to ease Donald's rebuke. "Great apes are much smarter than monkeys, and Seibu might recognize the photos for what they represent, but he doesn't know how to read."

"Could you teach him?" inquired Jessica.

Kaufman was about to say no but hesitated. "Well, some gorillas, chimpanzees, and orangutans have been taught sign language, and Seibu is special…"

Jessica interrupted. "Not special, just changed."

Kaufman regarded the girl and she matched his gaze. Did she know something? He would have to talk with her away from Donald later.

"Yes, well, whatever the case, I doubt he could ever learn a written language."

Jessica looked at Seibu and frowned as if she wasn't so sure. After a moment, she turned back to Kaufman.

"Why do you call him Seibu? I thought his name was Poo-Poo." Kaufman smiled and was again struck by the girl's guilelessness and aplomb. She made it easy for him to reveal himself.

"The world knows him as Pohon Sepupu, but as a teenager, I used to go visit the orangutans almost every day. After a while, they became like a family to me, so I gave them secret nicknames."

Donald scoffed a sharp snort that made Kaufman's ears burn. Oddly, he smiled at the reaction. Two days ago, he wouldn't have even registered it as an insult; now the embarrassment made him strangely happy.

"Definitely not your typical family, but more than I had growing up. Anyway, the big male Merah Gunung - Red Mountain - seemed too appropriate to change, but the older female Tua, I called Bibi, which means Aunt, and Seibu's mom was Pemalu Ibu or Shy Mother, and Pohon Sepupu became Seibu or Half Brother."

Hearing his name, Seibu looked up from his book and gave Kaufman a huge gummy equine grin. Jessica giggled.

"I know it's silly, but the name stuck, so that's why I call him Seibu."

Seibu clacked his teeth together in a grin.

Jessica looked at the orangutan thoughtfully, then back at Kaufman.

"It's not silly. He is your *seibu*," she said.

Kaufman blinked. "Well, technically… I mean we are both primates—"

"No!" Donald rumbled. Then pleadingly, "No, Jessica, sweetheart, listen to me; man is not related to that beast. We were created in the image of God, made just a little lower than the angels."

"I know that," said Jessica matter-of-factly, as if it was silly to have to tell her.

Donald stood. "And from the mouths of babes shall come words of wisdom, 1 Corinthians 12:8," he whispered.

Kaufman felt it was time to move the conversation along before Donald started sermonizing and Greasy reappeared.

"I plan to go to Shafter tomorrow."

Donald regarded him, and in a grave voice, said, "That is ill-advised."

Kaufman had expected an objection, but Donald's response seemed to indicate he knew more than he was letting on.

"Why not? What's at Shafter?"

"Don't you know? Haven't you figured that out by now?" said Donald leaning forward conspiratorially.

Kaufman found himself leaning forward expectantly, again wondering just what his friend might know.

"Damnation!" he drawled, rising to his feet. "Damnation is what you'll find; for cursed be the man that trusteth in man and maketh flesh his arm and whose heart departeth from the Lord, Jeremiah 17:5."

Kaufman sighed and sagged back in his seat, feeling foolish for being drawn in. "Then what do you suggest we do?"

"We should go to the hospital."

It was Matthew who'd responded. The boy hadn't said a word all night, and everyone turned to look at him. His expression was severe, but before anyone could ask him why an unfamiliar voice spoke from the far side of the room.

"I wouldn't do that if I were you."

Donald and Kaufman shot to their feet.

Standing in the entryway, looking like an earthquake victim who'd just crawled out from the rubble, was a woman in tattered and bloody clothes. She was short, no more than five-two, petite, but not frail.

Donald drew his Glock, and all at once, everyone was shouting.

"Who are you?" he demanded. "Why are you eavesdropping on us?"

"I apologize," said the woman, raising her hands. "I didn't mean to startle you; it's just—I heard your generator and saw the light. My name is Hollie Cunningham."

"*Doctor* Cunningham!?" Kaufman asked, taken aback. "Of NewLife?"

"Sorry, have we met?" she asked, her eyes widening with recognition. "Wait, I know you... I mean, I know who you are," she amended, a slightly embarrassed smile playing at the corner of her lips.

Of course, she knew him, the whole city did. He was the local celebrity, the freaky son of Göttlich Striker: the Droid. But this was the first time he could remember actually being grateful for that notoriety.

Hollie gave him another shy smile which waned into a tight, uneasy line and Kaufman suddenly realized it had less to do with the gossip she'd heard about him, and more to do with the fact that he was staring at her as unblinking as an infatuated schoolboy.

"Yes, well..." he stumbled, clearing his throat and trying to salvage some dignity. "We have food, and you're welcome to join us."

"How do we know we can trust her," Donald grumbled, his scrutinizing gaze full of suspicion.

"I guess we'll just have to have faith," countered Kaufman.

Donald snorted. "That we will." He holstered his gun, and Hollie sighed.

"Thank you."

Jessica and Matthew made a place for her as she sat and peppered her with questions. Hollie artfully handled the children's inquisitions, and Kaufman again found himself admiring her. He hadn't expected Dr. Cunningham to be a woman, especially not such an attractive one, and he wondered how someone like her could be involved in something as insane as Project Osiris; it certainly was a lot easier to reconcile the idea of a doddery old scientist playing god than this charismatic and unpretentious woman.

"But just why shouldn't we go to the hospital?" Matthew challenged.

Hollie weighed her response, noting the boy's anxious anticipation.

"Because I've just come from there and well…it isn't pretty."

"When is a hospital ever pretty?" Matthew asked sagely.

"She means everyone's dead," Donald supplanted.

Matthew darkened at that.

"Is that true? Did you not come across any other survivors?" Kaufman asked.

Hollie hesitated, her eyes darting over to Donald, who was covered in sweat. The quantity of moisture was unsettling, but it was the mercurial sheen that was genuinely alarming.

"Donald, are you alright?" Kaufman inquired.

"Never better," he said, although his glazed eyes told a different story, and the reassuring smile he gave looked slightly manic.

Hollie looked away. "No, no other survivors."

Kaufman nodded. He hadn't expected any other answer, but the confirmation was bitter.

Outside, the shrill scream of the mountain lion rolled over the still night like the tortured cry of a damn soul. The sound made Kaufman shiver, and Matthew and Jessica instinctively drew nearer to Hollie, who put her arms around them.

"Donald, why don't you let me take first watch," Kaufman suggested. "You look like you could use some sleep."

Actually, he looked like he could use an ambulance; a dark V of perspiration now stained the front of his shirt and his hair was damp and matted to his head.

Why was Donald sweating so much? The evening was warm, but not so hot as to be drenched with perspiration. Kaufman himself was dry as bone. Then, thinking about it, Kaufman realized he hadn't broken out into a sweat all day. Not once. Not while running around or biking, not even when he'd broken into the filing cabinet at NewLife. It had been an oven in there, but his body never had so much as flushed.

Was this another side effect of the alien DNA? Perhaps it affected everything it touched differently. Madness and instant death from most, advanced intelligence for Seibu, and rapid health and perfect body temperature regulation for him.

But then what was it doing to Donald?

In the dark night, the mountain lion screeched again. The cry was full of longing, suffering, and confusion - the now all too familiar accent of the remaining creatures in Decoy.

Kaufman watched Hollie watch Donald. The silvery sweat seemed to make her more nervous than Donald's gun, and although she lay down to sleep, she didn't close her eyes for a long, long time.

CHAPTER 16

Coming awake, Kaufman sensed someone standing over him. Without opening his eyes, he knew it was Jessica, just as he was somehow aware of the exact time: 6:17AM.

He hadn't awoken to any sound she'd made but had simply known she was there - the way he would know where his hand was if he'd been blindfolded. Was this clairvoyance? Another trait passed on from cells beyond this world?

It was a strange awareness this knowing, like déjà vu.

He had impressions of the others as well, and not just their proximity but their emotional states; Seibu was next to Jessica, who was upset; Hollie was at ease, sleeping deeply; Donald was further away and although his emotions were vague, like a shadow in fog, what was being emitted was out of balance, wrong somehow.

As Kaufman mentally swept the room, he realized he couldn't detect Matthew. Reaching out, he pushed harder, strained—

Kaufman opened his eyes.

He was exhausted and dizzy.

"Don't try to force it."

Looking at Jessica, Kaufman said, "He's gone."

It wasn't a question, but the girl confirmed it with a nod. In her hands was a folded piece of paper. She held it out to him.

I went to the hospital to find my mom. I'll be back.

-Matthew Sterling

"Damn," Kaufman mumbled. He reread the note.

"Did you see him leave?"

Jessica nodded. "He gave me the note after he wrote it."

Guilt clouded the girl's face, and she added hastily, "I couldn't stop him. His will was too strong."

Kaufman frowned.

That was an odd way to say that her brother had been determined to leave. Shaking his head, Kaufman suddenly felt stupid for not seeing this coming. Matthew had been obsessed with questions about the hospital last night.

He'd been planning his escape.

"When did he leave?"

"When everyone was sleeping."

Kaufman stiffened, "Everyone!?"

Jessica nodded.

Standing, Kaufman strode to the front door, where Donald was supposed to be keeping watch, where he was supposed to be on sentry duty but had apparently fallen asleep and let Matthew just saunter away.

And now the boy was out there.

Alone.

He might already be dead.

Rounding a shelf of tools, Kaufman spotted Donald. He was on his knees - a man in prayer, except instead of his head being bowed, it was flopped back. His mouth hung open and drool spilled out of one corner. Kaufman's breathing quickened as his mind flew back to the woman in the web video, frozen and spaced out.

Slowing his approach, Kaufman motioned for Jessica and Seibu to stay back. He didn't want them too close if Donald came to and started ripping himself apart, didn't want them to become collateral damage.

Stepping up to his vacant-eyed friend, Kaufman might have thought him meditating, except his detachment was too deep. He called Donald's name, waved his hand, and snapped his fingers.

Nothing.

Taking a breath, Kaufman reached out and took Donald by the shoulder. The moment he made contact, it was as if Kaufman had rammed Donald with an electric cattle prod. Snapping back to reality, Donald tumbled backward.

"What's going on?" he demanded, glancing about.

"You were in a trance," said Kaufman, stepping back.

Donald locked eyes with him, and he seemed irrationally irritated.

"No. I was praying."

More like you were hypnotized and completely out of it, thought Kaufman, but he didn't voice his objection, just held out the crumpled note.

"What's this?" asked Donald, as of he'd been handed soiled toilet paper.

Kaufman let him discover the answer for himself.

Eyes swept across the paper.

"Perfect!" Donald smiled. "I was wondering how I was going to get rid of that brat, but it looks like he took care of the matter himself."

"You what?"

The question had no sooner left his lips than Kaufman found himself staring down the barrel of Donald's gun. Again.

"The Lord has commanded, and I must obey. We have delayed too long." Donald looked past Kaufman. "Jessica, it's time to leave."

"No," she replied, straightening, one hand fisted by her side, the other holding tightly to Seibu's.

"I am your tutelary. Do *not* disobey me."

Hearing those words, Jessica's bravado drained away, and she became nothing more than a frightened, shy little girl. Turning to Seibu, she buried her face in his shoulder. The furry orangutan wrapped his long arms protectively around her, and he hissed at Donald.

Kaufman gawked, dumbfounded. He felt like he was in the middle of a play without ever having read the script. He had no clue what was going on, so he improvised, hoping to regain some objectivity.

"Donald look, this is not the Tribulation or the Rapture or any prophesied apocalypse from the Bible. This is all just a government SNAFU. NewLife was involved with the scientist at Shafter to implant extraterrestrial DNA into the human genome, and something went wrong, something got lose, something…" Kaufman stopped.

Soft chuckling filled the room.

"You want me to believe this is all some failed science experiment? The Invasion of the Body Snatchers?"

Donald's smiling laugh suddenly transformed into a sneer. "You want *me* - a man of God - to renounce my faith for some cheap science fiction plot!?"

"I have documents from NewLife," Kaufman asserted, "proof that they were experimenting with alien DNA. Proof—"

"Proof!" Donald exacerbated, "Proof? You have lies, just paper with man's words on it."

Kaufman didn't back down, but Donald was right. The documents themselves proved nothing without physical evidence, and all at once, he felt like a madman trying to convince another madman the other was the insane one. Donald's Bible was no more proof than his report, but he at least had conviction, faith in his theory, which was more than Kaufman had.

"Hollie - Dr. Cunningham, I mean - she was a scientist at NewLife. She'll corroborate this."

"Enough!" Donald bellowed. His eyes flashed in the rising sun like the moonshine disks of a wild animal.

Kaufman stepped back. Human eyes didn't reflect light like that.

This wasn't just Greasy enraged, but Greasy enraged and changed, tainted with celestial genetic material, altered by Project Osiris's fetid ET cells.

Donald's skin no longer just dripped with sweat but had the appearance of polished bronze.

"I *know* what has happened," said Donald, jabbing the gun at Kaufman. "I have seen an angel of the Almighty and have been given my calling; you, on the other hand, Kaufman Striker, are on the left hand of God. You have chosen darkness rather than light, and just like your father, you've decided to reject truth and embrace damnation. *You* who have been given every opportunity - so be it."

Kaufman blinked, his mind spinning.

Donald had never mentioned anything about an angel before…except he had. Kaufman remembered out on the country road, Donald saying that he'd been *told* to find Matthew and Jessica. Whether this vision happened as a result of the Decoy madness was of little importance. If Donald wasn't acting on faith alone, but on some conviction that he was receiving orders from a higher plane, then he was even more unstable than Kaufman had dared to imagine.

There was no way he could let him take Jessica.

"Don—" Kaufman started, but with the speed of a striking praying mantis, Donald lashed out and grabbed him by the throat. He pressed the barrel of the gun hard into Kaufman's temple.

"Your life is not mine to take," he spat, "but I *will* kill you if you try to impede me."

His finger tightened on the trigger. It was a hair's pressure away from blowing Kaufman's brains out.

"Now stand aside, serpent; lie on your belly like the snake you are and put your hands behind your head."

Kaufman obeyed.

Donald drove a knee hard into his back, and he took out a pair of zip ties. The plastic bit deep, broke skin.

Getting up, Donald yanked Kaufman by his shirt collar and dragged him over to a metal display case. With another pair of zip ties, he fastened his prisoner to the heavy rack.

Popping his knuckles and cracking his neck, Donald then advanced on Jessica and Seibu.

Kaufman wheezed and coughed, and watched on helplessly.

Seibu was doing his best to shelter Jess. He hooted, hissed, and bared his teeth, but Donald didn't so much as flinch. He seized Jessica by the arm and wrenched the girl away, sending Seibu sprawling.

Screaming, Jessica flailed as Donald picked her up by the waist and slung her over his shoulder.

As he turned, Jessica stretched out her arms, imploringly for Seibu and cried, "Brother!"

Donald's spine went rigid, snapped taunt like a soldier coming to attention.

He put Jessica down and grabbed her by the shoulders. Kneeling to be at eye level with her, Donald tried to keep from yelling, but his restrained voice shook violently. "God will not be mocked."

"He's not," Jessica responded in a completely calm and fearless voice. "He's been glorified."

Shooting to his feet, Donald erupted.

"Silence! Blasphemer!" he roared, grabbing his hair in anger. As he did, fistfuls of blond locks effortlessly fell away, as if merely touching them had caused the hair to come out. Looking at the tuft in his hand, Donald went wild. Screaming, he rubbed at his scalp, causing hundreds of yellow filaments to flutter to the ground.

"Nononono," Kaufman mumbled to himself. This was too much like the woman in the video.

After the frenzy, Donald breathed heavy and resembled a half-bald Barbie doll. His gaze locked onto Seibu.

Panic rose up in Kaufman.

Shouting some kind of garbled war cry, Donald charged. He drove a running kick into Seibu's side. Kaufman watched, paralyzed, as Seibu flew through the air, skidded and tumbled along the floor, and finally crashed into the wall.

Curled in a fetal position, Seibu moaned.

But Donald was not done.

"Disgusting troll," he grumbled, raising a glossy black boot.

Seibu shrieked as the foot slammed down, and Kaufman echoed his cry, struggling against the restraints.

"Leave him be," Kaufman begged.

But Donald didn't stop.

"Vile, loathsome creature," he spat, and again the boot came down, heel first to increase the damage.

Over and over, the foot stomped, kicked a jig of death.

Rushing over, Jessica grabbed Donald's hand and yelled at him to stop—

—and Donald stopped.

Foot frozen half in the air.

"Stop," she said again wearily, and Donald nodded in confused conformity. There was shame in his face, and his eyes pleaded for forgiveness.

It was the girl, Kaufman saw. She wasn't just steadying Donald; wasn't just a calming influence; she was making him obey her. Yet, as incredible as Jessica's ability was, Kaufman barely reacted to it - for his mind was consumed by Seibu's motionless body. He didn't want to accept what that stillness might mean. On the far side of the room, Hollie staggered into view.

"What the hell?" she murmured.

Donald wheeled around, and Jessica's hand slipped from his as quickly as a child lost in the press of a busy mall. With the contact broken, anger flooded back into Donald's face.

He brought up the gun.

Hollie halted.

Jessica grabbed Donald's hand again, but she didn't have control over him anymore. She was used up - a dead battery - and now could only plead with him.

"Let's go. We're going; we're leaving," she said, pulling him towards the door with both hands, using all her weight to tug him away.

Keeping the gun aimed at Hollie, Donald allowed himself to be led to the front entrance, but before crossing the threshold, he stopped.

His face was surly, except instead of being red with rage, it seemed to shine, and despite his manic appearance, he looked serene and strangely angelic.

He raised the gun and three deafening gunshots boomed in rapid succession.

"Do not come after us."

The door banged shut.

Kaufman wrenched and yanked against his restraints until it felt like his shoulders would pull out of their sockets. Muscles strained, and he overturned the shelf and broke free just as the patrol car rumbled to life, kicking up loose rocks as it peeled away.

On his feet, Kaufman ran over to Seibu and dropped to his knees. Hollie was only a second behind. She tried to undo the handcuffs, but Kaufman shrugged her off.

"Forget it, check Seibu."

Hollie looked uncertain for a moment, then set to work.

"What happened?" she asked as her hands probed the inert furry form.

Seibu moaned when her fingers touched bruised flesh. Kaufman shuddered with relief at the sound.

"I…" Kaufman swallowed and shook his head. He took a breath and whispered, "How's Seibu?"

"There don't appear to be any broken bones, at least none that I can feel, but without an x-ray, I can't be sure," replied Hollie.

Kaufman nodded.

Gently rolling Seibu on to his back, she looked into the orangutan's eyes.

"I think you're going to be all right, boy-o," she said, stroking his head. "I just wish there was more I could do."

Blinking, Seibu reached up and lightly caressed her face.

"Oh," she breathed in surprise. "Did he…ah, did he understand me?"

Kaufman found he couldn't answer. A lump was in his throat as he watched Seibu shakily get to his feet and step over to him. He threw his long, hairy arms around Kaufman and held him tight, his small body trembling.

Hollie's hand went to her heart, and tears filled her eyes. She'd heard the rumors about Kaufman; the Droid was supposed to be as mechanical inside as a clockwork doll, as unfeeling as a machine. But she didn't see any of that - there was only tenderness here and love.

After a moment, Kaufman lifted his head.

"It's alright, Seibu. I was scared too."

Wiping her eyes, Hollie snatching up a nearby pair of pruning scissors.

"Let's get those things off you," she said, making quick work of the plastic hand restraints.

"Why did Donald take Jessica?"

Kaufman rubbed his wrists.

"He didn't give a reason, just said he was her tutelary, and that God had commanded and he must obey. It doesn't really matter why; we have to go after them. Donald's lost it."

"Yeah, that poor puppy is as cracked up as Humpty Dumpty. Alright then, what are we waiting for? Let's go."

Hollie stood and took a step towards the door, then stopped. "Hold on, where's Matthew?"

Kaufman sighed. He picked up the note from the floor and let Hollie read it.

"Oh, sweet Jesus, no!" she gasped.

"The kid slipped out when Donald fell asleep, and when I confronted Donald about it, he snapped."

Hollie reread the note. "We have to go get him."

"What about Jessica?"

"I don't think Donald will hurt her, do you?"

Kaufman hesitated. Before the last day-and-a-half, he would have said no without batting an eye. He knew Donald to be good-hearted and well-meaning, if a little overbearing, but now…

"I don't know anymore."

"Well, I don't think he will. Not if he believes he's her tutelary."

"Are you willing to bet the girl's life on that?"

"Yes, I'll take that wager. Tutelary means guardian or protector, but of a divine nature or appointment."

Kaufman cocked a quizzical eyebrow at Hollie. "How do you know that?"

"I went to Catholic school," she said as if that answered everything.

Kaufman doubted that even the strictest Catholic school required their pupils to know the definition of such an archaic word. Hollie was either extremely devout or one of those passionate crossword fanatics that prided themselves in knowing the most obscure definitions.

"Plus," Hollie continued, "We have no idea where they might be going."

On that point, Kaufman did not question her. With the city empty, Donald could hole up anywhere.

"On the other hand, we know exactly where Matthew has gone, and unlike Jessica, he doesn't have anyone watching out for him. Except us. Are you willing to trade his life for his sister's?"

"No," Kaufman responded without hesitation.

"Besides," said Hollie, her features darkening with dread, "there are things there in that hospital, horrible things, things that nobody should see, let alone a little boy."

Kaufman didn't understand.

"Aren't they all dead?"

Hollie though about Capt. Mills, his murderous glee and demon-like fangs.

"God, let's hope so."

CHAPTER 17

Within minutes, their gear and Seibu were loaded in the Humvee.

It was at times like these that Kaufman's conditioning was a benefit. He hadn't argued with Hollie's reasoning, hadn't played the foolish hero, or gotten emotionally divided; he just did what needed to be done.

Yet as they were racing down the road, something nagged at him, plagued him as thoroughly as any cancer, something that made him uncomfortable in his own skin.

Then he realized what it was.

Guilt.

He felt insanely guilty for abandoning Jessica. It made no sense, was illogical, unreasonable. But there it was like a humiliating and painful STD.

Kaufman tightened his jaw. He ground his teeth and accelerated.

Regret and shame tormented him, and the more he thought about it, the deeper the discontent dug. Yet there was nothing he could do, and his impotency turned sour, turned outward, homed in on Hollie - on Dr. Cunningham. *The* Dr. Cunningham, the jokester with the picture of Einstein sticking out his tongue on her office wall - the Advanced Programs Director and Special Projects Leader who had a hand in all this mess, and who was possibly the catalyst of thousands of deaths.

Kaufman grew angry with himself. He gripped down hard on the steering wheel.

How could he ever have admired her? Was it just because she was attractive? That was such shallow reasoning, such a flimsy, superficial excuse that let too many conceited people use their looks to live above the law. Wasn't that the real deception of evil - that because it was rich, or charming, or powerful, that the admiring masses gave it a pass to be cruel and murderous?

With tight-lipped fury, Kaufman said, "I know what you did at NewLife."

Hollie's polygraph eyes scanned over him, and he could tell she didn't believe him or only believed he knew something inconsequential about her work. So, she remained silent, and her reserve pissed Kaufman off even more.

"What were you people thinking!?"

Hollie didn't reply, and Kaufman found himself having to hold back his anger, his rage.

A dam had broken in him; physically, he was shaking. He wanted to punch something, anything - punch until his arms ached, punch until his knuckles split.

In rising heat waves the passing steel and concrete buildings warped and bent under the merciless sun's rays. Taking a deep breath, Kaufman calmed himself. He didn't want to give Hollie the upper hand.

Recovering his composure, Kaufman spoke slowly.

"I know about Project Osiris."

That not only got a response, it completely floored Hollie.

"What? How?" she blurted, but Kaufman didn't pause to relish the fact that he'd finally caught her off guard, had finally slapped the smug demure look right off her pretty face. Instead, he plowed forward with his questions and accusations.

"It wasn't enough that you found Pandora's Box, but you had to open it too? What could you possibly hope to achieve by splicing human DNA with extraterrestrials!?"

"Ah..." Hollie breathed; mouth hung open. Then her lips curled into a smile and she clamped a hand over her mouth but wasn't fast enough to stifle a hiccup of a giggle.

That sound was like fingers on a chalkboard, and Kaufman slammed on the brakes. Seatbelts snapped taut and tires squealed.

As they crashed back into their seats, Kaufman whipped his head around and glared at this woman, this mocker of human life.

Exhaling sharply, Hollie pushed her bangs out of her face, and suddenly she was laughing again. And this was no muffled snicker, but a full-on tear-spilling, air-denying, uncontrollable convulsion.

For a moment, Kaufman honestly thought he might hit her. Hollie's hysteria was inexplicable, as out of place as a clown at a funeral, but it also had a dispelling quality, and soon, he could feel his anger deflating.

"I'm sorry," Hollie wheezed, dabbing at her eyes and chortling.

"What's so damn funny?" Kaufman asked, utterly confused.

"You didn't read the entire file, did you."

It wasn't a question.

"No," Kaufman admitted, "and I didn't understand most of what I read either. But it did say ET cells in the report."

Clearing her throat, Hollie said, "Yes, many times, and it did mean extraterrestrial, but it was also just a dumb joke."

Kaufman balked. "How could alien cells be a joke?"

"Because we didn't know what else to call them," Hollie confessed. "We meant ET in that the eukaryotes we were working with were more than earthly - no longer, strictly speaking, terrestrial."

The air in the cab was abruptly thin, and the rumbling engine jostled rather than soothed.

Kaufman knew the answer to his next question would turn everything he knew about the world upside down.

"What did you do? How could cells no longer be terrestrial?"

Hollie wasn't smiling anymore, and her sudden somberness closed in tight around Kaufman.

"We resurrected them," she said flatly.

For a long while, Kaufman just sat in silence. The sound of his breathing filled his ears, and everything around him slowed. A particle of dust turned lazily in the morning sun. It moved across the front of the windshield, bobbing and twirling until, in a climactic finale, it blew away.

Wetting his lips, Kaufman finally asked the question that was darting around in his head.

"How?"

Hollie sucked in a lung full of air as if the answer required more oxygen than a normal response.

"Clinically speaking, doctors bring people back from the dead every day, all around the world."

"But that's not what you're talking about," Kaufman conjectured.

"No, not exactly," she admitted, "but it's where it all started."

Slowly she exhaled. "What do you know about Adam Murakami?"

Kaufman shook his head. "Not much, just what I've read in newspapers. He founded NewLife; he's rich, and supposedly a brilliant scientist."

"He's not just rich, he's one of the wealthiest people in the world, and he isn't just brilliant, he's a Mozart to biology and an Einstein in genetics."

Hollie paused then.

"But on April 10th, 1998, Dr. Murakami died as a result of anaphylaxis."

"Wait; what?! He died?" asked Kaufman disconcerted. "But he just on the news—"

Hollie held up a hand, and he let his question go unanswered.

"Ten years ago, he was out fly fishing in Alaska with some business associates, and while looking for a better location to cast, he stumbled across a nest of bees. Dr. Murakami had never been stung before, but he quickly realized that he was highly allergic. In desperation - before anaphylactic shock set in - he jumped into the river. It was early spring, and the water was ice cold. It probably would have killed him even if the bee stings hadn't.

"The official report stated he was stung over four hundred times, enough to potentially threaten even a non-allergic individual.

"It took Dr. Murakami's fishing buddies over an hour to exhume his body, and even with a personal helicopter onsite, he'd been dead for more than two hours by the time doctors began to resuscitate him. It was almost pointless to try and revive him at that point. Yet somehow, after fifty minutes of working on him, the doctors successfully jumpstarted Dr. Murakami's heart, and, more astonishingly, he wasn't braindead or permanently comatose. In fact, he made a complete recovery."

Hollie stopped then and looked at Kaufman. He saw that she expected this news to astonish him, but he knew nothing of record medical resuscitations.

"So, three hours is pretty long," he guessed.

"It is completely unprecedented," she noted. "Only in clinically controlled deaths for surgery - where the body is cooled and drained of blood, and where brain activity is stopped through the administering of certain drugs - have longer deaths been documented without serious brain injury."

"Then why haven't I heard about it?" asked Kaufman, now genuinely intrigued.

"Because it hasn't been highly publicized. Dr. Murakami worked hard to keep it that way.

"The discharge files claim that the frigid water preserved him in a suspended state, which is what allegedly saved his life. But ask any doctor in the world to look at that report and they'll tell you that's nonsense.

"The water wasn't nearly cold enough, and his friends mistakenly warmed him on the flight to the hospital, not to mention the fact that his body was traumatized with toxins, or the sheer amount of time that oxygen wasn't flowing and blood wasn't circulating - allowing ischemic injuries to occur throughout all his major organs - and on, and on. The list of things that would have had to happen perfectly to account for his successful resuscitation - not to mention his full recovery - is almost as staggering as the list of things that went wrong.

"Pure and simple, what happened to Dr. Murakami was a miracle, and he'll be the first to admit as much."

Pausing in her explanation, Hollie cleared her throat.

"We really need to keep going; I'll tell you the rest as we drive."

Kaufman blinked; he'd forgotten they'd stopped. To him, his world had been in constant motion ever since Hollie told him the scientist at NewLife had scientifically resurrected cells.

He took his foot from the brake, and they set off again.

Hollie continued. "Many people pronounced clinically dead, and later revived, report no memory of the event. But others say they see themselves as they float over their bodies, or travel through a tunnel of light.

"Adam Murakami's Near-Death Experience was far more vivid and detailed. He doesn't speak about it openly, but dying changed his life - as it would for anyone - even without the vision."

Kaufman raised an eyebrow. "What vision?"

Hollie huffed, expelling a large lungful of air as if she wasn't comfortable with what she was about to share…or didn't believe it.

"Dr. Murakami claims he saw the creation of the universe - the beginning of life and its evolution thereafter; and he's adamant that this wasn't a vision in any traditional sense, not an emotional color and light show, nothing like seeing images projected onto a movie screen, but a deep and profound understanding of how the universe works on a biological level."

"That's some trip," said Kaufman. "I can see now why he doesn't publicly talk about it; the media would make him out as a crackpot."

Hollie nodded.

"Yet after being released from the hospital, he dove into the idea of resurrection - and not just in a religious sense, but in how it might be achieved using scientific means."

"He became a Victor Frankenstein," observed Kaufman.

"No, no, he didn't want to make monsters or zombies," insisted Hollie. "Resurrection isn't reanimating dead things - true resurrection means having the ability innate in a being to take back up their life once it has been taken from them. And this isn't as farfetched as you might think. We see resurrection in nature in many forms."

"Really?" asked Kaufman.

"Absolutely," Hollie asserted, "the most straightforward example being hibernation, in which metabolisms slow down to the point of almost being nonexistent; the core body temperature drops, breathing is minimized, and the heart beats are so far apart that the animal is barely alive. Many insects experience something even greater during winter months, a suspended state called dormancy or specifically diapause. The organism is all but dead until certain conditions are met, at which time chemical reactions take place to bring the insect back to life."

"Wait," Kaufman interrupted. "Isn't that just cryogenics?"

Hollie shook her head.

"Certain types of cryopreservation are used to conserve blood and DNA, and even embryos and eggs, but what you're thinking of is cryonics - which is the preservation of humans at low-temperatures after they are legally dead to hopefully be brought back to life in a thousand years.

"The idea is ridiculous; our pickling skills aren't anywhere near good enough for that, and those poor suckers that have actually undergone the process - which are very, very few - will be lucky if the methods used to preserve them haven't done more damage than the freezing was worth.

"Besides, that's 1950's sci-fi stuff. Nowadays, it makes way more sense just to take a sample of their DNA and pop them out in the future, when scientists are walking around the USS Enterprise in one-piece jumpsuits, and boldly going when no man has gone before."

"Oh," said Kaufman, pursing his lips. "Still, the proposition to resurrect humans must have been absurd at best. How could you have been persuaded to work on something so farfetched? And how was the military convinced to get involved?"

"You're still thinking about this in religious terms," said Hollie. "More to the point, full resurrection was never a real goal. If a person is completely burned up in a fire or a soldier horrendously blown up on a battlefield, the damage done would be too extensive to repair. There are many other scenarios, however, where this research could help every living person the world over.

"Our bodies already naturally repair themselves. Break a leg, and the bone grows back together, get cut, and the skin binds back up. It is these very regenerative properties that separate the terms living from dead. But there are even more extreme cases found in the animal kingdom where entire limbs can be severed, and the skin doesn't just close up - the organism re-grows the appendage."

"Like starfish and lizard's tails."

"Exactly, those are amazing abilities! Just think how it would revolutionize the world if humans were capable of that. Medical science, as we know it, would be eradicated or changed into something so completely different we wouldn't even recognize it.

"What army in the world wouldn't want soldiers who could take a bullet, rapidly heal from it, and be back on the battlefield in a few days? It would save billions of dollars in investments and training. Even more, it could wipe out war altogether."

"Or make it even more destructive and violent," said Kaufman, thinking of a world where limbs regenerated and where bullets didn't kill.

"That was always a dark possibility," Hollie admitted, "but we believed in the good, tried to focus on the positive."

"I wonder if the scientist on the Manhattan project said the same thing."

Hollie gave Kaufman a dark look. "They were at war and knew they were making a weapon."

"Perhaps," Kaufman acquiesced, "but limb regeneration and rapid healing isn't resurrection."

"No," Hollie agreed. "It was, however, the most realistic goal; because the ability to jumpstart a whole organism back to life is centuries away, and maybe even impossible for complex life."

"What about in simple life forms?" Kaufman inquired.

"Well, some worms when cut in half will not just grow back new bodies or heads, but those two halves will literally become two new individual worms."

"You're talking about cloning."

"Cloning is easy compared to self-resurrection," said Hollie. "Making a copy is a cinch when you have the schematics. But forget about worms for a minute and think sponges. Sponges are the only known animal that, if broken down to a cellular level, can miraculously reassemble - and we don't even have a good theory to explain how this is possible."

"But, you did it."

"No," objected Hollie.

"But the report…" Kaufman insisted flustered, feeling like a man on the tight rope, grasping at the air to try and keep from toppling over and plummeting to the ground.

"It was only a simulation," Hollie admitted, wearily running a hand over her face.

"For the first few years, we failed miserably, made almost no headway. We endlessly tried to keep cells alive in dead environments. We had cells that could live incredibly long with nothing to maintain them that would unexplainably mutate, or instantly stop functioning, or become cancerous.

"We continued to slowly make progress and expand our understanding, but for all intents and purposes, we'd come to a dead end. The project was on the verge of going bust when Dr. Murakami made an astounding breakthrough, a real Nobel Prize-type discovery. He was able to isolate key sequences in junk DNA that had profound effects on a cell's ability to not just survive, but to rebuild themselves."

"Wait, I'm not familiar with junk DNA," said Kaufman.

"No one is really," explained Hollie. "Junk, or non-coding DNA, has no known biological function. They are incredibly long sequences of chromosomes on a genome for which no purpose has been identified, yet ninety-eight percent of the human genome has been designated as 'junk', and this always bothered Dr. Murakami, for truly nonfunctional DNA seemed to defy evolutionary logic."

"You mean he looked at the human blueprint and questioned what all the extra light switches were for if they didn't do anything?" asked Kaufman.

"Exactly, said Hollie. "What Dr. Murakami discovered was that genomes are dynamic entities and that junk DNA - correctly manipulated - held functional properties. To use your example, those light switches that didn't turn anything on, if connected properly, could operate lights all over the house…or turn on your stove, or more astonishingly, even build a new room when flipped. But even with this quantum leap, we still weren't able to achieve what we hoped for. Self-sustaining, rebooting cells still eluded us."

Dazed, Kaufman looked away from the road and glanced at the speedometer. Although it indicated they were traveling at seventy-five miles per hour, his mind was racing at supersonic speeds: clinical death, junk DNA, resurrected cells - it was more absurd than his mistaken belief that Project Osiris had been about aliens. It was also far more incredible.

"The project continued, though," said Kaufman, encouraging Hollie to continue.

"Yes, that's when I went back and began to look over our earliest work. I realized we were operating off a faulty fundamental assumption. We were trying to keep specific key cells alive to get others operational, before the whole organism degraded past the point of supporting reanimated life. And while looking over those reports, it occurred to me that if we were genuinely trying to achieve resurrection, then the entire organism needed to die - even the little supercells we'd been creating. It was a completely illogical and contradictory idea. Surprisingly, the proposition wasn't immediately rejected; but after months without any shred of success, the concept was abandoned. Yet I felt certain that this was the key to the problem.

"However, with Dr. Murakami's junk DNA discovery, we were making major headway with limb regeneration and rapid healing. We could re-grow a rat's tail within days of it being cut off. We had mixed results with joints and major organs but felt confident it was only a matter of time before those problems were worked out."

"Is that when you teamed up with the military?" inquired Kaufman.

"Hardly. NewLife has always been in bed with Uncle Sam, and the military was far more ambitious than we were," said Hollie, recalling what Capt. Mills had told her about the brutal experiments his friend in the animal labs had been ordered to conduct.

"So, what went wrong?"

"You mean to ask what went right," said Hollie. "Somehow, the scientist at Shafter figured it out; they had the tools to bypass the paradox."

"What paradox?"

"How to end life for it to begin again: how to perform a resurrection."

"But they didn't!" exploded Kaufman. "They killed everybody! Killed hundreds. Thousands! I've seen them, hills of dead bodies piled up just outside the city limits; mountains of corpses - men, women, children, the old and the young. They wiped out an entire city!"

"Yes," Hollie admitted gravely. "Whatever procedure or technology was used obviously kills *living* organisms, but it was never meant to be implemented on such. You don't resurrect the living, only the dead."

Kaufman rolled into the hospital parking lot and stopped.

Hollie's words rang in his head, and just beyond his comprehension, something loomed, something massive, something fast approaching.

"You don't resurrect the living, only the dead," he repeated, remembering the way the noose had closed so tightly around his throat when his feet had slipped off the countertop. He also remembered coming to, finding himself so cold, his heart thudding, and he'd wondered if he was some kind of machine coming back to life.

Then, it hit him - understanding slammed into him with apocalyptic force, blasted him back into his seat and physically knocked the wind out of him.

"Jesus Christ!" Kaufman exclaimed, gasping.

"He is the most famous," Hollie agreed, fingering the cross around her neck.

Kaufman nodded.

It all made sense.

It had felt like his esophagus had been crushed when he'd accidentally hung himself - because it had!

"Then we didn't survive. That's what makes us different. We were all dead when it happened. We were resurrected!"

With the engine softy idling, Kaufman sat rubbing his throat.

"I really did hang myself; the rafter broke, but it didn't matter. I died."

Hollie nodded; she had a hand to her side.

"I was shot."

"And the kids?" Kaufman wondered.

"I don't know; a car accident, perhaps."

"What about Donald?"

"No," said Hollie, "he's dying it's…just killing him more slowly than everyone else."

Kaufman let his hand drop into his lap and looked out the window. Beyond, the brown landscape he'd known his whole life remained unchanged, but he would never be the same.

"What are we going to find in there?" he asked, noting the hospital and remembered why they were there.

"Nothing you haven't already seen," said Hollie, exiting the Humvee.

But it wasn't true.

There were plenty of dead bodies; however, these were nothing like the corpses Kaufman had seen out in the desert. The remains here were ghastly.

Most of the beds were empty at first, but as Hollie led them nearer the terminal ward, they were almost all filled with the abhorrent forms.

"What happened to them?"

"I'm not exactly sure," responded Hollie. "But whatever drove the healthy citizens of Decoy insane also speeds up diseases and enhances genetic defects."

Kaufman could see the evidence for himself.

It was even more disturbing when they reached Ms. Sterling's room. Her cancer had unnaturally metastasized throughout all of her body, turning the once beautiful woman into a grotesque cadaver. She was bloated with tumors and lumpy with mutations.

On the floor, at the foot of his mother's bed, lay Matthew, vacant-eyed and catatonic, with his knees tucked up under his chin. The boy reminded Kaufman of a haunting newspaper photograph he'd once seen of a lost and found dead, Cub Scout.

Hollie rushed in and dropped to her knees. She cradled Matthew in her arms, kissed his forehead, and stroked his face, but he didn't acknowledge the contact, didn't even blink.

Kaufman handed Hollie his shotgun and took Matthew into his arms.

"Come on, let's get him out of here," he said, leading the way.

The hospital wasn't large, but without the florescent bulbs washing everything in artificial light, the place felt shadowy and dirty. The incoming sunlight, instead of appearing clean, looked polluted, and as Kaufman hurried through the long murky corridors, he found it ironic that in the name of technological advancement, man had sterilized itself from nature, had truly become manmade.

From the gloominess of the hospital, the group emerged, batting their eyes at the hard sun. Kaufman sat Matthew on the bumper of the Humvee next to where Seibu had been resting, and Hollie wet a cloth with a bottle of water. As she wiped his face, he gradually came to.

"Where's Jess?" Matthew whispered.

Hollie turned away, unable to answer. She was uneasy, and her guilt was contagious. Kaufman could feel heat and shame burning in his face.

"Donald took her," he said, not knowing how to soften the blow.

Matthew squeezed shut his eyes and shook his head.

"It's my fault," he retorted. "I shouldn't have left her. I'm so selfish." Suddenly he clenched his fist and punched himself in the head.

"Matthew, no, oh no, sweetie," Hollie countered. She grabbed his arm so he couldn't hit himself again and pulled him tightly against her.

"There was nothing you could have done; you would have been as helpless as we were. But I promise you, I promise, we *will* find her."

Clutching Hollie as tightly as any bereaved graveside mourner, Matthew took comfort from her, but he didn't believe her. Kaufman could see in his youthful face the assurance that if he'd been present, he could have stopped his sister's abduction.

"Where'd he take her?" he asked, untangling himself from the embrace.

"We...we don't know, hun. We were hoping Donald might have said something to you, mentioned somewhere."

Matthew thought for a moment and scowled.

"No."

The boy looked defeated.

Hollie persisted. "Maybe he mentioned someplace in passing. It might have seemed unimportant at the time."

"No!" he said with more force. "I would have remembered."

Kaufman could taste the boy's self-reproach, his failed sense of responsibility - driving out here, he too had drunk from that bitter cup.

Fingering a tarnished silver angel pendant around his neck, Matthew began to cry. Clean white tears cut through the grime on his face as his eyes pleaded for an answer to the impossible, searched for something to make everything better.

"What good is it not being a cripple if you can't protect others? If everyone you love either gets taken or leaves? What's the point?"

Kaufman opened his mouth, then shut it, opened it again, but no words came out. He couldn't answer. He didn't know Matthew's circumstances, but he saw the boy's loneliness, saw his bitterness and path towards apathy. He saw himself - and he wanted desperately to help. For not only was Matthew a shadow of what he'd once been but of what he might have been, given half a chance.

Both compassion and despair filled Kaufman. He wanted to help, felt that if he could find Jessica, he could save Matthew and himself in the process. But he didn't know what to do, felt as directionless and debilitated as a ship adrift at sea. And thus consumed, he didn't notice Seibu take his hand until he found himself walking.

Guiding Kaufman over to one of the decorative landscape niches, Seibu pulled him into a keeling position and began smoothing out the soil. Still, in a fog, Kaufman wasn't sure what Seibu was doing until he used a callused finger to draw a square. Still, in a fog, Kaufman wasn't sure what Seibu was doing until he used a callused finger to draw a square.

Transfixed, Kaufman stared as Seibu topped the square with a triangle.

Blinking hard, feeling drunk and slow-witted, Kaufman gaped. Seibu had just drawn a house! And to make sure there was no mistake, a door was added with a knob.

In a day when his world had just gotten turned upside down, it now got flipped inside out. Seibu was communicating with him, talking in the only way he could - by drawing pictures. The experience was surreal, more fantastic than any Salvador Dalí dreamscape painting, and Kaufman felt his pulse race as he continued to watch the image unfold.

In the end, though, it wasn't a house.

At the point of the triangle, at the tip of the roof, Seibu drew two lines. One long vertical and one short horizontal: a cross.

Abruptly Kaufman stood and his eyes searched Seibu's, trying to find an answer to the impossible.

"Holy Christ on the Cross," he mumbled.
Seibu flashed his signature gummy broad toothed grin and nodded.

CHAPTER 18

"Holy Christ on the Cross," said Kaufman as they sped along the boulevard.

"What?" Hollie asked, confused.

"Holy Christ on the Cross - it's the name of Donald's church. I should have thought of it from the start. It makes sense for Donald to take Jessica there - he thinks this is Armageddon."

"I still don't understand how Seibu would know about the church."

"You saw the picture," replied Kaufman, taking a corner at too high a speed. The Humvee squealed as it jumped a curb, before swinging back hard onto the road. "He must have just deduced the most likely location to look."

"But *how* is that possible?" insisted Hollie.

"I don't know. Your resurrection serum made him smarter."

"It shouldn't have." Hollie frowned and sat silent for a moment, brooding. "And it wasn't a serum. I don't know what technology the government used to make this happen, but resurrection doesn't account for everything, certainly not Seibu's intelligence. Something else is at play here."

"Like what?"

"I wish I knew," she said musing. "Dr. Murakami must, though. We have to find him."

"First things first," said Kaufman, coming to a stop and pulling out the shotgun. He'd parked well short of the church, as he didn't want to be seen or heard as they approached. Matthew and Seibu both insisted on coming, but somehow Hollie convinced to stay put.

One step up from a trailer park, the subdivision all around was made up of HUD homes crammed together on both sides of the street, struggling to keep the vast desert at bay. A car sitting on a front lawn and a dozen smashed potted cacti might have been signs of the Decoy Madness, although it might also have just been the standard fare in this low-income neighborhood. It was hard to tell.

At the end of the block, the pavement gave way to gravel, and Kaufman stopped. He pointed out the chapel a few hundred yards away. Situated at the end of a long dusty road, the building was nestled in among a few low-lying hills, and despite its name - Holy Christ on the Cross - there was no crucifix on the steeple to indicate it was a place of worship.

Dry, dead weeds grew along the base of the walls like patchy stubble on a jawline, and eczema paint chips flaked off everywhere. Kaufman was never sure if Donald had built the church new or had remodeled an existing edifice, but whatever the case, very little money had been spent in making it appealing.

In contrast to the drab building sat Donald's sparkling patrol car - both a welcome and unwelcome sight.

"What's the plan?" Hollie asked.

"Donald told me it's just a single room, with only one entrance, and since there are no front-facing windows, he won't see us coming." Kaufman indicated directions with two fingers. "I'll go first and cover the right side; you take the left."

Hollie rubbed her arm nervously. She wasn't too keen on this commando crap, but she'd be damned if she let that lunatic cop hurt Jessica. Even if she wasn't the girl's mother, she felt a powerful maternal instinct.

"What happens once we're inside?"

"We're going to talk."

"And what if that doesn't work?" Hollie pressed.

"Then, our conversation will be with bullets instead of words." Kaufman snapped off the gun's safety.

Hollie shivered at the coolness in his tone, yet his stoicism didn't surprise her as much as her reaction to it. Instead of feeling afraid or repulsed, she found that she admired him for his fortitude. More, she was attracted to it. Kaufman seemed more solid than other men, more secure, more…stable, and she liked the safe feeling he gave her.

Catching his handsome hazel eyes, Hollie blushed and looked away.

I'm worse than a teenybopper with a crush, she thought, *and this has got to be the most fucked-up first date I've ever been on.* Hollie smiled, almost enjoying herself, in spite of what they were about to do.

"Okay, let's go," she said.

Kaufman put a hand on her shoulder. "Hang on."

He did a final sweep of the surrounding hills. Finally, he signaled they should go, and with guns pointed down, the two jogged up the driveway fast, like FBI agents initiating a raid. Reaching the front entrance, they briefly paused. Kaufman took a deep breath, and Hollie nodded.

With one swift kick, the double doors exploded inward, but no cry of surprise or alarm followed. Entering, Hollie and Kaufman swung their guns left and right, taking in their surroundings.

The inside of the building was the epitome of a bare-bones old frontier church down to the foundation - if it had any. No paint had ever touched these walls, nor were the pews on either side of the single-aisle stained. It was the kind of parish to appeal to a hellfire-and-damnation-type congregation, rather than the handclapping and arm-waving worshippers of mega TV evangelists.

Hard shafts of sunlight from the west-facing windows cut through the murky interior, and ahead, past a plain and thin pulpit, rose a massive oak tree that seemed to have grown up right out of the floorboards. The minimalist décor was highly effective for the colossal oak, which was pruned in such a way that the branches formed a natural cross - towering upwards, commanded attention and engendered wonder.

Here was the heart of Holy Christ on the Cross.

And on those white limbs, where all the bark had been stripped away, leaving the tree as smooth as polished marble, was nailed - not the son of Joseph and Mary - but Donald Graeci.

Hollie swore and crossed herself, and immediately felt disgusted.

Nails had been driven through both of Donald's palms as well as his wrists, the second set of nails having been hammered in to helped support the weight of his body and to keep his hands from ripping free. Through his feet, another massive spike secured him to the tree.

Sagging, chin against chest, Donald's head drooped low. Dark stains streamed down his arms, chest, and legs. Nearly every inch of skin not covered in blood was torn and bruised.

There had been a scourging before the crucifixion - a fierce and terrible one.

But beyond the beating, Donald was hardly recognizable. In the few hours they'd been separated, he'd withered, and his skin was stretched taut across his razor-thin frame. Also, the hair loss that had begun in the nursery was now complete and universal. It was as if Donald had undergone chemotherapy; even his signature mustache was gone.

Inexorably, Kaufman was drawn towards the bruised and broken flesh that was once his friend. His stomach turned as he caught a sharp whiff of sweat, blood, and excrement, but near the base of the ancient execution device, Kaufman came to an abrupt halt when Donald spoke - his voice low and raspy.

"Beware of false prophets which come to you in sheep's clothing but inwardly are ravenous wolves, Matth…"

A bloody cough cut off the reference.

"Donald, who did this to you?" Kaufman asked. But Donald didn't respond. He just hung with head perpetually bowed.

"Tell me who did this?" Kaufman demanded, his guts in knots, fearing he already knew the answer, recounting the *Face of God* painting in his living room.

Quivering, Donald painstakingly lifted his head.

"I was supposed to be her tutelary," he croaked, and the tears in his eyes were both unexpected and heartbreaking. Trembling, he fought to keep his face up, but eventually, he slumped.

Taking a knee, Kaufman looked up at his friend.

"Who did this? Where's Jessica?"

"Gone," Donald sobbed, regret and bitterness knitted like an elaborate tapestry in his horse voice.

"I couldn't even protect a little girl, let alone myself. God warned that in the last days even the very elect should be deceived, Matthew 24:24. No truer words could have been spoken of me."

"Okay, enough," said Kaufman firmly. "Don't worry about that; save your strength. I'm going to get you down."

Standing, Kaufman took a step back and looked around. There was no hammer on the ground, bloody or otherwise. Whoever had done this had either taken it with him or used his mind to drive in the spikes - which begged the question as to just how Donald had been lifted on the crucifix in the first place. The tree was solidly fixed in place. It couldn't have been lowered to allow Donald to be nailed to it and then hoisted back up. That meant, somehow, Donald been braced vertically against the tree while the nails were beaten in. Kaufman supposed Donald could have been tied up or held in place, but in both scenarios, it would have taken a team of executioners to do the work - two at a minimum.

That insight sent Kaufman's mind back to the police station, and to Anthony Green's filleted and suspended body. Surely that ritualistic murder was somehow connected. If that too had been the work of one killer, of the mock messiah, it begged the question of how it had been done as well. The implication that a solitary man had lifted both Donald and Anthony's bodies without accomplices bordered on the supernatural.

Hollie was right; resurrection didn't account for everything.

Unexpected anger sprang up in Kaufman.

What did it matter how such savagery had been committed? His father might not only be in collusion with someone capable of that level of sadism but might have masterminded those executions himself. Was Donald just the latest cattle deemed unworthy and unclean? Was the plan to butcher them all, one by one? Was Jessica next? Is that why she had been taken?

Seething, and virtually seeing red, Kaufman was on the verge of losing it. However, as unwilling a disciple of reason and logic as he might be, he was a disciple nonetheless; and he knew that with a couple of wenches and a ladder, a lone individual could have hoisted up both bodies singlehandedly.

Even if his father wasn't directly involved, his work and ideologies implicated him in the brazen killings of this religious assassin; and by correlation, Kaufman himself was connected. The association dirtied him, but he wouldn't let it define him. He would not let Donald die up there.

Reaching down, Kaufman yanked back on a loose floorboard.

As hard as petrified wood, the stiff grey plank groaned but refused to break - until suddenly, cracking as loudly as a gunshot, a five-foot section broke away, either as a result of the avalanche quantity of adrenaline racing through Kaufman's bloodstream, or more likely, as another enhanced quality of his resurrected body.

Makeshift crowbar inches from Donald's feet, Kaufman glanced at Hollie. She shook her head slowly, both in protest and disbelief.

"Kaufman, no, don't."

An oscillating handsaw would have been preferable. It certainly would have been cleaner, not to mention far gentler, but this was all Kaufman had. And he *had* to do something - for he could no longer accommodate the deluge of enmity and gall that inundated him.

"This is going to hurt," said Kaufman. "A lot."

"No plea—"

And Kaufman wrenched.

Blood gushed, and flesh tore as bone, nerves, and soft tissue were jammed upwards and crushed against the head of the nail. Grunting with the effort, Kaufman pulled and twisted with all his might, even while Donald screamed and screamed.

After an exhaustive minute, he let go.

"No more…" Donald implored, breathlessly. "Please! I beg you. No more, please…please."

Stepping back, Kaufman yanked out the worthless timber and hurled it across the room.

"Worthless piece of shit!" he shouted, plopping down dejectedly, and Hollie couldn't tell if he'd been talking about the board or himself.

"You can't free me," gasped Donald. "Besides...there's no point, this is God's punishment for me...for my sins, for my blindness and lasciviousness."

"What?" Kaufman blurted, outrage bringing him to his feet. "God is not punishing you."

"Then, I punish myself!" Donald snapped, and the words flew out with such venom, with such self-loathing and asperity that it caused Kaufman to stumble back.

"I punish myself!" he screamed again, straining against the nails, pulling himself up and away from the tree, quaking violently with the effort. And still, Donald stretched, stretched until he was as taut as a bowstring - stretched until his eyes bulged and muscles rippled, and it was possible to believe that he might actually tear free.

However, after a moment, Donald slumped again, utterly spent - his external torture only a fraction as great as his internal torment.

Time seemed to slow then, seemed to condense, and in the dense swatches of sunlight, dust drifted. Unable to speak, Kaufman looked over at Hollie, who was stunned silent as well. The only sound in the clapboard chapel was Donald's raspy, labored breathing.

Kaufman listened to that haunted sound for what seemed like an eternity and thought he might be trapped in that hellish instant forever, until Donald spoke, breaking the eerie spell.

"He used me."

"Who?" asked Kaufman.

"He manipulated me, knew how to prey upon my weaknesses, and exploit them for his own purposes."

"Who?"

"Shane!" Donald hissed, and Hollie gasped.

Kaufman turned to her. "You know him?"

She nodded, and the fear in her face revealed that not only did she know the name, she'd been dreading hearing it.

"Who's Shane?" Kaufman pressed, believing he already knew.

Donald sighed, sagging heavily on the cross, as if what he was about to reveal was what weigh him down, rather than gravity.

"Yesterday morning, I woke up in a ditch. I didn't know who I was or what had happened. One moment I was driving through Marshall Pass, the next I'd crashed into a gully. When I tried the radio, it didn't work, so I crawled out and headed back into town. As I walked, I sensed something was different. The day was different...*I* was different. At first, I thought it was shock. I was pretty beat up - bruises and cuts and stuff - except I didn't feel any pain. I felt stronger and more resilient as if God wasn't just with me but in me, and when I reached town, I immediately knew why. I knew what had happened: The Judgment.

"God had let loose his wrath upon the wicked, and the world would never be the same. The streets of Decoy were filled with people languishing in their sins, having a bright recollection of all their guilt. It was strange because everyone suffered in absolute silence; I'd always imagined the screams of the condemned would be loud and shrill, but it was like watching TV with the sound off. In terror, the muted damned fled town by the droves, as if they believed they could save themselves by running.

"Even the animals didn't receive mercy. Most were killed instantly, falling from the sky or rolling on the ground in contorted agony. The few that did survive went insane, became the hellhounds you've seen roaming around town.

"It was then, amid that prophetic and literal Hell on Earth, that I realized God had not chosen me. *Me* who had served the Almighty with diligence my entire life - I had been left to rot; I was one of the forsaken!

"In anger and confusion, I raced through the city and made my way here. In supplication, I knelt, and for hours I carved my sins into the cross until my hands were numb and my fingers bled."

Kaufman looked at the tree. It was only then that he noticed the confetti of wood scattered about the base of the oak cross. He also took in for the first time the fact that the entire trunk was scared with both old and fresh confessions. Donald - apparently not satisfied with only confessing his sins to God - had made them permanent for others to see as well.

The act was either one of complete contrition or insidious hypocrisy.

"My anguish consumed me," Donald continued, "and through the night and into the early morning, I beseeched the Lord, pleaded for forgiveness, and begged for a second chance. At some point, I lost consciousness, but when I awoke, an angel of the Almighty stood before.

"He was the most beautiful thing I have ever seen. He radiated holiness and power; the very air seemed to crackle with it. The angel then smiled and told me his name was Shane."

"Son of a bitch," Hollie whispered, and the hair on Kaufman's neck stood up.

Donald went on.

"The angel called me by name and commanded me not to be afraid. I obeyed. He told me God had a special task for me, and that I'd been spared to do an important work. Some innocence was still left in the world, and I had been appointed a warden, made the tutelary of two children."

Kaufman blew out a breath of pent-up air. He knew that in Donald's state of mind, someone - particularly a religious, self-serving madman versed in the dogmas of Dominism - could have effortlessly beguiled his god-fearing friend. But to what end? The children had been defenseless before Donald found them. Why not kidnap them directly?

"I know what you must be thinking," said Donald. "You believe that I was ripe to be manipulated, clay easily shaped, and that may have been true. I recognize now that Shane was not sent from God. But he *is* an angel...just a dark and evil one."

"He's not an angel, Donald," said Hollie gently. "He's just a man. I've met him and seen him bleed."

Lifting his head, Donald regarded Hollie. His eyes were clear, alert, and as lucid as a defense lawyer at the top of his game.

"No!" he admonished. "I was weak and confused when he came to me, but not just anyone could have deceived me. No mortal man could have tricked me the way he did. Shane saw into my very soul and played to my deepest, most hidden lusts."

"What are you talking about?" asked Kaufman.

Donald licked his lips. And in that pause, a quiet apprehension filled the room.

"He promised me the girl," he finally said, his voice bedeviled with regret.

"What?" Kaufman blanched, unsure he'd heard correctly.

"In the scriptures, it's not uncommon," blurted Donald. "Many men of God were given women - even young girls - as wives for their righteousness. But I swear I wouldn't have touched her."

The promise was a moot point now.

Turning away, Kaufman couldn't speak, he was too rattled to respond, but Hollie's words wiped out like a lash.

"You sick fuck!"

"Yes, go ahead and judge me," Donald spat back. "My flesh is full of the sinful lust for little girls, but I have never once acted upon that evil, have instead sought my whole life to purge that darkness from me. Yet, where is the judgment for my parents who turned a blind eye while *I* was being molested? Who saw it as their sacrifice, their gift to God, their tithe to the church? Where is the judgment for those priests who used and defiled me?"

Donald snorted, and fire burned in his eyes.

"Those were supposed to be men of God!"

Swallowing, Hollie looked away, red-faced and castigated.

"No one but my Father in Heaven knew of that unspoken vice within me. How then did Shane know about it? Because he looked into my soul and *saw* it - only someone divine could have done that. He saw inside me and knew that the only way I would give in was if the laws of men no longer applied and that my vile desire could be masked and promised to me as marriage - mocking even that sacred union."

Lowering his head, Kaufman thought Donald looked as broken and disgraced as any man could.

"And now that he's taken Jessica, he's left me with nothing but shame."

"Where?" asked Hollie.

"I don't know."

"What does he want with her?"

Somehow Donald seemed to sag even more.

"I don't know that either," he mewled, and dragged his eyes to Kaufman. "But I've paid for my sin."

Through the lacerations and contusions, through the blood, and sweat, and tears, Kaufman saw a look that he recognized. It was the pleading petition of the German Sheppard. The desire for death.

"No," he said without hesitation.

"Please, I'm finished," Donald beseeched.

And seeing him pinned up on that cross like some insect on an entomologist's pegboard, splayed out for the whole world to see, reduced to a battered, desolate, and desperate version of the formerly kind - if overzealous - man he'd once been, the only person in all of Decoy to give a damn about him, broke something inside of Kaufman - cut him to the very core.

"I beg you, show me mercy. Send me to meet my maker."

Kaufman licked his lips. He felt as ragged and spent as ash. "After all this," he croaked, "how can you still believe?"

With eyes full of need, Donald said, "After all this, how can I not?"

Kaufman nodded, and for the first time in his life, he understood his friend's faith, understood how similar they were, understood that they were just different casualties in the same tragedy, and so he turned to Hollie and asked for the revolver.

"No, Kaufman...don't," she whispered, shaking her head, a hand over her heart.

Everything in her told her to run to him, to put her arms around him and hold him.

But she couldn't.

Pouring out of Kaufman was an anguish so profound that she was nearly lost by just glimpsing it, and as much as she wanted to ease his burden and share his sorrow, she was terrified that in doing so she'd be devoured by it.

So, he made it easier for her.

Closing his eyes, he buried the pain, shut it out, and hardened his heart like only someone who's suffered ungodly amounts of neglect and abuse could do. And a moment later, when he looked back up, his countenance was as flat and lifeless as if he'd been lobotomized.

It was the saddest thing Hollie had ever seen.

Slowly she walked over to him, her footsteps echoing emptily, and when she handed him the Smith & Wesson, he turned away resolutely - a man resigned to his fate.

"Wait outside," he said.

Hollie left, and once he heard the door close, Kaufman finished filling himself with a void as bottomless and dark as the space between stars. It didn't surprise him how easily he could find that emptiness, but it did frighten him.

Stepping up on the dais, he raised the barrel of the gun.

There was no tremble in his hand, but everything inside screamed.

"God bless you," Donald murmured.

"God has nothing to do with this," said Kaufman, and he pulled the trigger.

Outside, and all the way back at the Humvee, the sharp crack made Hollie jump.

She held Matthew and Seibu close.

. . .

It was a long time before Kaufman appeared, but when he did, his eyes were still empty, and he held a Polaroid.

"Is this Shane?"

The photo showed a smiling man with dark hair.

"That's him," said Matthew, although the question and the snapshot were directed at Hollie.

"You've met him too?" Hollie exclaimed.

Matthew nodded. He then went on to explain how Jessica had drowned, and how he'd been dragging what he thought was her dead body back into town when Shane had come along. He described the creepy blessing about fear and how the guy had vanished just as suddenly as he'd appeared.

Hollie, too, recounted her tale, told about being abducted and watching Shane slit his own throat. She insisted that it was imperative that they find him, not only to rescue Jessica but because he held Dr. Murakami captive too.

"Shane swore Dr. Murakami was alive, held prisoner in his basement. He said Murakami was his doubting Thomas, but that he wouldn't be killed until he saw Shane in all his glory."

Hollie looked at Kaufman pointedly. "We can't let that happen. Dr. Murakami is the only one who really knows what's going on here, and he'll be able to tell us how to stop it."

"Can we Google his address?" asked Matthew.

"We don't need to," said Kaufman.

"What do you mean?" Hollie asked, turning in his direction.

But Kaufman didn't answer right away, just stared down at the man in the photo, stared as if he believed that, by looking long enough and hard enough, he could somehow change what he saw there.

"How could I have missed it?"

"Missed what?"

Kaufman went on, talking to himself rather than answering Hollie.

"You're not the protégé. You're the master."

"The master of what?" Hollie asked though she wasn't so sure she wanted the answer.

"Of Dominism," said Kaufman, finally looking up. "Shane is Göttlich. Shane is my father."

CHAPTER 19

"How is that possible?" demanded Hollie.

Kaufman remained silent.

"It's *not* possible," she answered for him. "I've seen the great Göttlich Striker, and he's a human lizard: bald, angular, and pale. Shane, on the other hand, could be George Clooney's twin."

"His baldness comes from shaving," Kaufman proffered.

"Did you ever see him with hair?"

"No…"

"And it wouldn't have mattered if he'd had a wig made identical to Shane's hair," asserted Hollie, "because they still wouldn't look alike."

"I'm, not so sure," said Kaufman, looking at the Polaroid more closely and trying to envision the smiling face of Shane as that of his father's.

The transformation was remarkably easy.

"He could have bulked up, grown out his hair, and had some plastic surgery and dental work done…he certainly had the money."

"But why?" Hollie challenged. "Why would he go to such lengths?"

Kaufman didn't immediately reply; instead, he turned the photograph in his hands, spun it as if it were a puzzle piece that, if positioned in just the right way, would click into place and bring enlightenment.

"Because of Dominism," he whispered, the answer coming as unexpectedly as a summer squall, and as Kaufman continued, his conviction grew. "Because conquering death would have been the crowning achievement in his quest of total self-mastery. Because resurrection would free him from the body's most fundamental weakness, and it would have proved that he'd succeeded in completely overcoming the human condition. Somehow Göttlich must have known what NewLife was working on; he may have even moved here just to be close."

"Impossible," said Hollie, pacing, her resolute denial refusing to allow her to keep still. "There is no way your father could have known about Project Osiris. But if he did - and that's a big if - it obviously would have appealed to him. Death is the one thing every living creature on this planet has in common. It is the great equalizer, the great unknown, the mystery that has spawned nearly every religion, philosophy, and mythos through all history and throughout every civilization."

"But he knew," insisted Kaufman.

"How?" Hollie snapped, throwing up her hands. She wasn't just annoyed by Kaufman's insistence; she couldn't comprehend it. He was acting like a stubborn child.

Taking a breath, Kaufman opened his mouth to speak, then closed it. Absently he rubbed at his throat.

In the Humvee, when Hollie had revealed that they'd been resurrected, he'd been so astounded that he'd let slip he'd inadvertently killed himself. Now he found it difficult to admit to his witless suicide. He didn't want Hollie thinking less of him, but since she already knew, what was the point in being embarrassed?

Sighing, Kaufman said, "Because before I accidentally hanged myself, I got a letter from Göttlich."

"Let me guess it was a birthday card with ten bucks in it and a note explaining how the government was bringing people back from the dead?" Hollie quipped.

"Not exactly," said Kaufman. "He sent me my own death certificate."

Scrunching up her face, Hollie stopped and shivered.

"Ugh, why would he do that?"

"At the time, I thought he was encouraging me to commit suicide to test my vulnerability to Dominique Green's death."

"Jeez," blurted Matthew, "and I thought my dad was a creep."

More surprised that Matthew had spoken than by what he'd said, Kaufman turned to the boy.

"Sorry," said Matthew looking chagrin, "it's just…that's messed up."

"You're right, it is," said Kaufman giving Matthew a reassuring smile; he was really starting to like the kid. "I think now, though, the reason Göttlich was so precise about the time I should kill myself - between ten and ten-thirty - was because he knew what was going to happen."

Hollie started pacing again.

"That's the first thing you've said that makes sense."

"Why?" asked Kaufman. "Why was it so important that I be dead at such a precise time?"

"Because, whatever the military used to resurrect us might not have worked if we'd been dead too long," she explained.

Nodding, Kaufman said, "Like you mentioned about a soldier being blown up in an explosion whose body would be too greatly damaged to repair?"

"Exactly," said Hollie, her memory turning back to the mineshaft yesterday morning, and suddenly she realized that even though Shane had known the precise time in which Shafter would be running their trial, he'd still sacrificed them both to experimental technology.

"Damn, that bastard had a seriously diamond-hard pair of cojones," she muttered, astounded by Shane's leap of faith.

"What?" Kaufman asked.

"Nothing," Hollie said, waving him off. "Still, even if that's the case, if whatever brought us back was only effective during a finite period of time, and we all died within that window, I've yet to be convinced of the Shane-Göttlich connection. Your father was eccentric; I'll give you that - downright Tom Cruise bonkers for all I know," she said, fixing Kaufman with a determined stare. "But Shane is a psychopath - a psychopath with a god complex - and I just can't imagine the iconoclast Göttlich had anything to do with Allah, Jesus, Buddha, or Elohim."

"But he did," said Kaufman holding up the Polaroid and explaining the painting on his living room wall entitled *The Face of God*.

"That only proves my point," Hollie declared. "Shane sees himself as a new messiah or avenging angel or something, and if he sent you that painting, then he probably also mailed you the death certificate and forged your father's signature."

"That's what I thought at first. I thought Shane might be working for Göttlich or had possibly killed him and that I was next. But now I know I had it wrong. The painting wasn't marking me for execution; it was telling me why I should commit suicide because I'd seen Göttlich's new face - *The Face of God*."

"Oh please! How could your father possibly expect you to recognize him if he'd undergone such a dramatic change?"

"Because Göttlich means God."

"Excuse me?" said Hollie, shaken.

Kaufman explained. "My father was always making sly puns with names - my own, our dog's - and his was no exception. Göttlich is German for divine,

206

or just Gott means God. See it's a joke: his name implies he's slapping divinity - Göttlich Striker - or, better yet, the joke is on other people when they call him God, which is exactly how Shane sees himself."

Hollie took a second to respond, her position less solid than it had been a moment ago. "That's stretching it a bit."

"Not at all," continued Kaufman. "You have to remember that before everything happened, I didn't know about Shane. I just had a piece of artwork whose title seemed to infer that looking at it required death. I also had a death certificate from my father telling me how and when I should take my own life for doing so. The signature at the bottom was the key. Göttlich - that is to say, God - had signed my life away because I'd seen his face in the painting. That's how I was to recognize his new look."

Hollie stopped pacing. "Do you know what you're saying?" A horrified and troubled expression darkened her face. "You're saying that it was your father who crucified Donald."

"I know," sighed Kaufman. "And Donald wasn't his only victim." He told them about Anthony. "Daddy's been busy."

Hollie bit her lip. "Is your father really capable of all that?"

"He's just capable period," Kaufman said, "of everything; entirely masterful and proficient."

Hollie shook her head. "Still," she said in a soft voice, hating herself for playing the devil's advocate but compelled by her scientific training. "You can't be positive. Even with your deduction, you have no proof that the signature on the death certificate wasn't faked."

"You're right, of course," Kaufman admitted. "There is one way to make certain, though." He looked out towards the east, and instantly Hollie knew what he was thinking, and wondered why she couldn't keep her big fat mouth shut.

"We have to go to The Dwelling."

• • •

From a distance, the garish skyline of Decoy blurred into a glossy flame, and the surrounding mountains seemed like old men hunkered around a dying ember.

As they left the old two-lane highway, Hollie noticed that Kaufman was driving far slower than the gravel road required. She wished there was something she could do to make this visit easier on him. Surely, he'd vowed never to set foot in The Dwelling again or even come within sight of it, yet she'd forced his hand; and as the miles went by, her guilt grew.

As they came within sight of The Dwelling, Hollie wanted to tell Kaufman to turn around, that they didn't have to do this - only he'd already hardened himself, shrugging off his feelings, just as he'd done back at the church before mercy-killing Donald. Hollie at first took this as a defense mechanism, but it was much more than that; Kaufman wasn't lapsing into denial to avoid some unpleasantness but had fortified himself as a survival mechanism because he knew what they were about to face.

Hollie, on the other hand, was caught completely off guard.

Although she'd seen photos of The Dwelling, nothing could have prepared her for being in its presence. No camera - no matter how advanced, nor how skilled the photographer - could fully capture the power and presence of such an edifice. Like all commanding architecture, it had to be experienced.

Standing prominently amongst a field of jagged and porous black volcanic boulders jutting up out of the sand at oblique angles, the asymmetrical domicile sprawled before them. Oily flat slabs of concrete shimmered and clashed with craggy barnacle surfaces. The monolith wasn't massive, yet somehow it made the surrounding desert seem…insignificant.

Sucking in sharply, Hollie slid down into her seat.

The building wasn't pure evil, but it wasn't benign either.

The Dwelling called to her, yet rather than being inviting, it compelled.

There was no line or angle, no material or texture, no single element that was the cause of this reaction, but the overall façade was nothing short of domineering. The place brought to mind the Ministry of Love building from George Orwell's *1984* dystopian novel, and Hollie could easily imagine citizens being "reeducated" within those walls, having their worst fears used against them to break them down and make them, not just faithful lovers of their government again, but unquestioning believers.

One look at the place, and it didn't require any persuasion to get Matthew and Seibu to stay in the Humvee this time. It took an act of will, however, for Hollie to leave the car, and, even then, she almost wasn't able to muster the courage. Kaufman, on the other hand, seemed to have no problems, at least not outwardly. Like a programmed drone, he exited the SUV and made his way towards the entrance.

"Wait," Hollie entreated, falling behind. "Are we sure this is necessary? What if Shane…or Göttlich or whoever, is waiting for us? What if this is exactly what he wants?"

Kaufman turned, and his answer made her sick, made her want to tuck tail and run.

"This is exactly what he wants," he said. "He's been luring us here from the very start."

Hollie bit her lip. *Then what the holy hell are we doing here?*

But she knew the answer to her own internal question.

You mean besides rescuing Jessica and saving Dr. Murakami? Well, you accepted the dare to kiss your new boyfriend in the most scary-assed haunted mansion in the freaking world, of course; so, no backing out now, chicken shit.

Hollie sighed, recognizing her humor as being driven by fear - the kind of nervous jesting people did when they were heading into a situation they knew they weren't likely to come out of alive.

"Well, he sure isn't subtle about his invitations, is he?"

"No," Kaufman agreed mirthlessly and went inside.

Pinching herself to steel her resolve, Hollie followed. But when she stepped through the front door, her determination dried up.

It was as if she'd just walked into the darkest corner of Tim Burton's imagination.

Everywhere, distorted lines threatened, and angles threw her off balance; everything was grey on grey on grey - a monochromatic palate of despair.

Hollie could feel herself growing edgy, anxious, and oppressed. She wanted to scream, and she was just across the threshold. How long before she couldn't deal with the taxation of The Dwelling anymore? Would she end up throwing herself off the roof as a handful of businessmen had done at Göttlich's only public building?

She shuddered at the possibility, and without thinking, she took Kaufman's hand.

"How did you ever get comfortable enough to sleep in this place?" she asked, squeezing tightly, trying to give sympathy as much as take comfort.

"You're not meant to get comfortable," Kaufman said, not registering the intimate gesture. "You're meant to master your feelings. Dominism is often described as an architectural form of Asceticism - that's why there are no beds or other furnishings. But at its heart, Dominism is about control, not enlightenment. You either control the internal or the external controls you."

He motioned to the crushing cubist space they were in as if to emphasize his point.

"Charming," she said with unrestrained sarcasm. "I can see now why your mother found your father so attractive."

"Attraction had nothing to do with it," Kaufman said, leading them deeper into the house. "My father specifically selected my mother as the best proving grounds for him to transcend his sexual and emotional desires for love."

Hollie pulled sharply to a stop.

"What!?" she gasped.

Kaufman shrugged.

"For Göttlich, mere denial of the body's emotions and appetites wasn't true mastery of them. One couldn't say they'd overcome the lust for wealth if they'd never had the opportunity to be rich. Even turning down the offer of millions isn't enough. To fully be in control, a person has to know the power, influence, and prestige money brings, and care nothing for it. And what better way for my father to distill his biological and psychological yearning for companionship into something less than breeding, than with a woman like my mother? A famous French actress, who was, by all accounts, an outspoken man-hater and lesbian? For her devotion to be authenticated, she would have to give up so much, change so radically that her affections could never be called into question. Göttlich then, in effect, had his substantial capital with which he could then choose to do without."

Hollie blinked and opened her mouth wide to give him a piece of her mind, but nothing came out; instead, she threw away his hand and crossed her arms in disgust.

Kaufman's callousness wasn't just repulsive; it was scary. He'd spoke of his mother as dispassionately as a sanitarium worker describing fecal matter. Could the stoicism she'd found so attractive in him when they'd stormed Donald's church have been nothing more than the kindest version of this cold indifference?

Realizing he'd done something to upset Hollie, Kaufman smiled apologetically. It was just the faintest flutter, but in that slight curl of lips, Hollie saw that his aloofness was only a mask, a way to cover up the terrible sadness and pain underneath.

And suddenly she wished she hadn't been so abrupt. This couldn't be easy for him, and here she was holding things his father had done before he was even born against him as if Kaufman himself were somehow responsible.

"I'm sorry," Hollie said, snatching up both his hands this time. "I shouldn't have done that; it's just…"

Kaufman shook his head and continued.

"Under any other circumstances I know my mother would have aborted me, for the pregnancy not only ruined her career but the rest of her life - especially as she wasn't able to refuse Göttlich when he asked her to raise me, even though she knew that, just like with her, he only sought to transcended the proprietary obligations of fatherhood."

Hollie again opened her mouth to speak, to make a wisecrack about such a horrible upbringing, except she could find no jest to lighten the mood, no jib appropriate enough to sooth. So instead, she crushed Kaufman's hands in her own, hoping to impart a fraction of the empathy she felt for him…but he didn't seem to notice. However, when he told her not to worry, that it was all in the past, she could see that his eyes told a far different story.

"Anyway, we should keep going."

Hollie nodded. She knew Kaufman was right, knew that this was no place for a heart-to-heart; therapy would have to wait. It was imperative they locate Dr. Murakami, but Hollie found she had to choke down hard on her emotions to get moving again. It was so unfair that after Kaufman had reopened the scab of his past, there wasn't time to properly bandage it, that he would have to, once again, bear its festering stinking rawness. Hollie vowed that when this was all over, she'd help him heal…somehow.

Moving through The Dwelling, they passed several rooms that were less than utilitarian and hardly recognizable. No decorations or personal effects adorned the walls, nor was there anything that even suggested the spaces were meant for people to live in. This led Hollie to quickly conclude that no hidden doorways led to secret basements in any of the rooms they stopped in.

In contrast, Kaufman took his time exploring each wall and floorboard, running his hands along every joint and seam.

"If Göttlich *is* Shane," said Kaufman as he worked, sensing Hollie's impatience to move on, "and if he does have Dr. Murakami locked away somewhere, then it's going to be well concealed. As a kid, I searched every inch of this place, so we need to be thorough."

Mentally Hollie whipped herself - of course, a *hidden* cellar wasn't going to be easy to find. Not ten minutes in, and she was already throwing in the towel. Although her perfunctory inspection was only a kneejerk reaction to the constant oppression of this place, she still felt like a coward, felt like she'd let Kaufman down.

She rejoined him in his more exhaustive examination; they searched several rooms but found nothing. However, Hollie noticed Kaufman deliberately avoiding a large brass door at the end of a long hallway. The tarnished and irregularly riveted door seemed to grow larger as they neared.

Hollie thought there must be some optical illusion in play. "What's in that room down there?"

"Göttlich's office."

Hollie waited for more, but Kaufman said nothing else.

"And we aren't checking in there because…"

"Because I'm not allowed in there."

For a second, Hollie thought he was joking, thought his reply had been a feeble attempt at humor.

"Are you serious?" she asked, half laughing.

"Yes, it's forbidden. I'm not allowed in unless—"

Kaufman let the sentence go unfinished, and Hollie could see awareness come into his face.

Even after all these years, even after he'd left and made a life for himself, Kaufman couldn't get away from the conditioning he'd received as a boy. Göttlich and his teaching still manacled him; and although Kaufman could recognize that brainwashing, he wasn't, at present, able to do anything about it.

An awkward silence filled the room, and Hollie knew she would have to be the one to act, which was okay with her – earlier, she'd wished to bear a part of Kaufman's burden, and here now was her opportunity.

"Right, there's probably nothing in there anyway," Hollie said quickly, hoping to minimize Kaufman's embarrassment. "You finish searching here, and I'll go take a look."

Even though he didn't speak or show any signs of indebtedness, Hollie could nonetheless feel Kaufman's silent gratitude. Her magnanimous feelings of helping him keep face were short-lived, though, because halfway down the hall, she felt completely alone and vulnerable.

Why had she thought it would be a good idea to go alone? If Göttlich *was* Shane, then as an architect, it would have been as easy for him to conceal a hidden room as a magician might flick a card into thin air and make it disappear. So, what made her think she could just waltz in and find it? She wasn't special - just a childless, sinful, vain woman that thought she knew it all.

Hollie stopped.

Where were these thoughts coming from? She'd never condemned herself like this before. But she knew. It was this place; The Dwelling had been in her head and under her skin since she first laid eyes on it.

Come on you pussy, if Kaufman endured this hellhole for his whole life, you can handle it for one afternoon.

But her motivational insult didn't help, and, with growing dread, she continued down the corridor. As she walked, Hollie clasped the heavy shotgun to her chest - except, rather than being reassuring, it felt cumbersome and as ungainly as a bazooka.

Reaching the warped and discolored door, Hollie would have sworn the thing wasn't inert but alive. She had no problem imagining it as the mouth to the underworld, waiting to swallow up unwitting souls. She also had no problem imagining Shane waiting for her on the other side, so instead of opening the door with her hand, she pushed it open with the tip of the shotgun, ready to blast away whatever might be lurking beyond.

The door swung soundlessly open, and Hollie's imagination wasn't vivid enough to conceive what lay beyond. The room was not some small bookshelf-lined office, but a massive, gym-sized space with a vaulted ceiling covered in bizarre cones. Massive stalactites, as thick as trees and nearly as long, hung from the ceiling, which gave the room tremendous weight; and the floor was dark paneled hardwood, arranged at jarring angles that created the illusion of movement.

A few drafting tables and a large desk stood like forgotten medieval torture devices in the windowless expanse, and the vast emptiness and weird architecture gave Hollie the impression of an art deco Stalinist bomb shelter.

However, apart from the daggered canopy and the vertigo floor, the room was the most functional she'd come across.

Taking a deep breath, Hollie entered, and in the glare of harsh lights, she should have felt confident of finding any secret door, but although her thoughts before had been self-defeating, those doubts about locating a concealed basement now were nevertheless confirmed. She had no idea what she was looking for, and the room was too bare and too explicit to be hiding anything.

However, even if she hadn't been looking, Hollie couldn't have missed it, might even have fallen down the damn thing - for the trap door had been left open.

A purposeful, mocking, arrogant taunt; as subtle as using hedge trimmers to give a haircut.

The black rectangle cut across the floor like digital camouflage. When closed, it would fit neatly and undetectably among the elaborate wooden mosaic slats.

For a long while, Hollie stood looking down into that dark hole and contemplated what lay below. Finally, she called out to Kaufman and instantly regretted her action. She felt like the dumb broad in a slasher movie yelling for help and letting the maniac with a hatchet know precisely where she was.

Luckily it was Kaufman, and not Shane, that came to her beckon.

At the threshold of the office, though, Kaufman hesitated.

Hollie watched.

A quiet war raged in Kaufman as he struggled to overcome the mental and emotional discipline his father had imposed on him as a child.

The battle was intense - nuclear - but brief, and when Kaufman did cross over, he let out the softest of exhalations.

Hollie marveled at the inner strength and resilience he'd just displayed. She wondered how many other people could have done what he'd just done. How many could have lived his childhood and not end up so completely unraveled and mentally cracked that they'd be locked up in some psych ward? Very few, she supposed. She doubted she could have endured half as much, and at the basement opening, Kaufman again displayed the tenacity and grit she so greatly admired.

He didn't waver in the least but descend the stairs whose very existence advocated that his father was indeed a killer, the orchestrator of the Decoy Madness, and a mass murderer.

"Come on," he said, and they plunged into darkness.

. . .

Outside, Matthew was growing impatient.

Hollie and Kaufman had been in the weird-looking house for a long time, so long that he worried something might have happened to them, something bad. Or worse, something had happened to Jess, and they didn't know how to come out and tell him about it.

Well, screw that. As nice as Kaufman and Hollie were, they weren't family. Jessica was *his* responsibility and he was done waiting.

Reaching out for the door handle, Matthew jumped as a sharp knock rapped the window behind him.

Snapping his head around, Matthew immediately recognized the smiling face that greeted him.

Shane.

Bringing up his hand, he gave Matthew a little wave.

The hand was covered in blood.

CHAPTER 20

Step by step, Kaufman and Hollie moved towards a light. They were like moths being drawn to a flame, and although the source of the illumination wasn't likely to physically destroy them, what it revealed wouldn't leave them unscathed.

Already the wrongness of the place was evident in the hard rubber that lined the ground, and all too soon, the inky blackness gave way to harsh phosphorescent light.

White and sterile, the incongruity of the surgical suite at the end of the hall went well beyond the thick partition of Plexiglas that sectioned off the space. No one with good intentions secreted away and soundproofed a room where human flesh was cut open.

Except this was no operating room. It was a morgue.

"Oh, God!" Hollie moaned and ran forward.

Kaufman stepped in front of her. Tried to turn her away, tried to shield her from the sight.

"We're too late," he said.

"Noooo!" she shrieked, tearing free and throwing herself at the Plexiglas.

Despairingly, Kaufman turned towards the cell.

There, on a kind of hydraulic autopsy table, was laid out an elderly Japanese man. Thick restraining straps held the swollen and dissected body in place, but this had been anything but a routine postmortem. Those bindings were a clear indicator that Adam Murakami had been alive when the cutting had started.

Kaufman put a hand against the wall. Irrational self-accusations dizzied him. Even though he was as much a casualty of Göttlich as anyone held in this prison under the floorboards, even though he'd only been a child carefully groomed with ignorance and controlled through naiveté, he still felt responsible.

He should have realized what was going on. Somehow, he should have known.

Nausea filled Kaufman, but rage kept it down.

How many people had his father held captive down here over the years? How many had been tortured and killed while he'd been studying in the next room?

Any number was too many, and Kaufman's logic and reasoning was obliterated by the tsunami of guilt that washed over him.

Wild with despair, and disoriented by self-loathing, Kaufman staggered over to Hollie, who was still hammering away at the plastic wall.

"Enough!" he shouted, grabbing her up in a bear hug and pulling her away from the Plexiglas.

But Hollie hadn't had enough, wasn't even close to being finished.

Breaking free, she ran over to the metal door that gave access to the cell and began beat out an irregular rhythm of grief and vexation; each blow rang out as dully as a mallet striking a steel drum. For what seemed like minutes, Hollie hammered away until an electronic scratching rose from the thunderous percussion.

"What was that?" Kaufman asked, spinning, thinking that the door above was rolling shut and that they were in the process of being locked in.

Hollie fell silent.

The electronic rasping came again, and this time the noise was unmistakable. A voice.

Set in the wall beside the glass barrier was an intercom. Over the years, the soundproof room had locked in untold terror, but right now, it admitted the weak voice of Dr. Murakami.

"W-Who's…there?"

Hollie rushed to the intercom and fumbled with the buttons.

"Dr. Murakami, it's me: Hollie Cunningham."

"Who's with you?" rasped the voice.

"A friend."

"My name's Kaufman Striker, sir."

Dr. Murakami winced then nodded as if he'd been expecting this.

"Shane's son."

Kaufman stiffened.

Although he'd accepted the idea of Göttlich being Shane, being addressed as his son stung.

"Your silence suggests you already knew."

"No," Kaufman mumbled. "No, I didn't know about any of this."

Hollie interrupted. "Dr. Murakami, don't talk now, you can tell us everything later once we get you out of here."

"Don't be a fool!" snapped Dr. Murakami with sudden intensity. "Even if you did somehow manage to get in here, I'd die the second you open the door, and you wouldn't learn anything; so, let go of the idea of saving me Hollie, I'm well beyond that."

Hollie bit her lip, both at the sharp rebuke and its double meaning.

"I'm sorry, Hollie," said Dr. Murakami, softer this time. "It's just…all I have left is talk."

He turned his head to look at her then, and although his body and face were horribly mutilated, his eyes - his eyes were untouched. They had intentionally been left unspoiled to supposedly witness Shane in all his glory and be able to weep bitterly.

Anger rose up fresh in Hollie, white-hot.

That bastard was going to pay for this.

From the speakers, the bruised voice of Dr. Murakami crackled again.

"Hollie listen, for many years now, I've lied to you about what I was trying to achieve."

"I know," Hollie whispered, hating Shane for making her once dignified mentor confess his deception. "And, it's okay."

"The hell it is!" barked Dr. Murakami, his pristine eyes narrowing. "I'm not telling you this so you'll forgive me, I'm telling you so that you'll understand what I've done - and stop it."

"How do you stop a resurrection?" Hollie asked, feeling as bewildered as she imagined Kaufman must have felt when she'd first explained to him what Project Osiris was. "Reverse it? That doesn't make any sense."

"No, no," chuckled Dr. Murakami, deep and haltingly. "That's not it at all. Resurrection was just the outlandish notion everyone thought I was secretly interested in - my eccentric fantasy - and I let you and the military go on believing that. But resurrection was only a steppingstone to what I truly hoped to accomplish. Resurrection was the easy-to-swallow goal."

Hollie scowled.

How was resurrection an easy-to-swallow goal? She had actually worked on the project and *been* resurrected, yet the reality that Shafter scientists had somehow accomplished this mystical feat was almost too much to fathom, even for her. Yet now Dr. Murakami was telling them that resurrection was the easy part. If resurrection was the easy part, what was the hard part?

"Steppingstone to what?" Hollie asked, feeling punch-drunk and uneasy, the possibilities stalking her imagination.

Dr. Murakami took a deep labored breath. His injured body resisted the work, but when he spoke again, his voice was strong and clear.

"After I died, everything I thought I knew about life changed. I came to know I had a soul, some essence that went beyond my defined biological anatomy. I knew it down to my very core, yet how could I reconcile that new spiritual view with my empirical knowledge? I was a man of science. I'd spent my entire life in the fields of biology and mathematics, made my fortune applying evolutionary principals to computers and software, and then tuned those innovations into cutting edge gene therapies. Was I to now throw that all away and jump on the Creationist bandwagon because I'd experienced consciousness beyond death?

"I could not. But neither could I completely believe that the modern evolutionary synthesis was *the* theory of life anymore, for one of its basic axioms states that all evolutionary phenomena can be accounted for in a way consistent with known genetic mechanisms, and I had experienced something inconsistent. For I could not dismiss my vivid revelation during my three hours of inert brain activity as just a delusion or some programming error brought on when my cerebral cortex rebooted after my body was resuscitated."

Dr. Murakami paused for a moment and licked his lips.

"Not only that, but I had been shown differently."

Cocking an eyebrow, Kaufman glanced over at Hollie. *Shown,* he mouthed, and she shrugged, but she knew exactly what he was thinking: Dr. Murakami sounded nuts, sounded like a religious lunatic, sounded like...like Shane. Was this some form of Stockholm syndrome? Had Dr. Murakami's torture been so intense that he now not only sympathized with Shane but believed him? The truth seemed obvious, and only Hollie's deep respect for her mentor kept her mouth closed.

"Your incredulity is understandable," Dr. Murakami wheezed, having caught Hollie and Kaufman's silent exchange. "Many of my colleges responded the same way. They thought I'd come back from my 'ordeal' - as they referred to my death - without all of my mental facilities intact.

"Talk of the soul is little appreciated in the scientific community, let alone talk of visions - especially ones that postulate the idea that science and religion aren't at odds."

"Wait…what?" said Hollie.

A slight smile crossed Dr. Murakami's face.

"I'm glad to see you haven't completely dismissed me as mad, Hollie."

Ashamed to have her misgivings so easily read, Hollie blushed and looked away.

"You have to understand," continued Dr. Murakami, "that although I awoke in that Anchorage hospital with faith in souls, I didn't come back believing in God. Not in any secular form anyway, which freed me from the catch-22 between creation and evolution. My belief in God didn't go beyond a higher power, one that set the universe in motion and established natural laws, and if you take God out of the equation or at least don't limit an omnipotent being in His use of creative tools - evolution being one of them - then that particular catch-22 goes away and what you're left with is an unclouded understanding of the history of life.

"You see, when humans made the great evolutionary leap forward, we not only separated ourselves from all other animals on earth and become the dominant species, we changed the world forever. But it wasn't because we'd grown bigger brains or started using tools or complex symbolic thoughts; it was because in that instant - in the pivotal crutch of evolution - man evolved a soul."

Kaufman cleared his throat. "Humans evolved a soul," he repeated as if the statement needed to be seconded to be believed.

"Yes." Dr. Murakami nodded. "That was part of what I was shown, but I was not content merely to just believe. Faith did not satiate me. I wanted proof, and I'm not talking in philosophical terms. I wanted biological evidence of the incorporeal human essence. I wanted to find the soul of man."

"You went searching for the Holy Grail," said Hollie.

"Hardly," croaked Dr. Murakami. "Finding anatomical corroboration of the spirit is not the pinnacle of genetic research. Actually, it's about as far from it as one can get. The Cup of Christ was a tangible object, but what I was looking for couldn't be perceived by any of our senses."

"But then, where would you even reasonably start to look?" Hollie asked.

Except she knew.

"You went digging in our junk DNA."

"Exactly," said Dr. Murakami. "If what I had been shown was true, if the soul truly came into being during the birth of consciousness and advanced intelligence, then I concluded that it must be coded somewhere in our DNA."

"And you found it!" Hollie gasped. "That's the discovery you made that brought Project Osiris back from the brink of failure."

"Yes, I found it; I found the soul and so much more. I found the true Holy Grail."

Kaufman frowned. What could possibly trump the biological evidence of the soul?

"You mentioned resurrection was only a steppingstone…to what exactly?"

"Actually, it's more of a doorway."

"To what end?" Kaufman pressed.

"Mankind's true potential."

Kaufman scoffed, but Hollie knew better, she knew the history of evolutionary thought.

"You're referring to Teleology," she said. "The idea that final causes exist, that design and purpose are intrinsic in nature and that evolution is proceeding to some ultimate long-term goal."

"Wait, what…?" sputtered Kaufman. "You aren't talking about a zoological ladder where humans are the highest life form, are you? Isn't that a bit outdated?"

"That is the great debate," said Dr. Murakami. "It's what science and many religions have been at odds with from the very beginning. Yet, the idea of evolution with an end goal is not a new theory. Before Darwin, Plato and Aristotle's Great Chain of Being, which ordered life in a strict hierarchy, was used by Jean-Baptiste Lamarck to form his theory of progressive life, which stated that simple creatures gradual improved over time towards a more perfect development.

"Even up until the 1950s, Orthogenetic, or progressive evolution, presented the notion that life has an inherent proclivity to move in a unilinear manner driven by an internal process rather random chance.

"However, these days it's politically incorrect to refer to a species as being more or less advanced than another, as this indicates intent in evolution where none should exist - according to the modern evolutionary synthesis, that is. Biologists prefer to say an organism is more or less complex, yet even this idea carries with it the semantic notion of evolutionary intent."

All at once, Dr. Murakami was seized by a coughing fit, and his body arched against the restraints. Hollie sucked in sharply as dark blood bubbled at the corners of Dr. Murakami's mouth, and he thrashed on the table.

It took a long time for him to regain enough strength to be able to speak again, and Hollie's inability to ease her mentor's pain felt like broken glass in her stomach. She was grateful when Kaufman put a hand on her shoulder. It was solid and reassuring, and without his presence, there was no way she could have held it together.

"Why don't you take a minute and rest," Kaufman suggested.

"No…it's okay…I'm fine…let me continue," panted Dr. Murakami.

After a moment, his breathing eased, and he went on.

"Don't get me wrong, I'm not suggesting that Darwin was incorrect, but he used natural selection as *the* fundamental mechanism of evolution, and that only works up to a point.

"For many centuries now, humans have risen above the direct influence of natural selection. We control our environment and are ten thousand times more common than the rule of the animal kingdom states we should be. We've reduced the opportunities for random change through our globalization of the world; we also intervene and correct genetic defaults in our DNA, and so avoid many mutations that might otherwise have changed our species or stopped us from reproducing. In other words, because we influence natural selection more than natural selection influences us, do we now no longer evolve? There are arguments to this effect. But if Neo-Darwinism accounts for only part of the picture, then what's remains?"

Dr. Murakami paused and cleared his throat.

"What if evolution was only a random process up to a point - the point where we as a species made the great leap forward of advanced intelligence - where we gained a soul and separated ourselves from all other species on earth? Where would we go then? What would evolution's next great leap be for us?

Dr. Murakami spat out a thick wad of blood; he was bleeding more freely now. Talking wasn't just taking a toll; it was killing him.

"That's what I was sought to achieve: the second great evolutionary leap. You yourselves are proof that death isn't infinite, and in the process have become living testaments of humanity's next plane of existence."

Hollie swallowed hard.

"What are you talking about, Dr. Murakami? We were resurrected, not changed into some new species."

But even as she spoke, Hollie knew she was wrong. So did Kaufman. They had changed…yet what exactly had they changed into?

"You yourself jokingly referred to resurrected cells as extraterrestrial," said Dr. Murakami, his voice vigorous now, tinged with excitement. "And so it is."

"Are you saying we've become aliens?" Kaufman asked, thinking of the Project Osiris report and wondering if he'd had it right all along.

"No, no, that's absurd. Extraterrestrial, in that sense, would imply that you weren't from Earth. What I'm saying is that you've evolved beyond this world and are no longer bound by mortality. What I'm saying," said Dr. Murakami, pausing for emphasis, "is that you've become angels."

Hollie balked. It was a half cough, half splutter. "Adam, please, you can't be serious."

"But I am. What would convince you? Wings?"

Hollie couldn't reply. Her mouth worked but formed no words. She looked at Kaufman for help, but he had no response either.

"Listen, a soul with a resurrected body is a celestial being," said Dr. Murakami with the solemnity of an Old Testament prophet. "Or in layman's terms, an angel, and this idea is not as farfetched as you may think. Many religions teach that with death, there will be a resurrection and then eternal glory where the righteous will worship God as glorified beings. Even non-Christian sects believe in an afterlife where the body will be transformed. In fact, almost all denominations preach of some kind of enlightenment where humans transcended their earthly existence.

"This is what I was shown in my vision - what an *angel* showed me - evolution's next great leap, and it's what's happened to you…or at least is happening. But you don't have to believe me; the truth is in you. Surely you're experiencing things that go beyond mere physical resurrection."

"What things?" Kaufman asked.

"Increased senses, telepathy, invulnerability, a refinement of features, I don't know what else. The text on angelic attributes is very convoluted, but you must have experienced some of these things."

Kaufman had indeed experienced all of those.

His broken collar bone had miraculously healed overnight, and his sense of taste had been heightened, not to mention he seemed to no longer need to sweat to regulate body temperature. And this morning, he'd sensed where everyone was without having opened his eyes. He hadn't just sensed them; he'd reached out his mind and known their emotional states. His physical appearance had also undergone a dramatic change. Hollie's own features looked flawless. Even with digital editing, Kaufman doubted, an artist could have enhanced her allure to a higher degree; she almost seemed to be glowing.

"How did you do it?" Hollie asked in a voice that was barely above a whisper. She seemed to have come to the same realizations Kaufman had.

With a sigh, Dr. Murakami said, "This is my great regret. Although I saw how our souls came into existence and saw what we were destined to become, I wasn't content to just sit by and let evolution take its course. I had glimpsed eternity and desired it for myself, so I set out to help things along."

"You forced evolution!?" Kaufman said tightly. As if opening God's cookbook wasn't enough, Dr. Murakami had hoped to speed up the baking time by turning up the temperature, and in the process, he'd destroyed an entire population.

"No, I just encouraged it."

"Actually, we direct evolution all the time," responded Hollie distractedly. "Directed evolution is a process used in labs all around the world," she explained. "Most commonly, it's implemented in protein engineering to exploit advantageous properties that aren't found in nature."

"Yes," agreed Dr. Murakami. "But that's just one application. However, long before DNA was discovered and we began experimenting with it in test tubes, we were domesticating livestock and developing agriculture - both of which produced plants and animals that would never have evolved naturally.

"In fact, since the beginning, homo sapiens have been intervening with evolution's design. All I did, in this case, was to promote our genes to take us where we were already headed. The information was there - just like the potential any piano has to be able to perform Beethoven's Moonlight Sonata - they just needed to be arranged in the correct order."

"But *how* did you do it?" Hollie asked again.

Dr. Murakami explained, his breathing growing more labored. "The government has a beautiful nanovirus that was the key - the perfect little Ludwig van Beethovens."

Hollie nodded thoughtfully.

"A virus would be the perfect vehicle for manipulating genetic sequences since they're already designed to do that. But are you controlling it?"

"Not entirely," Dr. Murakami confessed. "The nanovirus works with a Vibrotic pulse - a new experimental technology which acts much like a magnetic field, although it's far more than just a power source. Within the zone of the vibration, the virus manipulates junk DNA sequences, isolating certain genomes, specifically genes with angelus properties—"

"That's enough," interrupted Kaufman. "The technical details aren't important. What does my father have to do with all of this?"

Dr. Murakami regarded him.

"I assumed you knew."

Kaufman shook his head. "Call it a coincidental accident that I'm here," he said, thinking about his inadvertent suicide.

"I no longer believe in coincidences," Dr. Murakami pronounced.

Blood now flowed freely from his mouth, and one of the metal hooks in his abdomen had pulled loose, bringing with it a shiny purple organ. But Dr. Murakami was either too far gone or in too much pain to notice.

"Your father somehow learned of Project Osiris and was able to insert himself into the core group of those involved. He even changed his appearance and created a new identity to facilitate his infiltration, but how he successfully got access, I do not know.

"It was also never clear to me what his exact position was, but he generally acted as a liaison between the biotech companies and the military. It was as if he'd been waiting years for something like this to come along."

Kaufman nodded. "The idea of physical resurrection would have appealed to him; mastery over the physical body was central to his ideology."

"Yes," Dr. Murakami agreed, spitting blood with each word. "But he was interested in much more than that. Somehow, he deduced what I was really trying to achieve, and then he sabotaged the project to test the results on himself."

Hollie shuddered, and suddenly the words Shane had said to her after he'd shot her rang in her head.

You shall be my first angel.

He'd known! More, he'd believed.

"But it wasn't isolated," Hollie pointed out. "The whole town was infected. Is the nanovirus contagious?"

"No, it's not self-replicating; it has to be manufactured. But Shane flooded the base, and subsequently, Decoy was contaminated. He then set the pulse to magnify a hundred times what was intended during the trial experiment."

"So, all the bodies just beyond the city limits," said Kaufman, "that must be the radius of the pulse."

"Yes," Dr. Murakami agreed. "Shane knew when he turned on the power, the virus would kill anyone within the circumference of the pulse who wasn't already dead. He also knew it would keep people out."

"Why is that important?" asked Hollie.

"Because he needs prolonged exposure to the pulse to complete the evolutionary process."

"How long?"

"I don't know…" confessed Dr. Murakami. "It might not even be possible in its current configuration."

"Hold on," said Kaufman, interrupting Hollie's scientific inquiries again. "I still don't understand. If my father knew what was going on, if he was involved, then why did he torture you?"

Dr. Murakami closed his eyes then, gathering his strength. When he opened them, he asked, "Have you ever heard of the ONA?"

"No," Kaufman replied.

"I'm not surprised," said Dr. Murakami. "It's an acronym for a satanic organization called the Order of Nine Angels. The ONA is a highly individualized quest that aims to create the perfect self by undertaking challenges to allow a person to transcend their physical, emotional, and mental limits. And your father is a practitioner, although an extreme one even by that sect's standards."

Hollie could see that this was news to Kaufman, but it explained where Göttlich derived some of the underlining doctrines behind Dominism. It also explained his occult tattoos.

"Go on," said Kaufman in a dry voice.

"The ONA's ultimate goal is to evolve a superior race…and they encourage human sacrifice as a means of eliminating the weak and worthless. They believe in what they refer to as the 'Left-Hand Path' and in becoming Dark Warriors, and Göttlich is as devout as any Jihadist on any battlefield the world has ever known."

. . .

Outside, Shane smiled and waved.

In the bright sun, his bloody hand glistened.

Transfixed, Matthew numbly waved back.

Vaguely he wondered whose blood that was until Seibu pulled him into a protective embrace and started shrieking. Suddenly it wasn't really important whose blood it was. Shane had told him never to come near, and now they were at his house!

Matthew was struggling to free himself from Seibu when Shane opened the door and stuck in his smiling head.

That's when Seibu went apeshit.

Hissing and hooting, he rocked back and forth like an autistic child locked in a tantrum and stimming. Seibu bounced away from the open door and lashed out blindly, all the while clutching Matthew to him. The thick aroma of fur and fear filled Matthew's nose. He screamed at Seibu to let him go, but his voice was drowned out.

Pinned up against the far door, Matthew reached for the handle. He got hold of it and yanked, but it didn't open. Blindly he fumbled at the lock, and all at once, he and Seibu spilled out of the Humvee.

Untangling himself, Matthew leapt to his feet and ran; ran like he'd never been capable of before, ran like no mortal boy had ever been capable of.

"...five, six, seven, eight..."

The words shot out over the desert air like thunderclaps.

Legs pumping, muscles bunching Matthew looked back over his shoulder and saw Shane standing behind him laughing.

He knew what would happen when Shane reached ten.

Lowering his head, Matthew ran faster.

Except it wasn't fast enough.

"Ready or not, here I come."

And instantly, Shane was ahead of him.

As if stepping out from an invisible doorway, Shane pivoted into view, and Matthew only had a fraction of a second to register the outstretched arm coming at him like a clothesline.

A grand slam struck him across the chest, and the next thing he knew, he was rolling in the sand and scrub, gasping for air.

"You do well to run," said Shane, towering overhead with a predatory smile. "You are beginning to understand the doctrine of fear I have given you."

His hyena grin broadened.

"But, your fear is weak."

He knelt.

"That is why I sent you my Son. He will help thy unbelief."

Dazed, Matthew glanced over at The Dwelling, his chest hitching.

Was it possible? Was Kaufman really Shane's son? Had he been working with his father all along? Was he responsible for Jessica's kidnapping?

Yes.

Matthew snapped his head back around.

He had not asked the questions aloud.

Above Shane winked.

It is through him that you will know perfect fear, for the Son can do nothing of himself but only that which the Father has taught him.

Matthew's eyes went wide.

Shane was in his head!

Squirming at the invasion in his mind, a pressure grew at Matthew's temples as fine as the piercing tip of a drill bit. The pain intensified, grew until he not only heard a voice but saw a vision too.

On her knees, Hollie hunched over awkwardly. A gun was pressed hard at the back of her head. She held out her hands and pleaded for her life.

But Kaufman took no heed.

Extending the gun, he stepped back and executed her.

Hollie's body slumped to the ground, and Kaufman unloaded the rest of the clip into her lifeless body.

My judgment is just, because I seek not my own will, but the will of the Father that sent me.

Kaufman turned to Matthew and smiled.

His teeth were perfect, exactly like Shane's.

And greater works than these will the Son do; for he beareth witness of the Father.

The world burned, and ash swirled in the wind as Kaufman walked through a street paved with bodies. Maggots writhed in the empty eye sockets of the dead, and Matthew began pounding his head against the ground to try and rid himself of the nightmare images within.

Teeth clacked with each blow. Above him, Kaufman laughed...or was it, Shane, Matthew couldn't tell any more.

He that has seen my face has seen the Father; for the Father and I are one.

In a silent and desolate city, Kaufman approached a lone figure outlined against a sunset of blood. As he drew nearer, Matthew saw that the figure was a little girl - Jessica! Seeing Kaufman, she ran. Except Kaufman was faster, incredibly fast, and he snatched her up like a striking cobra.

Suddenly Matthew heard screaming, real screaming.

He was screaming.

Five feet above the ground, Jessica's legs flailed for purchase. She desperately searched for rescue. Hair whipped against her bluing face and her tiny fists beat ineffectively at the coarse hands wrapped around her throat.

In his mind, Matthew saw the bloodless lips and dead vacant eyes of his sister as Kaufman flung away her lifeless body.

Behold, said Kaufman, turning, *I do not my own will, but the will of the Father that sent me.*

He laughed and raised the gun.

Then Matthew's world went red.

. . .

"Göttlich couldn't have invented a religion that more closely matched his personal ideologies than the ONA does," said Dr. Murakami.

Kaufman nodded. He thought of Donald crucified, of the message written in Anthony Green's blood - *The Herd has been Thinned* - and of this place, and everything fit.

"How do we stop him?" he asked, but although his voice was level, inside a torrent of emotions churned. Everything bad that had ever happened to him, everything he'd had to endure, was now so much worse for knowing the truth.

Dr. Murakami opened his mouth to answer, but instead of a response, the intercom emitted a soft whirring sound like that of a small vacuum coming to life.

"What time is it?" Dr. Murakami shouted, his voice suddenly shrill and frantic.

A digital clock positioned conspicuously in the cell displayed the time in bright red.

"It's four fifty-nine," said Kaufman.

"Then, I have only one minute left."

"A minute left for what?" Hollie asked in a tone that was full of the same panic as her mentor.

"The nanovirus is going to be released into this chamber. So listen carefully."

"But that will kill you," protest Hollie.

"Then don't let me die in vain," lamented Dr. Murakami. "Stop Shane and redeem me from my hubris."

Hollie bit her lip and nodded.

"Alright," she said with tear-filled eyes.

"You must turn off the pulse," said Dr. Murakami, his words slurring. "It's located at Shafter in an underground facility accessed by an elevator in the biochemical lab on the main floor. That elevator requires a key card. I have one at NewLife locked in my safe, so you'll need the combination."

Dr. Murakami gave them the number.

As he did, a hissing filled the room.

Dr. Murakami's body began to twitch, and Hollie wailed.

Through the convulsions, he grunted, "Repeat...the number...back...to me."

Hollie tried but couldn't, so Kaufman did it for her, as he held her tight.

In the cell, Adam Murakami changed. The process was too slow for the naked eye, but in the end, he succumbed to his own forced evolution. His transformation, however, was not glorious; and his corpse would never be mistaken as a messenger for God.

Kaufman watched until the final death throes ceased, and the great scientist, who had once died and been brought back to life, now died indefinitely.

CHAPTER 21

The front door of The Dwelling slammed shut.

The boom rumbled through the house and funneled down into the hidden basement.

"What was that?" Hollie asked, pushing away from Kaufman's embrace.

From the stairwell came the sound of another door banging shut.

"Sounds like someone's looking for us."

Hollie wiped her eyes. "Matthew?"

Several more doors opened, then closed in quick succession. "Why doesn't he call out?" Kaufman murmured, stepping forward, listening. "He'd call out, wouldn't he?"

Hollie nodded, chewing on her lower lip.

"You think it's Shane?"

Kaufman shrugged, but his hand went to the revolver tucked into his waistband.

"He has to know we're down here. So, why's he being so deliberate?"

Kaufman drew the gun. "He doesn't want us to surprise him from behind."

"Can you really shoot him?" Hollie asked.

"Yes," Kaufman replied, and his certainty didn't surprise him in the least. Here in The Dwelling, he was unfettered by emotions, which made the decision to kill so much easier...cleaner.

But that wasn't entirely true.

With a protective hand holding Hollie back, Kaufman realized his decision to kill came less from a sense of self-preservation than from a need to make sure Hollie was safe.

When had she become so important to him? Kaufman had no idea.

"You alright?"

Kaufman blinked. He was staring at Hollie absentmindedly again, but she didn't seem to mind. She gave him a nod and smiled. Kaufman could have gone on looking at that smile forever, but shuffling feet in the office above brought him back into sharp focus.

At the opening of the trapdoor, the footsteps stopped.

Kaufman aimed the Smith & Wesson down the narrow hall. Slowly he inched forward, his breathing filling his ears

Suddenly there came the rap of knuckles.

Kaufman froze.

That was not Matthew up there. The boy wouldn't have knocked. He would have called out.

Shane was toying with them.

Kaufman tightened his grip on the gun.

The knocking rang out again, louder this time, more insistent. It also had a mocking quality, and with each repercussion, Kaufman flinched, and his muscles tightened.

The knocking went on and on until Kaufman felt on the verge of firing blindly up the stairs when something flashed in his mind. Suddenly he could sense everyone around him, could discern their identity just like he'd done when he'd woken up this morning.

Hollie was a golden beacon, but upstairs was nothing but static. It was like trying to tune in a radio station.

Kaufman reached out, got a blip, and a quick blurb, and knew.

"Seibu," he called out.

The orangutan hooted, and Hollie exhaled. "That furry guy has a serious death wish."

"No," said Kaufman, lowering the gun. "I think he knew that if he came down, he might startle us and get shot; that's why he knocked."

Hollie thought about it.

"You're right, that was smart."

"That's more than just smart," asserted Kaufman. "For Seibu to do what he did implies that he not only understood what a gun is, he also remembered that we were carrying them. He then anticipated how we might react to being surprised and reasoned how to approach the situation in a way that reduced the danger to himself. That's more than just smart, that's evolved sentient intelligence."

A line of worry formed over Hollie's eyes.

"If Seibu did all that, he had a good reason."

Seibu seemed to confirm this by hooting again.

"Something's wrong," said Hollie, and she was moving before she'd finished speaking.

Kaufman was right behind her.

At the top of the stairs, Seibu beckoned them to follow. Hollie and Kaufman chased after him, their shoes a squeaking counterpoint to their breathing. As they exited The Dwelling, heat buffeted them like a blast of hot air from an oven, but it was the unmistakable *whomp-whomp-whomp* of a helicopter overhead that grabbed their attention.

"Sounds like a military chopper," said Kaufman, shading his eyes and searching the sky.

"I was wondering when they were going to show up," Hollie replied, pointing out a black dot moving to the southwest. "Even out here in the middle of nowhere, you don't shut down a whole town for two days and not get noticed - especially when the government is conducting clandestine experiments."

Cresting a distant ridgeline, the helicopter disappeared.

"They obviously know something went wrong," said Hollie turning back to face Kaufman. "I'm sure they've already quarantined the surrounding area and are doing recon in preparation of sending in a team."

"Then we better not waste any time shutting off the pulse."

Hollie's face tightened.

"We need to do more than that."

"We need to do more than shut off the pulse?" Kaufman asked, uncertainly.

"Yes, we can't let the government have this technology. No one should have it," said Hollie. She was chewing on her bottom lip again. "It's too dangerous, too…omnipotent."

Slowly Kaufman nodded. He hadn't accepted everything Dr. Murakami had told them, but it seemed Hollie had.

"You don't really think we're angels, do you?"

Hollie remained silent.

"Do you?"

She touched the slender cross around her neck.

"I don't know," she finally admitted.

Kaufman nodded again. His affection and respect for Hollie had grown tremendously since meeting her, and so he tried to be especially sensitive with what he said next.

"I know this has been hard on you, Hollie, but you can't let that cloud your judgment. Dr. Murakami didn't evolve us into angels - the idea is romanticized to the point of being make-believe - especially when there's a much more logical explanation."

Hollie looked up, a guarded hope lying just below a mask of confusion; she seemed desperate for another answer, for some other explanation to what they'd become, to free her from the crushing heresy she'd assumed upon Adam Murakami's death.

"I thought you might have realized it, you being a scientist and all," Kaufman ventured.

"Realized what?" Hollie asked cautiously.

"That we're not celestial beings," said Kaufman, "but Posthuman."

Hollie raised an eyebrow and regarded Kaufman as if he might be a talking cockroach.

"What?"

Suddenly Kaufman felt sheepish.

"Uh…well…"

He cleared his throat.

"I guess maybe it makes for better science fiction than actual science. Anyway, Transhumanism is a movement to apply emerging biotechnologies to improve human's mental and physical abilities. The fundamental idea is human improvement by eliminating disease, aging, pain, even death - as well as perfecting the human physique. A branch of the theory is Posthumanism, which represents people who've been modified to no longer fall into the traditional classification of natural humans."

"What, like cyborgs?" Hollie snorted.

"That is one possibility," Kaufman said seriously, his confidence coming back to him. "Although cyborgs rely heavily on a combination of computers and machinery mixed with human anatomy, whereas Posthumans could come into existence through artificial intelligence, genetic engineering, psychopharmacology, or even nanotechnology."

That last bit made Hollie pause.

The notion of superhumans was not a new idea; it had been around for quite some time - Hitler's eugenics, his superior Aryan race, fell along those lines. And nowadays - with the leaps modern scientists were making, like 3D printed organs, neural implants, and bionic prosthetics - it was an even closer reality.

But Kaufman hadn't met the hellish Captain Mills in the farmhouse, and hadn't Donald referred to Shane as a *dark* angel? Did Transhumanism account for sin, good and evil, righteousness and wickedness? Did Posthumans who had their perceptions enhanced also have their moral tendencies intensified as well? That made more of a spiritual kind of sense than a biological one.

Hollie had always found the balance between science and faith to be delicate. The two were always at such odds, and now, with the fantastic confession of Dr. Murakami, they'd been smashed together like electrons in a particle accelerator to form some incomprehensible antimatter.

Hollie didn't know what to think. Still, Kaufman's rationale seemed more plausible than the notion of angels. It certainly was easier to swallow. Then again, logic - no matter how remote - always went down easier than faith.

"You're probably right," Hollie acquiesced without complete conviction. "But, in either case, we can't let anyone get their hands on this technology. It could so easily be misused - would be misused."

"I agree, but what do you suggest we do then? Blow the place up?"

A smirk formed on Hollie's lips.

That's exactly what she had in mind.

"Know anybody with some dynamite?"

"Actually, yes," said Kaufman, thinking of the supply of plastic explosives at Warrior Pete's and completely missing Hollie's banter. "It's C-4, though, which is better because it's one and a half times more powerful than TNT, and much more stable to transport."

Hollie laughed delightedly.

"Good, more bang for our buck," she teased and touched Kaufman lightly on the arm; he became self-conscious as he realized he'd taken literally what had been meant as a joke.

Fortunately, his mistake was short-lived as Seibu tugged at his hand, reminding him of their intended purpose for coming out here.

"Matthew!" Kaufman blurted, and Hollie's smile dropped from her face.

At the Humvee, both back doors stood wide open and the ground around the vehicle was scarred and pockmarked as if by a scuffle. Hollie rushed forward, propelled to action by the dubious scene before them, so she didn't see the smudge on the window, didn't notice that the rust-colored ink.

But Kaufman did. And more, he knew who'd left it.

He knew too what they were going to find.

Nearby, or in the back seat, they'd discover Matthew's small body - broken, lifeless…mutilated - and the thought made Kaufman ill.

He went weak in the knees and wondered if his father hadn't been right in wanting to purge him from caring like this. Was he weaker now because he felt?

Had he become just another of the worthless, emotional, irrational masses? What would happen if he really opened up his heart to someone?

Looking around, Kaufman sought something to steady him, searched for anything that might reassure him - and that's when he spotted Seibu doing something no Great Ape had ever done before.

"My God!" Hollie gasped from a few feet away.

Stunned, Kaufman didn't reply right away but stared on in amazement at Seibu *running* through the open desert.

It was a lopping, lunging type of jog, but it was upright running nonetheless, not knuckle-walking or waddling.

"Not God. Man," Kaufman finally said. "Dr. Murakami's nanovirus made Seibu's legs grow longer. But it's his pelvis that must have significantly altered for him to be moving like that."

"And his feet..." observed Hollie.

Kaufman hadn't noticed them, but indeed Seibu's feet seemed flatter and less like a second set of hands.

"That would make sense," he said.

Hollie frowned. She was the one with a Ph.D., and everything made about as much sense as people who liked SPAM.

"What does?" she asked.

"The bipedal dogs, the coyotes, Seibu - they're being manipulated by the nanovirus to have human characteristics. Since Dr. Murakami's little Ludwigs - as he called them - are designed to work on human DNA to change us into angels, then they must be trying to do the same thing within any biological system they find themselves in."

"I thought you believed we were Posthuman, not angels."

"I do, but Dr. Murakami said he was encouraging evolution; and as we share common genes with every animal on the planet, and this virus is programmed to focus on junk DNA that resembles *human* genes, that means, in non-human species, it's going to emphasize those same traits."

The light bulb went on for Hollie.

"Your right, I should have thought of that, and it explains Seibu's remarkable intelligence and his now more Homo-sapien like body."

Kaufman felt dizzy.

"Is he that far along?"

Hollie couldn't believe what she was about to say. "No, still a few species back, I think, but in the modern Homo genus anyway."

Continuing to gape at the spectacle before them, Hollie and Kaufman watched in wonder the lumbering gait of Seibu until they saw what he was running towards.

"Matthew!" Hollie cried.

From behind a large outcropping of igneous rock, the boy staggered into view and fell on his face.

. . .

Staring up at the pale cloudless sky, Matthew wondered how he'd gotten here.

To his right, jagged boulders protruded from the ground.

What had happened?

Rolling over, he stood up, and sand poured out from under his shirt. Whatever it was, he hoped it wouldn't happen again, because his head hurt - bad.

Brushing himself off, Matthew looked around and noticed Seibu bobbing towards him in a funny kind of jog, and memory suddenly came rushing back.

Shane. Kaufman. Kaufman killing everyone, killing him.

No, he was still alive...but for how long?

The vision he'd seen had to be a lie, didn't it? Kaufman wasn't going to kill Jess or Hollie or burn the world. He wasn't creepy like Donald, but that didn't mean he might not turn out to be crazy all the same.

Just look at the house he'd grown up in!

At school, several of his classmates had talked about Kaufman as if he were some kind of local Edward Scissorhands - a true freak of nature - though Matthew had never believed what was said. Having plastic legs, he'd heard kids say a lot of mean things, except now some of those stories, didn't seem so farfetched.

An image of Kaufman strangling Jess flashed through Matthew's mind, and he shuddered.

Deep down inside, doubt was growing.

Preoccupied with worry, Matthew didn't notice Seibu had reached him until he was enveloped in a flurry of orange fur. Hugging the purring orangutan, Matthew looked out past Seibu and stiffened.

The Son was coming.

. . .

Still several yards away, Kaufman put on a burst of speed.

Matthew was alive!

Kaufman's heart leapt, and he wanted to sweep up the boy in an embrace, but something in Matthew's eyes cause Kaufman to slow, and for a moment, he didn't recognize what he was seeing. Then it came to him - Matthew was afraid of him.

Immediately Kaufman dismissed the observation. He'd obviously misread what he'd seen. He was full of emotions as confusing as a foreign language, however as he drew nearer, Matthew stepped back.

"Are you okay?" Kaufman asked.

Matthew nodded, trying to cover his fear. He couldn't let on what he knew. But as he stood there, he could feel the Son apprising him, could feel the weight of his gaze as heavy as manacles. For what seemed like an eternity, Matthew endured that stare until Hollie appeared.

"What happened?" she asked, kneeling.

"Nothing, I-I just fell."

"You must have fallen pretty hard for Seibu to come get us," Kaufman said.

Was he suspicious? Matthew wasn't used to lying, and the fib had felt clumsy coming out.

"Uh, yeah, I must have hit my head, cause I blacked out."

At this, Hollie clasped his head in both hands and looked into his eyes.

"Follow my finger," she said and moved her hand back and forth. Matthew tracked it.

"I don't know; he seems fine," she said, blowing her bangs out of her eyes and standing. "Heck, his new body can probably take better care of him than I can anyway."

"But why did you leave the car in the first place?" Kaufman pressed.

Matthew didn't know what to say to that. He couldn't tell them the truth, couldn't say that Shane had come to him with bloody hands and bloody revelations, could he? No, definitely not. Instead, he shrugged and put his hands in his pants and gave them the I-know-I-wasn't-supposed-to look to stall for time.

In his pocket, his fingers touched the angel medallion, and something occurred to him.

"Are you really the Son, Shane's son?"

Kaufman regarded Mathew, grey eyes searching the boy as thoroughly as an X-ray, trying to understand what he was really asking, but Matthew gave nothing away. After a moment, Kaufman said, "Yes, Shane is Göttlich - my dad; there's no doubt anymore."

Matthew frowned.

Seibu and Hollie seemed to trust Kaufman, and that helped calm his apprehension. Still, they hadn't seen what he had.

I come in my Father's name.

Kaufman's smile had looked exactly like Shane's.

The Father and I are one.

There had been so many dead bodies.

Like out of some Bible comic book, Shane and Kaufman were the evil counterparts to God and Jesus, and they had plans to do terrible things, things Matthew couldn't let happen.

He gripped the necklace in his pants pocket tighter. He still had the chef's knife tucked away at the small of his back, and that was good, he decided. He might need it.

"We better get going," said Kaufman. "It's late, and we have a few stops to make before its dark. We'll have dinner tonight, and in the morning, we're going after Jess."

Matthew liked the idea of dinner.

He liked the promise of getting Jessica back even more.

And this time, he had no intention of being left in the car.

. . .

Hollie burst out laughing.

"Look at those lips!"

She dropped her fork and covered her mouth as Seibu slurped up a long spaghetti noodle.

Matthew giggled. "He looks like an anteater."

With his puckered lips, Kaufman thought Seibu did indeed resemble an anteater sticking out its long skinny tongue.

He shot Matthew a smile, and the boy grinned back.

Whatever had made the kid skittish out in the desert seemed to have evaporated, for he was as boisterous as any of them. Kaufman supposed he had every right to be jumpy. The city had gone mad, his sister had been kidnapped

- twice - and his mother had died in a horrible and unnatural fashion. If anything, Matthew's resiliency was a mark of true character. He was no diamond in the rough; instead, at the tender age of ten, he was already a dazzling gem.

Without warning, the end of the noodle suddenly came free and slapped the side of Seibu's face.

He smacked his lips appreciatively, and everyone laughed.

Kaufman had prepared one of his favorite meals: chicken carbonara. The creamy pasta dish with bacon and breaded chicken was a hit, especially for Seibu. There might not be electricity, but the gas still worked, and the group was highly enjoying their candlelit feast.

"This is amazing," said Hollie, through another mouthful of food. "You should seriously give up gardening and become a cook."

"Yeah, it's great," said Matthew through a mouthful of food.

"Normally, I'd be flattered by your compliments," said Kaufman, "but I think I could have burnt mud tonight and it would have tasted great."

Matthew chuckled, thinking it was a joke, but Hollie looked at him knowingly. Their enhanced taste buds were making every bite sensational.

"Well, we'll have to have mud pancakes in the morning then, Chef Striker," kidded Hollie.

"I might make you regret those words," Kaufman threatened and then stood. "Okay, who wants dessert."

Matthew raised his hand, and Seibu followed.

"Careful, you're likely to give me an orgasm with that chocolate delight you whipped up over there," Hollie teased.

"Yeah, I want a chocolate organism, too," said Matthew naively.

Kaufman and Hollie exploded.

"Well then, orgasms for everyone," Hollie decreed, waving a hand in the air. Kaufman shook his head, clearing plates, but he couldn't wipe the grin off his face.

After dessert, Matthew lay cocooned in a sleeping bag with Seibu next to him. Candlelight washed over the pair, and Kaufman watched as Seibu stared out into the night. The glass sliding door reflected his features, and in that almost human face was a display of emotion Kaufman felt sure had never been present on any of his kind ever before. It was the forlorn quality of a creature utterly alone in all of the universe and helplessly aware of it. It was the type of self-awareness that, until recently, only humans had been capable of. But it was also a burden that could lead to self-destruction. The German Shepherd had reached some level where it desired death over the pain and suffering of its twisted life, and Kaufman hoped Seibu wouldn't turn to that same avenue for escape.

"This was a great idea," said Hollie, interrupting Kaufman's thoughts.

"Hmm…" said Kaufman, still looking at Seibu, who must have sensed it; the orangutan turned his attention away from the vast starry sky towards the kitchen. He cocked his head and flashed Kaufman a big goofy grin, then curled up next to Matthew.

Hollie touched Kaufman's hand to get his attention.

"Oh, yeah, of course…we needed it."

"No, you don't understand," said Hollie. "I mean, it was important for us to have a nice evening, because…because it might be our last."

Kaufman scowled. "What do you mean?"

Taking a moment before replying, Hollie chose her words carefully.

"When we blow up the pulse, there's a chance we might not survive."

Kaufman put the cup he was holding down on the table. It clinked dully against the wooden surface.

"You don't mean getting caught in the explosion, do you?"

Hollie shook her head.

"How big of a chance?" he asked.

"I don't know…maybe fifty percent, maybe ninety, maybe none. I doubt even Dr. Murakami would have known, but there's definitely a possibility, and I wanted to let you know."

"You wouldn't have said anything if there wasn't a real risk. What are our odds?"

Hollie looked into her empty mug.

"Not good," she breathed. "Probably worse than bad. We're in completely uncharted waters here."

For a long while, Kaufman sat in silence, he looked at Matthew and Seibu.

"Shane's not going to let them live if we don't succeed." He turned to Hollie.

"We have to do it, even if there's a hundred percent chance."

Hollie smile gently.

"I was hoping you would feel that way."

She reached out and touched his hand again, but this time she didn't move to take it away, and Kaufman didn't want her to.

From the living room, Matthew snored softly, and for the first time in his life, Kaufman's house felt like home.

CHAPTER 22

From a distance, Shafter Army Base and Testing Grounds was as impressive as dockyard warehouses and seemed more likely to house cobwebs and dust than deadly top-secret weapons.

True to government standards, the base was drab and unassuming.

Six squat buildings were situated in a semi-circle with a large main central hub - it was the perfect example of tight-fisted spending and it-ain't-got-to-look-pretty-it's-got-to-work attitudes. But if the U.S. military was guilty of aesthetical blandness, it was overindulgent when it came to dumping money into projects - for under the surface of the compound was buried a state of the art BSL 4, the highest level biosafety lab there was, as well as the machine powering Dr. Murakami's clandestine evolution experiment.

Being this close to the epicenter, Kaufman's skin didn't merely tingle; it positively hummed.

"Do you feel that?" asked Kaufman, parking the Humvee behind the main gate.

Hollie nodded, but she didn't need to reply for Kaufman to know the answer. He could see that everyone in the car was experiencing the same sensations he was having. They were changing, evolving, and not on some incomprehensible scale of millions of years, but by the minute, and although it was still hard to believe, it was not unpleasant. Rather, the process was intoxicating to the point that Kaufman felt tempted just to sit there and let nature - or man's blasphemy, or whatever this was - run its course.

"Right," he said, clearing his throat, "let's do this."

As they exited the SUV, the morning air was warm and still. Kaufman led the group towards the compound with Hollie bringing up the rear. Matthew and

Seibu were unarmed in the center, but between the adults, they were toting the shotgun, the revolver, and a massive military-style duffle bag with enough plastic explosives to blow an island.

The plan was to get in, get Jessica, and destroy everything else once they got out. Neither Kaufman nor Hollie believed it would be that easy.

Shane wasn't going to cooperate.

Finding the elevator to the top-level security lab was relatively easy, given that the base was supplied with independent power. Kaufman and Hollie had agreed not to ask Matthew and Seibu to stay in the Humvee. They wanted them close because if something went wrong, the plan was to discharge the C-4 and allow them to be euthanized by the blast rather than let the government have them to run endless experiments on, or worse, leave them to Shane.

No, they would all make it, or they wouldn't. It was that simple.

At the elevator doors, Hollie said, "Matthew, we need you to stay here with Seibu and keep watch. We'll only be a minute getting Jessica, and when we come back, you've got to be ready to book it, so don't go anywhere, okay?"

Matthew nodded.

Kaufman thought he consented a little too quickly, thought the kid was putting on an act. Matthew had been standoffish all morning, and the joviality he'd displayed during dinner last night now seemed like a front.

What'd happened to him out in the desert? He hadn't just fallen off some rocks, Kaufman was certain about that. And there'd been what looked like bloody knuckles stamped on the window of the Humvee. Had Shane been there? Kaufman worried about the repercussions of not finding out, but speculation at this point was unproductive. He needed to focus.

Getting into the elevator, he and Hollie made sure there was a bullet in each chamber of their weapons and patted down their spare ammo. The safeties were off, and they were ready to go.

Kaufman pushed the button to descend.

The downward journey seemed to take well over five minutes. The underground lab was either very deep, or the elevator was extremely slow.

Hollies guessed it was deep - somewhere just above Hell.

"What happens if we can't kill Shane?"

"What do you mean?"

"Even if we aren't angels, but Posthuman like you suggest," said Hollie, "our bodies have been enhanced and are capable of rapid regeneration. A bullet might not be enough."

Kaufman shook his head. "No way. A shot in the heart or head will put him down. None of us can can't heal that quickly."

Hollie looked unconvinced. "The nanovirus is meant to restore otherwise lethal wounds and resurrect us. Our cells will continue to function even if major organs are damaged and, if what Dr. Murakami told us was accurate, then our bodies are undergoing a continual refinement to the point where we might, now, not even be capable of sustaining injuries."

Kaufman raised an eyebrow at that.

"You're making us sound like all-powerful angels again."

Hollie shrugged. "Well then, what if he's just inhumanly fast or strong?"

"Then we'll be that way too," countered Kaufman, yet he lacked conviction.

"But what if Shane uses some other ability that we haven't discovered yet?" insisted Hollie. "Like telekinesis?"

Under any other circumstances, Kaufman would have scoffed at the notion; but after everything he'd seen and experienced, after reaching out with his mind yesterday morning and sensing everyone's emotional states as physically and distinctly as if he was smelling their body odor, he knew Hollie was right to worry.

In this brave new world, they were no longer bound by mortal human limitations.

Anything, and everything seemed possible.

Looking into Hollie's scared yet determined face, Kaufman was again struck by the depth of his feelings for this woman he barely knew. What he feared was not the unknown, but that he wouldn't be able to protect her from it.

Reaching out, she touched his face, and he sensed that she knew what he was thinking - either by supernatural means or just through normal human connectedness.

"If our guns don't stop him," he said, "then we do what we planned. Detonate the explosives first chance we get and take away all his abilities."

"And our lives," said Hollie softly.

Kaufman nodded, contemplating his less-than-perfect resolve to this last-ditch solution.

The elevator doors slid open.

On the other side waited Shane.

He had a Desert Eagle fifty-caliber handgun and his Oscar-winning smile.

"I'm so glad you both could join me," he said pleasantly. "Now, drop your weapons."

"You first," said Hollie, snapping up the shotgun.

"My goodness, dying certainly hasn't diminished any of your spunk," laughed Shane.

Behind him, the lab arced outward like a small amphitheater.

In neat rows, the main compartment was laid out with computer workstations arranged on descending levels. Several huge monitors were mounted on the center wall. Below the LED screens were three floor-to-ceiling glass walls, the sides angling out at forty degrees to the center. A biosafety and chemical lab was situated on the right next to several ultra-high-tech ICU suites. On the opposite side, in a circular silo lined with mirrored black hexagonal titles, was a machine that could only be the Vibrotic pulse. Reaching upwards, the massive tubular antenna blinked and throbbed. The multicolor spectrum reflected in the obsidian paneling.

As impressive as the apparatus was, though, it was Jessica - tied up in a steel chair in the center observation room - that drew Kaufman and Hollie's attention.

Head lolled back, mouth slack, and eyes rolled up to reveal the whites, she looked hypnotized.

"What have you done to her?" Kaufman demanded.

"Ah, yes…don't let her youth fool you. That girl is quite the dangerous little anomaly. I never expected anyone like her, yet when I realized what she was, I'd hoped to scare her off; I even sent Donald to keep her in check. But she's grown too powerful, so I had to take her out of the equation."

Kaufman's head was spinning. What she *was*? His father hadn't just drunk the Kool-Aid; he was mainlining it.

"She's nothing but a little girl, Göttlich."

Shane chuckled ironically. "Göttlich…yes, now more than ever; such an appropriate name, don't you think Dr. Cunningham? A real self-fulfilling prophecy, all thanks to you."

"I had nothing to do with this," spat Hollie.

"Oh, but you had everything to do with it," countered Shane. "I wouldn't have been able to achieve my divinity without your brilliance. And as for all the deaths, well don't think your hands are clean just because somebody else pushed the button on the bomb you created."

Hollie glared at him, but she didn't have a retort.

"And Kaufman, my boy, I wasn't sure you'd take my advice about offing yourself. Your obedience, however, is…inspiring. You truly have proven yourself. You were willing to die for me, and as a reward, you too have been glorified. But greater gifts than these doth the Father have for thee. You shall take the spot on my right hand and shall be my voice, and through you, my will shall be done."

For a moment, Kaufman was speechless, then he laughed hard and a little manic.

"If you think I killed myself out of devotion, you're even more delusional than I could have ever imagined." Abruptly his voice turned bitter, and he hissed, "I hung myself to try and *feel* something inside this empty husk of a person you made me."

"No!" Shane reprimanded softly and fervently. "I helped rid you of unnecessary baggage, baggage that makes humanity weak and mere cattle to those who are masters of themselves. I didn't leave you empty, I stripped you down to your most powerful essence, and I prepared you for this day - when you would become like a god!"

"Shut up," Hollie shouted. "Shut up and put your gun down or so help me, I'm going to blow those flapping lips of yours right out the back of your damn head."

Shane frowned and regarded Hollie.

"Now, now, Hollie, I took you for a woman of action. Why threaten me? If you're going to shoot someone, shoot them, don't talk about it."

And he pulled the trigger.

The Desert Eagle bucked, and Hollie's left kneecap disintegrated, exploded into a hundred shards of biological shrapnel. Hollie crumpled to the floor, screaming.

"Seems like me shooting you is becoming a habit in our relationship, Hollie dear," said Shane. "But I'll wager that although Adam Murakami explained to you what he did, you didn't fully believe, and as a result, you haven't learned to control those new abilities of yours. Which means that destroyed knee of yours hurts far more than it would for a normal person."

Writhing in agony, Hollie clutched her leg; eyes pinched shut, spittle flexing at the corner of her mouth.

"See, what you're experiencing now is divine pain," continued Shane grinning excitedly. "We are no longer restricted by finite minds, no longer limited by mortal boundaries, which means Hollie, your ability to experience suffering is…limitless, eternal even."

Kaufman knelt, ready to take off his t-shirt and apply pressure to the wound, except there was almost no blood - which was impossible because the .50 caliber ammunition had nearly severed the leg in two. Where Hollie's knee used to be, there was now nothing but a gaping hole the size of a grapefruit. The wound should have been bleeding out, should have already soaked the floor - but the ragged flesh was only lightly beaded with blood as if it had sustained nothing more than road rash.

Inspecting the damage more closely, Kaufman watched in amazement as the skin began reattaching itself. It was like watching a time-lapse video - muscle, tendon, cartilage, and bone were knitting back together in blurred wriggling spurts.

"That's right, her body will eventually heal, and in a little while, she'll be as good as new, but for the time being, Hollie's become a non-factor - which means, Kaufman my boy, it's your move."

Getting to his feet, Kaufman hefted up the canvas duffle bag.

"This bag is full of C-4," he said, moving forward. "I'll blow us all to hell if you don't throw that gun over here."

"Then you'll only kill yourself," said Shane calling his son's bluff. "I would just simply remove myself before I was hurt."

"Maybe," replied Kaufman. "But what happens to you when the pulse is destroyed? Have you finished evolving yet? Or should I say, completely ascending?"

That caused Shane to hesitate.

"Very well," he said, tossing the gun aside. "It saddened me to be reduced to using such lowly means of persuasion anyway."

Through clenched teeth, Hollie shouted, "Go now - plant the explosives."

Keeping his gun trained on Shane, Kaufman made his way towards Jessica and the Vibrotic pulse. As he moved, it crossed his mind more than once to put a few bullets into dear old dad.

"You want to shoot me, don't you?" said Shane with a smirk. "You should, you know, because it makes logical tactical sense. Shooting me takes out your biggest threat. I would be incapacitated just like Hollie, but you're not thinking with your head anymore, are you? You're thinking with your heart. You want to shoot me because you think I deserve it."

Göttlich did deserve it, and Kaufman's grip tightened on the gun. He knew he was being baited, but there was too much hate in him, too much anger, too many years of unrequited wrongs heaped upon him not to shoot.

"Well then, go ahead."

So, Kaufman pulled the trigger—

And it was like being hit by a taser.

Suddenly his whole body seized up. There was no pain, his mind was clear, but Kaufman couldn't move, couldn't so much as blink an eyelid.

"Let me explain what's happened," said Shane stepping forward. "Mankind started out smashing rocks together to shape blades and to crush and kill. We haven't made much progress since. We still burn and ignite, still explode and obligate the elements to our will through compulsory means. Even our transportation - from whipping a horse to the combustion engine - is propelled through force."

Shane moved closer. "Humans only know how to force things. Celestial beings, on the other hand," he said emphatically, "they only have to ask and are obeyed."

Kaufman's eyes went wide as he recognized Shane as a presence in his mind.

Yes, I'm there, and you won't do a thing I don't tell you too. You will obey me as the very molecules do. Now drop the gun.

Kaufman did.

Fingers uncoiled, and the Smith and Wesson clattered to the ground. Kaufman hadn't told himself to, had tried in fact to stop himself, but that didn't seem to matter. As much as he wanted to keep his hand wrapped tightly around the handle of the revolver, as hard as he tried to hold fast, he couldn't. It was as if he were a passenger in a remote-control plane, and no matter what levers he pulled or buttons he pushed, nothing responded.

Good, the bag too.

Kaufman obeyed.

"Perhaps I was wrong about you," Shane mused aloud. "I thought you were stronger than this; I thought I'd taught you better."

Kaufman railed against his unresponsive body.

Göttlich *had* taught him better, had shown him how to be his own master, to not let external influences manipulate him. He hadn't come all this way - through all the years of living in The Dwelling and through all the years after ridding himself of it - to only end up a child shackled to his father's bidding.

So Kaufman went down into himself, deep down, where everything was cold and hard and passionless.

"Your weakness is a blight on me!" Shane spat.

Trembling, Kaufman willed his foot forward, ignoring his father's influence on him. He turned his mind to his own volition and slowly took a step.

"Good, good," Shane encouraged, laughing delightedly. "I knew you'd be a challenge; knew you couldn't be passive. I molded you better than that, and that's why I wanted you by my side. You are my greatest creation, my masterpiece."

Kaufman locked eyes with his father and whispered, "I'm not your anything. I am."

Standing, Kaufman jerked up. In his hand was the revolver, and though his father's will weighed on him like ten thousand fathoms of ocean, he brought up the gun.

"Interesting," Shane said, bemused.

He was thoroughly enjoying this.

He was also toying with Kaufman, for the moment the barrel was centered on him, he snapped up his son's arm like a puppeteer yanking on the strings of a marionette.

Yet Kaufman would not be deterred.

Moving past his dispassionate core, he located his recently acquired zeal for life, focused on his affection for Hollie and Matthew and Jessica - centered himself on his friendship with Seibu and leveraged those emotions to bolster his will, turned those feelings that his father had taught him were a weakness to his advantage.

Caring for others wasn't inhibiting - it empowered, gave focus and purpose, and Kaufman used that, made it his strength, and inch by excruciating inch, he brought the crosshairs back on target.

"Is this enough challenge for you?" Kaufman asked and squeezed off a shot.

The boom was deafening in the underground bunker, and Shane scowled as the wall overhead exploded, raining down concrete and grey ash.

"Oh, we're just getting started," he said, forcing Kaufman to direct the gun into his mouth. "Why don't you try that again?"

Kaufman growled as the steel barrel pushed its way in through clenched teeth and pressed up hard against the roof of his mouth, hard enough to break skin. The iron was hot and tasted of gunpowder, as he was made to bite down on the Smith and Wesson.

Hollie screamed at him, but Kaufman couldn't make out what she was saying over the thought of a bullet punching through his brain, and his finger rattling around in the trigger guard. Hollie kept shouting at him, and when the elevator doors binged open, he knew what she'd been saying.

Matthew!

. . .

It'd been a no-brainer to get on the elevator after Hollie and Kaufman. There was no way he was just going to wait around.

Jess was *his* sister, *his* responsibility.

Matthew didn't know what to expect when he got to the bottom and stepped out, but the scene before him was way more screwed up and scarier than anything he'd imagined.

The Star Wars-like control room might have been cool if it hadn't been filled with the pained screams of Hollie, who was rolling around on the floor trying to hold her leg together and if Kaufman hadn't been sucking on his gun like a lollypop, seemingly on the verge of swallowing a bullet.

The flashing, oscillating engine thingy in the black room was definitely cool, except right next to it was Jess, and she looked freaking possessed.

Eyeballs rolled back and fluttering in their sockets, mouth agape - she was completely out of it. But that apparently wasn't enough for whoever had done that to her, because they'd also tied her up.

Jess was only five, and she'd been tied up with fishing wire!

Matthew saw that and went cold.

He pulled out the chef's knife.

The steel felt heavy and right in his hand.

He might not understand everything that was happening in Decoy, but he knew who was responsible for tying up his sister.

Without a second thought, he rushed Shane.

Matthew went three feet, then something invisible slammed into him. He was still able to move, but it felt as if he'd belly-flopped into a swimming pool and was now walking around at the bottom of the deep end. Only this was way, way more intense; every movement took massive concentration.

Looking around for an explanation to this weird resistance, Matthew saw Shane turn the death stare he'd been locked in with Kaufman right at him.

Eyes narrow and face pinched, Shane was pissed.

That's when Matthew knew what the tension in the room was about. He'd felt tension like this before when his parents would fight, and a quiet strain would fill the house as thick as fog until one or the other gave in.

In this case, though, Matthew was aware that giving in wouldn't just result in Shane looking smug and superior, but in him killing them all. So Matthew swam forward, pulled himself along in a labored over-hand style breaststroke, full of wrath and brotherly vengeance; and as he advanced, he watched Kaufman remove the revolver he'd been sucking on and take aim.

The gun cracked sharp and loud, and incredibly, Matthew *saw* the bullet fly through the air. In slow motion, the brass slug speed right for Shane's head, but at the last moment, it bent away and lodged in the wall.

"Let's try something different, shall we?" said Shane through tight lips, trembling with the effort of splitting his will.

He released Matthew, and the boy stumbled forward and went sprawling.

For a moment, Matthew lay motionless, feeling angry with himself, feeling clumsy and stupid - feeling as if he still had his leg braces on.

As he lay there, a voice rang out in his head.

Arise, Matthew, my first disciple.

Matthew looked up.

Shane smiled at him, and it wasn't scary at all; it was…it was beautiful.

Well done, my good and faithful servant.

Beaming, Shane stretched forth his arms, and Matthew wondered why he had ever been afraid. There was nothing to fear; there was only awe and devotion.

Matthew look; behold the deceiver, the Evil One.

And he saw.

Just like in the vision in the desert, Matthew watched Kaufman pop his knuckles and start towards Jessica.

She cried out when he picked her up by the throat and started choking her.

Flailing, her pigtails whipped about and her eyes bulged wide, pleading, pleading for Matthew to save her.

And he would.

. . .

Springing to his feet, Matthew shouted low and gutturally, brandishing the knife high above his head.

Still locked in a stalemate of wills with Shane, Kaufman was unable to divide even a fraction of his attention to Matthew. He knew the boy's mind had been poisoned, that Shane had gotten in there and deceived him, turned him traitor. That's what must have happened to him in the desert yesterday too. But the revelation did nothing to impede Matthew's murderous charge.

Fast as a snapped rubber band, Matthew reached Kaufman and thrust upward, using both hands to drive the blade in deep. The sharp steel pierced skin and muscle, slipped in between ribs, grated bone, and nicked cartilage as it found its way to puncturing a lung.

And the world for Kaufman turned to pain.

Never had he known such agony. It was as if every injury, burn, sickness, and contusion, every cut, stubbed toe, and broken bone he'd ever experienced was served to him at once. His mind reeled and lurched - but...he...did...not...pass...out.

Crumpling to the floor, sweet oblivion eluded Kaufman. Unconsciousness, apparently, was a safety mechanism that no longer existed in him. Fighting the sharp all-consuming pain, Kaufman came to understand that in order to stop his suffering, he would have to choose not to acknowledge it.

That's when Matthew stabbed him again.

Thrown back into a realm of blinding white pain, Kaufman no longer knew what was going on. Endless waves of physical and mental suffering washed over him, dragged him away from coherent thought, and pinned him against a sharp reef of madness. One moment he was back on the kitchen floor with the noose around his neck; the next, he was a motherless child scared and alone, only to morph into an adolescent being force-fed the tenets of Dominism.

From far away, a woman called his name; Shane laughed, and Matthew brought up the knife to strike.

Feebly Kaufman put out a hand to defend against the incoming blow when an orange streak blurred past him, slammed into Shane.

Even through the disorienting pain, Kaufman recognized what had happened. Seibu had saved him like this before. Back in The Paradise Hotel and Casino, he'd taken out Merah Gunung in a similar fashion - only this time, the intrepid orangutan didn't have a metal pipe to give him the advantage. Seibu might have tipped the balance of power, but it wouldn't last long, for Shane had weapons at his disposal that were far greater than fist and tooth and claw.

Kaufman knew he had to act quickly.

Summing up his reserves, he pushed away the torment in his mind and sat up. Beside him, Matthew stood babbling. Tears of shame streamed down his face, and he let slip the bloody knife.

"Matthew, look at me," said Kaufman locking eyes with the boy. "It's alright...I'm alright."

He picked up the knife and slapped it back into the boy's hand.

"I need you to go and cut your sister free."

Matthew nodded, wiping away tears and snot. He took the knife and hurried over to his sister. Kaufman watched him go. The kid was a marvel. Damned if he was going to let either of those two down.

Getting to his feet, Kaufman lugged the fifty bricks of C-4 over to the Vibrotic pulse. It was difficult going. His chest burned where he'd been stabbed, and he could feel the perforation in his lung.

Shane and Seibu fought on in a contorted heap of limbs.

Suddenly, Seibu was launched into the air. He slammed into the ceiling, and aluminum panels rained to the ground, but Seibu remained suspended.

Shane stared at the orangutan and narrowed his eyes.

The pressure in the room grew, and Kaufman felt his ears pop. He started the timer for the charges - ten minutes - and ran back for his gun just as Seibu began to shriek in pain.

A few feet from the revolver, Kaufman was hit by the mental Taser again.

Invisible hands wrenched back his arms, and lifted him until he stood on tiptoes. Kaufman tried to fight it, but his injuries left him too weak to assert his will.

"You need to show more deference, boy," growled his father. "It's time I reminded you of your lessons."

"Please, no," Kaufman whispered, as he was rotated to face Seibu, whose eyes were wide and confused and beseeching.

The pressure in the room increased again, and Seibu screams grew louder. His body twisted and was wrenched until bones broke.

Each dry crack stabbed Kaufman in the chest. It was infinitely more piercing than the knife had been.

"Stop," he moaned as Seibu, contorted and broken, reached out a trembling hand to him.

"Stop!"

But Shane didn't stop.

"You went soft over a pet?" he sneered, and Seibu's chest abruptly crumpled inward, cutting off his scream.

"No!" wailed Kaufman, head pinned forwards and eyelids forced open.

Seibu's soft brown eyes trembled and searched Kaufman's.

"It's okay," he whispered, "let go."

Seibu sighed and his body went limp.

Kaufman wept.

Shane saw those tears and grinned.

"You are so weak, Kaufman! Look at you, sniveling like a child whose toy has been taken away! And for what? For nothing."

"No," said Kaufman, and he exerted all his will, returning an outstretched arm to his friend.

"You think that by killing Seibu, you've taken something from me." Kaufman looked at his father. "You can never take anything away from me ever again."

"Good, yes, that's right. No possession. You just might yet learn to master Dominism."

Kaufman shook his head.

He was not crying because of loss, but because of what Seibu had given him.

All those years ago, the young orangutan had given him the key to his heart, the key he'd been searching for his whole life. Seibu had taught him empathy. To love, to care for another, to be vulnerable, to be willing to lose and hurt; it was these qualities that ennobled man, that made a soul.

"He saved me. From myself, from you."

Shane roared with laughter.

"Pathetic. You think because you cared about another creature, you're better for it? That it somehow made you stronger? False, it has gotten you nowhere. You are more lost now than ever."

Shane yanked back Kaufman's arm and raised him higher in the air.

"*I* will show you salvation. It comes from power."

The molecules around Kaufman pressed in, and he felt his body being crushed.

"This is my final lesson," said Shane, and he exerted his will.

Kaufman screamed.

"*I* giveth, and *I* taketh away."

Kaufman's mind swam, his vision darkened, and he knew this was the end. He had nothing left. He couldn't best his father.

"Enough!" A voice commanded, full of power and authority.

Seibu and Kaufman dropped to the ground, and Shane turned towards the sound.

Out of the observation room, Jessica walked, wrapped in an aura of white.

"You have roamed unchecked for too long," she said.

"Don't come any closer," Shane snarled. He suddenly had his own aura - black and thick as tar.

But Jessica didn't heed him.

She took another step and another.

"Stay back!"

The light around Jessica grew brighter.

She took another step, and her features lost all imperfection. Skin radiating, eyes blazing, Jessica's mouth glowed as she spoke.

"Get thee behind me, O ye follower of the Son of the Morning."

The biblical vernacular caused Kaufman to straighten.

"Your banishment is upon you."

"No!" Shane hissed, and he seemed to writhe in the light as if it burned.

Jessica's next step lifted her into the air, and she was now so bright that the light washed out everything in the room. Shadows fled as illumination filled every corner, seemed to shine *through* things. Kaufman found he wasn't squinting, despite the light. With his enhanced eyes, he had no trouble seeing Jessica; her light was pure, not blinding.

Unrestrained by the laws of gravity, Jessica spoke again, and her voice boomed.

"Look what you have forsaken for darkness."

She spread her arms, displaying her glory.

Shane knelt and cowered.

Jessica's eyes were orbs of pure electricity, and she no longer seemed to have a physical form. She was a being of pure light - glittering gold.

"There are laws in the universe, cause and effect, balance, order," declared Jessica, although she no longer spoke aloud - rather, her words rang out in everyone's mind. *And you, fiend* - she pointed a radiant finger as Shane - *have overstepped your bounds.*

Shane gnashed his teeth and rent his clothes.

Ruby tattoos flashed in Jessica's glorious light as the evil symbols and occult ciphers on Shane's muscled body smoked.

"Nooooo!" Shane growled. "I am divine. I rebuke you."

Jessica responded by saying something in a language that was lyrical, powerful, and as ancient as time, and Shane reacted to it like a spoiled child throwing a tantrum.

Light bloomed out of Jessica's chest and she arched backwards, flexing against the glowing brightness.

"I cast thee out," she sang aloud and exploded.

Her radiance consumed all, obliterated everything, and for an instant, light and life, and joy filled the universe, and Kaufman could not distinguish himself from Hollie or Matthew, and time did not exist. He was everything and everywhere, but apart, separate, unique, eternal.

All at once, the room winked back into existence, and neither Jessica nor Shane remained.

For a moment, Kaufman, Hollie, and Matthew remained motionless. No one wanted to disturb the moment, its sacredness.

But a jarring beeping blared, loud and insistent.

"Come on!" Kaufman shouted. "We have to get out of here."

Hollie - whose knee was nearly mended - limped over to Matthew. He had tears streaming down his face. Hollie realized she did too.

Kaufman scooped up Seibu's body, and the group made their escape.

Bursting out of the elevators, they ran for the exit.

When they were 100 yards from the Humvee, the earth bucked. They looked back in time to see the concrete building crumble in on itself as a plume of smoke and dirt spewed upwards.

The ground rumbled and groaned. Sandy soil rained down in an apocalyptic hailstorm, and Kaufman suddenly felt violently ill. Pressure grew in his head. He looked at Hollie and Matthew.

Blood was streaming out of their noses and ears.

They collapsed, screaming, clenching their skulls.

But Kaufman didn't hear them. There was only a ringing silence between his ears as he fell to the ground, gasping for air.

It felt like he was dying all over again.

Then his skin stopped tingling and he closed his eyes.

Beside him, Hollie and Matthew did the same.

EPILOGUE

A rare cool breeze blew.

The landscape rustled, and a lush spot of green caught the wind. Kaleidoscope flowers trembled, while perennials and slender-stalked trees shifted.

The small, lush garden was a beautiful oasis in the otherwise barren and dry desert - a fitting final resting place for Seibu, the native Nevadan, so far from his ancestral home.

In this secret spot at the edge of Kaufman's property, three figures stood around a freshly covered mound of earth.

They each took turns saying a few last words, and when the opportunity came for Kaufman, he simply said, "He was my brother."

There was a break in his voice, and Hollie led Matthew away.

From a distance, she heard Kaufman weeping softly, and after a while, he returned to them. But this time, unlike when he'd come out of Donald's church, he didn't bury his pain and grief - and this time, Hollie didn't hold back. She went to him, opened her arms, and held him.

For what felt like ages, Kaufman hugged her back, squeezed like a man lost but now found.

Looking up, he saw Matthew standing a few feet away. The kid had been through as much as any of them. He motioned for him, and the boy tentatively stepped forward. He added his arms to the embrace. They were a family now - of a sort, anyway - and with them, Kaufman believed he would be able to finish the journey he'd started a lifetime ago when he'd left The Dwelling.

"Okay, let's go," he said, and the trio departed.

. . .

Hollie led them up the mountain. The road was rarely used, but she'd found it easy enough. Soon they were at the secluded mine Shane had brought her to.

After concealing the Humvee, they went in.

The plan now was to lie low, hide out until they could slip away one night unnoticed by the military or news crew that were already circle in the distance. They would have to change their identities, might even have to leave the country, but life was out there, and they were determined to have a piece of it. Nothing seemed more desirable than a quiet existence, some friends, and each other.

Walking down the carved-out stone tunnel, Matthew listened while Hollie and Kaufman talked.

"So, do you still think we're Posthuman?"

Kaufman thought for a moment.

"You mean, do I still think we're genetically enhanced people who have amazing abilities? Yes…no…I don't know."

They walked for a while in silence, the beams of their flashlights slashing lazily through the darkness.

"Are you still of the angel persuasion?"

Hollie sighed.

"If you told me what I've seen, I wouldn't have believed you. I'd have called you nuts and looked to see what insane asylum you'd escaped from. I hardly believe it myself, and I lived through it."

Nearing the staging area where Shane had stockpiled his food and supplies, she added, "I guess seeing isn't always believing."

"Then what's left?" asked Kaufman.

"Faith," she said, "and hope."

Kaufman stopped and looked at her.

"Hope?" he said, and the word didn't seem foreign to him, didn't taste like poison as it once had when he'd been a child.

"Yeah, okay, I can live with that."

From behind, Matthew watched Kaufman take Hollie's hand in his own. He thought their fingers looked interlaced as tightly as their futures.

The two had tried to explain to him what had happened, how their bodies had changed, and how they weren't sure what changes would be permanent and what wouldn't or even how long they might live, but Matthew didn't care about that. They'd told him a lot of stuff he didn't understand or care about. What did matter was that they weren't going to leave him. Not ever.

From his pants pocket, he withdrew the angel pendant his mother had given him. He'd tried to give the necklace to Jess back in the base after he'd cut her free; her eyes had snapped forward like the rotating glass orbs of a porcelain doll, and she'd smiled her pixie smile - the smile that always banished dark thoughts and brightened every day - but she'd refused. She'd known that the small cherubim would forever remind him of her.

It hurt that she'd gone away, but he'd kept his promise. He'd watched out for her, he'd protected her the best he knew how, and she'd helped the world out just like he always knew she would - whether the world realized it or not.

Turning the pendant over and over in his hand, Matthew rubbed the tarnished surface until it shone. He put it over his head and tucked it into his shirt, then ran to catch up with his new family.

Over his heart, he could feel the metal angel.

"Hang on, mom, hang on Jess," he said, as his legs pumped and skipped him along, unfettered by disease or abjection. "I'm coming. Maybe not soon, but someday…someday I'll come."

Author's Note

Thank you for reading! I hope you enjoyed the book. I had a blast writing it. If you liked it, please head over to Amazon @ www.amazon.com/dp/B07WRL35FX and leave a review. Every review helps a ton.

Also, follow me on Facebook @ authorMCHansen. Find news about upcoming novels I'm working on, read some of my short stories, and check out other projects, content, and videos.

Cheers!
-*M.C. Hansen*